Visions &
Imaginings:
Classic Fantasy Fiction

Visions &
Imaginings:

Classic Fantasy Fiction

EDITED BY
ROBERT H. BOYER AND
KENNETH J. ZAHORSKI

Academy
Chicago
Publishers

Published in 1992 by
Academy Chicago Publishers
213 West Institute Place
Chicago, Illinois 60610

Copyright © 1991 by Robert H. Boyer and Kenneth J. Zahorski
Published by arrangement with the authors.

Printed and bound in the USA.

Library of Congress Cataloging–in–Publication Data

Visions & Imaginings : classic fantasy fiction / edited by Robert
H. Boyer & Kenneth J. Zahorski.
    p.   cm.
    Includes bibliographical references.
    ISBN 0-89733-361-6
     1. Fantastic fiction. I. Boyer, Robert H. 1937–
II. Zahorski, Kenneth J., 1939–   . III. Title: Visions and
imaginings.
PN6120.95.F25V5 1991
808.83'8766—dc20   91-10641
                                        CIP

Cover art by Barbara Corey
Cover design by B. Spann

ACKNOWLEDGMENTS

We are pleased to re-introduce a number of stories that we made available to readers in our previous anthologies. We have listed below, in abbreviated form, the earlier anthologies from which we have selected the present list: FI = *The Fantastic Imagination*; FI-II = *The Fantastic Imagination II*; DI = *Dark Imaginings: Gothic Fantasy*; PT = *The Phoenix Tree: Myth Fantasy*; VW=*Visions of Wonder: Christian Fantasy*.

George MacDonald, "The Light Princess" (FI): reprinted from *The Gifts of the Christ Child: Fairy Tales and Stories for the Childlike*, Vol. I, (Grand Rapids, Michigan: William Eerdmans Publishing Company, 1973), edited by Glenn E. Sadler. Originally published in *Adela Cathcart*, 1864.

Frank R. Stockton, "The Accommodating Circumstance" (FI): reprinted from *The Storyteller's Pack: A Frank R. Stockton Reader*, (New York: Charles Scribner's Sons, 1968).

John Buchan, "The Grove of Ashtaroth" (FI): reprinted from *The Moon Endureth: Tales and Fancies*, (Edinburgh: Blackwood, 1912).

Kenneth Morris, "Red-Peach-Blossom Inlet" (FI-II): reprinted from *The Secret Mountain and Other Tales*, (London: Faber & Gwyer, 1926).

Selma Lagerlöf, "The Legend of the Christmas Rose" (FI-II): reprinted from *Sweden's Best Stories*, (New York: W.W. Norton & Company, Inc., 1928), edited by Hanna Astrup Larsen, and translated by Charles Wharton Stork. Reprinted by permission of the American-Scandinavian Foundation, New York.

Eric Linklater, "The Abominable Imprecation" (FI–II): reprinted from *God Likes Them Plain: Short Stories*, (London: Jonathan Cape, Ltd., 1935); reprinted by permission of Jonathan Cape, Ltd., and the Peters Fraser & Dunlop Group, Ltd.

T.H. White, "The Troll" (DI): reprinted by permission of David Higham Associates, Ltd.

Lord Dunsany, "The Bride of the Man-Horse" (PT): reprinted from *The Sword of Welleran and Other Tales of Enchantment* (New York: The Devin-Adair Company, 1954). Copyright © 1954 by Edward John Moreton Drax Plunkett, Lord Dunsany; Copyright renewed © 1982 by Lady Dunsany. Reprinted by permission of The Devin-Adair Company, Inc.

Félix Martí-Ibáñez, M.D., "Niña Sol" (PT): reprinted from *All the Wonders We Seek: Thirteen Tales of Surprise and Prodigy* (New York: Clarkson N. Potter, Inc., 1963). Copyright © 1963 by Félix Martí-Ibáñez, M.D. Reprinted by permission of Verna Sabelle.

Ursula K. Le Guin, "April in Paris" (FI–II): reprinted from *The Wind's Twelve Quarters* (New York: Harper & Row, Inc., 1975). Copyright © 1962, 1975 by Ursula K. Le Guin; reprinted by permission of the author and the author's agent, Virginia Kidd.

Isaac Bashevis Singer, "Jachid and Jechidah" (VW): reprinted from *Short Friday and Other Stories*, (New York: Farrar, Straus & Giroux, Inc., 1964). Copyright © 1961, 1962, 1963, 1964 by Isaac Bashevis Singer. Reprinted by permission of Farrar, Straus and Giroux, Inc., and Laurence Pollinger Limited.

Lloyd Alexander, "The Foundling" (FI): reprinted from *The Foundling and Other Tales of Prydain* (New York: Holt, Rinehart and Winston, Inc., 1973). Copyright © 1973 by Lloyd Alexander. Reprinted by permission of the author, Brandt and Brandt Literary Agents, Inc., and Henry Holt and Company, Inc.

We are pleased to express our gratitude to those who, in various ways, shared with us the excitement and the labors involved in compiling this anthology: to Maria Quinlan, our research assistant, who provided invaluable help in the beginning stages of the project; to Chris Utech and Arlene Schlapman, whose secretarial expertise lightened our editorial burden; to Academy Chicago Publishers' editor Sarah Leslie Welsch; to Bill Senior and John Douglas to whom we turned for information about current trends in fantasy; to Robert L. Horn, Dean of St Norbert College, for his continuing support and encouragement; and to Barb and Marijean, our wives and muses.

Contents

Introduction

This collection is a distillation of stories which were published by Dell and Avon in the late seventies and early eighties, contained in five separate volumes: *The Fantastic Imagination* (1977), *Dark Imaginings* (1978), *The Fantastic Imagination II* (1978), *The Phoenix Tree* (1980) and *Visions of Wonder* (1981).

By 1985, all five volumes had gone out of print, victims of a temporary decline in the popularity of classic Fantasy. Since that time, many readers have written to us about the books and we were gratified to have received a special award for these anthologies from Fantasy fans at Mythcon XVI in 1985.

More than 2000 stories were read for this five-volume series and now, at last, a new compilation out of that series has been created — *Visions and Imaginings* — a kind of "best of the best".

The question of how to define Fantasy haunts us to this day. When we began teaching SF and Fantasy some eighteen years ago there was a dearth of critical literature on these genres. So with a little help from a few writers such as E.M. Forster and J.R.R. Tolkien we developed our own theory based on a broad sampling of the literature itself. It was a challenging and exciting process and (we hope readers agree) our critical position seems to have endured, even if we have made a number of refinements.

Our basic premise is that Fantasy literature is characterized by the presence of *non-rational*, rather than irrational elements ("irrational" suggests aberration); that is, by phenomena that cannot be readily explained in reasonable or scientific terms. In fact, it is this premise which has allowed us to find Fantasy within general literary tradition. For instance, Tolkien's "secondary worlds" as well as creatures of faerie and the God or gods of creation are all examples of non-rational phenomena, elements of which are found in the Bible, *The Iliad*, *The Odyssey*, *A Thousand and One Nights*, medieval Romance, Greek and Renaissance drama as well as the courtly tales of Charles Perrault, including "Sleeping Beauty" and "Cinderella".

These works in fact occupied a large and honorable place in the literary mainstream of their time. And it wasn't until the latter part of the 17th century that the light of Fantasy dimmed, only to be rekindled in the mid-19th century by the Romantic movement in European literature and by the reappearance in print of fairy tales, both folk — from the Grimm Brothers, Jacob and Joseph — and literary — by Hans Christian Anderson. This resurgence of the genre was then taken up by George MacDonald, considered by many to be the founder of modern British Fantasy. He, in turn, influenced Lewis Carroll, C.S. Lewis and, of course, Tolkien whose The *Lord of the Rings*, published in paperback in the '60's, became the catalyst for the wave of enthusiasm for Fantasy which ensued.

The operative term "non-rational" helps also, we think, to separate Fantasy from other, similar types of literature. Poe's horror stories, for example, seem to be non-rational, but in the end prove to be explicable, which thus disqualifies them. Stories, too, in which the narrator is dreaming or suffers psychotic delusions are not fantasies, either, because the non-rational elements radiate from the dreamer's or psychotic's mind. For instance, two works of Fantasy — *The Wizard of Oz* and *A Connecticut Yankee in King Arthur's Court* — were actually de-fantasized in their film versions because their protagonists were "bumped on the head", robbing them of their natural Fantasy elements.

Science Fiction, because it is based on scientific data or pseudo-scientific explanation, is clearly different from Fantasy, although the aura of awe and wonder which SF produces is quite similar to the effects evoked by Fantasy.

However, the main focus of this volume is the imaginary or so-called secondary world, a setting which is unique to "high" Fantasy (as opposed to "low" Fantasy) and exemplified by Middle Earth, Narnia and the Forest Sauvage. As noted above these secondary worlds are themselves the non-rational phenomena that place these works within the Fantasy realm.

Within the secondary, high Fantasy settings, however, events are regulated by an internal logic or system peculiar to these worlds. Consequently, they do not qualify as non-rational elements, even if they do evoke, as Tolkien put it, an "arresting strangeness". And, as it happens, all the stories in this volume except for two, "Lila the Werewolf" and "The Troll", are examples of high Fantasy.

Low Fantasy differs from high Fantasy in that the former is set in the world of everyday reality and thus, in the total absence of scientific or rational elements, is all the more startling. In Peter Beagle's "Lila the Werewolf", the title character lives an apparently ordinary life in Manhattan with her boyfriend, but on nights of the full moon she turns into a ravening beast. There is no plausible explanation for her metamorphosis — it is non-rational — just as there is no logical reason why the properties of silver bullets are fatal to werewolves.

This kind of implausibility is also exemplified by T.H. White's story , "The Troll", set in a resort hotel in Lapland. It is precisely this bizarre, matter-of-fact and unexplained appearance of the creature which gives the story its impact and also illustrates how the non-rational can stand out as a more effective threat in low Fantasy than in high. The fear of the unknown or the inexplicable which is present in these two tales also characterizes good ghost stories such as those written by H. P. Lovecraft or Algernon Blackwood. Unquestionably, the low Fantasy tales are more successful than their high Fantasy counterparts in producing fear in those who read them, thus linking them to the genre of Gothic stories.

However, as we have said, most of the works in this collection are high Fantasy stories, of which there are two types: Myth and Faery Tale. In the case of Myth, the explanation of the Fantasy phenomena is through supernatural causality or divine agency. For example, it is the divine or "super-terrestrial" light that causes the forest to bloom in midwinter in "The Legend of the Christmas Rose."

On the other hand, if the changes effected are through the agency of beings other than God or gods — wizards, say, or enchantresses — then the causation is a product of magic and the work is a Faery Tale. In "The Light Princess", for example, it is a very disgruntled witch named Makemnoit who causes the Princess to lose her gravity; the witch's powers are magical, not divine, and thus the story is a Faery Tale.

Secondary world settings and supernatural or magical causality are thus the principal characteristics that define high Fantasy and account for the sense of awe and wonder it evokes. And there are three literary ingredients that figure prominently in Fantasy works and which support the setting and causality: (1) the Everyman character; (2) an elevated style; and (3) archetypes. The Everyman character — King Arthur or Bilbo Baggins — is a person like the rest of us, but who rises above the ordinary in critical circumstances.

The high or elevated style enables fantasists to depict the secondary world by using the language of comparison or metaphor, and to characterize the inhabitants of this world through their speech as different from those of the primary world. For example, characters in faerie such as Gandalf the Wizard know the proper way to address noble beasts like eagles.

And, thirdly, archetypes: those symbols, characters, plot motifs or themes which powerfully move the reader and elicit an instinctive response are more prominent in Fantasy than perhaps in any other form of literature. This is why Freud thought Fantasy a fertile area of study. The sacrifice of the Prince and its redemptive effects throughout the realm in "The Light Princess" is one of the most enduring, evocative and universal archetypes in all of literature.

Naturally, all the stories in this collection qualify as

Fantasy, but we have used other criteria as well for their selection. To begin with, we wanted all five of our earlier volumes to be represented in *Visions and Imaginings*, making it a true omnibus edition. The abbreviations in the Acknowledgments section above indicate the volume from which each story was taken. Some volumes are more heavily represented than others because we did not try for strict numerical equality, but, rather, aimed for variety and balance. As might be expected, we relied more heavily upon our general anthologies, *The Fantastic Imagination* (I & II) and *The Phoenix Tree,* rather than the more specialized *Visions of Wonder and Dark Imaginings.*

We have also tried to include as wide a variety of Fantasy authors as possible. The earliest work, "The Light Princess" by George MacDonald was written in 1864. The most recent piece, written by another remarkable English writer, Vera Chapman, is "The Thread". Although she is in her nineties, she continues to publish, and her contribution to this volume appeared for the first time in 1980 in *The Phoenix Tree.* Our selection covers more than 100 years and also has an international flavor with the inclusion of authors from Sweden, Scotland, Wales and Spain, although the majority of the stories are by English and American fantasists, since they accurately reflect the high proportion of Fantasy works produced in these two countries.

As in earlier anthologies, we have also tried to include relatively inaccessible or neglected stories. For example, both Vera Chapman's "The Thread" and Evangeline Walton Ensley's "The Mistress of Kaer-Mor" made their publishing debuts in *The Phoenix Tree* and have not been reprinted as often since as they should. More attention, too, should be accorded the stories of Kenneth Morris and Félix Martí-Ibáñez; and while T.H. White's Arthurian classic *The Once and Future King* remains a perennial favorite, his "The Troll", a most intriguing low Fantasy work, is far less well known and deserves further promotion. Some writers, such as Selma Lagerlöf and Eric Linklater, although highly regarded in their own countries, are not widely reprinted elsewhere.

Perhaps the most important requirement for works included in this omnibus edition was that the selections be good literature. While it was not easy to separate "the cream from the cream", as it were, we were lucky enough to be able to draw on the views of our students, of outside readers and of critics. Obviously, the treasure house of "classics" expands over the years. The anthologies we edited in the seventies and early eighties necessarily reflected the extant Fantasy masterpieces. Were we to inventory our store now, in 1991, we would undoubtedly have included stories by writers such as Anne McCaffrey, Nicholas Stuart Gray, Molly Hunter and Katherine Kurtz. Still, we stand by the selections made as the very best of the time.

One of the most delightful discoveries we made while compiling our other anthologies was the remarkable diversity within the genre. Following the approach we used in those earlier works, in *Visions and Imaginings* we have also tried to take full advantage of this rich diversity by including stories which display a wide variety of settings, characters, styles and archetypes such as those discussed above.

An equally delightful aspect of Fantasy is its dynamism. From the advent of Fantasy literature's modern era in the mid-nineteenth century to the present, the genre has undergone remarkable change. Especially dramatic have been the changes of the past quarter of a century. Since the publication of Tolkien's *Lord of the Rings* in 1965, the genre's physical appearance, personality, and literary status have altered considerably. While we will not attempt an in-depth historical treatment of the genre, we will paint a few broad strokes on the contemporary historical canvas, focusing on some of the most significant permutations of the past dozen years or so.

Our approach will be to compare what we see today with the primary trends we identified in the General Introduction to *Fantasy Literature,* a bibliographical study published in 1979, just two years after the appearance of our first anthology, *The Fantastic Imagination.* In *Fantasy Literature* we identified the following developments and trends: (1) the high priority given Fantasy by publishing houses; (2) the attention lavished upon the genre by teachers, scholars and critics; (3) the emergence of a strong contingent of home-grown fantasists; (4) the increasing number of women entering the field; (5) the rediscovery of neglected major talents; (6) the popularity of cinema and television adaptations of Fantasy works; and (7) the extraordinary interest in Fantasy among adult readers.

What has happened to each of these developments during the past decade?

To begin with, publishing houses, especially American and British firms, have continued to give Fantasy high priority treatment. Throughout the 1980s, publishers printed scores of new Fantasy works, reissued many of those long out of print, and introduced dozens of handsome reprint and facsimile editions of Fantasy classics. Some types of Fantasy, as well as some packaging formats, however, were given preferential treatment. Recognizing the reading public's seemingly insatiable hunger for gore and horror, for example, publishers stocked bookstore shelves with Gothics aplenty. Perhaps the biggest winner in the Gothic Fantasy sweepstakes of the '80s was Stephen King, whose phenomenal success epitomizes a decade which could not seem to get enough of ghosts, ghouls and gremlins. We will also remember the '80s as the era of the sequel. Noting the popularity of Tolkien's *Ring* series, publishers flooded the market with trilogies, tetralogies and sometimes even longer series. This predisposition toward multi-part "epic Fantasy" such as Stephen Donaldson's *Chronicles of Thomas Covenant* promises to make its power felt well into the '90s. This and other current publishing trends have their negative side as we will show later.

Furthermore, instructors, scholars and critics have maintained their interest in Fantasy. The trend toward developing Fantasy literature courses which began in the mid-sixties seems to be continuing on both the secondary school and college levels. Scholars, too, continue to enter the Perilous

Realm. Starting with Tzvetan Todorov in the early 1970's, a substantial number of critical, bibliographic and encyclopedic works have appeared, stimulating lively debate and discussion of all aspects of Fantasy. The annual International Conference on the Fantastic and its "Selected Essays" series have provided a focus for scholarly activity, adding further evidence of the genre's vitality.

In short, the pedagogical and critical attention paid to Fantasy in the '70s and '80s has continued unabated during the past decade. However, to say Fantasy scholarship within Academe has assumed the same prestige as have studies of mainstream fiction is to paint too rosy a picture. There is still considerable evidence that Fantasy criticism remains somewhat suspect among some academics. And the snobbery still exists which created the Science Fiction/ Fantasy Ghetto, though it may be less pronounced than it was a decade or two ago.

In *Fantasy Literature* we suggested that British domination of modern Fantasy had at last come to an end, noting the large numbers of fine home-grown fantasists then entering the field. Specifically, we pointed out that the ranks of veteran American fantasists (*e.g.* C.L.Moore, Andre Norton, Poul Anderson, L. Sprague de Camp, Fritz Leiber, and Evangeline Walton Ensley) were being bolstered by relative newcomers such as Ursula K. Le Guin, Lloyd Alexander, Peter S. Beagle, Patricia McKillip, Carol Kendall, Jane Langton, Sanders Anne Laubenthal, Nancy Bond, Katherine Kurtz, C.J. Cherryh, Elizabeth Scarborough, Stephen Donaldson and Robin McKinley. What began as a trend in the late '70s has now become the *status quo*. Although much top-notch Fantasy still comes from England, and although the genre is fast taking on an international character, the '80s belonged to American fantasists. For evidence of this, one need only turn to the recent lists of nominees and winners of the William L. Crawford Award, given yearly by the International Association for the Fantastic in the Arts to an outstanding new author of Fantasy fiction. The 1987 list is a good indicator: Greg Bear (for

The Infinity Concerto/The Serpent Image); Timothy Findley (for *Not Wanted on the Voyage*); Paul Hazel (for *The Finnbranch Trilogy*); Guy Gavriel Kay (for *The Fionavar Trilogy*); Dan Simmons (for *Song of Kali*); Judith Tarr (for *The Hound and the Falcon Trilogy*); and Tad Williams (for *Tailchaser's Song*). Findley and Kay are from Canada; all the others are from the United States.

Still another trend which began within the last twenty years is the influx of women fantasists. Charlotte Spivach's *Merlin's Daughters: Contemporary Women Writers of Fantasy* attests to this. We are pleased to note that with the rise in numbers of women fantasists has come a corresponding increase in the numbers of strong female protagonists, righting the imbalance which existed for far too long.

Unfortunately, some exciting developments of the '70s have not fulfilled their promise. For example, one of the most heartening events at that time was the rediscovery of neglected major talents in the field. In *Fantasy Literature* we mentioned writers such as Kenneth Morris, Barry Pain, and James Branch Cabell. Beginning with Ian and Betty Ballantine's Adult Fantasy Series in the late-sixties (1969-1975) there seemed to be a healthy move afoot to make the works of such writers more accessible. The Ballantine Series provided an excellent and encouraging start. Since then, however, the reintroduction of Fantasy classics has been sporadic. In our own anthologies, we helped to bring back the short fantasy works of authors such as Félix Martí-Ibáñez, Vera Chapman, John Buchan, H.E. Bates, Selma Lagerlöf, Frank Stockton, Richard Garnett, as well as the aforementioned James Branch Cabell, and Evangeline Walton Ensley, to name only a handful. But few anthologists have followed suit and the tendency these days seems to be to reprint only those authors who sell.

Another trend of the '70s which still has not fulfilled its rich promise, it seems to us, is the adaptation of fantasy literature to the screen. In 1979 we were excited about the potential of television versions of Tolkien's *The Hobbit* and Lewis's *The Lion, The Witch and the Wardrobe*, as well as cinematic treatments of *The Lord of the Ring* and Richard Adams's *Watership Down*. This renewed interest in Fantasy classics, coupled with the use of innovative cinematic techniques (especially in the area of animation), seemed to promise even more sophisticated and compelling adaptations in the '80s. Since then, however, we have not seen a steady improvement in technique. This is not to say that movies such as *The Black Cauldron*, *The Princess Bride*, *The Adventures of Baron Munchausen*, *The Neverending Story*, *Laputa—The City in the Clouds*, *The Little Mermaid*, *Big*, and *Edward Scissorhands* were without merit. Indeed, these, and other such fantasy films, were not only good entertainment, but did advance the state of the art. The degree and rate of advancement have not, however, met our expectations.

While cinema and television may not have done as much as we had hoped for in the areas of faery tale and myth fantasy, they did provide aficionados of horror and sword-and-sorcery fantasy with abundant fare. The success of this sub-genre can be measured by the record number of sequels for such films as *Halloween*, *Friday the 13th*, *Nightmare on Elm Street*, *Psycho*, and *Poltergeist*. In addition, cinematic renditions of Stephen King novels appeared almost monthly, vampire movies abounded, the "Living Dead" did indeed return, and the theme song from *Ghostbusters* became one of the biggest hits of the '80s. Nearly as ubiquitous as werewolves, vampires, ghouls, ghosts, and gremlins were the muscular men and women of sword-and-sorcery. From *Conan the Destroyer* through *Ladyhawke* and *Willow*, the loincloth and double ax have been very evident the past few years.

In our Introduction to *Fantasy Literature* we also noted that at the end of the '70s there was an extraordinary interest in fantasy among adult readers. As Patrick Merla pointed out in an insightful and thought-provoking article which appeared in the November 4, 1972 issue of *Saturday Review*, "Children [were] forsaking innocence in their reading habits to peruse stark realities, while adults, paradoxically, [were] wandering more and more into fictional never-never lands." The paradoxical trend Merla recognized in the early seventies persists today. But this is not to say that young readers have forsaken the fields of Fantasy. They, too, continue their love affair with the genre even as they read quality realistic fiction written for young adults. Happily, this broad readership for Fantasy literature seems likely to continue for at least the next decade, given the continual production of works in this field.

Also worthy of mention are two or three more recent trends and developments not dealt with in any of our previous Introductory essays. To begin with, many fine contemporary fantasists (especially Americans) have moved away from the conventional orientation toward northern European settings to a more international orientation. Bill Senior, Fantasy scholar and Chair of the Crawford Harvard Committee, pointed this out to us in one of three recent telephone interviews. Although what Tolkien called "the Northern Thing" has not lost its appeal, readers are now just as likely to be introduced to aboriginal cultures (Michaela Roessner's *Walkabout Woman*), the culture of Medieval China (Jeanne Larsen's *Silk Road*), life in The Middle East (Susan Schwartz's *Heirs to Byzantium*), and Mayan Culture (Lewis Shiner's *Deserted Cities of the Heart*) as to the more traditional Celtic realms.

Deserving mention as a second significant trend is the emergence of the Latin American School of Magical Realism, a movement being helped along considerably by the Avon Books Latin American reprinting program under the very capable editorship of John Douglas, Avon's fantasy editor. In a recent interview, Douglas cites Cortazar and Garcia Marquéz as prime examples of the type of fantasy in which the magical is accepted as part of reality. Significant, too, is the unabated interest in Arthurian scholarship and fantasy. Geoffrey Ashe's *The Discovery of King Arthur* (1985) might have been more aptly titled "The Ongoing Discovery of King Arthur," given the recent outpouring of articles, books, novels, and stories dealing with the Arthurian legend.

A final note. In the April 29, 1990 issue of *The New York Times Book Review,* David Hartwell, consulting editor for William Morrow & Company and Tor Books, discusses the current state of Fantasy literature in an article entitled, "Dollars and Dragons: The Truth about Fantasy." In his thought-provoking essay, Hartwell identifies still another trend worth watching. He contends that in the last two decades American publishing houses have succeeded in doing with Fantasy what they did earlier with the Gothic romance and the contemporary Romance genre: they have created what Hartwell calls a "mass-market sub-genre." This sub-genre exists by slavishly reproducing in book after book the ingredients that made Tolkienian fantasy popular. Hartwell, while perhaps overstating his argument, justifiably quotes readers who complain, "Hey, I've read this book already, in fact I've read this book about fourteen times." Furthermore, says Hartwell, "Fantasy, like the marketing genres before it, has been made more predict-able, has eliminated new ideas and can now be sold as product." Later in his article Hartwell does temper his dreary views somewhat by pointing out that "there are signs that the dominance of the genre by the best-selling, intensively marketed book, while it prevails, does provide a publishing home and a supportive audience for writers and for works of quality otherwise unsupported by fashion."

John Douglas agrees with Hartwell's more temperate assessment by pointing to the recent appearance of "a double handful of excellent books" in the Fantasy area, books containing "something new or beguiling in the re-telling." He cites Jonathan Carroll as one example. None-theless, the mass marketing trend, because of its very serious negative implications, deserves not only our atten-tion, but our assistance in preventing formula fantasy from blocking the sunlight from the tender shoots of serious, innovative fantasy that is pushing toward the light of public and critical attention.

While the updating of general trends and developments in the field of Fantasy has been a primary goal in this

"Introduction," we would now like to engage briefly in a more specific update. Just as the landscape of Fantasy has changed over the past decade, so too have the lives and careers of our authors in *Visions and Imaginings* who are still living. Here, in our opinion, are some of the most noteworthy developments.

Let us begin with Evangeline Walton Ensley and Peter S. Beagle, both of whom — after long hiatuses — brought forth long-awaited novels. In 1983, Ensley published an historical fantasy, *The Sword is Forged*, her first major work since *The Prince of Annwn* in 1974. Beagle broke an even longer silence in 1986 when *The Folk of the Air* was issued nearly two decades after the publication in 1968 of his classic, *The Last Unicorn*. These novels brought a resurgence of critical and popular interest in both authors.

Similarly, Vera Chapman, who was very active in the '70's, has not published a great deal since. We are pleased, however, to report that Mrs Chapman, now in her nineties, will soon see in print her picaresque novel featuring the mysterious and adventurous Abbess of Shaston. Tentatively entitled *The Notorious Abbess*, it should appear within the next year, also from Academy Chicago Publishers .

Unlike the above authors, Lloyd Alexander has continued to be prolific. Though the quality of his writing has remained high, he has, however, taken an interesting turn in recent years, moving away from Fantasy. The Westmark Trilogy (1981–1984) takes place in an historical timeframe, but in a fictitious realm. The five books in the Vesper Holly series (1986–1990) are adventure stories set in 19th century Philadelphia and various exotic, but real, locations.

Joan Aiken is another productive writer who has continued her output of young adult and adult novels and short stories. Among her fantasy collections, *A Touch of Chill: Tales of Sleepless Nights* (1980) and *A Whisper in the Night: Tales of Terror and Suspense* (1984) received especially positive reviews. *The Last Slice of Rainbow and Other Stories* (1988) is one of her more recent collections.

In recent years, Ursula K. Le Guin has continued her pattern of experimentation with various forms, including Fantasy, Science Fiction, and Metafiction, and for various audiences, including young adults and adults. *The Beginning Place* (1980), *Always Coming Home* (1984), and her new and final "Earthsea" novel, *Tehanu: The Last Book of Earthsea* (1990) are certainly important milestones that mark the decade for her.

And, finally, there is Isaac Bashevis Singer. We had written the following statement about Singer before his death on July 24, 1991, and would like to leave it unchanged as a tribute to his extraordinary vitality. "The remarkable Singer, even at his advanced age, continues to write for readers of all ages. He has had published a number of novels, short story collections, and children's story books over the past decade, collecting along the way well-deserved awards such as the Handel Medallion (1986)."

In several of our previous anthologies we speculated on the causes of the remarkable resurgence of Fantasy literature in the second half of the 20th century. Why, we asked, is it only in recent years that it has been discovered—or rediscovered? The answer we gave in the past remains as valid now as then. Ours is a frenetic and dangerous age. Today, perhaps more than ever before, we have a deeply felt need to escape for a time in order to restore our sense of awe and wonder and to regain a fresh perspective on our lives and this world. It is our hope now, as it was when we compiled our other anthologies from which the works of *Visions and Imaginings* have been chosen, that the present volume will serve as a rich and dependable source of readings to those readers who wish to explore the restorative realms of Fantasy.

Visions & Imaginings:
Imaginings:
Classic Fantasy Fiction

❦ GEORGE MAC DONALD ❦

(1825–1905)

George Mac Donald, Scottish novelist, poet, and writer of children's stories, was born at Huntley, Aberdeenshire, the son of a farmer. He was educated at Aberdeen University and Highbury Theological College. In 1850, Mac Donald became a Congregationalist minister at Arundel, but after a few years he retired, partly because of health problems, and partly because of theological considerations. Devoting the rest of his long life to the writing of literature, he published scores of books, including popular novels of Scottish peasant life and volumes of collected sermons and theological treatises. The latter attracted the attention of C. S. Lewis, who was greatly impressed by the deep religious feeling which permeates all Mac Donald's works.

In the past decade or so, Mac Donald's fantasy writings have gained great popularity. *Phantastes: A Faerie Romance* (1858) and *Lilith* (1895) are generally considered to be two of the best adult fantasy novels ever written. Of equally fine quality are his collections of children's stories, including *At the Back of the North Wind* (1871), *Ranald Bannerman's Boyhood* (1871), and *The Princess and the Goblin* (1872). Although troubled by ill health, Mac Donald seems to have lived a happy, eventful, and rewarding life. He became a famous and popular writer, and established a number of close friendships with some of the leading literary figures of the day. He seemed happiest, however, when reading one of his stories to his huge, and adoring, family of eleven children.

"The Light Princess" is one of Mac Donald's most

1

charming and inventive fairy tales. It is full of surpris-
ing events and clever contrivances. Perhaps the most
ingenious device is the central one, the Princess's
weightlessness. Once her sour aunt's evil spell has deprived the Princess of her "gravity" she gets into one
embarrassing predicament after another, much to the
chagrin of her royal parents. It is not princess-like, after
all, to be used as a ball by the servants of the castle.
Another memorable device is the mysterious "White
Snake of Darkness" which is used by the evil aunt later
in the narrative. The story is also distinctive because of
its subtle, but devastating, satire. Especially poignant
are the epsiodes involving the two court Metaphysi-
cals—Hum-Drum the Materialist and Kopy-Keck the
Spiritualist. But perhaps the most amazing thing about
this story is that it remains a fairy tale in the finest and
purest sense of the term, even while mercilessly paro-
dying many of the stock ingredients of the genre.

The Light Princess
George Mac Donald

I

WHAT! NO CHILDREN?

Once upon a time, so long ago that I have quite forgotten the date, there lived a king and queen who had no children.

And the king said to himself, "All the queens of my acquaintance have children, some three, some seven, and some as many as twelve; and my queen has not one. I feel ill-used." So he made up his mind to be cross with his wife about it. But she bore it all like a good patient queen as she was. Then the king grew very cross indeed. But the queen pretended to take it all as a joke, and a very good one too.

"Why don't you have any daughters, at least?" said he. "I don't say *sons;* that might be too much to expect." "I am sure, dear king, I am very sorry," said the queen.

"So you ought to be," retorted the king; "you are not going to make a virtue of *that,* surely."

But he was not an ill-tempered king, and in any matter of less moment would have let the queen have her own way with all his heart. This, however, was an affair of state.

The queen smiled.

3

"You must have patience with a lady, you know, dear king," said she.

She was, indeed, a very nice queen, and heartily sorry that she could not oblige the king immediately.

The king tried to have patience, but he succeeded very badly. It was more than he deserved, therefore, when, at last, the queen gave him a daughter—as lovely a little princess as ever cried.

II

WON'T I, JUST?

The day grew near when the infant must be christened. The king wrote all the invitations with his own hand. Of course somebody was forgotten.

Now it does not generally matter if somebody *is* forgotten, only you must mind who. Unfortunately, the king forgot without intending to forget; and so the chance fell upon the Princess Makemnoit, which was awkward. For the princess was the king's own sister; and he ought not to have forgotten her. But she had made herself so disagreeable to the old king, their father, that he had forgotten her in making his will; and so it was no wonder that her brother forgot her in writing his invitations. But poor relations don't do anything to keep you in mind of them. Why don't they? The king could not see into the garret she lived in, could he?

She was a sour, spiteful creature. The wrinkles of contempt crossed the wrinkles of peevishness, and made her face as full of wrinkles as a pat of butter. If ever a king could be justified in forgetting anybody, this king was justified in forgetting his sister, even at a christening. She looked very odd, too. Her forehead was as large as all the rest of her face, and projected over it like a precipice. When she was angry, her little eyes flashed blue. When she hated anybody, they shone yellow and green. What they looked like when she loved anybody, I do not know; for I never heard of her loving anybody but herself, and I do not think she could have managed that if she had not somehow got used to herself. But what made it highly imprudent in the king to forget her was—that she was awfully clever. In fact, she was a witch; and when she bewitched anybody, he very soon had enough of it; for she beat all the wicked fairies in wickedness, and all the clever ones in cleverness. She despised all the modes we read of in history, in which offended fairies and witches have taken their revenges; and therefore, after waiting and waiting in vain for an invitation, she made up her mind at last to go without one, and make the whole family miserable, like a princess as she was.

So she put on her best gown, went to the palace, was kindly received by the happy monarch, who forgot that he had forgotten her, and took her place in the procession to the royal chapel. When they were all gathered about the font, she contrived to get next to it, and throw something into the water; after which she maintained a very respectful demeanour till the water was applied to the child's face. But at that moment she turned round in her place three times, and muttered the following words, loud enough for those beside her to hear:—

"Light of spirit, by my charms,
Light of body every part,
Never weary human arms—
Only crush thy parents' heart!"

They all thought she had lost her wits, and was repeating some foolish nursery rhyme; but a shudder went through the whole of them notwithstanding. The baby, on the contrary, began to laugh and crow; while the nurse gave a start and a smothered cry, for she thought she was struck with paralysis: she could not feel the baby in her arms. But she clasped it tight and said nothing.

The mischief was done.

III

SHE CAN'T BE OURS

Her atrocious aunt had deprived the child of all her gravity. If you ask me how this was effected, I answer, "In the easiest way in the world. She had only to destroy gravitation." For the princess was a philosopher, and knew all the *ins* and *outs* of the laws of gravitation as well as the *ins* and *outs* of her boot-lace. And being a witch as well, she could abrogate those laws in a moment; or at least so clog their wheels and rust their bearings, that they would not work at all. But we have more to do with what followed than with how it was done.

The first awkwardness that resulted from this unhappy privation was, that the moment the nurse began to float the baby up and down, she flew from her arms towards the ceiling. Happily, the resistance of the air brought her ascending career to a close within a foot of it. There she remained, horizontal as when she left her nurse's arms, kicking and laughing amazingly. The nurse in terror flew to the bell, and begged the footman, who answered it, to bring up the house-steps directly. Trembling in every limb, she climbed upon the steps, and had to stand upon the very top, and reach up, before she could reach the floating tail of the baby's long clothes.

When the strange fact came to be known, there was a terrible commotion in the palace. The occasion of its discovery by the king was naturally a repetition of the nurse's experience. Astonished that he felt no weight when the child was laid in his arms, he began to wave her up and—not down; for she slowly ascended to the ceiling as before, and there remained floating in perfect comfort and satisfaction, as was testified by her peals of tiny laughter. The king stood staring up in speechless amazement, and trembled so that his beard shook like grass in the wind. At last, turning to the queen, who was just as horror-struck as himself, he said, gasping, staring, and stammering,—

"She *can't* be ours, queen!"

Now the queen was much cleverer than the king, and had begun already to suspect that "this effect defective came by cause."

"I am sure she is ours," answered she. "But we ought to have taken better care of her at the christening. People who were never invited ought not to have been present."

"Oh, ho!" said the king, tapping his forehead with his forefinger, "I have it all. I've found her out. Don't you see it, queen? Princess Makemnoit has bewitched her."

"That's just what I say," answered the queen.

"I beg your pardon, my love; I did not hear you.— John! bring the steps I get on my throne with."

For he was a little king with a great throne, like many other kings.

The throne-steps were brought, and set upon the dining-table, and John got upon the top of them. But he could not reach the little princess, who lay like a baby-laughter-cloud in the air, exploding continuously.

"Take the tongs, John," said his Majesty; and getting up on the table, he handed them to him.

John could reach the baby now, and the little princess was handed down by the tongs.

IV

WHERE IS SHE?

One fine summer day, a month after these her first adventures, during which time she had been very carefully watched, the princess was lying on the bed in the queen's own chamber, fast asleep. One of the windows was open, for it was noon, and the day was so sultry that the little girl was wrapped in nothing less ethereal than slumber itself. The queen came into the room, and not observing that the baby was on the bed, opened another window. A frolicsome fairy wind, which had been watching for a chance of mischief, rushed in at the one window, and taking its way over the bed where the child was lying, caught her up, and rolling and floating her along like a piece of flue, or a dandelion seed, carried her with it through the opposite window, and away. The queen went down-stairs, quite ignorant of the loss she had herself occasioned.

When the nurse returned, she supposed that her Majesty had carried her off, and, dreading a scolding, delayed making inquiry about her. But hearing nothing, she grew uneasy, and went at length to the queen's boudoir, where she found her Majesty.

"Please, your Majesty, shall I take the baby?" said she.

"Where is she?" asked the queen.

"Please forgive me. I know it was wrong."

"What do you mean?" said the queen, looking grave.

"Oh! don't frighten me, your Majesty!" exclaimed the nurse, clasping her hands.

The queen saw that something was amiss, and fell down in a faint. The nurse rushed about the palace, screaming, "My baby! my baby!"

Every one ran to the queen's room. But the queen

could give no orders. They soon found out, however, that the princess was missing, and in a moment the palace was like a beehive in a garden; and in one minute more the queen was brought to herself by a great shout and a clapping of hands. They had found the princess fast asleep under a rose-bush, to which the elvish little wind-puff had carried her, finishing its mischief by shaking a shower of red rose-leaves all over the little white sleeper. Startled by the noise the servants made, she woke, and, furious with glee, scattered the rose-leaves in all directions, like a shower of spray in the sunset.

She was watched more carefully after this, no doubt; yet it would be endless to relate all the odd incidents resulting from this peculiarity of the young princess. But there never was a baby in a house, not to say a palace, that kept the household in such constant good humour, at least below-stairs. If it was not easy for her nurses to hold her, at least she made neither their arms nor their hearts ache. And she was so nice to play at ball with! There was positively no danger of letting her fall. They might throw her down, or knock her down, or push her down, but couldn't *let* her down. It is true, they might let her fly into the fire or the coal-hole, or through the window; but none of these accidents had happened as yet. If you heard peals of laughter resounding from some unknown region, you might be sure enough of the cause. Going down into the kitchen, or *the room,* you would find Jane and Thomas, and Robert and Susan, all and sum, playing at ball with the little princess. She was the ball herself, and did not enjoy it the less for that. Away she went, flying from one to another, screeching with laughter. And the servants loved the ball itself better even than the game. But they had to take some care how they threw her, for if she received an upward direction, she would never come down again without being fetched.

V

WHAT IS TO BE DONE?

But above-stairs it was different. One day, for instance, after breakfast, the king went into his counting-house, and counted out his money.

The operation gave him no pleasure.

"To think," said he to himself, "that every one of these gold sovereigns weighs a quarter of an ounce, and my real, live, flesh-and-blood princess weighs nothing at all!"

And he hated his gold sovereigns, as they lay with a broad smile of self-satisfaction all over their yellow faces.

The queen was in the parlour, eating bread and honey. But at the second mouthful she burst out crying, and could not swallow it. The king heard her sobbing. Glad of anybody, but especially of his queen, to quarrel with, he clashed his gold sovereigns into his money-box, clapped his crown on his head, and rushed into the parlour.

"What is all this about?" exclaimed he. "What are you crying for, queen?"

"I can't eat it," said the queen, looking ruefully at the honey-pot.

"No wonder!" retorted the king. "You've just eaten your breakfast—two turkey eggs, and three anchovies."

"Oh, that's not it!" sobbed her Majesty. "It's my child, my child!"

"Well, what's the matter with your child? She's neither up the chimney nor down the draw-well. Just hear her laughing."

Yet the king could not help a sigh, which he tried to turn into a cough, saying,—

"It is a good thing to be light-hearted, I am sure, whether she be ours or not."

"It is a bad thing to be light-headed," answered the queen, looking with prophetic soul far into the future.

" 'Tis a good thing to be light-handed," said the king.

" 'Tis a bad thing to be light-fingered," answered the queen.

" 'Tis a good thing to be light-footed," said the king.

" 'Tis a bad thing—" began the queen; but the king interrupted her.

"In fact," said he, with the tone of one who concludes an argument in which he has had only imaginary opponents, and in which, therefore, he has come off triumphant—"in fact, it is a good thing altogether to be light-bodied."

"But it is a bad thing altogether to be light-minded," retorted the queen, who was beginning to lose her temper.

This last answer quite discomfited his Majesty, who turned on his heel, and betook himself to his counting-house again. But he was not half-way towards it, when the voice of his queen overtook him.

"And it's a bad thing to be light-haired," screamed she, determined to have more last words, now that her spirit was roused.

The queen's hair was black as night; and the king's had been, and his daughter's was, golden as morning. But it was not this reflection on his hair that arrested him; it was the double use of the word *light*. For the king hated all witticisms, and punning especially. And besides, he could not tell whether the queen meant light-*haired* or light-*heired*; for why might she not aspirate her vowels when she was ex-asperated herself?

He turned upon his other heel, and rejoined her. She looked angry still, because she knew that she was guilty, or, what was much the same, knew that he thought so.

"My dear queen," said he, "duplicity of any sort is exceedingly objectionable between married people of any rank, not to say kings and queens; and the most objectionable form duplicity can assume is that of punning."

"There!" said the queen, "I never made a jest, but I broke it in the making. I am the most unfortunate woman in the world!"

She looked so rueful, that the king took her in his arms; and they sat down to consult.

"Can you bear this?" said the king.

"No, I can't," said the queen.

"Well, what's to be done?" said the king.

"I'm sure I don't know," said the queen. "But might you not try an apology?"

"To my older sister, I suppose you mean?" said the king.

"Yes," said the queen.

"Well, I don't mind," said the king.

So he went the next morning to the house of the princess, and, making a very humble apology, begged her to undo the spell. But the princess declared, with a grave face, that she knew nothing at all about it. Her eyes, however, shone pink, which was a sign that she was happy. She advised the king and queen to have patience, and to mend their ways. The king returned disconsolate. The queen tried to comfort him.

"We will wait till she is older. She may then be able to suggest something herself. She will know at least how she feels, and explain things to us."

"But what if she should marry?" exclaimed the king, in sudden consternation at the idea.

"Well, what of that?" rejoined the queen.

"Just think! If she were to have children! In the course of a hundred years the air might be as full of floating children as of gossamers in autumn."

"That is no business of ours," replied the queen. "Besides, by that time they will have learned to take care of themselves."

A sigh was the king's only answer.

He would have consulted the court physicians; but he was afraid they would try experiments upon her.

VI

SHE LAUGHS TOO MUCH

Meantime, notwithstanding awkward occurrences, and griefs that she brought upon her parents, the little princess laughed and grew—not fat, but plump and tall. She reached the age of seventeen, without having fallen into any worse scrape than a chimney; by rescuing her from which, a little bird-nesting urchin got fame and a black face. Nor thoughtless as she was, had she committed anything worse than laughter at everybody and everything that came in her way. When she was told, for the sake of experiment, that General Clanrunfort was cut to pieces with all his troops, she laughed; when she heard that the enemy was on his way to besiege her papa's capital, she laughed hugely; but when she was told that the city would certainly be abandoned to the mercy of the enemy's soldiery—why, then she laughed immoderately. She never could be brought to see the serious side of anything. When her mother cried, she said,—

"What queer faces mamma makes! And she squeezes water out of her cheeks! Funny mamma!"

And when her papa stormed at her, she laughed, and danced round and round him, clapping her hands, and crying—

"Do it again, papa. Do it again! It's such fun! Dear, funny papa!"

And if he tried to catch her, she glided from him in an instant, not in the least afraid of him, but thinking it part of the game not to be caught. With one push of her foot, she would be floating in the air above his head; or she would go dancing backwards and forwards and sideways, like a great butterfly. It happened several times, when her father and mother were holding a consultation about her in private, that they were interrupted by vainly repressed outbursts of laughter over their heads; and looking up with indignation, saw her floating at full length in the air above them, whence she regarded them with the most comical appreciation of the position.

One day an awkward accident happened. The princess had come out upon the lawn with one of her attendants, who held her by the hand. Spying her father at the other side of the lawn, she snatched her hand from the maid's, and sped across to him. Now when she wanted to run alone, her custom was to catch up a stone in each hand, so that she might come down again after a bound. Whatever she wore as part of her attire had no effect in this way: even gold, when it thus became as it were a part of herself, lost all its weight for the time. But whatever she only held in her hands retained its downward tendency. On this occasion she could see nothing to catch up but a huge toad, that was walking across the lawn as if he had a hundred years to do it in. Not knowing what disgust meant, for this was one of her peculiarities, she snatched up the toad and bounded away. She had almost reached her father, and he was holding out his arms to receive her, and take from her lips the kiss which hovered on them like a butterfly on a rosebud, when a puff of wind blew her aside into the arms of a young page, who had just been receiving a message from his Majesty. Now it was no great peculiarity in the princess that, once she was set agoing, it always cost her time and trouble to check herself. On this occasion there was no time. She *must* kiss—and she kissed the page. She did not mind it much; for she had no shyness in her composition; and she knew, besides, that she could not help it. So she only laughed, like a musical box. The poor page fared the worst. For the princess, trying to correct the unfortunate tendency of the kiss, put out her hands to keep her off the page; so that along with the kiss, he received, on the other cheek, a slap with a huge black toad, which she poked right into his eye. He tried to

laugh, too, but the attempt resulted in such an odd
contortion of countenance, as showed that there was no
danger of his pluming himself on the kiss. As for the
king, his dignity was greatly hurt, and he did not speak
to the page for a whole month.

I may here remark that it was very amusing to see
her run, if her mode of progression would properly be
called running. For first she would make a bound,
then, having alighted, she would run a few steps and
make another bound. Sometimes she would fancy she
had reached the ground before she actually had, and
her feet would go backwards and forwards, running
upon nothing at all, like those of a chicken on its back.
Then she would laugh like the very spirit of fun; only
in her laugh there was something missing. What it was,
I find myself unable to describe. I think it was a certain
tone, depending upon the possibility of sorrow—*mor-
bidezza,* perhaps. She never smiled.

VII

TRY METAPHYSICS

After a long avoidance of the painful subject, the king
and queen resolved to hold a council of three upon it;
and so they sent for the princess. In she came, sliding
and flitting and gliding from one piece of furniture to
another, and put herself at last in an arm-chair, in a
sitting posture. Whether she could be said *to sit,* seeing
she received no support from the seat of the chair, I do
not pretend to determine.

"My dear child," said the king, "you must be aware
by this time that you are not exactly like other people."

"Oh, you dear funny papa! I have got a nose, and
two eyes, and all the rest. So have you. So has
mamma."

"Now be serious, my dear, for once," said the queen.

"No, thank you, mamma; I had rather not."

"Would you not like to be able to walk like other people?" said the king.

"No indeed, I should think not. You only crawl. You are such slow coaches!"

"How do you feel, my child?" he resumed, after a pause of discomfiture.

"Quite well, thank you."

"I mean, what do you feel like?"

"Like nothing at all, that I know of."

"You must feel like something."

"I feel like a princess with such a funny papa, and such a dear pet of a queen-mamma!"

"Now really!" began the queen; but the princess interrupted her.

"Oh, yes," she added, "I remember. I have a curious feeling sometimes, as if I were the only person that had any sense in the whole world."

She had been trying to behave herself with dignity; but now she burst into a violent fit of laughter, threw herself backwards over the chair, and went rolling about the floor in an ecstasy of enjoyment. The king picked her up easier than one does a down quilt, and replaced her in her former relation to the chair. The exact preposition expressing this relation I do not happen to know.

"Is there nothing you wish for?" resumed the king, who had learned by this time that it was useless to be angry with her.

"Oh, you dear papa!—yes," answered she.

"What is it, my darling?"

"I have been longing for it—oh, such a time!—ever since last night."

"Tell me what it is."

"Will you promise to let me have it?"

The king was on the point of saying *Yes,* but the wiser queen checked him with a single motion of her head.

"Tell me what it is first," said he.

"No no. Promise first."

"I dare not. What is it?"

"Mind, I hold you to your promise.—It is—to be tied to the end of a string—a very long string indeed, and be flown like a kite. Oh such fun! I would rain rose-water, and hail sugar-plums, and snow whipped-cream, and—and—and—"

A fit of laughing checked her; and she would have been off again over the floor, had not the king started up and caught her just in time. Seeing that nothing but talk could be got out of her, he rang the bell, and sent her away with two of her ladies-in-waiting.

"Now, queen," he said, turning to her Majesty, "what *is* to be done?"

"There is but one thing left," answered she. "Let us consult the college of Metaphysicians."

"Bravo!" cried the king; "we will."

Now at the head of this college were two very wise Chinese philosophers—by name Hum-Drum, and Kopy-Keck. For them the king sent; and straightway they came. In a long speech he communciated to them what they knew very well already—as who did not?— namely, the peculiar condition of his daughter in relation to the globe on which she dwelt; and requested them to consult together as to what might be the cause and probable cure of her *infirmity*. The king laid stress upon the word, but failed to discover his own pun. The queen laughed; but Hum-Drum and Kopy-Keck heard with humility and retired in silence.

Their consultation consisted chiefly in propounding and supporting, for the thousandth time, each his favourite theories. For the condition of the princess afforded delightful scope for the discussion of every question arising from the division of thought—in fact, of all the Metaphysics of the Chinese Empire. But it is only justice to say that they did not altogether neglect the discussion of the practical question, *what was to be done*.

Hum-Drum was a Materialist, and Kopy-Keck was a

Spiritualist. The former was slow and sententious; the latter was quick and flighty: the latter had generally the first word; the former the last.

"I reassert my former assertion," began Kopy-Keck, with a plunge. "There is not a fault in the princess, body or soul; only they are wrong put together. Listen to me now, Hum-Drum, and I will tell you in brief what I think. Don't speak. Don't answer me. I *won't* hear you till I have done.—At that decisive moment, when souls seek their appointed habitations, two eager souls met, struck, rebounded, lost their way, and arrived each at the wrong place. The soul of the princess was one of those, and she went far astray. She does not belong by rights to this world at all, but to some other planet, probably Mercury. Her proclivity to her true sphere destroys all the natural influence which this orb would otherwise possess over her corporeal frame. She cares for nothing here. There is no relation between her and this world.

"She must therefore be taught, by the sternest compulsion, to take an interest in the earth as the earth. She must study every department of its history—its animal history; its vegetable history; its mineral history; its social history; its moral history; its political history; its scientific history; its literary history; its musical history; its artistical history; above all, its metaphysical history. She must begin with the Chinese dynasty and end with Japan. But first of all she must study geology, and especially the history of the extinct races of animals—their natures, their habits, their loves, their hates, their revenges. She must—"

"Hold, h-o-o-old!" roared Hum-Drum. "It is certainly my turn now. My rooted and insubvertible conviction is that the causes of the anomalies evident in the princess's condition are strictly and solely physical. But that is only tantamount to acknowledging that they exist. Hear my opinion.—From some cause or other, of no importance to our inquiry, the motion of her heart has been reversed. The remarkable combination of the suction and the force-pump works the wrong way—I mean in the case of the unfortunate princess: it draws in where it should force out, and forces out where it should draw in. The offices of the auricles and the ventricles are subverted. The blood is sent forth by the veins, and returns by the arteries. Consequently it is running the wrong way through all her corporeal organism—lungs and all. Is it then at all mysterious, seeing that such is the case, that on the other particular of gravitation as well, she should differ from normal humanity? My proposal for the cure is this:—

"Phlebotomize until she is reduced to the last point of safcty. Let it be effected, if necessary, in a warm bath. When she is reduced to a state of perfect asphyxy, apply a ligature to the left ankle, drawing it as tight as the bone will bear. Apply, at the same moment, another of equal tension around the right wrist. By means of plates constructed for the purpose, place the other foot and hand under the receivers of two airpumps. Exhaust the receivers. Exhibit a pint of French brandy, and await the result."

"Which would presently arrive in the form of grim Death," said Kopy-Keck.

"If it should, she would yet die in doing our duty," retorted Hum-Drum.

But their Majesties had too much tenderness for their volatile offspring to subject her to either of the schemes of the equally unscrupulous philosophers. Indeed, the most complete knowledge of the laws of nature would have been unserviceable in her case; for it was impossible to classify her. She was a fifth imponderable body, sharing all the other properties of the ponderable.

VIII

TRY A DROP OF WATER

Perhaps the best thing for the princess would have been to fall in love. But how a princess who had no gravity could fall into anything is a difficulty—perhaps *the* difficulty. As for her own feelings on the subject, she did not even know that there was such a beehive of honey and stings to be fallen into. But now I come to mention another curious fact about her.

The palace was built on the shores of the loveliest lake in the world; and the princess loved this lake more than father or mother. The root of this preference no doubt, although the princess did not recognise it as such, was, that the moment she got into it, she recovered the natural right of which she had been so wickedly deprived—namely, gravity. Whether this was owing to the fact that water had been employed as the means of conveying the injury, I do not know. But it is certain that she could swim and dive like the duck that her old nurse said she was. The manner in which this alleviation of her misfortune was discovered was as follows.

One summer evening, during the carnival of the country, she had been taken upon the lake by the king and queen, in the royal barge. They were accompanied by many of the courtiers in a fleet of little boats. In the middle of the lake she wanted to get into the lord chancellor's barge, for his daughter, who was a great favourite with her, was in it with her father. Now though the old king rarely condescended to make light of his misfortune, yet, happening on this occasion to be in a particularly good humour, as the barges approached each other, he caught up the princess to throw her into the chancellor's barge. He lost his balance, however, and dropping into the bottom of the barge, lost his hold of his daughter; not, however, before imparting to her the downward tendency of his own person, though in a somewhat different direction; for, as the king fell into the boat, she fell into the water. With a burst of delighted laughter she disappeared in the lake. A cry of horror ascended from the boats. They had never seen the princess go down before. Half the men were under water in a moment; but they had all, one after another, come up to the surface again for breath, when—tinkle, tinkle, babble, and gush! came the princess's laugh over the water from far away. There she was, swimming like a swan. Nor would she come out for king or queen, chancellor or daughter. She was perfectly obstinate.

But at the same time she seemed more sedate than usual. Perhaps that was because a great pleasure spoils laughing. At all events, after this, the passion of her life was to get into the water, and she was always the better behaved and the more beautiful the more she had of it. Summer and winter it was quite the same; only she could not stay so long in the water when they had to break the ice to let her in. Any day, from morning till evening in summer, she might be descried—a streak of white in the blue water—lying as still as the shadow of a cloud, or shooting along like a dolphin; disappearing, and coming up again far off just where one did not expect her. She would have been in the lake of a night too, if she could have had her way; for the balcony of her window overhung a deep pool in it; and through the shallow reedy passage she could have swum out into the wide wet water, and no one would have been any the wiser. Indeed, when she happened to wake in the moonlight, she could hardly resist the temptation. But there was the sad difficulty of getting into it. She had as great a dread of the air as some children have of the water. For the slightest gust of wind would blow her away; and a gust might arise in the stillest moment. And if she gave herself a push towards the water and just failed of reaching it, her situation would be dreadfully awkward, irrespective of the wind; for at best there she would have to remain, suspended in her night-gown, till she was seen and angled for by somebody from the window.

"Oh! if I had my gravity," thought she, contemplating the water, "I would flash off this balcony like a long white sea-bird headlong into the darling wetness. Heigh-ho!"

This was the only consideration that made her wish to be like other people.

Another reason for her being fond of the water was that in it alone she enjoyed any freedom. For she could not walk out without a *cortège,* consisting in part of a troop of light-horse, for fear of the liberties which the wind might take with her. And the king grew more apprehensive with increasing years, till at last he would not allow her to walk abroad at all without some twenty silken cords fastened to as many parts of her dress, and held by twenty noblemen. Of course horseback was out of the question. But she bade good-by to all this ceremony when she got into the water.

And so remarkable were its effects upon her, especially in restoring her for the time to the ordinary human gravity, that Hum-Drum and Kopy-Keck agreed in recommending the king to bury her alive for three years; in the hope that, as the water did her so much good, the earth would do her yet more. But the king had some vulgar prejudices against the experiment, and would not give his consent. Foiled in this, they yet agreed in another recommendation; which, seeing that one imported his opinions from China and the other from Thibet, was very remarkable indeed. They argued that, if water of external origin and application could be so efficacious, water from a deeper source might work a perfect cure; in short, that if the poor afflicted princess could by any means be made to cry, she might recover her lost gravity.

But how was this to be brought about? Therein lay all the difficulty—to meet which the philosophers were not wise enough. To make the princess cry was as im-

possible as to make her weigh. They sent for a professional beggar; commanded him to prepare his most
touching oracle of woe; helped him out of the court
charade-box, to whatever he wanted for dressing up,
and promised great rewards in the event of his success.
But it was all in vain. She listened to the mendicant
artist's story, and gazed at his marvellous make-up, till
she could contain herself no longer, and went into the
most undignified contortions for relief, shrieking, positively screeching with laughter.

When she had a little recovered herself, she ordered
her attendants to drive him away, and not give him a
single copper; whereupon his look of mortified discomfiture wrought her punishment and his revenge, for it
sent her into violent hysterics, from which she was with
difficulty recovered.

But so anxious was the king that the suggestion
should have a fair trial, that he put himself in a rage
one day, and, rushing up to her room gave her an awful whipping. Yet not a tear would flow. She looked
grave, and her laughing sounded uncommonly like
screaming—that was all. The good old tyrant, though
he put on his best gold spectacles to look, could not
discover the smallest cloud in the serene blue of her
eyes.

IX

PUT ME IN AGAIN

It must have been about this time that the son of a
king, who lived a thousand miles from Lagobel, set out
to look for the daughter of a queen. He travelled far
and wide, but as sure as he found a princess, he found
some fault in her. Of course he could not marry a mere
woman, however beautiful; and there was no princess
to be found worthy of him. Whether the prince was so

near perfection that he had a right to demand perfection itself, I cannot pretend to say. All I know is, that he was a fine, handsome, brave, generous, well-bred, and well-behaved youth, as all princes are.

In his wanderings he had come across some reports about our princess; but as everybody said she was bewitched, he never dreamed that she could bewitch him. For what indeed could a prince do with a princess that had lost her gravity? Who could tell what she might not lose next? She might lose her visibility, or her tangibility; or, in short, the power of making impressions upon the radical sensorium; so that he should never be able to tell whether she was dead or alive. Of course he made no further inquiries about her.

One day he lost sight of his retinue in a great forest. These forests are very useful in delivering princes from their courtiers, like a sieve that keeps back the bran. Then the princes get away to follow their fortunes. In this they have the advantage of the princesses, who are forced to marry before they have had a bit of fun. I wish our princesses got lost in a forest sometimes.

One lovely evening, after wandering about for many days, he found that he was approaching the outskirts of this forest; for the trees had got so thin that he could see the sunset through them; and he soon came upon a kind of heath. Next he came upon signs of human neighbourhood; but by this time it was getting late, and there was nobody in the fields to direct him.

After travelling for another hour, his horse, quite worn out with long labour and lack of food, fell, and was unable to rise again. So he continued his journey on foot. At length he entered another wood—not a wild forest, but a civilized wood, through which a footpath led him to the side of a lake. Along this path the prince pursued his way through the gathering darkness. Suddenly he paused, and listened. Strange sounds came across the water. It was, in fact, the princess laughing. Now there was something odd in her laugh, as I have already hinted; for the hatching of a real hearty laugh requires the incubation of gravity; and perhaps this was how the prince mistook the laughter for screaming. Looking over the lake, he saw something white in the water; and, in an instant, he had torn off his tunic, kicked off his sandals, and plunged in. He soon reached the white object, and found that it was a woman. There was not light enough to show that she was a princess, but quite enough to show that she was a lady, for it does not want much light to see that.

Now I cannot tell how it came about,—whether she pretended to be drowning, or whether he frightened her, or caught her so as to embarrass her,—but certainly he brought her to shore in a fashion ignominious to a swimmer, and more nearly drowned than she had ever expected to be; for the water had got into her throat as often as she had tried to speak.

At the place to which he bore her, the bank was only a foot or two above the water; so he gave her a strong lift out of the water, to lay her on the bank. But, her gravitation ceasing the moment she left the water, away she went up into the air, scolding and screaming.

"You naughty, *naughty,* NAUGHTY, *NAUGHTY* man!" she cried.

No one had ever succeeded in putting her into a passion before.—When the prince saw her ascend, he thought he must have been bewitched, and have mistaken a great swan for a lady. But the princess caught hold of the topmost cone upon a lofty fir. This came off; but she caught at another; and, in fact, stopped herself by gathering cones, dropping them as the stalks gave way. The prince, meantime, stood in the water, staring, and forgetting to get out. But the princess disappearing, he scrambled on shore, and went in the direction of the tree. There he found her climbing down one of the branches towards the stem. But in the darkness of the wood, the prince continued in some bewilderment as to what the phenomenon could be; until, reaching the ground, and seeing him standing there, she caught hold of him, and said,—

"I'll tell papa."

"Oh no, you won't" returned the prince.

ot the air? I never did you any harm."

"Pardon me. I did not mean to hurt you."

"I don't believe you have any brains; and that is a worse loss than your wretched gravity. I pity you."

The prince now saw that he had come upon the bewitched princess, and had already offended her. But before he could think what to say next, she burst out angrily, giving a stamp with her foot that would have sent her aloft again but for the hold she had of his arm,—

"Put me up directly."

"Put you up where, you beauty?" asked the prince.

He had fallen in love with her almost, already; for her anger made her more charming than any one else had ever beheld her; and, as far as he could see, which certainly was not far, she had not a single fault about her, except, of course, that she had not any gravity. No prince, however, would judge of a princess by weight. The loveliness of her foot he would hardly estimate by the depth of the impression it could make in mud.

"Put you up where, you beauty?" asked the prince.

"In the water, you stupid!" answered the princess.

"Come, then," said the prince.

The condition of her dress, increasing her usual difficulty in walking, compelled her to cling to him; and he could hardly persuade himself that he was not in a delightful dream, notwithstanding the torrent of musical abuse with which she overwhelmed him. The prince being therefore in no hurry, they came upon the lake at quite another part, where the bank was twenty-five feet high at least; and when they had reached the edge, he turned towards the princess, and said,—

"How am I to put you in?"

"That is your business," she answered, quite snappishly. "You took me out—put me in again."

"Very well," said the prince; and, catching her up in his arms, he sprang with her from the rock. The princess had just time to give one delighted shriek of laughter before the water closed over them. When they came to the surface, she found that, for a moment or two, she could not even laugh, for she had gone down with such a rush, that it was with difficulty she recovered her breath. The instant they reached the surface—

"How do you like falling in?" said the prince.

After some effort the princess panted out,—

"Is that what you call *falling in?*"

"Yes," answered the prince, "I should think it a very tolerable specimen."

"It seemed to me like going up," rejoined she.

"My feeling was certainly one of elevation too," the prince conceded.

The princess did not appear to understand him, for she retorted his question:—

"How do *you* like falling in?" said the princess.

"Beyond everything," answered he; "for I have fallen in with the only perfect creature I ever saw."

"No more of that: I am tired of it," said the princess.

Perhaps she shared her father's aversion to punning.

"Don't you like falling in, then?" said the prince.

"It is the most delightful fun I ever had in my life," answered she. "I never fell before. I wish I could learn. To think I am the only person in my father's kingdom that can't fall!"

Here the poor princess looked almost sad.

"I shall be most happy to fall in with you any time you like," said the prince, devotedly.

"Thank you. I don't know. Perhaps it would not be proper. But I don't care. At all events, as we have fallen in, let us have a swim together."

"With all my heart," responded the prince.

And away they went, swimming, and diving, and floating, until at last they heard cries along the shore, and saw lights glancing in all directions. It was now quite late, and there was no moon.

"I must go home," said the princess. "I am very sorry, for this is delightful."

"So am I," returned the prince. "But I am glad I haven't a home to go to—at least, I don't exactly know where it is."

"I wish I hadn't one either," rejoined the princess, "it is so stupid! I have a great mind," she continued, "to play them all a trick. Why couldn't they leave me alone? They won't trust me in the lake for a single night!—You see where that green light is burning? That is the window of my room. Now if you would just swim there with me very quietly, and when we are all but under the balcony, give me such a push—*up* you call it—as you did a little while ago, I should be able to catch hold of the balcony, and get in at the window: and then they may look for me till tomorrow morning!"

"With more obedience than pleasure," said the prince, gallantly; and away they swam, very gently.

"Will you be in the lake to-morrow night?" the prince ventured to ask.

"To be sure I will. I don't think so. Perhaps," was the princess's somewhat strange answer.

But the prince was intelligent enough not to press her further; and merely whispered, as he gave her the parting lift, "Don't tell." The only answer the princess returned was a roguish look. She was already a yard above his head. The look seemed to say, "Never fear. It is too good fun to spoil that way."

So perfectly like other people had she been in the water, that even yet the prince could scarcely believe his eyes when he saw her ascend slowly, grasp the balcony, and disappear through the window. He turned, almost expecting to see her still by his side. But he was alone in the water. So he swam away quietly, and watched the lights roving about the shore for hours after the princess was safe in her chamber. As soon as they disappeared, he landed in search of his tunic and sword, and after some trouble, found them again. Then he made the best of his way round the lake to the other side. There the wood was wilder, and the shore steeper—rising more immediately towards the mountains which surrounded the lake on all sides, and kept sending it messages of silvery streams from morning to night, and all night long. He soon found a spot whence he could see the green light in the princess's room, and where, even in the broad daylight, he would be in no danger of being discovered from the opposite shore. It was a sort of cave in the rock, where he provided himself a bed of withered leaves, and lay down too tired for hunger to keep him awake. All night long he dreamed that he was swimming with the princess.

X

LOOK AT THE MOON

Early the next morning the prince set out to look for something to eat, which he soon found at a forester's hut, where for many following days he was supplied with all that a brave prince could consider necessary. And having plenty to keep him alive for the present, he would not think of wants not yet in existence. Whenever Care intruded, this prince always bowed him out in the most princely manner.

When he returned from his breakfast to his watch-cave, he saw the princess already floating about in the lake, attended by the king and queen—whom he knew by their crowns—and a great company in lovely little boats, with canopies of all the colours of the rainbow, and flags and streamers of a great many more. It was a very bright day, and soon the prince burned up with the heat, began to long for the cold water and the cool princess. But he had to endure till twilight; for the boats had provisions on board, and it was not till the sun went down that the gay party began to vanish. Boat after boat drew away to the shore, following that of the king and queen, till only one, apparently the princess's own boat, remained. But she did not want to

go home even yet, and the prince thought he saw her
order the boat to the shore without her. At all events,
it rowed away; and now, of all the radiant company,
only one white speck remained. Then the prince began
to sing.

And this is what he sang:—

> "Lady fair,
> Swan-white,
> Lift thine eyes,
> Banish night
> By the might
> Of thine eyes.
>
> "Snowy arms,
> Oars of snow,
> Oar her hither,
> Plashing low.
> Soft and slow,
> Oar her hither.
>
> "Stream behind her
> O'er the lake,
> Radiant whiteness!
> In her wake
> Following, following for her sake,
> Radiant whiteness!
>
> "Cling about her,
> Waters blue;
> Part not from her,
> But renew
> Cold and true
> Kisses round her.
>
> "Lap me round,
> Waters sad
> That have left her;
> Make me glad,
> For ye had
> Kissed her ere ye left her."

Before he had finished his song, the princess was just under the place where he sat, and looking up to find him. Her ears had led her truly.

"Would you like a fall, princess?" said the prince, looking down.

"Ah! there you are! Yes, if you please, prince," said the princess, looking up.

"How do you know I am a prince, princess?" said the prince.

"Because you are a very nice young man, prince," said the princess.

"Come up then, princess."

"Fetch me, prince."

The prince took off his scarf, then his sword-belt, then his tunic, and tied them all together, and let them down. But the line was far too short. He unwound his turban, and added it to the rest, when it was all but long enough; and his purse completed it. The princess just managed to lay hold of the knot of money, and was beside him in a moment. This rock was much higher than the other, and the splash and the dive were tremendous. The princess was in ecstasies of delight, and their swim was delicious.

Night after night they met, and swam about in the dark clear lake; where such was the prince's gladness, that (whether the princess' way of looking at things infected him, or he was actually getting light-headed) he often fancied that he was swimming in the sky instead of the lake. But when he talked about being in heaven, the princess laughed at him dreadfully.

When the moon came, she brought them fresh pleasure. Everything looked strange and new in her light, with an old, withered, yet unfading newness. When the moon was nearly full, one of their great delights was to dive deep in the water, and then, turning round, look up through it at the great blot of light close above them, shimmering and trembling and wavering, spreading and contracting, seeming to melt away, and again grow solid. Then they would shoot up through the blot; and lo! there was the moon, far off, clear and steady and cold, and very lovely, at the bottom of a deeper and bluer lake than theirs, as the princess said.

The prince soon found out that while in the water the princess was very like other people. And besides this, she was not so forward in her questions or pert in her replies at sea as on shore. Neither did she laugh so much; and when she did laugh, it was more gently. She seemed altogether more modest and maidenly in the water than out of it. But when the prince, who had really fallen in love when he fell in the lake, began to talk to her about love, she always turned her head towards him and laughed. After a while she began to look puzzled, as if she were trying to understand what he meant, but could not—revealing a notion that he meant something. But as soon as ever she left the lake, she was so altered, that the prince said to himself, "If I marry her, I see no help for it: we must turn merman and mermaid, and go out to sea at once."

XI

HISS!

The princess's pleasure in the lake had grown to a passion, and she could scarcely bear to be out of it for an hour. Imagine then her consternation, when diving with the prince one night, a sudden suspicion seized her that the lake was not so deep as it used to be. The prince could not imagine what had happened. She shot to the surface, and, without a word, swam at full speed toward the higher side of the lake. He followed, begging to know if she was ill, or what was the matter. She never turned her head, or took the smallest notice of his question. Arrived at the shore, she coasted the rocks with minute inspection. But she was not able to come to a conclusion, for the moon was very small, and so she could not see well. She turned therefore and swam home, without saying a word to explain her conduct to the prince, of whose presence she seemed no longer conscious. He withdrew to his cave, in great perplexity and distress.

Next day she made many observations, which, alas! strengthened her fears. She saw that the banks were too dry; and that the grass on the shore, and the trailing plants on the rocks, were withering away. She caused marks to be made along the borders, and examined them, day after day, in all directions of the wind; till at last the horrible idea became a certain fact—that the surface of the lake was slowly sinking.

The poor princess nearly went out of the little mind she had. It was awful to her to see the lake, which she loved more than any living thing, lie dying before her eyes. It sank away, slowly vanishing. The tops of rocks that had never been seen till now, began to appear far down in the clear water. Before long they were dry in the sun. It was fearful to think of the mud that would soon lie there baking and festering, full of lovely creatures dying, and ugly creatures coming to life, like the unmaking of a world. And how hot the sun would be without any lake! She could not bear to swim in it any more, and began to pine away. Her life seemed bound up with it; and ever as the lake sank, she pined. People said she would not live an hour after the lake was gone.

But she never cried.

Proclamation was made to all the kingdom, that whosoever should discover the cause of the lake's decrease, would be rewarded after a princely fashion. Hum-Drum and Kopy-Keck applied themselves to their physics and metaphysics; but in vain. Not even they could suggest a cause.

Now the fact was that the old princess was at the root of the mischief. When she heard that her niece found more pleasure in the water than anyone else had out of it, she went into a rage, and cursed herself for her want of foresight.

"But," said she, "I will soon set all right. The king and the people shall die of thirst; their brains shall boil and frizzle in their skulls before I will lose my revenge."

And she laughed a ferocious laugh, that made the hairs on the back of her black cat stand erect with terror.

Then she went to an old chest in the room, and opening it, took out what looked like a piece of dried seaweed. This she threw into a tub of water. Then she threw some powder into the water, and stirred it with her bare arm, muttering over it words of hideous sound, and yet more hideous import. Then she set the tub aside, and took from the chest a huge bunch of a hundred rusty keys, that clattered in her shaking hands. Then she sat down and proceeded to oil them all. Before she had finished, out from the tub, the water of which had kept on a slow motion ever since she had ceased stirring it, came the head and half the body of a huge gray snake. But the witch did not look round. It grew out of the tub, waving itself backwards and forwards with a slow horizontal motion, till it reached the princess, when it laid its head upon her shoulder, and gave a low hiss in her ear. She started— but with joy; and seeing the head resting on her shoulder, drew it toward her and kissed it. Then she drew it all out of the tub, and wound it round her body. It was one of those dreadful creatures which few have ever beheld—the White Snakes of Darkness.

Then she took the keys and went down to her cellar; and as she unlocked the door she said to herself—

"This is worth living for!"

Locking the door behind her, she descended a few steps into the cellar, and crossing it, unlocked another door into a dark, narrow passage. She locked this also behind her, and descended a few more steps. If any one had followed the witch-princess, he would have heard her unlock exactly one hundred doors, and descend a few steps after unlocking each. When she had unlocked the last, she entered a vast cave, the roof of which was supported by huge natural pillars of rock. Now this room was the underside of the bottom of the lake.

She then untwined the snake from her body, and held it by the tail high above her. The hideous creature stretched up its head towards the roof of the cavern, which it was just able to reach. It then began to move its head backwards and forwards, with a slow oscillating motion, as if looking for something. At the same moment the witch began to walk round and round the cavern, coming nearer to the centre every circuit; while the head of the snake described the same path over the floor, for she kept holding it up. And still it kept slowly oscillating. Round and round the cavern they went, ever lessening the circuit, till at last the snake made a sudden dart, and clung to the roof with its mouth.

"That's right, my beauty!" cried the princess, "drain it dry."

She let it go, left it hanging, and sat down on a great stone, with her black cat, which had followed her all round the cave, by her side. Then she began to knit and mutter awful words. The snake hung like a huge leech, sucking at the stone; the cat stood with his back arched, and his tail like a piece of cable, looking up at the snake; and the old woman sat and knitted and muttered. Seven days and seven nights they remained thus; when suddenly the serpent dropped from the roof as if exhausted, and shrivelled up till it was again like a piece of dried seaweed. The witch started to her feet, picked it up, put it in her pocket, and looked up at the roof. One drop of water was trembling on the spot where the snake had been sucking. As soon as she saw that, she turned and fled, followed by her cat. Shutting the door in a terrible hurry, she locked it, and having muttered some frightful words, sped to the next, which also she locked and muttered over; and so with all the hundred doors, till she arrived in her own cellar. There she sat down on the floor ready to faint, but listening with malicious delight to the rushing of the water, which she could hear distinctly through all the hundred doors.

But this was not enough. Now that she had tasted revenge, she lost her patience. Without further measures, the lake would be too long in disappearing. So the next night, with the last shred of the dying old moon rising, she took some of the water in which she had revived the snake, put it in a bottle, and set out, accompanied by her cat. Before morning she had made the entire circuit of the lake, muttering fearful words as she crossed every stream, and casting into it some of the water out of her bottle. When she had finished the circuit she muttered yet again, and flung a handful of water towards the moon. Thereupon every spring in the country ceased to throb and bubble, dying away like the pulse of a dying man. The next day there was no sound of falling water to be heard along the borders of the lake. The very courses were dry; and the mountains showed no silvery streaks down their dark sides. And not alone had the fountains of mother Earth ceased to flow; for all the babies throughout the country were crying dreadfully—only without tears.

XII

WHERE IS THE PRINCE?

Never since the night when the princess left him so abruptly had the prince had a single interview with her. He had seen her once or twice in the lake; but as far as he could discover, she had not been in it any more at night. He had sat and sung, and looked in vain for his Nereid; while she, like a true Nereid, was wasting away with her lake, sinking as it sank, withering as it dried. When at length he discovered the change that was taking place in the level of the water, he was in great alarm and perplexity. He could not tell whether the lake was dying because the lady had forsaken it; or whether the lady would not come because the lake had begun to sink. But he resolved to know so much at least.

He disguised himself, and, going to the palace, requested to see the lord chamberlain. His appearance at once gained his request; and the lord chamberlain, being a man of some insight, perceived that there was more in the prince's solicitation than met the ear. He felt likewise that no one could tell whence a solution of the present difficulties might arise. So he granted the prince's prayer to be made shoeblack to the princess. It was rather cunning in the prince to request such an easy post, for the princess could not possibly soil as many shoes as other princesses.

He soon learned all that could be told about the princess. He went nearly distracted; but after roaming about the lake for days, and diving in every depth that remained, all that he could do was to put an extra polish on the dainty pair of boots that was never called for.

For the princess kept her room, with the curtains drawn to shut out the dying lake. But could not shut it out of her mind for a moment. It haunted her imagination so that she felt as if the lake were her soul, drying up within her, first to mud, then to madness and death. She thus brooded over the change, with all its dreadful accompaniments, till she was nearly distracted. As for the prince, she had forgotten him. However much she had enjoyed his company in the water, she did not care for him without it. But she seemed to have forgotten her father and mother too.

The lake went on sinking. Small slimy spots began to appear, which glittered steadily amidst the changeful shine of the water. These grew to broad patches of mud, which widened and spread, with rocks here and there, and foundering fishes and crawling eels swarming. The people went everywhere catching these, and looking for anything that might have dropped from the royal boats.

At length the lake was all but gone, only a few of the deepest pools remaining unexhausted.

It happened one day that a party of youngsters found themselves on the brink of one of these pools in the very centre of the lake. It was a rocky basin of considerable depth. Looking in, they saw at the bottom something that shone yellow in the sun. A little boy jumped in and dived for it. It was a plate of gold covered with writing. They carried it to the king.

On one side of it stood these words:

> "Death alone from death can save.
> Love is death, and so is brave.
> Love can fill the deepest grave.
> Love loves on beneath the wave."

Now this was enigmatical enough to the king and courtiers. But the reverse of the plate explained it a little. Its writing amounted to this:

"If the lake should disappear, they must find the hole through which the water ran. But it would be useless to try to stop it by any ordinary means. There was but one effectual mode—The body of a living man should alone stanch the flow. The man must give himself of his own will; and the lake must take his life as it filled. Otherwise the offering would be of no avail. If the nation could not provide one hero, it was time it should perish."

XIII

HERE I AM

This was a very disheartening revelation to the king— not that he was unwilling to sacrifice a subject, but that he was hopeless of finding a man willing to sacrifice himself. No time was to be lost, however, for the princess was lying motionless on her bed, and taking no nourishment but lake-water, which was now none of the best. Therefore the king caused the contents of the wonderful plate of gold to be published throughout the country.

No one, however, came forward.

The prince, having gone several days' journey into the forest, to consult a hermit whom he had met there on his way to Lagobel, knew nothing of the oracle till his return.

When he had acquainted himself with all the particulars, he sat down and thought—

"She will die if I don't do it, and life would be nothing to me without her; so I shall lose nothing by doing it. And life will be as pleasant to her as ever, for she will soon forget me. And there will be so much more beauty and happiness in the world!—To be sure, I shall not see it." (Here the poor prince gave a sigh.) "How lovely the lake will be in the moonlight, with that glorious creature sporting in it like a wild goddess!—It is rather hard to be drowned by inches, though. Let me see—that will be seventy inches of me to drown." (Here he tried to laugh, but could not.) "The longer the better, however," he resumed: "For can I not bargain that the princess shall be beside me all the time? So I shall see her once more, kiss her perhaps,—who knows? and die looking in her eyes. It will be no death. At least, I shall not feel it. And to see the lake filling for the beauty again!—All right! I am ready."

He kissed the princess's boot, laid it down, and hurried to the king's apartment. But feeling, as he went, that anything sentimental would be disagreeable, he resolved to carry off the whole affair with nonchalance. So he knocked at the door of the king's counting-house, where it was all but a capital crime to disturb him.

When the king heard the knock he started up, and opened the door in a rage. Seeing only the shoeblack, he drew his sword. This, I am sorry to say, was his

usual mode of asserting his regality when he thought
his dignity was in danger. But the prince was not in the
least alarmed.

"Please your majesty, I'm your butler," said he.

"My butler! you lying rascal! What do you mean?"

"I mean, I will cork your big bottle."

"Is the fellow mad?" bawled the king, raising the
point of his sword.

"I will put a stopper—plug—what you call it, in
your leaky lake, grand monarch," said the prince.

The king was in such a rage that before he could
speak he had time to cool, and to reflect that it would
be great waste to kill the only man who was willing to
be useful in the present emergency, seeing that in the
end the insolent fellow would be as dead as if he had
died by his majesty's own hand.

"Oh!" said he at last, putting up his sword with difficulty, it was so long; "I am obliged to you, you young
fool! Take a glass of wine?"

"No, thank you," replied the prince.

"Very well," said the king. "Would you like to run
and see your parents before you make your experiment?"

"No, thank you," said the prince.

"Then we will go and look for the hole at once,"
said his majesty, and proceeded to call some attendants.

"Stop, please your majesty; I have a condition to
make," interposed the prince.

"What!" exclaimed the king, "a condition! and with
me! How dare you?"

"As you please," returned the prince, coolly. "I wish
your majesty a good morning."

"You wretch! I will have you put in a sack, and
stuck in the hole."

"Very well, your majesty," replied the prince, becoming a little more respectful, lest the wrath of the
king should deprive him of the pleasure of dying for
the princess. "But what good will that do your

majesty? Please to remember that the oracle says the victim must offer himself."

"Well, you *have* offered yourself," retorted the king.

"Yes, upon one condition."

"Condition again!" roared the king, once more drawing his sword. "Begone! Somebody else will be glad enough to take the honor off your shoulders."

"Your majesty knows it will not be easy to get another to take my place."

"Well, what is your condition?" growled the king, feeling that the prince was right.

"Only this," replied the prince: "that, as I must on no account die before I am fairly drowned, and the waiting will be rather wearisome, the princess, your daughter, shall go with me, feed me with her own hands, and look at me now and then to comfort me; for you must confess it *is* rather hard. As soon as the water is up to my eyes, she may go and be happy, and forget her poor shoeblack."

Here the prince's voice faltered, and he very nearly grew sentimental, in spite of his resolution.

"Why didn't you tell me before what your condition was? Such a fuss about nothing!" exclaimed the king.

"Do you grant it?" persisted the prince.

"Of course I do," replied the king.

"Very well. I am ready."

"Go and have some dinner, then, while I set my people to find the place."

The king ordered out his guards, and gave directions to the officers to find the hole in the lake at once. So the bed of the lake was marked out in divisions and thoroughly examined, and in an hour or so the hole was discovered. It was in the middle of a stone, near the centre of the lake, in the very pool where the golden plate had been found. It was a three-cornered hole of no great size. There was water all round the stone, but very little was flowing through the hole.

XIV

THIS IS VERY KIND OF YOU

The prince went to dress for the occasion, for he was resolved to die like a prince.

When the princess heard that a man had offered to die for her, she was so transported that she jumped off the bed, feeble as she was, and danced about the room for joy. She did not care who the man was; that was nothing to her. The hole wanted stopping; and if only a man would do, why, take one. In an hour or two more everything was ready. Her maid dressed her in haste, and they carried her to the side of the lake. When she saw it she shrieked, and covered her face with her hands. They bore her across to the stone, where they had already placed a little boat for her. The water was not deep enough to float it, but they hoped it would be, before long. They laid her on cushions, placed in the boat wines and fruits and other nice things, and stretched a canopy over all.

In a few minutes the prince appeared. The princess recognized him at once, but did not think it worthwhile to acknowledge him.

"Here I am," said the prince. "Put me in."

"They told me it was a shoeblack," said the princess.

"So I am," said the prince. "I blacked your little boots three times a day, because they were all I could get of you. Put me in."

The courtiers did not resent his bluntness, except by saying to each other that he was taking it out in impudence.

But how was he to be put in? The golden plate contained no instructions on this point. The prince looked at the hole, and saw but one way. He put both his legs into it, sitting on the stone, and stooping forward, covered the corner that remained open with his two hands. In this uncomfortable position he resolved to abide his fate, and turning to the people, said,—

"Now you can go."

The king had already gone home to dinner.

"Now you can go," repeated the princess after him, like a parrot.

The people obeyed her and went.

Presently a little wave flowed over the stone, and wetted one of the prince's knees. But he did not mind it much. He began to sing, and the song he sang was this:

"As a world that has no well,
Darkly bright in forest dell;
As a world without the gleam
Of the downward-going stream;
As a world without the glance
Of the ocean's fair expanse;
As a world where never rain
Glittered on the sunny plain:—
Such, my heart, thy world would be,
If no love did flow in thee.

"As a world without the sound
Of the rivulets underground;
Or the bubbling of the spring
Out of darkness wandering;
Or the mighty rush and flowing
Of the river's downward going;
Or the music-showers that drop
On the outspread beech's top;
Or the ocean's mighty voice,
When his lifted waves rejoice;—
Such, my soul, thy world would be,
If no love did sing in thee.

"Lady, keep thy world's delight;
Keep the waters in thy sight.
Love hath made me strong to go,

> For thy sake, to realms below,
> Where the water's shine and hum
> Through the darkness never come:
> Let, I pray, one thought of me
> Spring, a little well, in thee;
> Lest thy loveless soul be found
> Like a dry and thirsty ground."

"Sing again, prince. It makes it less tedious," said the princess.

But the prince was too much overcome to sing any more, and a long pause followed.

"This is very kind of you, prince," said the princess at last, quite coolly, as she lay in the boat with her eyes shut.

"I am sorry I can't return the compliment," thought the prince; "but you are worth dying for, after all."

Again a wavelet, and another, and another flowed over the stone, and wetted both the prince's knees; but he did not speak or move. Two—three—four hours passed in this way, the princess apparently asleep, and the prince very patient. But he was much disappointed in his position, for he had none of the consolation he had hoped for.

At last he could bear it no longer.

"Princess!" said he.

But at the moment up started the princess, crying,—

"I'm afloat! I'm afloat!"

And the little boat bumped against the stone.

"Princess!" repeated the prince, encouraged by seeing her wide awake and looking eagerly at the water.

"Well?" said she, without looking round.

"Your papa promised that you should look at me, and you haven't looked at me once."

"Did he? Then I suppose I must. But I am so sleepy!"

"Sleep then, darling, and don't mind me," said the poor prince.

"Really, you are very good," replied the princess. "I think I will go to sleep again."

"Just give me a glass of wine and a biscuit first," said the prince, very humbly.

"With all my heart," said the princess, and gaped as she said it.

She got the wine and the biscuit, however, and leaning over the side of the boat toward him, was compelled to look at him.

"Why, prince," she said, "you don't look well! Are you sure you don't mind it?"

"Not a bit," answered he, feeling very faint indeed. "Only I shall die before it is of any use to you, unless I have something to eat."

"There, then," said she, holding out the wine to him.

"Ah! you must feed me. I dare not move my hands. The water would run away directly."

"Good gracious!" said the princess; and she began at once to feed him with bits of biscuit and sips of wine.

As she fed him, he contrived to kiss the tips of her fingers now and then. She did not seem to mind it, one way or the other. But the prince felt better.

"Now, for your own sake, princess," said he, "I cannot let you go to sleep. You must sit and look at me, else I shall not be able to keep up."

"Well, I will do anything I can to oblige you," answered she, with condescension; and, sitting down, she did look at him, and kept looking at him with wonderful steadiness, considering all things.

The sun went down, and the moon rose, and, gush after gush, the waters were rising up the prince's body. They were up to his waist now.

"Why can't we go and have a swim?" said the princess. "There seems to be water enough just about here."

"I shall never swim more," said the prince.

"Oh, I forgot," said the princess, and was silent.

So the water grew and grew, and rose up and up on the prince. And the princess sat and looked at him. She fed him now and then. The night wore on. The waters rose and rose. The moon rose likewise higher and higher, and shone full on the face of the dying prince. The water was up to his neck.

"Will you kiss me, princess?" said he, feebly. The nonchalance was all gone now.

"Yes, I will," answered the princess, and kissed him with a long, sweet, cold kiss.

"Now," said he, with a sigh of content, "I die happy."

He did not speak again. The princess gave him some wine for the last time: he was past eating. Then she sat down again, and looked at him. The water rose and rose. It touched his chin. It touched his lower lip. It touched between his lips. He shut them hard to keep it out. The princess began to feel strange. It touched his upper lip. He breathed through his nostrils. The princess looked wild. It covered his nostrils. Her eyes looked scared, and shone strange in the moonlight. His head fell back; the water closed over it, and the bubbles of his last breath bubbled up through the water. The princess gave a shriek, and sprang into the lake.

She laid hold first of one leg, and then of the other, and pulled and tugged, but she could not move either. She stopped to take breath, and that made her think that he could not get any breath. She was frantic. She got hold of him, and held his head above the water, which was possible now his hands were no longer on the hole. But it was of no use, for he was past breathing.

Love and water brought back all her strength. She got under the water, and pulled and pulled with her whole might, till at last she got one leg out. The other easily followed. How she got him into the boat she never could tell; but when she did, she fainted away. Coming to herself, she seized the oars, kept herself steady as best she could, and rowed and rowed, though she had never rowed before. Round rocks, and over shallows, and through mud she rowed, till she got to the landing-stairs of the palace. By this time her people were on the shore, for they had heard her shriek. She made them carry the prince to her own room, and lay him in her bed, and light a fire, and send for the doctors.

"But the lake, your highness!" said the chamberlain, who, roused by the noise, came in, in his nightcap.

"Go and drown yourself in it!" she said.

This was the last rudeness of which the princess was ever guilty; and one must allow that she had good cause to feel provoked with the lord chamberlain.

Had it been the king himself, he would have fared no better. But both he and the queen were fast asleep. And the chamberlain went back to his bed. Somehow, the doctors never came. So the princess and her old nurse were left with the prince. But the old nurse was a wise woman, and knew what to do.

They tried everything for a long time without success. The princess was nearly distracted between hope and fear, but she tried on and on, one thing after another, and everything over and over again.

At last, when they had all but given it up, just as the sun rose, the prince opened his eyes.

XV

LOOK AT THE RAIN!

The princess burst into a passion of tears, and *fell* on the floor. There she lay for an hour, and her tears never ceased. All the pent-up crying of her life was spent now. And a rain came on, such as had never been seen in that country. The sun shone all the time, and the great drops, which fell straight to the earth, shone likewise. The palace was in the heart of a rainbow. It was a rain of rubies, and sapphires, and emeralds, and topazes. The torrents poured from the mountains like molten gold; and if it had not been for its subterraneous outlet, the lake would have overflowed and inundated the country. It was full from shore to shore.

But the princess did not heed the lake. She lay on the floor and wept. And this rain within doors was far more wonderful than the rain out of doors. For when it abated a little, and she proceeded to rise, she found, to her astonishment, that she could not. At length, after many efforts, she succeeded in getting upon her feet. But she tumbled down again directly. Hearing her fall, her old nurse uttered a yell of delight, and ran to her, screaming,—

"My darling child! she's found her gravity!"

"Oh, that's it! is it?" said the princess, rubbing her shoulder and her knee alternately. "I consider it very unpleasant. I feel as if I should be crushed to pieces."

"Hurrah!" cried the prince from the bed. "If you've come round, princess, so have I. How's the lake?"

"Brimful," answered the nurse.

"Then we're all happy."

"That we are indeed!" answered the princess, sobbing.

And there was rejoicing all over the country that rainy day. Even the babies forgot their past troubles, and danced and crowed amazingly. And the king told stories, and the queen listened to them. And he divided the money in his box, and she the honey in her pot, among all the children. And there was such jubilation as was never heard of before.

Of course the prince and princess were betrothed at once. But the princess had to learn to walk, before they could be married with any propriety. And this was not so easy at her time of life, for she could walk no more than a baby. She was always falling down and hurting herself.

"Is this the gravity you used to make so much of?" said she one day to the prince, as he raised her from the floor. "For my part, I was a great deal more comfortable without it."

"No, no, that's not it. This is it," replied the prince,

as he took her up, and carried her about like a baby, kissing her all the time. "This is gravity."

"That's better," said she. "I don't mind that so much."

And she smiled the sweetest, loveliest smile in the prince's face. And she gave him one little kiss in return for all his; and he thought them overpaid, for he was beside himself with delight. I fear she complained of her gravity more than once after this, notwithstanding.

It was a long time before she got reconciled to walking. But the pain of learning it was quite counterbalanced by two things, either of which would have been sufficient consolation. The first was, that the prince himself was her teacher; and the second, that she could tumble into the lake as often as she pleased. Still, she preferred to have the prince jump in with her; and the splash they made before was nothing to the splash they made now.

The lake never sank again. In process of time, it wore the roof of the cavern quite through, and was twice as deep as before.

The only revenge the princess took upon her aunt was to tread pretty hard on her gouty toe the next time she saw her. But she was sorry for it the very next day, when she heard that the water had undermined her house, and that it had fallen in the night, burying her in its ruins; whence no one ever ventured to dig up her body. There she lies to this day.

So the prince and princess lived and were happy; and had crowns of gold, and clothes of cloth, and shoes of leather, and children of boys and girls, not one of whom was ever known, on the most critical occasion, to lose the smallest atom of his or her due proportion of gravity.

❦ FRANK RICHARD STOCKTON ❦
(1834–1902)

Frank R. Stockton, noted American humorist, was born in Philadelphia and received his formal education from the common schools of that city. After graduation, he became a successful wood engraver, but writing remained his first love. As a young boy he voraciously read fairy tales, and while still in school he began writing his own. Many of these were good enough to be accepted for publication. He kept at his writing while practicing the art of engraving, but the success of *Ting-a-Ling* (1870), a collection of short stories for children, prompted him to devote all his time and energy to writing. Thus, in 1872, he turned to journalism, and spent the next ten years or so working for newspaper and magazine concerns. During this period he also continued to write many children's works, including *Roundabout Rambles in Lands of Fact and Fancy* (1872), *Tales Out of School* (1875), *A Jolly Fellowship* (1880), *The Floating Prince and Other Fairy Tales* (1881), and *The Story of Viteau* (1884). In 1879 Stockton published the book that was to make him famous, *Rudder Grange*. It was so successful that he wrote two sequels: *The Rudder Grangers Abroad* (1891) and *Pomona's Travels* (1894). After Stockton retired from the magazine business he wrote his most popular novel, *The Casting Away of Mrs. Lecks and Mrs. Aleshine* (1886). Stockton's humorous novels are truly delightful, but he is probably best remembered for his short stories, the most widely known of which is "The Lady or the Tiger" (1884). Those who knew him well described him

51

as a gentle man with an enviable capacity for always looking at the bright and humorous side of life.

In many respects "The Accommodating Circumstance" resembles the traditional fairy tale. Within its pages the reader will find a cruel prince, narrow escapes, chivalrous deeds, an abundance of magic, and the inevitable marriage of beautiful maiden and charming hero. However, the quaint and whimsical humor of Stockton simply will not allow one of his stories to become typical or commonplace, and so the reader can expect to find a number of delightful surprises. Most obvious, is the device of the accommodating circumstance itself. Brought into being through a magical incantation, the sprightly "Green Goblin of the Third Word" literally becomes the accommodating circumstance of this memorable tale. The device is effectively handled by Stockton, and creates much of the narrative's lively and engaging action. Unique, too, is the central episode of the story, which features a curious "School for Men," where the students (full-grown men, of course) are taught the proper treatment of boys—by schoolmasters who are boys. Depend upon Stockton to develop such a delightful and satiric reversal of situation and perspective.

The Accommodating Circumstance
Frank R. Stockton

It was on a bright afternoon, many, many years ago, that a young baron stood on the stone steps that led down from the door of his ancestral home. That great castle was closed and untenanted, and the baron was taking leave of it forever. His father, who was now dead, had been very unfortunate, and had been obliged to sell his castle and his lands. But he had made it a condition that the nobleman who bought the estate should allow the young baron to occupy it until he was twenty-one years of age.

This period had now arrived, and although the purchaser, who did not need the castle, had told the baron that he might remain there as long as he chose, the young man was too high-spirited to depend upon the charity of anyone, and he determined to go forth and seek a fortune for himself. His purpose was to go to the town of the Prince of Zisk, a journey of a few days, and to offer to join an army which the prince intended to lead against a formidable band of robbers who had set up a stronghold in his dominions. If he should distinguish himself in this army, the young baron hoped that he might rise to an honorable position. At any rate, he would earn a livelihood for himself and be dependent upon no one.

But it was a very sad thing for him to leave this home where he was born and where he had spent most of his life. His parents were dead, he had no relatives, and now he was to leave the house which had been so

dear to him. He stood with one foot upon the ground
and the other upon the bottom step and looked up to
the great hall door, which he had shut and locked behind him, as if he were unwilling to make the movement which would finally separate him from the old
place.

As he stood thus, he heard someone approaching,
and turning, he saw an old woman and a young girl
coming toward the castle. Each carried a small bundle,
and besides these, the young girl had a little leathern
bag, which was fastened securely to her belt.

"Good sir," said the woman, "can you tell me if we
can rest for the night in this castle? My granddaughter
and I have walked since early morning, and I am very
tired. It is a long time since we have passed a house,
and I fear we might not come to another one today."

The baron hesitated for a moment. It was true that
there was no other house for several miles, and the old
woman looked as if she was not able to walk any farther. The castle was shut up and deserted, for he had
discharged his few servants that morning and he was
just about to leave it himself; but for all that, he could
not find it in his heart to say that there was no refuge
there for these two weary travelers. His family had always been generous and hospitable, and although there
was very little that he could offer now, he felt that he
must do what he could and not send away an old
woman and a young girl to perish on the road in the
cold winter night which was approaching.

"The castle is a bare and empty place," he said,
"but you can rest here for the night." And so saying,
he went up the steps, opened the door, and invited the
travelers to enter.

Of course if they stayed there that night, he must do
so also, for he could not leave the castle in the care of
strangers, although these appeared to be very inoffen-
sive people. And thus he very unexpectedly re-entered
the home he thought he had left forever.

There was some wood by the fireplace in the great
hall, and the baron made a fire. He had left no provi-

sions in the house, having given everything of the kind to the servants, but he had packed into his wallet a goodly store of bread, meat, and cheese, and with these he spread a meal for the wayfarers. When they had been strengthened by the food and warmed by the fire, the old woman told her story.

"You must not think, kind sir," she said, "that we are poor outcasts and wanderers. I have a very pleasant little home of my own, where my granddaughter and myself have lived very happily ever since she was a little baby, and now, as you see, she is quite grown up. But Litza—that is her name—has a godmother who is a very peculiar person, whom we are all obliged to obey; and she came to us yesterday and gave Litza a little iron box, which is in that leathern bag she carries, and charged her to start with me the next morning and take it to its destination."

In order to account for the condition of his house, the baron then told his story. Litza and her grandmother were grieved to hear the account of the young nobleman's ill fortune, and the old woman said if they prevented his journey they might yet try to go on.

"Oh, no," said the baron. "I was starting too late anyway, for it had taken me so long to bid good-bye to my old home. It will be just as well for me to go tomorrow. So you and your granddaughter shall have a room here tonight, and all will be well."

The next morning, after a breakfast which quite finished the baron's provisions, the three set out together, as their roads lay in the same direction. About noon the old woman became very tired and hungry. There was no house in sight, and the road seemed quite deserted.

"If I had known it would be so far," she said to herself, "we would not have come. I am too old to walk for two days. If I could only remember the meaning of the words, I would surely try them now. But I cannot remember—I cannot remember."

When this old woman was a little girl, she had lived with Litza's godmother, who was the daughter of a magician and was now over a hundred years old. From this person she had learned five magical words, which, when repeated, would each bring up a different kind of goblin or spirit. In her youth Litza's grandmother had never used these words, for she was a timid girl; and now for years, although she remembered the words, she had entirely forgotten what sort of creature each one would call forth. Some of these beings were good, and some she knew were very bad, and so, for fear of repeating the wrong word, she had never used any one of them. But now she felt that if ever she needed the help of goblin or fairy, she needed it this day.

"I can walk no farther," she said, "and that young man cannot carry me. If I do not use my words, I must perish here. I will try one of them, come what may." And so, with fear and trembling, she repeated aloud the third word.

Instantly there appeared before her a strange being. He was of a pale pea-green color, with great black eyes, and long arms and legs which seemed continually in motion. He jumped into the air, he snapped his fingers over his head, and suddenly taking from his pockets two empty bottles and an earthern jar, he began tossing them in the air, catching them dexterously as they fell.

"Who on earth are you?" said the old woman, much astonished.

"I am the Green Goblin of the Third Word," replied the other, still tossing up his jar and bottles, "but I am generally known as the Accommodating Circumstance."

"I don't know exactly what that may be," said the old woman, "but I wish that instead of a juggler with empty bottles and jars you were a pastrycook with a basket full of something to eat."

Instantly the goblin changed into a pastrycook carrying a large basket filled with hot meat pies and buns. The old woman jumped to her feet with delight and beckoned to the others, who had just turned around to see where she was.

"Come here," she cried. "Here is a pastrycook who has arrived just in the nick of time."

The party now made a good meal, for which the old woman would not allow the baron to pay anything, as it was a repast to which she had invited him. And then they moved on again, the pastrycook following. But although the grandmother was refreshed by the food, she was still very tired. She fell back a little and walked by the side of the pastrycook.

"I wish," she said, "that you were a man with a chair on your back. Then you might carry me."

Instantly the pastrycook changed into a stout man in a blue blouse, with a wooden armchair strapped to his back. He stooped down, and the old woman got into the chair. He then walked on and soon overtook the baron and Litza.

"Ah!" cried the old woman. "See what good fortune has befallen me! The pastrycook has gone, and this man with his chair has just arrived. Now I can travel with ease and comfort."

"What wonderful good fortune!" cried Litza.

"Wonderful good fortune, indeed!" exclaimed the baron, equally pleased.

The four now pursued their way, the old woman comfortably nodding in the chair, to which the baron had secured her with his belt. In about an hour the road branched, and the baron asked the chair man which way led to the town of Zisk. But the man, who was a dull, heavy fellow, did not know, and the baron took the road to the right. After walking two or three miles, they came to a wide river, at the edge of which the road stopped. On a post was a signboard on which was painted "Blow ye horn for ye ferryman." Below this hung a large horn, with a small pair of bellows attached to the mouthpiece.

"That is a good idea," said the baron. "One ought to be able to blow a horn very well with a pair of bellows." And so saying, he seized the handle of the bellows and blew a blast upon the horn that made Litza and her grandmother clap their hands to their ears. "I think that will bring the ferryman," said the baron, as he helped the old woman to get out of her chair.

In a few minutes they heard the sound of oars, and a boat made its appearance from behind a point of land to the right. To their surprise it was rowed by a boy about fourteen years old. When the boat touched the shore, they all got in.

"I am afraid you cannot row so heavy a load," said the baron to the boy; "but perhaps this good man will help you."

The boy, who was well dressed and of a grave demeanor, looked sternly at the baron. "Order must be kept in the boat," he said. "Sit down, all of you, and I will attend to the rowing." And he began to pull slowly but steadily from the shore. But instead of rowing directly across the river, he rounded the high point to the right and then headed toward an island in the stream.

"Where are you taking us?" asked the baron.

"This is the place to land," replied the boy gruffly. And in a few strokes he ran the boat ashore at the island.

A large house stood not far away from the water, and the baron thought he would go there and make some inquiries, for he did not like the manner of the boy in the boat. He accordingly stepped ashore and, followed by the rest of his party, approached the house. When they reached it, they saw over the door, in large black letters, the words "School for Men." Two boys, well dressed and sedate, came out to meet them and ushered them in.

"What is this place?" asked the baron, looking about him.

"It is a school," was the reply, "established by boys for the proper instruction and education of men. We have found that there are no human beings who need to be taught so much as men; and it is to supply this long-felt want that we have set up our school. By diverting the ferry from its original course we have obtained a good many scholars who would not otherwise have entered."

"What do you teach men?" asked the baron.

"The principal thing we try to teach them," said the other, "is the proper treatment of boys. But you will know all about this in good time."

"What I wish most now to know," said the baron, smiling, "is whether or not we can all obtain lodging here tonight. It is already growing dark."

"Did these two ladies come with you?" asked the boy.

"Yes," answered the baron.

"It was very good of them," said the boy. "Of course they can stay here all night. We always try to accommodate friends who come with scholars."

It was past suppertime at the school, but the baron and his party were provided with a good meal, and Litza and her grandmother were shown to a guest chamber on the ground floor. One boy then took charge of the chair-carrier, while another conducted the baron to a small chamber upstairs, where he found everything very comfortable and convenient.

"You can sit up and read for an hour or two," said the boy. "We don't put our scholars all into one great room like a barrack and make them put out their lights and go to bed just at the time when other people begin to enjoy the evening."

When the baron arose the next morning, he was informed that the principal wished to see him, and he was taken downstairs into a room where there was a very solemn-looking boy sitting in an armchair before a fire. This was the principal, and he arose and gravely shook hands with the baron.

"I am glad to welcome you to our school," he said, "and I hope you will do honor to it."

"I have no intention of remaining here," said the baron.

The principal regarded him with a look of great severity. "Silence, sir!" he said. "It pains me to think of the sorrow which will fill the hearts of your children or your young relatives if they could hear you deliberately declare that you did not wish to avail yourself of the extraordinary educational opportunities which are offered to you here."

The principal then rang a bell, and two of the largest scholars, who acted as monitors, entered the room. "Take this new pupil," he said to them, "to the schoolroom and have him entered in the lowest class. He has much to learn."

The baron saw that it would be useless to resist these two tall fellows, who conducted him from the room, and he peacefully followed them to the large schoolroom where he was put in a class and given a lesson to learn.

The subject of the lesson was the folly of supposing that boys ought not to be trusted with horses, battleaxes, and all the arms used in war and hunting. There were twelve reasons proving that men were very wrong in denying these privileges to boys, and the baron was obliged to learn them all by heart.

At the other end of the room he saw the chair-carrier, who was hard at work over a lesson on the wickedness of whipping boys. On the wall, at one end of the room, was the legend, in large letters, "The Boy: Know Him, and You Are Educated." At the other end were the words "Respect Your Youngers."

In the afternoon the baron studied sixteen rules which proved that boys ought to be consulted in regard to the schools they were sent to, the number of their holidays, the style of their new clothes, and many other things which concerned them more than anyone else. At the end of the afternoon session the principal made a short address the school, in which he said that in four days it would be Christmas, at which time the scholars would have a month's holiday.

"We believe," he said, "that scholars ought to have at least that much time at Christmas; and besides, your instructors need relaxation. But," said he, with a severe look at the baron, "disaffected newcomers must not suppose that they will be allowed this privilege. Such pupils will remain here during the holidays."

After this speech, school was dismissed, and the scholars were allowed three hours to play.

The baron was disturbed when he found that he would not be permitted to leave. He had heard that the Prince of Zisk intended to start on his expedition immediately after Christmas; and if he did not get to the town very soon, he could not join his army. So he determined to escape.

Walking about, he met Litza and her grandmother. The old woman was much troubled. She had been told that she could leave whenever she chose, but she felt she could not go away without the chair-carrier, and he was detained as a pupil. She would not explain her trouble to her granddaughter, for she did not wish her to know anything about the magical nature of the assistance she had received. In a few moments the chair-carrier also made his appearance, and then the baron, seeing that none of the boys were in sight, proposed that they should go down to the beach and escape in a ferryboat.

The boat was found there, with the oars, and they all jumped in. The baron and the chair-carrier then each seized an oar and pushed off. They were not a dozen yards from the shore when several of the boys, accompanied by some of the larger pupils, came running down to the beach. The baron could not help smiling when he saw them, and resting on his oar, he made a little speech.

"My young friends," he said, "you seem to have forgotten, when you set up your school, that men, when they become scholars, are as likely to play truant as if they were boys."

To these remarks the boy teachers made no answer, but the big scholars on shore looked at each other and grinned. Then they all stooped down and took hold of a long chain that lay coiled in the shallow water. They began to pull, and the baron soon perceived that the other end of the chain was attached to the boat. He and the chair man pulled as hard as they could at the oars, but in spite of their efforts they were steadily drawn to shore. Litza and her grandmother were then sent to their room, while the baron and the chair man were put to bed without their suppers.

The next day the old grandmother walked about by herself, more troubled than ever, for she was very anxious that Litza should fulfill her mission and that they should get back home before Christmas. And yet she would not go away and leave her magical companion. Just then she saw the chair-carrier looking out of a second-story window, with a blanket wrapped around him.

"Come down here," she said.

"I can't," he answered. "They say I am to stay in bed all day, and they have taken away my clothes."

"You might as well be back with your goblin companions," said the old woman, "for all the use you are to me. I wish you were somebody who could set things straight here."

Instantly there stood by her side a school trustee. He was a boy of grave and pompous demeanor, handsomely dressed, and carrying a large gold-headed cane.

"My good woman," he said, in a stately voice, "is there anything I can do to serve you?"

"Yes, sir," she replied. "My granddaughter and I"—she pointed to Litza, who just then came up—"wish to leave this place as soon as possible and to pursue our journey."

"Of course you may do so," said he. "This is not a school for women."

"But, Grandma," said Litza, "it would be a shame to go away without the poor baron, who is as anxious to get on as we are."

"There is a gentleman here, sir," said the old woman, "who does not wish to stay."

"Did you bring him?" asked the trustee.

"Yes, sir; he came with us."

"And you wish to take him away again?" said he.

"Yes, sir; we do," said Litza.

"Very well, then," said the trustee, severely; "he

shall be dismissed. We will have no pupils here whose children or guardians desire their removal. I will give orders in regard to the matter."

In a few moments the baron's clothes were brought to him, and he was told that he might get out of bed and leave the establishment. When he came down and joined Litza and her grandmother, he looked about him and said, "Where is the chair-carrier? I cannot consent to go away and leave him here."

"Do not trouble yourself about that man," said the grandmother. "He has already taken himself away."

The party, accompanied by the trustee, proceeded to the boat, where the boy ferryman was waiting for them. To the surprise of the baron the trustee got in with them, and they were all rowed to the other side of the river, where they found the road that led to Zisk. The school trustee walked with them, delivering his opinions in regard to the education of men. The baron grew very tired of hearing this talk.

"I am much obliged to this person," he thought, "for having enabled me to get away from that queer school; but he certainly is a dreadful bore. I wish he were going on some other road."

Litza and her grandmother agreed with the baron, and the old woman would gladly have changed the trustee into a chair-carrier again, but she had no opportunity of doing so, for the pompous little fellow never fell back behind the rest of the party, where he could be transformed unobserved. So they all walked on together until they reached the middle of a great plain, when suddenly a large body of horsemen appeared from behind a clump of trees at no great distance.

"It is a band of robbers!" said the baron, stopping and drawing his sword. "I know their flag. And they are coming directly toward us."

The grandmother and Litza were terribly frightened, and the baron turned very pale, for what could his one sword do against all those savage horsemen? As for the school trustee, he was glad to fall back now, and he crouched behind the baron, nearly scared out of his wits. He even pushed the old woman aside, so as to better conceal himself.

"You wretched coward!" she exclaimed. "I wish you were somebody able to defend us against these robbers."

Instantly there was a great clank of steel, and in the place of the trustee there stood an immense man, fully eight feet high, clothed in mail, and armed to the teeth. At his left side he carried a great sword, and on the other a heavy mace. In his hand he held a strong bow, higher than himself. His belt was filled with daggers and arrows, and at his back was an immense shield.

"Hold this in front of your party," he said to the baron, setting the shield down before him, "and I will attend to these rascals."

Quickly fitting a long arrow to his bow, he sent it directly through the foremost horseman and killed a man behind him. Arrow after arrow flew through the air, until half the robbers lay dead on the field. The rest turned to fly, but the armed giant sprang in among them, his sword in one hand and his mace in the other, and in less than five minutes he had slain every one of them.

"Now, then," said he, returning and taking up his bow and shield, "I think we may proceed without further fear."

The baron and Litza were no less delighted at their deliverance than surprised at the appearance of this defender, and the old woman was obliged to explain the whole matter to them. "I did not want you to know anything about it," she said to Litza, "for a young girl's head should not be filled with notions of magic; but the case was very urgent, and I could not hesitate."

"I am very glad you did not hesitate," said the baron, "for in a few minutes we should all have been killed. There was certainly never anything so useful as your Accommodating Circumstance."

The armed giant was a quiet and obliging fellow,

and he offered to carry the old woman on his shoulder, which she found a very comfortable seat.

Toward evening they arrived in sight of the town of Zisk, and the baron said to the grandmother, "I am very much afraid you will lose your giant, for when the prince sees such a splendid soldier he will certainly enlist him into his army."

"Oh, dear!" cried the old woman, slipping down from the giant's shoulder. "I wish this great fellow was somebody who could not possibly be of any use to the prince as a soldier."

Instantly there toddled toward her a little baby about a year old. She had a white cap on her funny little head and was very round and plump. She had scarcely taken three steps when she stumbled and sat down very suddenly, and then she began to try to pull off one of her little shoes. They all burst out laughing at this queer little creature, and Litza rushed toward the baby and snatched her up in her arms.

"You dear little thing!" she said. "The prince will never take you for a soldier."

"No," said the baron, laughing, "and she can never grow up into one."

It was too late for the baron to see the Prince of Zisk that day, and the party stopped for the night at a little inn in the town. The next morning, as the baron was about to go to the palace, he asked Litza what was her business in Zisk and if he could help her.

"All my godmother told me to do," said the young girl, "was to give this box to the noblest man in Zisk, and of course he is the prince."

"Yes," said the baron; "and as I am on my way to the palace, I may help you to see him."

"Go you with the baron," said the grandmother to Litza, "and I will stay here and take care of this baby. And as soon as you come back I will change her into a long-legged man with two chairs on his back, and we will get home to my cottage as fast as we can."

When the baron and the young girl reached the palace they found the prince in his audience chamber, surrounded by officers and courtiers. Litza stood by the door, while the baron approached the prince and respectfully told him why he had come.

"You are the very man we want!" cried the prince. "I have conceived a most admirable plan of conquering my robber foes, and you shall carry it out. The day after tomorrow is Christmas, and these highwaymen always keep this festival as if they were decent people and good Christians. They gather together all their wives and children and their old parents, and they sing carols and make merry all day long. At this time they never think of attacking anybody or of being attacked, and if we fall upon them then, we can easily destroy them all, young and old, and thus be rid of the wretches forever. I have a strong body of soldiers ready to send, but they must be led by a man of rank, and all my officers of high degree wish to remain here with their families to celebrate Christmas. Now, you are a stranger and have nothing to keep you here, and you are the very man to lead my soldiers. Destroy that colony of robbers, and you shall have a good share of the booty that you find there."

"Oh, Prince!" exclaimed the baron. "Would you have me, on holy Christmas Day, when these families are assembled together to celebrate the blessed festival, rush upon them with an armed band and slay them, old and young, women and children, at the very foot of the Christmas tree? No man needs occupation more than I, but this is a thing I cannot do."

"Impudent upstart!" cried the prince in a rage. "If you cannot do this, there is nothing for you here. Begone!"

Without an answer the baron turned and left the hall. Litza, who still stood by the door, did not now approach the prince but ran after the baron, who was walking rapidly away. "This is yours," she said, taking the iron box from her little bag. "You are the noblest man."

The baron, surprised, objected to receiving the box,

but Litza was firm. "I was told," she said, "to give it to the noblest man in Zisk, and I have done so."

When the baron found that he must keep the box, he asked Litza what was in it.

"I do not know," said Litza; "but the key is fastened to the handle."

They sat down under a tree in a quiet corner of the palace grounds and opened the box. Something inside was covered with a piece of velvet, on top of which lay a golden locket. The baron opened it and beheld a portrait of the beautiful Litza. "Why, you have given me yourself!" he cried, delighted.

"So it appears," said Litza, looking down upon the ground.

"And will you marry me?" he cried.

"If you wish it," said Litza. So that matter was settled.

The two then went to the inn and told the grandmother what had occurred. She looked quite pleased when she heard this story, and then she asked what else was in the box.

"I found so much," said the baron, "that I did not think of looking for anything more." He then opened the box, and lifting the piece of velvet, found it filled with sparkling diamonds.

"That is Litza's dowry," cried the old woman. "It was a wise thing in her godmother to send her out to look for a noble husband, for one would never have come to my little cottage to look for her. But it seems to me that the box might as well have been given to you at your castle. It would have saved us a weary journey."

"But if we had not taken that journey," said Litza, "we should not have become so well acquainted, and I would not have known he was the noblest man."

"It is all right," said the grandmother, "and your dowry will enable the baron to buy his castle again and to live there as his ancestors did before him."

The grandmother desired to leave Zisk immediately, but the baron objected. "There is something I wish to do today," he said; "and if we start early tomorrow morning on horseback, we can reach my castle before dark."

The old woman agreed to this, and the baron continued: "I would like you to lend me the baby for the rest of the day; and when the sundial in the courtyard shall mark three hours after noon, you will please open this piece of paper and wish what I have written upon it."

The grandmother took the folded piece of paper and let him have the baby. She and Litza wondered much what he was going to do, but they asked no questions.

The baron had learned that it was a three hours' walk from the town to the stronghold of the robbers, and just at noon he set out for that place, carrying the baby in his arms. Before he had gone a mile he wished that the baby had been changed into somebody who could walk, but it was too late now.

At three hours after noon the grandmother was about to open the paper when Litza exclaimed, "Before you wish anything, dear Grandmother, let me read what the baron has written."

Litza then took the paper and read it. "It is just what I expected," she cried. "He has gone out to fight the robbers, and he wants you to change the baby into that great armed giant to help him. But don't you do it, for the baron will certainly be killed, there are so many robbers in that place. Please change the baby into a very strong, fleet man who knows the country and who will take the baron in his arms and bring him back here just as fast as he can."

"I will wish that," said the grandmother. And she did so.

The baron had just arrived in sight of the robbers' stronghold when he was very much surprised to find that, instead of carrying a baby in his arms, he himself was in the grasp of a tall, powerful man who was carrying him at the top of his speed toward the town. The baron kicked and struggled much worse than the baby had, but the man paid no attention to his violent remonstrances and soon set him down in the courtyard of the inn.

"This is your doing," he said to Litza. "I wished to show the prince that it was not fear that kept me from fighting the robbers, and you have prevented me."

"You have proved that you are brave," said Litza, "and that is enough. The prince is a bad man; let him fight his own robbers."

The baron could not be angry at this proof of Litza's prudent affection. And the next morning the party left the town on three horses, which the baron bought with one of his diamonds. The tall, fleet man who knew the country acted as guide and led them by a byroad which did not pass near the School for Men. They arrived at the castle early on Christmas Eve, and the baron sent for his servants, his friends, and a priest, and he and Litza were married amid great rejoicing, for everybody was glad to see him come to his own again.

The next day Litza and the baron asked the grandmother to show them her magical servant in his original form. The old woman called the tall, fleet guide and transformed him into the Green Goblin of the Third Word. This strange creature wildly danced and skipped before them, and taking a watermelon and three pumpkins from his pocket, he tossed them up, keeping two of them always in the air.

The baron and his wife were very much amused by the antics of the goblin, and Litza exclaimed, "Oh, Grandmother, if I were you I would keep him this way always. He would be wonderfully amusing, and I am sure he could carry you about and scare away robbers, and do ever so many things."

"A merry green goblin might suit you," said the old woman, shaking her head, "but it would not suit me. I want to return to my own little home, and what I now wish is a suitable companion."

Instantly the goblin changed into a healthy middle-aged woman of agreeable manners and willing to make herself useful. With this "suitable companion" the old grandmother returned after the holidays to her much-loved cottage, where she was often visited by the young baron and his wife; but although they sometimes asked it, she never let them see the green goblin again.

"When a circumstance is just as accommodating as you want it to be," she said, "the less you meddle with it the better."

❦ JOHN BUCHAN ❦
(1875-1940)

John Buchan, distinguished statesman and writer, was born in Perth, Scotland, the son of a minister. He was educated at Glasgow University and Oxford, where he established a reputation as an outstanding scholar. In 1901, he was called to the Bar at the Middle Temple, and in the same year he became private secretary to Lord Milner, High Commissioner for South Africa. After a two-year term in Africa, he returned to England and joined a publishing firm. During World War I, he became Director of Information and wrote a twenty-four-volume history of the War. In 1935, he was appointed Governor-General of Canada and raised to the peerage. The newly titled first Baron Tweedsmuir became chancellor of Edinburgh University in 1938. The life of this extraordinarily gifted man came to a tragic end in 1940 as a result of a brain concussion brought on by an accidental fall.

Although Buchan had a busy professional life in government, he somehow found time for writing. During a literary career as a journalist, novelist, biographer, and historian he wrote over sixty works. He is probably best known for his adventure stories, of which the most popular are *The Watcher by the Threshold* (1902), *Prester John* (1910), *The Thirty-Nine Steps* (1915), *Greenmantle* (1916), *Mr. Standfast* (1919), and *The Three Hostages* (1924). Those familiar with C. S. Lewis's *That Hideous Strength* might recall Lewis saying that Mark Studdock had missed reading Buchan—along with Mac Donald—and

71

that, as a consequence, he lacked an appreciation for mystery.

At first glance, Africa might seem a highly unlikely setting for a work of high fantasy, but one must remember that a century ago this vast and mysterious continent seemed as other-worldly to the Englishman as any fictional creation. The writings of Joseph Conrad, H. Rider Haggard, and John Buchan will attest to the enchanting spell this land exercised upon its visitors. In "The Grove of Ashtaroth," the reader will find Buchan's enchantment manifested in the rich and memorable descriptions of Welgevonden, Lawson's lush and exotic estate. This verdant expanse is an almost perfect example of the archetypal Eden where irresistible evil lurks in the paradisaical garden. The pagan presence of the goddess Ashtaroth seems as natural here as a supernatural agent in an Edgar Allen Poe thriller. "Ashtaroth" is not only an exceptionally fine example of myth fantasy, but one of the rare instances of high fantasy built upon a foundation of scriptural myth.

The Grove of Ashtaroth

John Buchan

ờ

"C'est enfin que dans leurs prunelles
Rit et pleure—fastidieux—
L'amour des choses éternelles,
Des vieux morts et des anciens dieux!"
—PAUL VERLAINE

I

We were sitting around the camp fire, some thirty miles north of a place called Taqui, when Lawson announced his intention of finding a home. He had spoken little the last day or two, and I had guessed that he had struck a vein of private reflection. I thought it might be a new mine or irrigation scheme, and I was surprised to find that it was a country house.

"I don't think I shall go back to England," he said, kicking a sputtering log into place. "I don't see why I should. For business purposes I am far more useful to the firm in South Africa than in Throgmorton Street. I have no relation left except a third cousin, and I have never cared a rush for living in town. That beastly house of mine in Hill Street will fetch what I gave for it—Isaacson cabled about it the other day, offering for furniture and all. I don't want to go into Parliament, and I hate shooting little birds and tame deer. I am one of those fellows who are born Colonial at heart, and I don't see why I shouldn't arrange my life as I please.

73

Besides, for ten years I have been falling in love with this country, and now I am up to the neck."

He flung himself back in the camp chair till the canvas creaked, and looked at me below his eyelids. I remember glancing at the lines of him, and thinking what a fine make of a man he was. In his untanned field-boots, breeches and grey shirt, he looked the born wilderness hunter, though less than two months before he had been driving down to the City every morning in the sombre regimentals of his class. Being a fair man, he was gloriously tanned, and there was a clear line at his shirt-collar to mark the limits of his sunburn. I had first known him years ago, when he was a broker's clerk working on half-commission. Then he had gone to South Africa, and soon I heard he was a partner in a mining house which was doing wonders with some gold areas in the North. The next step was his return to London as the new millionaire—young, good-looking, wholesome in mind and body, and much sought after by the mothers of marriageable girls. We played polo together, and hunted a little in the season, but there were signs that he did not propose to become the conventional English gentleman. He refused to buy a place in the country, though half the Homes of England were at his disposal. He was a very busy man, he declared, and had not time to be a squire. Besides, every few months he used to rush out to South Africa. I saw that he was restless, for he was always badgering me to go big-game hunting with him in some remote part of the earth. There was that in his eyes, too, which marked him out from the ordinary blond type of our countrymen. They were large and brown and mysterious, and the light of another race was in their odd depths.

To hint such a thing would have meant a breach of friendship, for Lawson was very proud of his birth. When he first made his fortune he had gone to the Heralds to discover his family, and these obliging gentlemen had provided a pedigree. It appeared that he was a scion of the house of Lowson or Lowieson, an ancient and rather disreputable clan on the Scottish side of the Border. He took a shooting in Teviotdale on the strength of it, and used to commit lengthy Border ballads to memory. But I had known his father, a financial journalist who never quite succeeded, and I had heard of a grandfather who sold antiques in a back street at Brighton. The latter, I think, had not changed his name, and still frequented the synagogue. The father was a progressive Christian, and the mother had been a blonde Saxon from the Midlands. In my mind there was no doubt, as I caught Lawson's heavy-lidded eyes fixed on me. My friend was of a more ancient race than the Lowsons of the Border.

"Where are you thinking of looking for your house?" I asked. "In Natal or in the Cape Peninsula? You might get the Fishers' place if you paid a price."

"The Fishers' place be hanged!" he said crossly. "I don't want any stuccoed, overgrown Dutch farm. I might as well be at Roehampton as in the Cape."

He got up and walked to the far side of the fire, where a lane ran down through the thornscrub to a gully of the hills. The moon was silvering the bush of the plains, forty miles off and three thousand feet below us.

"I am going to live somewhere hereabouts," he answered at last.

I whistled. "Then you've got to put your hand in your pocket, old man. You'll have to make everything, including a map of the countryside."

"I know," he said, "that's where the fun comes in. Hang it all, why shouldn't I indulge my fancy? I'm uncommonly well off, and I haven't chick or child to leave it to. Supposing I'm a hundred miles from railhead, what about it? I'll make a motor-road and fix up a telephone. I'll grow most of my supplies, and start a colony to provide labour. When you come and stay with me, you'll get the best food and drink on earth, and sport that will make your mouth water. I'll put Lochleven trout in these streams,—at six thousand feet you can do anything. We'll have a pack of hounds,

too, and we can drive pig in the woods, and if we want
big game there are the Mangwe flats at our feet. I tell
you I'll make such a country-house as nobody ever
dreamed of. A man will come plumb out of stark sav-
agery into lawns and rose-gardens." Lawson flung himself into his chair again and smiled dreamily at the fire.

"But why here, of all places?" I persisted. I was not
feeling very well and did not care for the country.

"I can't quite explain. I think it's the sort of land I
have always been looking for. I always fancied a house
on a green plateau in a decent climate looking down on
the tropics. I like heat and colour, you know, but I like
hills too, and greenery, and the things that bring back
Scotland. Give me a cross between Teviotdale and the
Orinoco, and by Gad! I think I've got it here."

I watched my friend curiously, as with bright eyes
and eager voice he talked of his new fad. The two
races were very clear in him—the one desiring gorge-
ousness, the other athirst for the soothing spaces of the
North. He began to plan out the house. He would get
Adamson to design it, and it was to grow out of the
landscape like a stone on the hillside. There would be
wide verandahs and cool halls, but great fireplaces
against winter time. It would all be very simple and
fresh—"clean as morning" was his odd phrase; but
then another idea supervened, and he talked of bringing the Tintorets from Hill Street. "I want it to be a
civilised house, you know. No silly luxury, but the best
pictures and china and books. . . . I'll have all the furniture made after the old plain English models out of
native woods. I don't want second-hand sticks in a new
country. Yes, by Jove, the Tintorets are a great idea,
and all those Ming pots I bought. I had meant to sell
them, but I'll have them out here."

He talked for a good hour of what he would do, and
his dream grew richer as he talked, till by the time we
went to bed he had sketched something more like a
palace than a country-house. Lawson was by no means
a luxurious man. At present he was well content with a
Wolseley valise, and shaved cheerfully out of a tin

mug. It struck me as odd that a man so simple in his habits should have so sumptuous a taste in bric-a-brac. I told myself, as I turned in, that the Saxon mother from the Midlands had done little to dilute the strong wine of the East.

It drizzled next morning when we inspanned, and I mounted my horse in a bad temper. I had some fever on me, I think, and I hated this lush yet frigid tableland, where all the winds on earth lay in wait for one's marrow. Lawson was, as usual, in great spirits. We were not hunting, but shifting our hunting-ground, so all morning we travelled fast to the north along the rim of the uplands.

At midday it cleared, and the afternoon was a pageant of pure colour. The wind sank to a low breeze; the sun lit the infinite green spaces, and kindled the wet forest to a jewelled coronal. Lawson gaspingly admired it all, as he cantered bareheaded up a bracken-clad slope. "God's country," he said twenty times. "I've found it." Take a piece of Sussex downland; put a stream in every hollow and a patch of wood; and at the edge, where the cliffs at home would fall to the sea, put a cloak of forest muffling the scarp and dropping thousands of feet to the blue plains. Take the diamond air of the Gornergrat, and the riot of colour which you get by a West Highland lochside in late September. Put flowers everywhere, the things we grow in hothouses, geraniums like sun-shades and arums like trumpets. That will give you a notion of the countryside we were in. I began to see that after all it was out of the common.

And just before sunset we came over a ridge and found something better. It was a shallow glen, half a mile wide, down which ran a blue-grey stream in linns like the Spean, till at the edge of the plateau it leaped into the dim forest in a snowy cascade. The opposite side ran up in gentle slopes to a rocky knoll, from which the eye had a noble prospect of the plains. All down the glen were little copses, half moons of green edging some silvery shore of the burn, or delicate clusters of tall trees nodding on the hill brow. The place so satsified the eye that for the sheer wonder of its perfection we stopped and stared in silence for many minutes.

Then "The House," I said, and Lawson replied softly, "The House!"

We rode slowly into the glen in the mulberry gloaming. Our transport wagons were half an hour behind, so we had time to explore. Lawson dismounted and plucked handfuls of flowers from the water meadows. He was singing to himself all the time—an old French catch about *Cadet Rousselle* and his *trois maisons*.

"Who owns it?" I asked.

"My firm, as like as not. We have miles of land about here. But whoever the man is, he has got to sell. Here I build my tabernacle, old man. Here, and nowhere else!"

In the very centre of the glen, in a loop of the stream, was one copse which even in that half light struck me as different from the others. It was of tall, slim, fairy-like trees, the kind of wood the monks painted in old missals. No, I rejected the thought. It was no Christian wood. It was not a copse, but a "grove,"—one such as Artemis may have flitted through in the moonlight. It was small, forty or fifty yards in diameter, and there was a dark something at the heart of it which for a second I thought was a house.

We turned between the slender trees, and—was it fancy?—an odd tremor went through me. I felt as if I were penetrating the *temenos* of some strange and lovely divinity, the goddess of this pleasant vale. There was a spell in the air, it seemed, and an odd dead silence.

Suddenly my horse started at a flutter of light wings. A flock of doves rose from the branches, and I saw the burnished green of their plumes against the opal sky. Lawson did not seem to notice them. I saw his keen eyes staring at the centre of the grove and what stood there.

It was a little conical tower, ancient and lichened, but, so far as I could judge, quite flawless. You know the famous Conical Temple at Zimbabwe, of which prints are in every guidebook. This was of the same type, but a thousandfold more perfect. It stood about thirty feet high, of solid masonry, without door or window or cranny, as shapely as when it first came from the hands of the old builders. Again I had the sense of breaking in on a sanctuary. What right had I, a common vulgar modern, to be looking at this fair thing, among these delicate trees, which some white goddess had once taken for her shrine?

Lawson broke in on my absorption. "Let's get out of this," he said hoarsely, and he took my horse's bridle (he had left his own beast at the edge) and led him back to the open. But I noticed that his eyes were always turning back and that his hand trembled.

"That settles it," I said after supper. "What do you want with your medieval Venetians and your Chinese pots now? You will have the finest antique in the world in your garden—a temple as old as time, and in a land which they say has no history. You had the right inspiration this time."

I think I have said that Lawson had hungry eyes. In his enthusiasm they used to glow and brighten; but now, as he sat looking down at the olive shades of the glen, they seemed ravenous in their fire. He had hardly spoken a word since we left the wood.

"Where can I read about these things?" he asked, and I gave him the names of books.

Then, an hour later, he asked me who were the builders. I told him the little I knew about Phoenician and Sabaean wanderings, and the ritual of Sidon and Tyre. He repeated some names to himself and went soon to bed.

As I turned in, I had one last look over the glen, which lay ivory and black in the moon. I seemed to hear a faint echo of wings, and to see over the little

grove a cloud of light visitants. "The Doves of Ashtaroth have come back," I said to myself. "It is a good
omen. They accept the new tenant." But as I fell
asleep I had a sudden thought that I was saying something rather terrible.

II

Three years later, pretty nearly to a day, I came back
to see what Lawson had made of his hobby. He had
bidden me often to Welgevonden, as he chose to call
it—though I do not know why he should have fixed a
Dutch name to a countryside where Boer never trod.
At the last there had been some confusion about dates,
and I wired the time of my arrival, and set off without
an answer. A motor met me at the queer little wayside
station of Taqui, and after many miles on a doubtful
highway I came to the gates of the park, and a road on
which it was a delight to move. Three years had
wrought little difference in the landscape. Lawson had
done some planting,—conifers and flowering shrubs
and such-like,—but wisely he had resolved that Nature
had for the most part forestalled him. All the same, he
must have spent a mint of money. The drive could not
have been beaten in England, and fringes of mown turf
on either hand had been pared out of the lush
meadows. When we came over the edge of the hill and
looked down on the secret glen, I could not repress a
cry of pleasure. The house stood on the farther ridge,
the viewpoint of the whole neighbourhood; and its
brown timbers and white rough-cast walls melted into
the hillside as if it had been there from the beginning
of things. The vale below was ordered in lawns and
gardens. A blue lake received the rapids of the stream,
and its banks were a maze of green shades and glorious
masses of blossom. I noticed, too, that the little grove
we had explored on our first visit stood alone in a big
stretch of lawn, so that its perfection might be clearly

seen. Lawson had excellent taste, or he had had the best advice.

The butler told me that his master was expected home shortly, and took me into the library for tea. Lawson had left his Tintorets and Ming pots at home after all. It was a long, low room, panelled in teak half-way up the walls, and the shelves held a multitude of fine bindings. There were good rugs on the parquet floor, but no ornaments anywhere, save three. On the carved mantelpiece stood two of the old soapstone birds which they used to find at Zimbabwe, and between, on an ebony stand, a half moon of alabaster, curiously carved with zodiacal figures. My host had altered his scheme of furnishing, but I approved the change.

He came in about half-past six, after I had consumed two cigars and all but fallen asleep. Three years make a difference in most men, but I was not prepared for the change in Lawson. For one thing, he had grown fat. In place of the lean young man I had known, I saw a heavy, flaccid being, who shuffled in his gait, and seemed tired and listless. His sunburn had gone, and his face was as pasty as a city clerk's. He had been walking, and wore shapeless flannel clothes, which hung loose even on his enlarged figure. And the worst of it was, that he did not seem over-pleased to see me. He murmured something about my journey, and then flung himself into an armchair and looked out of the window.

I asked him if he had been ill.

"Ill! No!" he said crossly. "Nothing of the kind. I'm perfectly well."

"You don't look as fit as this place should make you. What do you do with yourself? Is the shooting as good as you hoped?"

He did not answer, but I thought I heard him mutter something like "shooting be damned."

Then I tried the subject of the house. I praised it extravagantly, but with conviction. "There can be no place like it in the world," I said.

He turned his eyes on me at last, and I saw that they were as deep and restless as ever. With his pallid face they made him look curiously Semitic. I had been right in my theory about his ancestry.

"Yes," he said slowly, "there is no place like it—in the world."

Then he pulled himself to his feet. "I'm going to change," he said. "Dinner is at eight. Ring for Travers, and he'll show you your room."

I dressed in a noble bedroom, with an outlook over the garden-vale and the escarpment to the far line of the plains, now blue and saffron in the sunset. I dressed in an ill temper, for I was seriously offended with Lawson, and also seriously alarmed. He was either very unwell or going out of his mind, and it was clear, too, that he would resent any anxiety on his account. I ransacked my memory for rumours, but found none. I had heard nothing of him except that he had been extraordinarily successful in his speculations, and that from his hill-top he directed his firm's operations with uncommon skill. If Lawson was sick or mad, nobody knew of it.

Dinner was a trying ceremony. Lawson, who used to be rather particular in his dress, appeared in a kind of smoking suit with a flannel collar. He spoke scarcely a word to me, but cursed the servants with a brutality which left me aghast. A wretched footman in his nervousness spilt some sauce over his sleeve. Lawson dashed the dish from his hand, and volleyed abuse with a sort of epileptic fury. Also he, who had been the most abstemious of men, swallowed disgusting quantities of champagne and old brandy.

He had given up smoking, and half an hour after we left the dining-room, he announced his intention of going to bed. I watched him as he waddled upstairs, with a feeling of angry bewilderment. Then I went to the library and lit a pipe. I would leave first thing in the morning—on that I was determined. But as I sat gazing at the moon of alabaster and the soapstone birds my anger evaporated, and concern took its place. I remembered what a fine fellow Lawson had been, what good times we had had together. I remembered especially that evening when we had found this valley and given rein to our fancies. What horrid alchemy in the place had turned a gentleman into a brute? I thought of drink and drugs and madness and insomnia, but I could fit none of them into my conception of my friend. I did not consciously rescind my resolve to depart, but I had a notion that I would not act on it.

The sleepy butler met me as I went to bed. "Mr. Lawson's room is at the end of your corridor, sir," he said. "He don't sleep over well, so you may hear him stirring in the night. At what hour would you like breakfast, sir? Mr. Lawson mostly has his in bed."

My room opened from the great corridor, which ran the full length of the front of the house. So far as I could make out, Lawson was three rooms off, a vacant bedroom and his servant's room being between us. I felt tired and cross, and tumbled into bed as fast as possible. Usually I sleep well, but now I was soon conscious that my drowsiness was wearing off and that I was in for a restless night. I got up and laved my face, turned the pillows, thought of sheep coming over a hill and clouds crossing the sky; but none of the old devices were of any use. After about an hour of make-believe I surrendered myself to facts, and, lying on my back, stared at the white ceiling and the patches of moonshine on the walls.

It certainly was an amazing night. I got up, put on a dressing-gown, and drew a chair to the window. The moon was almost at its full, and the whole plateau swam in a radiance of ivory and silver. The banks of the stream were black, but the lake had a great belt of light athwart it, which made it seem like a horizon, and the rim of land beyond it like a contorted cloud. Far to the right I saw the delicate outlines of the little wood which I had come to think of as the Grove of Ashtaroth. I listened. There was not a sound in the air. The land seemed to sleep peacefully beneath the moon, and yet I had a sense that the peace was an illusion. The place was feverishly restless.

I could have given no reason for my impression, but there it was. Something was stirring in the wide moonlit landscape under its deep mask of silence. I felt as I had felt on the evening three years ago when I had ridden into the grove. I did not think that the influence, whatever it was, was maleficent. I only knew that it was very strange, and kept me wakeful.

By-and-by I bethought me of a book. There was no lamp in the corridor save the moon, but the whole house was bright as I slipped down the great staircase and across the hall to the library. I switched on the lights and then switched them off. They seemed a profanation, and I did not need them.

I found a French novel, but the place held me and I stayed. I sat down in an arm-chair before the fireplace and the stone birds. Very odd those gawky things, like prehistoric Great Auks, looked in the moonlight. I remember that the alabaster moon shimmered like translucent pearl, and I fell to wondering about its history. Had the old Sabaeans used such a jewel in their rites in the Grove of Ashtaroth?

Then I heard footsteps pass the window. A great house like this would have a watchman, but these quick shuffling footsteps were surely not the dull plod of a servant. They passed on to the grass and died away. I began to think of getting back to my room.

In the corridor I noticed that Lawson's door was ajar, and that a light had been left burning. I had the unpardonable curiosity to peep in. The room was empty, and the bed had not been slept in. Now I knew whose were the footsteps outside the library window.

I lit a reading-lamp and tried to interest myself in *La Cruelle Enigme*. But my wits were restless, and I could not keep my eyes on the page. I flung the book aside and sat down again by the window. The feeling came over me that I was sitting in a box at some play. The glen was a huge stage, and at any moment the players might appear on it. My attention was strung as high as

if I had been waiting for the advent of some world-fa-
mous actress. But nothing came. Only the shadows
shifted and lengthened as the moon moved across the
sky.

Then quite suddenly the restlessness left me and at
the same moment the silence was broken by the crow
of a cock and the rustling of trees in a light wind. I felt
very sleepy, and was turning to bed when again I heard
footsteps without. From the window I could see a figure moving across the garden towards the house. It
was Lawson, got up in the sort of towel dressing-gown
that one wears on board ship. He was walking slowly
and painfully, as if very weary. I did not see his face,
but the man's whole air was that of extreme fatigue
and dejection.

I tumbled into bed and slept profoundly till long after daylight.

III

The man who valeted me was Lawson's own servant. As he was laying out my clothes I asked after the
health of his master, and was told that he had slept ill
and would not rise till late. Then the man, an anxious-
faced Englishman, gave me some information on his
own account. Mr. Lawson was having one of his bad
turns. It would pass away in a day or two, but till it
had gone he was fit for nothing. He advised me to see
Mr. Jobson, the factor, who would look to my entertainment in his master's absence.

Jobson arrived before luncheon, and the sight of him
was the first satisfactory thing about Welgevonden. He
was a big, gruff Scot from Roxburghshire, engaged, no
doubt, by Lawson as a duty to his Border ancestry. He
had short, grizzled whiskers, a weather-worn face, and
a shrewd, calm blue eye. I knew now why the place
was in such perfect order.

We began with sport, and Jobson explained what I

could have in the way of fishing and shooting. His exposition was brief and business-like, and all the while I could see his eye searching me. It was clear that he had much to say on other matters than sport.

I told him that I had come here with Lawson three years before, when he chose the site. Jobson continued to regard me curiously. "I've heard tell of ye from Mr. Lawson. Ye're an old friend of his, I understand."

"The oldest," I said. "And I am sorry to find that the place does not agree with him. Why it doesn't I cannot imagine, for you look fit enough. Has he been seedy for long?"

"It comes and it goes," said Mr. Jobson. "Maybe once a month he has a bad turn. But on the whole it agrees with him badly. He's no' the man he was when I first came here."

Jobson was looking at me very seriously and frankly. I risked a question.

"What do you suppose is the matter?"

He did not reply at once, but leaned forward and tapped my knee.

"I think it's something that doctors canna cure. Look at me, sir. I've always been counted a sensible man, but if I told you what was in my head you would think me daft. But I have one word for you. Bide till to-night is past and then speir your question. Maybe you and me will be agreed."

The factor rose to go. As he left the room he flung me back a remark over his shoulder—"Read the eleventh chapter of the First Book of Kings."

After luncheon I went for a walk. First I mounted to the crown of the hill and feasted my eyes on the unequalled loveliness of the view. I saw the far hills in Portuguese territory, a hundred miles away, lifting up thin blue fingers into the sky. The wind blew light and fresh, and the place was fragrant with a thousand delicate scents. Then I descended to the vale, and followed the stream up through the garden. Poinsettias and oleanders were blazing in coverts, and there was a paradise of tinted water-lilies in the slacker reaches. I saw good trout rise at the fly, but I did not think about fishing. I was searching my memory for a recollection which would not come. By-and-by I found myself beyond the garden, where the lawns ran to the fringe of Ashtaroth's Grove.

It was like something I remembered in an old Italian picture. Only, as my memory drew it, it should have been peopled with strange figures—nymphs dancing on the sward, and a prick-eared faun peeping from the covert. In the warm afternoon sunlight it stood, ineffably gracious and beautiful, tantalising with a sense of some deep hidden loveliness. Very reverently I walked between the slim trees, to where the little conical tower stood half in the sun and half in shadow. Then I noticed something new. Round the tower ran a narrow path, worn in the grass by human feet. There had been no such path on my first visit, for I remembered the grass growing tall to the edge of the stone. Had the Kaffirs made a shrine of it, or were there other and strange votaries?

When I returned to the house I found Travers with a message for me. Mr. Lawson was still in bed, but he would like me to go to him. I found my friend sitting up and drinking strong tea—a bad thing, I should have thought, for a man in his condition. I remember that I looked about the room for some sign of the pernicious habit of which I believed him a victim. But the place was fresh and clean, with the windows wide open, and, though I could not have given my reasons, I was convinced that drugs or drink had nothing to do with the sickness.

He received me more civilly, but I was shocked by his looks. There were great bags below his eyes, and his skin had the wrinkled puffy appearance of a man in dropsy. His voice, too, was reedy and thin. Only his great eyes burned with some feverish life.

"I am a shocking bad host," he said, "but I'm going

to be still more inhospitable. I want you to go away. I hate anybody here when I'm off colour."

"Nonsense," I said; "you want looking after. I want to know about this sickness. Have you had a doctor?"

He smiled wearily. "Doctors are no earthly use to me. There's nothing much the matter I tell you. I'll be all right in a day or two, and then you can come back. I want you to go off with Jobson and hunt in the plains till the end of the week. It will be better fun for you, and I'll feel less guilty."

Of course I pooh-poohed the idea, and Lawson got angry. "Damn it, man," he cried, "why do you force yourself on me when I don't want you? I tell you your presence here makes me worse. In a week I'll be as right as the mail, and then I'll be thankful for you. But get away now; get away, I tell you."

I saw that he was fretting himself into a passion. "All right," I said soothingly; "Jobson and I will go off hunting. But I am horribly anxious about you, old man."

He lay back on his pillows. "You needn't trouble. I only want a little rest. Jobson will make all arrangements, and Travers will get you anything you want. Good-bye."

I saw it was useless to stay longer, so I left the room. Outside I found the anxious-faced servant. "Look here," I said, "Mr. Lawson thinks I ought to go, but I mean to stay. Tell him I'm gone if he asks you. And for Heaven's sake keep him in bed."

The man promised, and I thought I saw some relief in his face.

I went to the library, and on the way remembered Jobson's remark about First Kings. With some searching I found a Bible and turned up the passage. It was a long screed about the misdeeds of Solomon, and I read it through without enlightenment. I began to re-read it, and a word suddenly caught my attention—

"For Solomon went after Ashtaroth, the goddess of the Zidonians."

That was all, but it was like a key to a cipher. Instantly there flashed over my mind all that I had heard or read of that strange ritual which seduced Israel to sin. I saw a sunburnt land and a people vowed to the stern service of Jehovah. But I saw, too, eyes turning from the austere sacrifice to lonely hill-top groves and towers and images, where dwelt some subtle and evil mystery. I saw the fierce prophets, scourging the votaries with rods, and a nation penitent before the Lord; but always the backsliding again, and the hankering after forbidden joys. Ashtaroth was the old goddess of the East. Was it not possible that in all Semitic blood there remained transmitted through the dim generations, some craving for her spell? I thought of the grandfather in the back street at Brighton and of those burning eyes upstairs.

As I sat and mused my glance fell on the inscrutable stone birds. They knew all those old secrets of joy and terror. And that moon of alabaster! Some dark priest had worn it on his forehead when he worshipped like Ahab, "all the host of Heaven." And then I honestly began to be afraid. I, a prosaic, modern Christian gentleman, a half-believer in casual faiths, was in the presence of some hoary mystery of sin far older than creeds or Christendom. There was fear in my heart—a kind of uneasy disgust, and above all a nervous eerie disquiet. Now I wanted to go away, and yet I was ashamed of the cowardly thought. I pictured Ashtaroth's Grove with sheer horror. What tragedy was in the air? What secret awaited twilight? For the night was coming, the night of the Full Moon, the season of ecstasy and sacrifice.

I do not know how I got through that evening. I was disinclined for dinner, so I had a cutlet in the library and sat smoking till my tongue ached. But as the hours passed a more manly resolution grew up in my mind. I owed it to old friendship to stand by Lawson in this extremity. I could not interfere—God knows, his reason seemed already rocking,—but I could be at hand in case my chance came. I determined not to undress, but

to watch through the night. I had a bath, and changed
into light flannels and slippers. Then I took up my
position in a corner of the library close to the window,
so that I could not fail to hear Lawson's footsteps if he
passed.

Fortunately I left the lights unlit, for as I waited I
grew drowsy, and fell asleep. When I woke the moon
had risen, and I knew from the feel of the air that the
hour was late. I sat very still, straining my ears, and as
I listened I caught the sound of steps. They were
crossing the hall, stealthily, and nearing the library
door. I huddled into my corner as Lawson entered.

He wore the same towel dressing-gown, and he
moved swiftly and silently as if in a trance. I watched
him take the alabaster moon from the mantelpiece and
drop it in his pocket. A glimpse of white skin showed
that the gown was his only clothing. Then he moved
past me to the window, opened it, and went out.

Without any conscious purpose I rose and followed,
kicking off my slippers that I might go quietly. He was
running, running fast, across the lawns in the direction
of the Grove—an odd shapeless antic in the moonlight.
I stopped, for there was no cover, and I feared for his
reason if he saw me. When I looked again he had disappeared among the trees.

I saw nothing for it but to crawl, so on my belly I
wormed my way over the dripping sward. There was a
ridiculous suggestion of deer-stalking about the game
which tickled me and dispelled my uneasiness. Almost
I persuaded myself I was tracking an ordinary sleep-
walker. The lawns were broader than I imagined, and
it seemed an age before I reached the edge of the
Grove. The world was so still that I appeared to be
making a most ghastly amount of noise. I remember
that once I heard a rustling in the air, and looked up to
see the green doves circling about the tree-tops.

There was no sign of Lawson. On the edge of the
Grove I think that all my assurance vanished. I could
see between the trunks to the little tower, but it was
quiet as the grave, save for the wings above. Once

more there came over me the unbearable sense of anticipation I had felt the night before. My nerves tingled with mingled expectation and dread. I did not think that any harm would come to me, for the powers of the air seemed not malignant. But I knew them for powers, and felt awed and abased. I was in the presence of the "host of Heaven," and I was no stern Israelitish prophet to prevail against them.

I must have lain for hours waiting in that spectral place, my eyes riveted on the tower and its golden cap of moonshine. I remember that my head felt void and light, as if my spirit were becoming disembodied and leaving its dew-drenched sheath far below. But the most curious sensation was of something drawing me to the tower, something mild and kindly and rather feeble, for there was some other and stronger force keeping me back. I yearned to move nearer, but I could not drag my limbs an inch. There was a spell somewhere which I could not break. I do not think I was in any way frightened now. The starry influence was playing tricks with me, but my mind was half asleep. Only I never took my eyes from the little tower. I think I could not, if I had wanted to.

Then suddenly from the shadows came Lawson. He was stark-naked, and he wore, bound across his brow, the half-moon of alabaster. He had something, too, in his hand,—something which glittered.

He ran round the tower, crooning to himself and flinging wild arms to the skies. Sometimes, the crooning changed to a shrill cry of passion, such as a maenad may have uttered in the train of Bacchus. I could make out no words, but the sound told its own tale. He was absorbed in some infernal ecstasy. And as he ran, he drew his right hand across his breast and arms, and I saw that it held a knife.

I grew sick with disgust,—not terror, but honest physical loathing. Lawson, gashing his fat body, affected me with an overpowering repugnance. I wanted to go forward and stop him and I wanted, too, to be a hundred miles away. And the result was that I stayed

still. I believe my own will held me there, but I doubt
if in any case I could have moved my legs.

The dance grew swifter and fiercer. I saw the blood
dripping from Lawson's body, and his face ghastly
white above his scarred breast. And then suddenly the
horror left me; my head swam; and for one second—
one brief second—I seemed to peer into a new world.
A strange passion surged up in my heart. I seemed to
see the earth peopled with forms not human, scarcely
divine, but more desirable than man or god. The calm
face of Nature broke up for me into wrinkles of wild
knowledge. I saw the things which brush against the
soul in dreams, and found them lovely. There seemed
no cruelty in the knife or the blood. It was a delicate
mystery of worship, as wholesome as the morning song
of birds. I do not know how the Semites fround Ashtaroth's ritual; to them it may well have been more
rapt and passionate than it seemed to me. For I saw in
it only the sweet simplicity of Nature, and all riddles of
lust and terror soothed away as a child's nightmares
are calmed by a mother. I found my legs able to move,
and I think I took two steps through the dusk towards
the tower.

And then it all ended. A cock crew, and the homely
noises of earth were renewed. While I stood dazed and
shivering, Lawson plunged through the Grove toward
me. The impetus carried him to the edge, and he fell
fainting just outside the shade.

My wits and common-sense came back to me with
my bodily strength. I got my friend on my back, and
staggered with him towards the house. I was afraid in
real earnest now, and what frightened me most was the
thought that I had not been afraid sooner. I had come
very near the "abomination of the Zidonians."

At the door I found the scared valet waiting. He had
apparently done this sort of thing before.

"Your master has been sleep-walking and has had a
fall." I said. "We must get him to bed at once."

We bathed the wounds as he lay in a deep stupor,
and I dressed them as well as I could. The only danger

lay in his utter exhaustion, for happily the gashes were
not serious, and no artery had been touched. Sleep and
rest would make him well, for he had the constitution
of a strong man. I was leaving the room when he
opened his eyes and spoke. He did not recognize me,
but I noticed that his face had lost its strangeness, and
was once more that of the friend I had known. Then I
suddenly bethought me of an old hunting remedy
which he and I always carried on our expeditions. It is
a pill made up from an ancient Portuguese prescrip-
tion. One is an excellent specific for fever. Two are invaluable if you are lost in the bush, for they send a
man for many hours into a deep sleep, which prevents
suffering and madness, till help comes. Three give a
painless death. I went to my room and found the little
box in my jewel-case. Lawson swallowed two, and
turned wearily on his side. I bade his man let him sleep
till he woke, and went off in search of food.

IV

I had business on hand which would not wait. By
seven, Jobson, who had been sent for, was waiting for
me in the library. I knew by his grim face that here I
had a very good substitute for a prophet of the Lord.

"You were right," I said. "I have read the eleventh
chapter of First Kings, and I have spent such a night as
I pray God I shall never spend again."

"I thought you would," he replied. "I've had the
same experience myself."

"The Grove?" I said.

"Ay, the wud," was the answer in broad Scots.

I wanted to see how much he understood.

"Mr. Lawson's family is from the Scottish Border?"

"Ay. I understand they come off Borthwick Water
side," he replied, but I saw by his eyes that he knew
what I meant.

"Mr. Lawson is my oldest friend," I went on, "and I
am going to take measures to cure him. For what I am

going to do I take the sole responsibility. I will make that plain to your master. But if I am to succeed I want your help. Will you give it me? It sounds like madness, and you are a sensible man and may like to keep out of it. I leave it to your discretion."

Jobson looked me straight in the face. "Have no fear for me," he said: "there is an unholy thing in that place, and if I have the strength in me I will destroy it. He has been a good master to me, and, forbye, I am a believing Christian. So say on, sir."

There was no mistaking the air. I had found my Tishbite.

"I want men," I said,—"as many as we can get."

Jobson mused. "The Kaffirs will no' gang near the place, but there's some thirty white men on the tobacco farm. They'll do your will, if you give them an indemnity in writing."

"Good," said I. "Then we will take our instructions from the only authority which meets the case. We will follow the example of King Josiah." I turned up the twenty-third chapter of Second Kings, and read—

"And the high places that were before Jerusalem, which were on the right hand of the Mount of Corruption, which Solomon the king of Israel had builded for Ashtaroth the abomination of the Zidonians . . . did the king defile.

"And he brake in pieces the images, and cut down the groves, and filled their places with the bones of men.

"Moreover the altar that was at Beth-el, and the high place which Jeroboam the son of Nebat, who made Israel to sin, had made, both the altar and the high place he brake down, and burned the high place, and stamped it small to powder, and burned the grove."

Jobson nodded. "It'll need dinnymite. But I've plenty of yon down at the workshops. I'll be off to collect the lads."

Before nine the men had assembled at Jobson's house. They were a hardy lot of young farmers from home, who took their instructions docilely from the masterful factor. On my orders they had brought their shotguns. We armed them wtih spades and woodmen's axes, and one man wheeled some coils of rope in a handcart.

In the clear, windless air of morning the Grove, set amid its lawns, looked too innocent and exquisite for ill. I had a pang of regret that a thing so fair should suffer; nay, if I had come alone, I think I might have repented. But the men were there, and the grim-faced Jobson was waiting for orders. I placed the guns, and sent beaters to the far side. I told them that every dove must be shot.

It was only a small flock, and we killed fifteen at the first drive. The poor birds flew over the glen to another spinney, but we brought them back over the guns and seven fell. Four more were got in the trees, and the last I killed myself with a long shot. In half an hour there was a pile of little green bodies in the sward.

Then we went to work to cut down the trees. The slim stems were an easy task to a good woodman, and one after another they toppled to the ground. And meantime, as I watched, I became conscious of a strange emotion.

It was as if someone were pleading with me. A gentle voice, not threatening, but pleading—something too fine for the sensual ear, but touching inner chords of the spirit. So tenuous it was and distant that I could think of no personality behind it. Rather it was the viewless, bodiless grace of this delectable vale, some old exquisite divinity of the groves. There was the heart of all sorrow in it, and the soul of all loveliness. It seemed a woman's voice, some lost lady who had brought nothing but goodness unrepaid to the world. And what the voice told me was that I was destroying her last shelter.

That was the pathos of it—the voice was homeless. As the axes flashed in the sunlight and the wood grew

thin, that gentle spirit was pleading with me for mercy
and a brief respite. It seemed to be telling of a world
for centuries grown coarse and pitiless, of long sad
wanderings, of hardly-won shelter, and a peace which
was the little all she sought from men. There was nothing terrible in it. No thought of wrong-doing. The spell,
which to Semitic blood held the mystery of evil, was to
me, of the Northern race, only delicate and rare and
beautiful. Jobson and the rest did not feel it, I with my
finer senses caught nothing but the hopeless sadness of
it. That which had stirred the passion in Lawson was
only wringing my heart. It was almost too pitiful to
bear. As the trees crashed down and the men wiped
the sweat from their brows, I seemed to myself like the
murderer of fair women and innocent children. I
remember that the tears were running over my cheeks.
More than once I opened my mouth to countermand the
work, but the face of Jobson, that grim Tishbite, held
me back.

I knew now what gave the Prophets of the Lord
their mastery, and I knew also why the people sometimes stoned them.

The last tree fell, and the little tower stood like a ra-
vished shrine, stripped of all defense against the world.
I heard Jobson's voice speaking. "We'd better blast
that stane thing now. We'll trench on four sides and lay
the dinnymite. Ye're no' looking weel, sir. Ye'd better
go and sit down on the braeface."

I went up the hillside and lay down. Below me, in
the waste of shorn trunks, men were running about,
and I saw the mining begin. It all seemed like an aim-
less dream in which I had no part. The voice of that
homeless goddess was still pleading. It was the innocence of it that tortured me. Even so must a merciful
Inquisitor have suffered from the plea of some fair girl
with the aureole of death on her hair. I knew I was
killing rare and unrecoverable beauty. As I sat dazed
and heartsick, the whole loveliness of Nature seemed to
plead for its divinity. The sun in the heavens, the mel-
low lines of upland, the blue mystery of the far plains,

were all part of that soft voice. I felt bitter scorn for
myself. I was guilty of blood; nay, I was guilty of the
sin against light which knows no forgiveness. I was
murdering innocent gentleness—and there would be no
peace on earth for me. Yet I sat helpless. The power of
a sterner will constrained me. And all the while the
voice was growing fainter and dying away into unutterable sorrow.

Suddenly a great flame sprang to heaven, and a pall
of smoke. I heard men crying out, and fragments of
stone fell around the ruins of the grove. When the air
cleared, the little tower had gone out of sight.

The voice had ceased and there seemed to me to be
a bereaved silence in the world. The shock moved me
to my feet, and I ran down the slope to where Jobson
stood rubbing his eyes.

"That's done the job. Now we maun get up the tree
roots. We've no time to howk. We'll just blast the feck
o' them."

The work of destruction went on, but I was coming
back to my senses. I forced myself to be practical and
reasonable. I thought of the night's experience and
Lawson's haggard eyes, and I screwed myself into a
determination to see the thing through. I had done the
deed; it was my business to make it complete. A text in
Jeremiah came into my head: *"Their children remem-*
ber their altars and their groves by the green trees
upon the high hills." I would see to it that this grove
should be utterly forgotten.

We blasted the tree-roots, and, yoking oxen, dragged
the debris into a great heap. Then the men set to work
with their spades, and roughly levelled the ground. I
was getting back to my old self, and Jobson's spirit was
becoming mine.

"There is one thing more," I told him. "Get ready a
couple of ploughs. We will improve upon King Josiah."
My brain was a medley of Scripture precedents, and I
was determined that no safeguard should be wanting.

We yoked the oxen again and drove the ploughs

over the site of the grove. It was rough ploughing, for the place was thick with bits of stone from the tower, but the slow Afrikander oxen plodded on, and sometime in the afternoon the work was finished. Then I sent down to the farm for bags of rock-salt, such as they use for cattle. Jobson and I took a sack apiece, and walked up and down the furrows, sowing them with salt.

The last act was to set fire to the pile of tree-trunks. They burned well, and on the top we flung the bodies of the green doves. The birds of Ashtaroth had an honorable pyre.

Then I dismissed the much-perplexed men, and gravely shook hands with Jobson. Black with dust and smoke I went back to the house, where I bade Travers pack my bags and order the motor. I found Lawson's servant, and heard from him that his master was sleeping peacefully. I gave him some directions, and then went to wash and change.

Before I left I wrote a line to Lawson. I began by transcribing the verses from the twenty-third chapter of Second Kings. I told him what I had done, and my reason. "I take the whole responsibility upon myself," I wrote. "No man in the place had anything to do with it but me. I acted as I did for the sake of our old friendship, and you will believe it was no easy task for me. I hope you will understand. Whenever you are able to see me send me word, and I will come back and settle with you. But I think you will realise that I have saved your soul."

The afternoon was merging into twilight as I left the house on the road to Taqui. The great fire, where the Grove had been, was still blazing fiercely, and the smoke made a cloud over the upper glen, and filled all the air with a soft violet haze. I knew that I had done well for my friend, and that he would come to his senses and be grateful. My mind was at ease on that score, and in something like comfort I faced the future. But as the car reached the ridge I looked back to the vale I had outraged. The moon was rising and silvering the smoke, and through the gaps I could see the tongues of fire. Somehow, I know not why, the lake, the stream, the garden-coverts, even the green slopes of hill, wore an air of loneliness and desecration.

And then my heartache returned, and I knew that I had driven something lovely and adorable from its last refuge on earth.

❦ KENNETH VENNOR MORRIS ❦

(1879–1937)

Kenneth Morris is one of the finest but least known of the writers of contemporary fantasy. We are indebted to Ursula K. Le Guin for bringing him to our attention. In her essay on style, "From Elfland to Poughkeepsie," Le Guin includes him as one of three "master stylists" of modern fantasy, along with E. R. Eddison and J. R. R. Tolkien. She refers to Morris's *The Book of the Three Dragons* (1930) as "a singularly fine example of the recreation of a work magnificent in its own right (the *Mabinogion*)—a literary event rather rare except in fantasy, where its frequency is perhaps proof, if one were needed, of the ever-renewed vitality of myth." Le Guin strongly recommends Morris, but warns that the prospective reader will have to search for him on the dusty back shelves, and usually in the section devoted to outdated children's works. Only a small portion of *Three Dragons*, Morris's last published book, has been reproduced for a wider audience, in Lin Carter's adult fantasy series. Nor, surprisingly, can one find Morris listed in any of the standard biographical references devoted to adult or children's authors. We are grateful to The Theosophical Society–International, in which Morris was active most of his life, for the following information. We hope that this information, and more importantly, the story that follows, will bring Morris some measure of the attention he deserves.

Kenneth Morris was born in Potamman, South Wales, on July 31, 1879. His family was modestly wealthy, thanks to his grandfather. The family suffered a series of misfortunes, however: Morris's father died in 1884, his grandfather in 1885, and shortly afterwards the family business was ruined by the American Tariff Law. When the family moved to London in 1885 or 1886, Morris enrolled in Christ's Hospital, a school that had been attended by such luminaries as Coleridge, Lamb, and Leigh Hunt. He left school at the age of sixteen and, in 1896, spent some time with a group of writers in Dublin. There he formed close ties with the poet and short-story writer A.E. (George Russell). He also joined the Theosophical Society, an organization that profoundly influenced his life. By 1899 he was back in Wales, contributing prose and poetry to the magazine published by the Theosophical Society in Cardiff. In 1908 he came to the United States, where he became professor of literature and history at the Theosophical University in Point Loma, California. He remained in that position, teaching and writing, until he returned to Wales in 1930. He published the monthly magazine *Y Fforum Theosophaid* from 1930 until his death on April 21, 1937.

The twenty-two years that Morris spent in the United States seem to have been his most productive in terms of his writing. While teaching at Point Loma, he also wrote a good deal, including works of history, literary criticism, poetry, and fiction. In his myth-based fiction, Morris blends his two great loves, theosophy and Wales. His first book, *The Fates of the Princes of Dyfed* (1913), is a close retelling of parts of the *Mabinogion,* the medieval compendium of Welsh mythology. In *The Secret Mountain and Other Tales* (1926), his second major publication, Morris expanded his interest in myth to include tales from a number of other countries. A.E., who reviewed the collection for the April 23, 1927, edition of *The Irish Statesman of Dublin,* admired Morris's ability to capture the authentic spirit of various mythologies, including those of India and China. A.E. also compared Morris's tales favorably with those of Dunsany for their inventiveness and convincing other-world settings. But Morris's stories have, according to A.E., a more "mystical character," being the product of "long mystical meditation." *Three Dragons,* Morris's third and last major fiction publication, is a continuation of his 1913 rendering of the *Mabinogion.* Morris also applied his genius to New-World myth in an unpublished story about ancient Mexico, *The Chalchuhuite Dragon*.

Morris's theosophy instilled in the man and his work a catholicity of outlook that was at the same time profound and penetrating. His writings thus attain to the sort of universality that Morris saw as the proper aim of fantasy. He defines the function of romance as "proclaiming indestructable truth in terms of the imagination; using the symbols provided by the poetic or creative imagination to show forth those truths which are permanent, because they lie at the heart of life, not on its surface; and which belong to all ages, because all eternity is the birthday of the soul" (quoted in *The San Diego Union,* May 15, 1927).

"Red-Peach-Blossom Inlet" is a myth fantasy, with Chinese Taoism as its source. Lao-tse the Master, whom Wang Tao-chen meets in the story, was the founder of Taoism in the seventh century B.C. But, as in any good fantasy of this type, both the myth and its expression are universal. Recognizable archetypes such as the quest, the crossing of the waters, the garden, and the tree of knowledge and immortality underly the story. The style fits the contents. In this respect "Red-Peach-Blossom Inlet" sets a standard that few stories by other writers will be able to match. The inlet is a paradise of sight, smell, and taste delights, all of which are vividly conveyed by Morris's sensuous imagery. The archetypes and imagery, however, are not the only memorable aspects of the tale. Its conclusion will linger in the memory, causing the reader to reflect for some time on the meaning of Wang Tao-chen's fate.

Red-Peach-Blossom Inlet
Kenneth Morris

❧

Wang Tao-chen loved the ancients: that was why he was a fisherman. Modernity you might call irremediable: it was best left alone. But far out in the middle lake, when the distances were all a blue haze and the world a sapphirean vacuity, one might breathe the atmosphere of ancient peace and give oneself to the pursuit of immortality. By study of the Classics, by rest of the senses, and by cultivating a mood of universal benevolence, Wang Tao-chen proposed to become superior to time and change: a Sennin—an adept, immortal.

He had long since put away the desire for an official career. If, thought he, one could see a way, by taking office, to reform the administration, the case would be different. One would pass one's examinations, accept a prefecture, climb the ladder of promotion, and put one's learning and character to use. One would establish peace, of course; and presently, perhaps, achieve rewelding into one the many kingdoms into which the empire of Han had split. But unfortunately there were but two roads to success: force and fraud. And, paradoxically, they both always led to failure. As soon as you had cheated or thumped your way into office, you were marked as the prey of all other cheaters and thumpers; and had but to wait a year or two for the most expert of them to have you out, handed over to the Board of Punishments, and perchance shortened of stature by a head. The disadvantages of such a career outweighed its temptations; and Wang Tao-chen had decided it was not for him.

So he refrained from politics altogether, and transplanted his ambitions into more secret fields. Inactive, he would do well by his age; unstriving, he would attain possession of Tao. He would be peaceful in a world disposed to violence; honest where all were cheats; serene and unambitious in an age of fussy ambition. Let the spoils of office go to inferior men; for him the blue calmness of the lake, the blue emptiness above: the place that his soul should reflect and rival, and the untroubled noiseless place that reflected and rivalled heaven.—Where, too, one might go through the day unreminded that that unintelligent Li Kuang-ming, one's neighbour, had already obtained his prefecture, and was making a good thing of it; or that Fan Kao-sheng, the flashy and ostentatious, had won his *chin shih* degree, and was spoken well of by the undiscerning on all sides. Let *him* examine either of them in the Classics! . . .

Certainly there was no better occupation for the meditative than fishing. One suffered no interruption—except when the fish bit. He tolerated this vile habit of theirs for a year or two; and brought home a good catch to his wife of an evening, until such time as he had shaken off—as it seemed to him—earthly ambitions and desires. Then, when he could hear of Li's and Fan's successes with equanimity, and his own mind had grown one-pointed towards wisdom, he turned from books to pure contemplation, and became impatient even of the attentions of the fish. He would emulate the sages of old: in this respect a very simple matter. One had but to bend one's hook straight before casting it, and everything with fins and scales in Lake Tao-ting might wait its turn to nibble, yet shake down none of the fruits of serenity from the branches of his mind. It was an ingenious plan, and worked excellently.

You may ask, What would his wife say?—he, fortunately, had little need to consider that. He was lucky, he reflected, in the possession of such a spouse as Pu-hsi; who, though she might not tread with him his elected path, stood sentry at the hither end of it, so to say, without complaint or fuss. A meek little woman, lazily minded yet withal capable domestically, she gave him no trouble in the world; and received in return unthinking confidence and complete dependence in all material things—as you might say, a magnanimous marital affection. His home in the fishing village was a thing not to be dispensed with, certainly; nor yet much to be dwelt upon in the mind by one who sought immortality. No doubt Pu-hsi felt for him the great love and reverence which were a husband's due, and would not presume to question his actions.

True, she had once, soon after their marriage, mildly urged him to follow the course of nature and take his examinations; but a little eloquence had silenced her. In this matter of the fish, he would let it dawn on her in her own time that there would be no more, either to cook or to sell. Having realized the fact she would, of course, dutifully exert herself the more to make things go as they should. There would be neither inconvenience nor disturbance, at home.

Which things happened. One night, however, she examined his tackle and discovered the unbent hook; and meditated over it for months. Then a great desire for fish came over her; and she rose up while he slept and bent the hook back to its proper shape with care, and baited it; and went to sleep again, hoping for the best.

Wang Tao-chen never noticed it; perhaps because, as he was gathering up his tackle to set out, a neighbour came to the door and borrowed a net from him, promising to return it that same evening. It was an interruption which Wang resented inwardly; and the resentment made him careless, I suppose. He was far out on the lake, and had thrown his line, before composure quite came back to him; and it had hardly come when there was a bite to frighten it away again,—and such a bite as might not be ignored. Away went the fish, and Wang Tao-chen after it: speeding over the water so swiftly that he had no thought even to drop the rod. Away and away, breathless, until noon; then suddenly the boat stopped and the line hung loose. He drew it in, and found the baited hook untouched; and fell to pondering on the meaning of it all. . . .

He had come into a region unknown to him, lovelier than any he had visited before. He had left the middle lake far behind, and was in the shadow of lofty hills. The water, all rippleless, mirrored the beauty of the mountains; and inshore, here reeds greener than jade, there hibiscus splendid with bloom. High up among the pines a little blue-tiled temple glowed in the magical air. Above the bluff yonder, over whose steep sheer face little pinetrees hung jutting half-way between earth and heaven, delicate feathers of cloud, bright as polished silver, floated in a sky bluer than glazed porcelain. From the woods on the hillsides came birdsong strangely and magically sweet. Wang Tao-chen, listening, felt a quickening of the life within him: the rising of a calm sacred quality of life, as if he had breathed airs laden with immortality from the Garden of Siwangmu in the western world. Shore and water seemed bathed in a light at once more vivid and more tranquil than any that shone in familiar regions.

Quickening influences in the place stirred him to curiosity, to action; and he took his oar and began to row. He passed round the bluff and into the bay beyond; and as he went, felt himself drawing nearer to the heart of beauty and holiness. A high pine-clad island stood in the mouth of the bay; so that, unless close in shore, you might easily pass the latter undiscovered. Within—between the island and the hills, the whole being of him rose up into poetry and peace. The air he breathed was keenness of delight, keenness of perception. The pines on the high hills on either side blushed into deep and exquisite green. Blue long-tailed birds like fiery jewels flitted among the trees and out from the boscage over the bay; the water, clear as a diamond, glassed the wizardry of the hills and pines and the sweet sky with its drifting delicacy of cloudlets; glassed, too, the wonder of the lower slopes where, and in the valley-bottom, glowed an innumerable multitude of peach-trees, red-blossomed, and now all lovely like soft clouds of sunset with bloom.

He rowed shoreward, and on under the shadow of the faery peach-trees, and came into a narrow inlet, deep-watered, that seemed the path for him into bliss and the secret places of wonder. The petals fell about him in a slow roseate rain; even in midstream, looking upward, one could see but inches and glimpses of interstitial blueness. He went on until a winding of the inlet brought him into the open valley: to a thinning of the trees,—a house beside the water,—and then another and another: into the midst of a scattered village and among a mild, august and kindly people, unlike, in fashion of garb and speech, any

whom he had seen—any, he would have said, that had
lived among the Hills of Han[1] these many hundred years.

They had an air of radiant placidity, passionless joy and
benevolence, lofty and calm thought. They appeared to
have expected his coming: greeted him majestically, but
with affability; showed him, presently, a house in which,
they said, he might live as long as he chose. They had no
news, he found, of the doings in any of the contemporary
kingdoms, and were not interested; they were without
politics entirely; wars nor rumours of wars disturbed them.
Here, thought Wang, he would abide for ever; such things
were not be be found elsewhere. In this lofty peace he
would grow wise: would blossom, naturally as a flower,
but into immortality. They let fall, while talking to him,
sentences strangely illuminating—yet strangely tantalizing
too, as it seemed to him: one felt stupendous wisdom
concealed—saw a gleam of it, or as it were a corner trailing away; and missed the satisfaction of its wholeness.
This in itself was supreme incitement; in time one would
learn and penetrate all. Of course he would remain with
them forever; he would supply them with fish in gratitude
for their hospitality. Falling asleep that night, he knew that
none of his days had been flawless until that day—until
the latter part of it, at least. . . .

The bloom fell from the trees; the young fruit formed,
and slowly ripened in a sunlight more caressing than any
in the world of men. With their ripening, the air of the
valley became more wonderful, more quickening and in-
spiring daily. When the first dark blush appeared on the
yellow-green of the peaches, Wang Tao-chen walked
weightless, breathed joy, was as one who had heard tidings
glorious and never expected. Transcendent thoughts had
been rising in him continually since first he came into the
valley; now, his mind became like clear night-skies among
the stars of which luminous dragons sail always, liquid,
gleaming, light-shedding, beautiful. By his door grew a
tree whose writhing branches overhung a pool of golden
carp; as he came out one morning, he saw the first of the
ripe peaches drop shining from its bough, and fall into the

[1] i.e. in China.

water; diffusing the sweetness of its scent on the diamond light of the young day. Silently worshipping heaven, he picked up the floating peach, and raised it to his mouth. As he did so he heard the leisurely tread of oxhoofs on the road above: it would be his neighbour So-and-so, who rode his ox down to drink at the inlet at that time each morning. (Strange that he should have learnt none of the names of the villagers; that he should never, until now, have thought of them as bearing names.) As the taste of the peach fell on his palate, he looked up, and saw the Ox-rider . . . and fell down and made obeisance; for it was Laotse the Master, who had ridden his ox out of the world, and into the Western Heaven, some seven or eight hundred years before.

Forthwith and thenceforward the place was all new to him, and a thousand times more wonderful. What had seemed to him cottages were lovely pagodas of jade and porcelain, the sunlight reflected from their glaze of transparent azure or orange or vermilion, of luminous yellow or purple or green. Through the shining skies of noon or evening you might often see lordly dragons floating: golden and gleaming dragons; or that shed a violet luminance from their wings; or whose hue was the essence from which blue heaven drew its blueness; or white dragons whose passing was like the shooting of a star. As for his neighbours, he knew them now for the Mighty of old time: the men made one with Tao, who soared upon the Lonely Crane; the men who had eaten the Peaches of Immortality. There dwelt the founders of dynasties vanished millennia since: Men-Dragons and Divine Rulers: the Heaven-Kings and the Earth-Kings and the Man-Kings: all the figures who emerge in dim radiance out of the golden haze on the horizon of Chinese prehistory, and shine there quaintly wonderful. Their bodies emitted a heavenly light; the tones of their voices were an exquisite music; for their amusement they would harden snow into silver, or change the nature of the cinnabar until it became yellow gold. And sometimes they would bridle the flying dragon, and visit the Fortunate Isles of the Morning; and sometimes they would mount upon the hoary crane, and soaring through the empyrean, come into the Enchanted Gardens of the West: where Siwangmu is Queen of the

Evening, and whence her birds of azure plumage fly and sing unseen over the world, and their singing is the love, the peace, and the immortal thoughts of mankind. Visibly those wonder-birds flew through Red-Peach-Blossom Inlet Valley; and lighted down there; and were fed with celestial food by the villagers, that their beneficent power might be increased when they went forth among men.

Seven years Wang Tao-chen dwelt there: enjoying the divine companionship of the sages, hearing the divine philosophy from their lips: until his mind became clarified to the clear brightness of the diamond; and his perceptions serenely overspread the past, the present and the future; and his thoughts, even the most commonplace of them, were more luminously lovely than the inspirations of the supreme poets. Then one morning while he was fishing his boat drifted out into the bay, and beyond the island into the open lake.

And he fell to comparing his life in the valley with his life as it might be in the outer world. Among mortals, he considered, with the knowledge he had won, he would be as a herdsman with his herd. He might reach any pinnacle of power; he might reunite the world, and inaugurate an age more glorious than that of Han. . . . But here among these Mighty and Wise Ones, he would always be.— Well; was it not true that they must look down on him? He remembered Pu-hsi, the forgotten during all these years; and thought how astounded she would be,—how she would worship him more than ever, returning, so changed, after so long an absence. It would be nothing to row across the lake and see; and return the next day—or when the world of men bored him. He landed at the familiar quay in the evening, and went up with his catch to his house.

But Pu-hsi showed no surprise at seeing him, nor any rapturous satisfaction until she saw the fish. It was a cold shock to him; but he hid his feelings. To his question as to how she had employed her time during his absence, she answered that the day had been as other days. There was embarrassment, even guilt, in her voice, if he had noticed it. "The day?" said he; "the seven years!" —and her embarrassment was covered away with surprise and uncomprehension. But here the neighbour came to the door, "to return the net," he said, "that he had borrowed in the morning";—the net Wang Tao-chen had lent him before he went away. And to impart a piece of gossip, it seemed: "I hear," said he, "that Ping Yang-hsi and Po Lo-hsien are setting forth for the provincial capital to-morrow, to take their examination." Wang Tao-chen gasped. "They should have passed," he began; and bit off the sentence there, leaving "seven years ago" unsaid. Here were mysteries indeed.

He made cautious inquiries as to the events of this year and last; and the answers still further set his head spinning. He had only been away a day: everything confirmed that. Had he dreamed the whole seven years then? By all the glory of which they were compact; by the immortal energy he felt in his spirit and veins; *no!* He would prove their truth to himself; and he would prove himself to the world! He announced that he too would take the examination.

He did; and left all competitors to marvel: passed so brilliantly that all Tsin was talking about it; and returned to find that his wife had fled with a lover. That was not likely to trouble him much: he had lived forgetting her for seven years. But she, at least, should repent: she should learn what a Great One she had deserted. Without delay he took examination after examination; and before the year was out was hailed as the most brilliant of rising stars. Promotion followed promotion, till the Son of Heaven called him to be prime minister. At every success he laughed to himself: he was proving to himself that he had lived with the Immortals. His fame spread through all the kingdoms of China; he was courted by the emissaries of many powerful kings. Yet nothing would content him: he must prove his grand memory still further; so he went feeding his ambition with greater and greater triumphs. Heading the army, he inflicted disaster upon the Huns, and imposed his will on the west and north. The time was almost at hand, people said, when the Black-haired people should be one again, under the founder of a new and most mighty dynasty.

And still he was dissatisfied: he found no companionship in his greatness: no one whom he loved or trusted, none to give him trust or love. His emperor was but a puppet in his hands, down to whose level he must painfully diminish his inward stature; his wife—the emperor's daughter—flattered and feared, and withal despised him. The world sang his praises and plotted his downfall busily; he discovered the plots, punished the plotters, and filled the world with his splendid activities. And all the while a voice was crying in his heart: *In Red-Peach-Blossom-Inlet Valley you had peace, companionship, joy!*

Twenty years yassed, and his star still rose: it was whispered that he was certainly no common mortal, but a genie, or a *sennin,* possessor of Tao. For he grew no older as the years went by, but still had the semblance of young manhood, as on the day he returned from the Valley. And now the Son of Heaven was dying, and there was no heir to the throne but a sickly and vicious boy; and it was thought everywhere that the great Wang Tao-chen would assume the Yellow. The dynasty had exhausted the mandate of heaven.

It was night; and he sat alone; and home sickness weighed upon his soul. He had just dismissed the great court functionaries, the ministers and ambassadors, who had come to offer him the throne. The people were everywhere crying out for reunion, an end of dissensions, and the revival of the ancient glories of Han: and who but Wang Tao-chen could bring these things to pass? He had dismissed the courtiers, promising an answer in the morning. He knew that not one of them had spoken from his heart sincerely, nor voiced his own desire; but had come deeming it politic to anticipate the inevitable. For alas! in all the world there was none who was his equal. . . . Of these that had pressed upon him sovereignty especially, there was none to whom he could speak his mind—none with the greatness to understand. He saw polite enmity and fear under their bland expressions, and heard it beneath their courtly phrases of flattery. To be Son of Heaven—among such courtiers as these!

But in Red-Peach-Blossom-Inlet Valley one might talk daily with the Old Philosopher and with Such-a-One [2];

[2] Laotse and Confucius.

with the Duke of Chow and with Muh Wang and Tang the Completer; with the Royal Lady of the West; with Yao, Shun and Ta Yü themselves, those stainless Sovereigns of the Golden Age;—ah! with Fu-hsi the Man-Dragon Emperor and his seven Dragon Ministers; with the August Monarchs of the three August Periods of the world-dawn: the Heaven-Kings and the Earth-Kings and the Man-Kings. . . .

He did off his robes of state, and donned an old fisherman's costume which he had never had the heart to part with; and slipped away from his palace and from the capital; and set his face westward towards the shores of Lake Tao-ting. He would get a boat, and put off on the lake, and come to Red-Peach-Blossom-Inlet Valley again; and consult with Fu-hsi and the Yellow Emperor as to this wearing of the Yellow Robe,—as to whether it was Their will that he, the incompetent Wang Tao-chen, should dare to mount Their throne. But when he had come to his native village, and bought a boat and fishing-tackle, and put forth on the lake in the early morning, his purpose had changed: never, never, never would he leave the company of the Immortals again. Let kinghood go where it would; he would dwell with the Mighty and Wise of old time, humbly glad to be the least of their servants. He had won a name for himself in history; *They* would not wholly look down on him now. And he knew that his life in that bliss would be forever: he had eaten of the Peaches of Immortality, and could not die. He wept at the blue lonely beauty of the middle lake when he came to it; he was so near now to all that he desired. . . .

In due time he came to the far shore; and to one bluff after another that he thought he recognized; but rounding it, found no island, no bay, no glazed-tile roofed temples, no grove of red-bloomed peaches. The place must be farther on . . . and farther on. . . . Sometimes there would be an island, but not *the* island; sometimes a bay, but not *the* bay; sometimes an island and a bay that would pass, and even peach-trees; but there was no inlet running in beneath the trees, with quiet waters lovely with a rain of petals—least of all that old divine red rain. Then he remembered the great fish that had drawn him into that sacred vicinity; and threw his line, fixing his hopes on that . . . fixing his desperate hopes on that.

All of which happened some sixteen hundred years ago. Yet still sometimes, they say, the fishermen on Lake Tao-ting, in the shadowy hours of evening, or when night has overtaken them far out on the waters, will hear a whisper near at hand: a whisper out of vacuity, from no boat visible: a breathless despairing whisper: *It was here . . . surely it must have been here! . . . No, no; it was yonder!* And sometimes it is given to some few of them to see an old, crazy boat, mouldering away —one would say the merest skeleton or ghost of a boat dead ages since, but still by some magic kept floating; and in it a man dressed in the rags of an ancient costume, on whose still young face is to be seen unearthly longing and immortal sadness, and an unutterable despair that persists in hoping. His line is thrown; he goes by swiftly, straining terrible eyes on the water, and whispering always: *It was here; surely it was here. . . . No, no; it was yonder . . . it must have been yonder. . . .*

❦ SELMA LAGERLÖF ❦

(1858-1940)

Selma Ottiliana Lovisa Lagerlöf is one of the most eminent names in Scandinavian literature, ranking in importance with writers like Henrik Ibsen and August Strindberg. Her fiction, for children and adults, has been translated into at least thirty languages, and it brought her national and international recognition during the early part of this century. She received an honorary Doctor of Philosophy degree from Uppsala University in 1904. Then, in 1909, she became the first woman ever to win the Nobel Prize in Literature. A few years later, in 1914, she became the first woman to be admitted to the Swedish Academy. Her seventieth birthday was the occasion for a national holiday in Sweden; at that time she received numerous awards, including the diploma of the French Legion of Honor and the Danish Distinguished Service Medal. The latter award was particularly significant: Lagerlöf's fiction for younger people had become second in popularity only to that of Hans Christian Andersen.

Lagerlöf owes a great deal of her success and popularity to her early childhood. She spent this childhood, as well as the majority of her eighty-one years, on a one hundred and forty acre farm named Mårbacka in the county of Värmland in southern Sweden. In "The Story of a Story," her slightly fictionalized account of the genesis of her first novel, she says of her early environment, "they seemed to have a greater love for books and reading there than elsewhere, and an air of restfulness and peace always pervaded it." Her love of reading and listening to stories became in fact her "keenest enjoyment,"

115

since, because of chronically poor health, she couldn't romp and play with her numerous brothers, sisters, and cousins. The stories she listened to so avidly were about the "many legends and traditions" which "hovered about the farm" and about the rugged lands and dense forests of the Värmland province.

Lagerlöf immortalized the Mårbacka farmhouse as the setting for *Gösta Berling,* the first and best known of her novels, which was published in part in 1891 and in completed form in 1894. The book became an instant success and after 1895 helped to free her from her teaching duties. She had been teaching in a school in Skåne, in the far southern portion of Sweden, since 1885. She then travelled to Italy, Palestine, and the Orient, all of which became scenes for her fiction. But her most successful writings remained those about Swedish country gentry and peasants, works like her volume of short stories, *From a Swedish Homestead* (1899), or her novel *The Emperor of Portugallia* (1914), which are set in the rural lands and deep, legend-laden forests of Värmland. This is also the setting for her children's stories *The Adventures of Nils* (1906–07).

Perhaps the outstanding trait of Lagerlöf's writing is her descriptive style, which is rich in imagery and suggestive comparisons. This style is the more remarkable for coming into being during the reign in Northern literature of an austere realism. In fact, Lagerlöf admired this literature and at first tried to apply its style to her subjects. In her fictionalized account of herself she describes the conflict: "Although her brain was filled to overflowing with stories of ghosts and mad love, of wondrously beautiful women and adventure-loving cavaliers, she tried to write about it all in calm, realistic prose." She recognized the impossibility of this and made the rather courageous decision to turn away from the prevailing fashion and to gamble with a more colorful and emotional style. Her success enabled her to write about real subjects, but subjects about whom a magical past still lingered and could at any moment come to the fore.

It is the evocative style that more than anything else makes "The Legend of the Christmas Rose" a successful story and an admirable example of high fantasy. In the pages that describe the transformation of the desolate waste of Göinge Forest into a Christmas garden, it is the style that creates this secondary world by flooding all of our senses and convincing us of the genuine beauty and goodness of nature; it is the style that enables us to sense what the pre-Fall garden of the Bible must have been like. The story, however, also expresses the dark note of human cynicism and lack of trust that sully this innocence and for which we all, like the monk, must do penance. Fortunately, there are those who, like Abbot Hans and Robber Mother, with their childlike simplicity, remind us—often at their own peril—of a lost but not irretrievable rose of innocence.

Legend of the Christmas Rose
Selma Lagerlöf
(Translated By Charles Wharton Stork)

❦

Robber Mother, who lived in the robbers' cave in Göinge Forest, went down to the village one day on a begging tour. Father Robber himself was an outlawed man, and dared not leave the forest; he could only plunder wayfarers who ventured within the borders of the wood. But in those days travellers were not very plentiful in northern Skåne, and if the husband had had a few weeks of bad luck, the wife would take to the road. Her five children in their ragged buckskin tunics and birch-bark shoes— each child with a bag on his back as long as himself— always accompanied her. When Robber Mother stepped inside the door of a cottage, nobody dared refuse her anything she demanded—for she was not above coming back in the night and setting fire to a house where she had not been well received. Robber Mother and her brats were worse than a pack of wolves, and many a man felt tempted to run a spear through them. But everyone knew, of course, that the husband was back in the forest, and that he would take revenge, were anything to happen to his wife or his children.

Now that Robber Mother went from place to place begging, she appeared one day at Övid, which was then a monastery. She rang the bell and asked for food. The watchman opened a small wicket in the gate and handed her out six round loaves of bread, one for herself and one for each of the five children. While the mother stood quietly at the gate, the youngsters were running about. And now one of them came and pulled at her skirt, which meant that he had found something which she should come and see, and she went at once.

118

The monastery was enclosed by a high, strong wall, and the youngster had discovered a narrow back gate that stood ajar. Robber Mother pushed the gate wide-open and walked in, as was her custom, without asking leave.

Övid Monastery was under the priorship of Abbot Hans, who was a collector of herbs. Just inside the cloister wall he had planted a little herb garden, and it was into this the woman had forced her way.

Robber Mother was so astonished at first that she paused for a moment and only looked. It was high summer, and the Abbot's garden was so full of bright flowers that her eyes were fairly dazzled by all the reds, blues, and yellows. But a smile of satisfaction overspread her features, as she walked down the narrow path between the many flower-beds.

A friar was at work in the garden, pulling up weeds. It was he who had left the gate half-open, that he might throw the couch grass and pigweed on the rubbish heap outside. When he saw Robber Mother in the garden and all her youngsters, he ran over to her and ordered her out. The beggar woman walked right on, now glancing at the stiff white lilies that spread before her feet, now at the climbing ivy that covered the cloister wall —and took no notice of the friar. He, thinking that she had not understood him, was about to take her by the arm and turn her round toward the gate when she gave him a look that made him draw back. She had been walking quite bent under the weight of her beggar's pack, but now she drew herself up to her full height, and said:

"I am Robber Mother of Göinge Forest, so touch me if you dare!"

It was obvious that she was as sure of being left in peace as if she had announced that she was the Queen of Denmark. All the same the friar dared to disturb her, though now that he knew who she was he tried to reason with her.

"You must know, Robber Mother, that this is a monastery, and that no woman is allowed within these walls. If you do not go away, the monks will be angry at me for leaving the gate open, and perhaps they may drive me out of the cloister and the garden."

But such prayers were wasted on Robber Mother. She continued her stroll among the flower-beds, looking at the hyssop with its magenta flowers, and at the honeysuckles with their rich clusters of deep orange.

The friar then saw nothing for it but to run to the cloister and call for help. He came back directly with two stalwart monks. Robber Mother realized that now they meant business! She planted her feet firmly in the path and began to shout in a strident voice all the awful things she would do to the monastery if she were not allowed to remain in the garden as long as she wished. The monks did not appear to be alarmed by her threats; they thought only of getting her out.

Of a sudden Robber Mother, with a wild shriek, threw herself upon the monks, clawing and biting at them. And so did all her children. The men soon found that she was too much for them, and went back for reinforcements.

They were running through the passage leading into the cloister, when they met Abbot Hans, hurrying out to see who was raising all this racket in the garden. They had to tell him that Robber Mother of Göinge Forest was in the garden, that they had not been able to drive her out and must call for assistance.

Abbot Hans rebuked the men for resorting to force and forbade their calling for help. He sent the two monks back to their work, and although he himself was a frail old man, he took with him only the friar.

When he came out, Robber Mother was still walking about among the flower-beds, and he could not help regarding her with admiration and wonder. He was quite certain that she had never seen an herb garden before, yet she sauntered leisurely between the many beds, each of which had its own species of rare plant, and looked at them as if they were old acquaintances; at some she smiled, at others she shook her head.

Now the Abbot loved his garden as much as he could love anything that was earthly and perishable. Savage and terrible as the intruder looked, he could not help liking her for having fought with three monks for the privilege of viewing his garden in peace. He went up to her and asked her meekly whether she was pleased with the garden.

Robber Mother turned upon Abbot Hans defiantly, expecting to be trapped and overpowered; but when she saw his white hair and frail, bent form, she answered quietly:

"I thought at first that I had never seen a more beautiful garden, but now I see that it can't be compared with the one I know."

Abbot Hans had expected quite a different answer. So, when Robber Mother declared she had seen a garden more beautiful than his, it brought a faint flush to his wizened cheek. The friar, who was standing close by, began to admonish the woman.

"This is Abbot Hans," he said, "who has collected from far and near, with the utmost care and diligence, the herbs you see in his garden. We all know there is not a finer garden to be found in all Skåneland, and it is not for you who live in the wild forest the whole year round to pass judgment on his work."

"I've no wish to set myself up as a judge of either him or you," said Robber Mother. "I am only saying that if you could see the garden I'm thinking of, you'd uproot all the flowers planted here and cast them out as weeds."

The Abbot's assistant was hardly less proud of the flowers than the Abbot himself, and he said with a scornful laugh:

"It must be a grand garden you have made for yourself among the pines of Göinge Forest! I'll wager my soul's salvation that you have never been inside the walls of an herb garden before."

Robber Mother went crimson with wrath to think that her word was doubted. "It may be true," she said, "that until to-day I was never inside the walls of an herb garden. But you monks, who are holy men, must know that every year on Christmas Eve the Göinge Forest is transformed into a pleasure garden, to celebrate the birth night of our Lord. We who live in the forest have witnessed this miracle every year. And in that garden I have seen flowers so lovely that I did not dare so much as to put out a hand to pluck them."

The friar wanted to retort, but Abbot Hans motioned to him to keep silent. For, from his early childhood, the Abbot had heard tell how on every Christmas Eve the forest clothed itself in festal verdure. He had always longed to see it, but had never had the pleasure. And now he begged Robber Mother fervently to let him come up to the robbers' cave on Christmas Eve. If she would only send one of her children to show him the way, he would ride thither alone, and he would never betray her or hers. On the contrary, he would reward them to the full extent of his power.

Robber Mother refused at first, for she was thinking of Robber Father and the harm that might befall him were she to permit Abbot Hans to visit their cave; but her desire to prove to the monk that the garden she knew was more beautiful than his prevailed, and she finally assented.

"But you cannot take with you more than one person, and you are not to waylay us or trap us, on your word as a holy man."

Abbot Hans gave his word, and Robber Mother went her way. The Abbot then commanded the friar not to reveal to a living soul that which had just been arranged. He was afraid that his monks, if they heard of it, would never allow a man so advanced in years to ride up to the robbers' cave.

Nor did the Abbot himself intend to speak of his project to any one. But it so happened that Archbishop Absalon of Lund came one day to Övid and stayed over night. While Abbot Hans was showing the Bishop his garden, he got to thinking of Robber Mother's visit, and the friar, who was at work in the garden, heard the Abbot tell the Bishop about Robber Father, who for many years had been an outlaw in the forest, and ask him for a letter of ransom for the man, that he might again lead an honest life in common with others. "As things are now," said the Abbot, "his children are growing up to be a worse menace than the Father himself, and you will soon have a whole band of robbers to deal with up in the forest."

Archbishop Absalon replied that he could not think of letting the wicked robber run loose on the countryside among honest folk; it was best for all that he stayed in his forest.

Then Abbot Hans waxed zealous, and told the bishop about Göinge Forest, how every year at Christmastide it arrayed itself in summer bloom around the robbers' cave. "If these outlaws are not too wicked to have revealed to them the glory of God, surely they cannot be too bad for the grace of mortals."

The Archbishop knew how to answer the Abbot. "This much I can promise you, Abbot Hans," he said with a smile, "any day that you send me a blossom from the Christmas garden at Göinge Forest, I will give you letters of ransom for all the robbers you may choose to plead for."

The friar understood that Archbishop Absalon no more believed this story of Robber Mother's than he himself did. But Abbot Hans had no such thought; he thanked the Archbishop for his kind promise, and said that he would surely send him the flower.

It was Christmas Eve, and Abbot Hans was on his way to Göinge Forest. Before him ran one of Robber Mother's wild youngsters, and behind him rode the friar who had talked with Robber Mother in the herb garden.

Abbot Hans had looked forward to this journey with longing, and was very happy now that it had come about. With the friar, however, it was quite a different matter. He loved Abbot Hans devotedly and would have been loath to let another attend and guard him; but he did not think they would see any Christmas garden. To his mind, the whole thing was a snare, cunningly laid by Robber Mother, to get Abbot Hans into the clutches of her husband.

As the Abbot rode northward toward the forest, he saw everywhere preparations for the celebration of Christmas. On every farm fires were burning in the bath-house to warm it for the afternoon bathing. Great quantities of bread and meat were being carried from the larders to the houses, and from the byres came the men with big sheaves of straw to be strewn over the floors. At each little church along the way the priest, with the help of his sexton, was decorating his sanctuary. And when he

came to the road leading to Bossjö Cloister he saw the
poor of the parish coming with armfuls of bread and with
long candles which they had received at the cloister gate.

The sight of all these Christmas preparations made the
Abbot the more eager to reach the forest; for he was
thinking of the festival in store for him, which was so
much greater than any that others would be permitted to
enjoy.

But the friar fretted and complained, as he saw how
at every lowly cabin they were preparing to celebrate
Christmas. He became more and more apprehensive of
danger, and begged and implored Abbot Hans to turn
back, and not throw himself into the hands of the robber.

Abbot Hans rode on, paying no heed to the friar's
lamentations. The open country was at last behind him,
and he rode into a wild and desolate region, where the
road was only a rocky, burr-grown path, with neither
bridge nor plank to help them over brook and river.
The farther they rode, the colder it grew, and after a
while they came upon snow-covered ground.

It was a long and hazardous ride. They climbed steep,
slippery by-paths, crossed marshes and swamps, and
pushed their way through windfalls and brambles. Just as
daylight was waning, the robber boy led them across a
woodland meadow, skirted by tall fir trees and denuded
leaf trees. Just beyond the meadow rose a mountain
wall, in which there was a door made of thick pine
boards.

Abbot Hans, understanding that they had arrived, dismounted. As the child opened the heavy door for him,
he found himself looking into a poor mountain grotto
with only bare stone walls. Robber Mother was sitting
by a log fire that burned in the middle of the floor. Along
the walls were beds of spruce-fir and moss, and on one
of the beds lay Robber Father, asleep.

"Come in, you out there!" Robber Mother shouted
without rising. "And fetch the horses in with you, so they
won't freeze to death in the cold night air."

Abbot Hans bravely walked into the cave, the friar
following. Here were wretchedness and poverty! Nothing
had been done to celebrate Christmas. Robber Mother
had neither brewed nor baked. Nor had she washed or

scoured. The children sprawled on the bare floor around a kettle, from which they were eating. The only fare provided them was a thin water-gruel.

Robber Mother now said in a tone as haughty and dictatorial as that of any well-to-do peasant woman:

"Sit down by the fire and warm yourself, Abbot Hans. If you've any food with you, eat; for the food we prepare in the forest I don't think you'd care to taste. And if you feel tired after your long ride, you can lie down on one of these beds, and rest. There's no fear of your oversleeping, for I'm sitting here by the fire, keeping watch. I'll wake you in time to see what you've come here to see."

Abbot Hans opened his food bag, but he was too fatigued to eat, and as soon as he had stretched out on the bed, he fell asleep.

The friar had also been given a bed to rest on. But he thought he had better keep an eye on Father Robber, lest he should jump up and try to bind Abbot Hans. However, he too was so exhausted that after a little he dropped into a doze.

When he awoke, Abbot Hans was sitting by the fire, talking with Robber Mother. The outlaw, a tall, thin man, with a sluggish and gloomy appearance, also sat by the fire. He had his back turned toward the Abbot as if he were not listening to the conversation.

Abbot Hans was telling Robber Mother about all the Christmas preparations he had seen on the journey, and reminding her of jolly feasts and Christmas games in which she had participated in her youth, when she lived at peace with mankind.

"I am sorry for your children," he said, "who can never run on the village street in fantastic array, or tumble about in the Christmas straw."

Robber Mother at first made short, gruff replies; but after a little she became rather subdued, and listened intently. Suddenly Robber Father turned round and shook his clenched fist in the Abbot's face.

"You miserable monk!" he cried. "Did you come here to lure away my wife and children? Don't you know that I'm an outlawed man, and cannot leave the forest?"

Abbot Hans, unafraid, looked him straight in the eyes.

"I propose to obtain a letter of ransom for you from Archbishop Absalon," he said.

Whereupon the outlaw and his wife burst out laughing. They knew well enough the kind of mercy a forest robber could expect from Bishop Absalon!

"Oh," said Robber Father, "if I get a letter of ransom from Absalon, I'll promise never again to steal so much as a goose."

The friar was indignant at their daring to laugh at Abbot Hans. Otherwise he was well pleased. Never had he seen the Abbot sitting more tranquil and meek with his own monks at Övid than he now sat with these robber folk.

Of a sudden, Robber Mother arose. "You sit here talking, Abbot Hans," she said, "so that we are forgetting to look at the forest. I can hear, even in this cave, that the Christmas bells are ringing."

And now they all jumped up and ran out. It was still black night in the forest and raw winter weather. They saw nothing, but they heard a distant chime, borne hither on a light south wind.

"How can this bell-ringing ever awaken the sleeping forest?" Abbot Hans wondered. For now, as he stood outside in the dark of winter, it seemed far less likely to him that a summer garden could bloom here than it had seemed before.

The chimes had pealed but a few seconds, when a wave of light broke upon the forest; it was gone in a moment, and then suddenly returned. Now it came floating through the dark trees like a luminous mist, and the night was merged in a faint daybreak.

Abbot Hans noted that the snow had disappeared from the ground, as if some one had removed a carpet, and that the earth was turning green. The ferns shot up through the soil, their fronds curling like a bishop's staff; the heather growing on the hill and the bog-myrtle rooted in the marsh quickly put on fresh green. The moss-tufts expanded and rose, and the spring flowers came out with swelling buds, which already had a touch of color.

Abbot Hans' heart beat fast at the first signs of the awakening of the forest. "Shall I, old man that I am, behold so great a miracle?" he mused, the tears springing to his eyes.

Then it grew so hazy that he feared the night darkness would again prevail; but immediately there came a new rush of light, which brought with it the murmur of brooks and the roar of water-falls. And now the trees put out their leaves so rapidly it looked as if millions of green butterflies had flown up and settled on the branches. It was not only trees and plants that had awakened, but grossbeaks hopped from branch to branch and woodpeckers hammered on the boughs till the splinters flew about them. A flock of starlings on the wing alighted in a spruce top to rest, and every time the birds moved, the bright red tips of their feathers glittered like precious jewels.

It darkened again for a moment, and again came a new light-wave. A warm, fresh south wind came up and scattered over the forest meadow all the little seeds brought from southern lands by birds and ships and winds. These seeds took root and sprouted the moment they touched the earth.

The next warm wave ripened the blueberries and whortleberries. Cranes and wild geese came shrieking their calls; bulfinches began building their nests, and squirrels played in the trees.

Everything went so swiftly now that Abbot Hans had no time to meditate on the wonder of the miracle that was taking place. He could only use his eyes and ears.

The wave of light that now came rolling in brought the scent of newly plowed fields, and from far, far away were heard the voices of milkmaids coaxing their cows, and the tinkle of sheep bells. Pine trees and spruce trees were so thickly laden with small red cones they shone like crimson mantles. The berries on the juniper changed their color every second, and wood-flowers covered the ground till it was all white, blue, and yellow.

Abbot Hans bent down, broke off a wild-strawberry blossom, and as he straightened his body, the berry ripened in his hand. The mother fox came out of her lair with a big litter of black-legged young. She went over to Robber Mother and scratched at her skirt.

Robber Mother leant down to her and praised her babies.
The horned owl, who had just started out on his nightly
hunt, blinded by the light, flew back to his ravine to
perch until dark. The cock cuckoo crowed, and the hen
cuckoo, with an egg in her bill, stole up into the nest of
another bird.

Robber Mother's children sent up twittering cries of
delight as they ate their fill of berries from the bushes,
where they hung large as pine cones. One of the children
played with a litter of baby hares; another raced with
some young crows that had ventured down from the nest
before their wings were quite ready for flying; a third
picked up an adder from the ground and wound it round
his neck and arm.

Robber Father stood out in the marsh eating cloudber-
ries. When he looked up he saw a big black bear at his
side. He broke off a willow twig and switched the bear
on the nose.

"You keep to your own ground," he said; "this is
my turf." The huge bear then turned and lumbered off
in another direction.

And all the while new waves of light and warmth kept
coming. The chatter of ducks could be heard from the
wood-pond. Golden pollen from rye fields filled the air;
and now came butterflies so big they looked like flying
lilies. The beehive in a hollow oak was so full of honey,
it oozed out and dripped down the stem. All the plants
which had come up from seeds blown hither from foreign
lands suddenly burst into bloom. The most gorgeous
roses clambered up the side of the mountain in a race
with the blackberry vines, and down in the meadow
bloomed flowers large as a human face.

Abbot Hans thought of the flower he was to pluck for
Archbishop Absalon, but each flower that came out was
more beautiful than the last, and he wanted to pick for
the Bishop the most beautiful flower in the garden.

Wave upon wave of light rolled in, until the sky became so dazzlingly bright that it fairly glittered. All the
life and beauty and joy of summer smiled on Abbot
Hans. He felt that the earth could hold no greater bliss
than that which welled about him.

"I do not know what new glories another wave may bring," he said.

But there came more and more light; and now it seemed to Abbot Hans that it brought with it something from an infinite distance. He felt himself being enwrapped, as it were, by an atmosphere superterrestrial, and, trembling with awe, he awaited the approaching glories of Heaven.

There was a hush, a stillness in the forest. The birds were silent, the young foxes played no more, and the flowers stopped growing. The glory now drawing nigh was such as to make the heart stand still and the soul long to rise to the Eternal. From far, far away came faint strains of harp music and celestial song.

Abbot Hans folded his hands and went down upon his knees. His face shone with bliss. Never had he dreamed that in this life he was to taste the joys of Heaven and hear the angels sing Christmas carols!

But close by stood the friar who had come with the Abbot, and in his mind dark thoughts arose. "This cannot be a true miracle," he thought, "since it is revealed to criminals. It can never have come from God, but must have been sent hither by Satan. The powers of evil are bewitching us and compelling us to see that which has no existence."

Angel harps and angel voices sounded in the distance; but the friar believed that the spirits of Hell were approaching. "They would charm and seduce us," he sighed, "and we shall be bound and sold into perdition."

The angel hosts were now so near that Abbot Hans could see their shining forms through the trees. The friar saw them too, but he thought that behind all this wondrous beauty lay something malevolent. To him, it was the Devil who worked these wonders on the night of our Saviour's birth. He thought it was done only in order to delude poor human beings the more effectually and lay a snare for them.

All this time the birds had been circling round the head of Abbot Hans, and had let him take them in his hands. But the birds and animals were afraid of the friar; no bird perched on his shoulder, no snake played at his feet. There was a little forest dove who, seeing the

angels draw near, took courage and flew down to the
friar's shoulder and laid her head against his cheek. The
friar, thinking the Adversary himself had come right
upon him, to tempt and corrupt him, struck at the dove
and cried in a loud voice, that reverberated through the
whole forest:

"Get thee back to Hell, whence thou art come!"

Just then the angels were so near that the motion of
their great wings fanned the face of Abbot Hans, and he
bowed his head to the earth in reverent salutation. But
the moment the friar uttered those words the singing
stopped, and the holy visitors turned and fled. At the
same time, the light and the warmth departed in unspeak-
able terror of the darkness and cold in a human heart.
Black night descended upon the earth; the frost came,
the plants shrivelled, the animals ran to cover, the roar
of the rapids was hushed, the leaves fell off the trees
with a rustling noise that sounded like a shower of rain.

Abbot Hans felt his heart—which had just been so full
of bliss—contract with insufferable agony.

"I can never get over this," he thought, "that the
angels of Heaven had been so near and were driven
away; that they wanted to sing Christmas carols for me,
and were put to flight!" He remembered the flower he
had promised Bishop Absalon, and in the last moment
he fumbled among the leaves and moss for a blossom.
But he could feel the ground freezing beneath his fingers
and the snow that came gliding over the earth. His heart
gave him still further trouble; he tried to rise, and fell
prostrate on the ground.

When the robber folk and the friar had groped their
way, in utter darkness, back to the cave, they missed
Abbot Hans. They snatched brands from the fire and went
out to search for him. . . . And they found him lying
dead upon a blanket of snow.

The friar wept and wailed—for he knew that he had
killed Abbot Hans by dashing from his lips the cup of
happiness which he had been thirsting to drain to its last
drop.

When Abbot Hans had been carried back to Övid the
monks who took charge of his body noticed that the right
hand was locked tightly around something which must

have been grasped at the moment of death. And when they finally got the hand open they found that that which had been held in so firm a grip was a pair of white root-bulbs, which had been pulled up from the moss.

The friar who had accompanied Abbot Hans to the forest took the bulbs and planted them in the Abbot's garden. He nursed and guarded them the whole year, hoping to see a flower come up from them. He waited in vain through the spring, the summer, and the autumn; and when winter set in and all the leaves and flowers were dead, he ceased caring for them.

But when Christmas Eve came again it brought Abbot Hans so vividly before his mind that he went out into the garden to think of him. When he came to the spot where he had planted the bare root-bulbs, he saw that from them had sprung flourishing green stalks which bore beautiful flowers, with silvery white petals.

He called out all the monks at Övid, and when they beheld the plant that bloomed on Christmas Eve, when all the other plants were dead, they knew that this flower had indeed been plucked by Abbot Hans in the Christmas Garden at Göinge Forest.

The friar then asked for permission to take a few flowers to Archbishop Absalon. When he appeared before the Archbishop and gave him the flowers, he said:

"Abbot Hans sends you these; they are the flowers he promised to pluck for you in the Christmas Garden of Göinge Forest."

And when Archbishop Absalon saw the flowers which had sprung from the earth in darkest winter, and heard the message, he went pale as if he had met a ghost. He sat silent for a long moment, whereupon he said:

"Abbot Hans has faithfully kept his word, and I shall keep mine." He ordered a letter of ransom to be drawn up for the robber who had been outlawed and compelled to live in the forest from the days of his youth. He entrusted the letter to the friar, who left at once for the forest.

When the friar stepped into the robbers' cave on Christmas Day, Robber Father came toward him with axe uplifted.

"I'd like to hack you monks to pieces, many as you are!" he said. "It must be your fault that the forest was not dressed last night in Christmas bloom."

"The fault is mine alone," the friar replied, "and I am ready to die for it; but first I must deliver a message from Abbot Hans." He drew forth the Archbishop's letter and told the outlaw that he was now a free man.

"Hereafter," he said, "you and your children shall play in the Christmas straw and celebrate your Christmas among men, as Abbot Hans wished to have you."

The robber stood there pale and speechless, but Robber Mother answered in his name:

"Abbot Hans has kept his promise, and Robber Father will keep his."

When the robber and his family left their cave, the friar moved into it; and there he lived all alone, in the solitude of the forest, in penance and prayer.

But Göinge Forest never again celebrated the natal hour of our Saviour, and of all its glory there remains today only the flower which Abbot Hans plucked. It has been named the Christmas Rose. And every year at Yuletide it sends up from the mold its green stalks and white blossoms, as if it could never forget that it once grew in the great Christmas Garden.

❦ ERIC LINKLATER ❦
(1899-1974)

Eric Linklater, like his somewhat older countrymen Lord Dunsany and John Buchan, fits the mold of the English gentleman: sophisticated, educated, and widely traveled yet deeply rooted in his native soil. Linklater was born in Dounby on the Orkney Islands, Scotland. While the relative isolation of northern Scotland remained his focal point, he ventured forth on numerous occasions to sample life elsewhere, and to write about it.

His first adventure took him to France in World War I as an enlistee in the Black Watch. After the war, and after recovering from his wounds, he went to the University of Aberdeen, where he earned a master's degree in literature. His next journey took him to Bombay, where he held a post as an assistant editor of *The Times of India*. He returned to Scotland and in 1927 became a lecturer at the University of Aberdeen. He next spent two years, 1928–30, in the United States on a Commonwealth Fellowship to Cornell and the University of California. But since he had decided to be a writer, he spent more time seeing the country than studying. When he returned to Scotland, he was indeed able to support himself as a writer. He married Marjorie MacIntyre in 1933 and the couple had two daughters. World War II drew him forth once again. He was a major in the Royal Engineers, defending the British fleet at Scapa Flow, and later he served as a military historian with British troops in Italy. Home once again from the wars, he served as rector of the University of Aberdeen from 1945 to 1948. In 1951 he traveled to the Pacific, to Shanghai and Japan.

Linklater's many travels, as well as his Orkney home,

furnished a prodigious amount of material for his equally prodigious literary output. The last volume of his three-volume autobiography, *Fanfare for a Tin Hat* (1970), lists sixty-one book-length works. These include novels; children's books; collections of short stories; plays; historical, biographical, and autobiographical works; and collections of essays. His second book, *Juan in America* (1931), is a thinly veiled autobiographical account of his coast-to-coast travels in the United States. It remains, in the eyes of many, one of his best works. Another book that received notice in this country is *The Wind in the Moon,* which won the Carnegie Award as the best children's book of 1944. His 1946 novel, *Private Angelo,* was later made into a movie starring Peter Ustinov. Nonetheless, he now appears to be relatively unknown to American readers. While his books, both hard- and soft-cover, are readily available on English bookshelves, he has, unfortunately, received scant critical or popular attention in the United States in recent years.

Characteristic of Linklater's writing are his madcap wit and exuberance. These qualities are nicely balanced by a polished style and a gentle but firm advocacy of responsible conduct. His fantasy stories, which exhibit this blend of humor and seriousness, are consequently reminiscent of the fantasies of his fellow Scotsman George Mac Donald, although Linklater tips the scales a bit more towards humor and moralizes much less explicitly or religiously than does Mac Donald.

"The Abominable Imprecation" is one of Linklater's most successful fantasies. On the level of plot, it is an engaging tale of adventure and romance, with punishments and rewards meted out, appropriate to the participants' conduct. The descriptive style is elegant and vivid, creating numerous memorable and moving scenes. Yet the work bristles with humor, stemming largely from incongruities. One of these is, of course, the situation in which Perigot finds himself as a result of the story's central device, the abominable imprecation. Another incongruity is the style of the dialogue. Kings and queens, heroes and nymphs, all speak, for the most part, in a most comically commonplace fashion. There is yet another dimension to the story: its erotic overtones (the curse)

and undertones (the sickle and the flute). Such erotic
elements are relatively rare in high fantasy, but rather
frequent in Linklater's case, making it quite clear that
while his stories are by no means offensive to children,
many of them are written primarily with adults in mind.

The Abominable Imprecation
Eric Linklater

❧

Unlike so many musicians, Perigot was handsome. His
eyes were blue and his hair was black. A lock of it fell
with engaging disorder over his broad forehead. Even
while he played upon his pipe, his upper lip, pursed for
its melodious task, retained a whimsical fascination, and
when he put down his reed and yawned, he showed white
teeth that looked the whiter for his brown skin, and the
arms he stretched were long and muscular.

The river-nymph, Cleophantis, hiding in a clump of
yellow irises, felt her natural shyness conquered by a
much stronger force, and first cutting, with a silver sickle
she carried, a few of the tall flowers to supplement her
exiguous costume, emerged from her shelter and walked
towards him. Her voice was a little uncertain with mingled
excitement and shame, and as she spoke a blush played
prettily on her pale cheeks.

"I don't want you to think that I am one of those im-
pressionable creatures who lose their heads on every possible occasion," she said, "but really, I've never heard
anything so lovely as that last little dancing tune. Of
course it's impertinent of me to speak like this to an utter
stranger, and quite unforgivable to ask him a favour, but
you would make me so happy if you were to play it
again!"

Perigot, at first, was amused rather than surprised by
her appearance and ingenuous request; for his playing had
often attracted, from their river-homes or dark-blossoming
corners of the wood, nymphs and dryads whose fervent
admiration of his skill upon the pipe had invariably been
succeeded by a declaration of their tenderness towards

himself. To begin with he had been flattered by their ad-
dresses, but after some dozen encounters he had discovered an unsubstantial airy monotony in their company.
They were agreeable to look at, they pattered a few pretty
sentences, but they had no personality and their charm
was vapid and standardized; so Perigot had long since
ceased to be impressed by the undines, sylphs, and hama-
dryads, errant glimpses of whom threw so many of his
contemporaries, less gifted than himself, into a perfect
fever of desire. Now, thinking that here was only another
of that kind, he was not very interested by the nymph's
appearance, but before she had finished speaking he perceived in her something different, a quality that made her
far superior to the trivial sprites of his previous acquaintance, and hurriedly rising he led her, with pleasant words
of welcome, to a cushion of comfortable green turf.

Putting down her silver sickle and discreetly arranging
her bunch of flags and yellow irises, she smiled and said,
"My name is Cleophantis, and I am, so far as we know,
the youngest daughter of the Moon King."

Perigot played his dancing tune, and all the birds within
hearing flew near to listen, while a brock came out of the
wood with a small deer following it, and from the river-
bank tumbled a sleek family of otters.

"That was beautiful," said Cleophantis when he had
finished. "Oh, so beautiful! I could sit and listen to you
for ever."

Her voice and eyes, however, betrayed a regard for
Perigot greater than that for his music, which Perigot quite
clearly recognized; for though he was not conceited he
was intelligent. Generally, when he noticed this transfer-
ence of interest in his audience, he was displeased and
bored, for he knew how readily a nymph was taken by
mere outward appearance, and as an artist he was de-
pressed to find that his music had never more than
a minor appeal for women. But now he was delighted to
see the brightness of Cleophantis' eyes, their bashful veil-
ing by long lashes, and to note the tremor in her voice. He
sat down beside her.

"Your father won't be up for hours yet," he said, and
kissed her with a warmth of which she, in the coolness of
her river, had never dreamed.

She sprang from him, dropping her flags and flowers, red as a lily-pool at sunset, and Perigot, laughing and eager, pursued her. He caught her easily, but when he found her shyness was real, and not assumed, he became gentle and courteous with her, though her beauty, of which he became ever more sensible, constantly tempted him into little sallies of ardour. These Cleophantis rebuked with increasing distress, for she had fallen deeply in love with the handsome shepherd, and only her early training in the chaste schoolroom of the osier beds prevented her from yielding to the persuasion which intermittently escaped his disciplined politeness. At last she said she would have to go, and nothing Perigot could say would make her tarry longer, for she was afraid of the awful lengths to which love might lead her.

"But you will come back?" said Perigot, pleading.

"Perhaps," said Cleophantis, and meant, "You know I will!"

"And you will not always keep me at arm's length, or even a finger-breadth away?"

"I am going to speak to my elder sister about you," answered Cleophantis, and though Perigot groaned, for he thought this was an ill omen for love, Cleophantis continued, "She is extraordinarily wise, and I have the greatest respect for her opinion. It is true that she has never had a lover, but in spite of that she is very broadminded. Oh, Perigot, if she says we are right to love, how happy I shall be!"

"You will come to-morrow?" said Perigot.

"At noon," said Cleophantis, "and for a pledge that I shall return, keep this sickle. Its blade is silver from the Mountains of the Moon, forged with the last heat of the moon, and tempered in its coldest stream. No man or beast can resist its edge, and the handle is an emerald that will keep its owner always in health."

While Perigot was examining the sickle, Cleophantis, fearing her resolution would fail, ran to the edge of the nearby stream. She stood for a moment on the bank, looked back, and whispered, "Perigot, my heart!" But Perigot's head was still bent over the flashing blade, and so she stepped unseen into the welcoming river. When Perigot looked up she had gone.

The sun was low and he realized that it was time to go home, so he whistled to the sheep-dogs that were lying far afield, guarding the fringes of the flock, and they gathered the sheep before them while Perigot, thrusting the sickle under his belt, played on his pipe the merriest song the meadows had ever heard, and strode briskly towards the hill on the far side of which stood his father's house. It seemed to him that the quicker he walked the sooner tomorrow would come, and with it Cleophantis— if her sister let her; and his tune grew so glad and so exciting that the lambs capered madly, and the old ewes were puzzled, and the half-grown rams leapt like mountain goats as they followed him over the hill.

Perigot's mother sighed when he came in to supper, for she at once perceived he was in love again, and she was always nervous when her sons were in that state of mind; but his father, a heartless and wealthy man who owned several thousand sheep, two rich valleys, and much hillland, asked in a gruff voice if the flock was safe, and finding it was told Perigot to keep quiet while he ate, for only children or idiots, he said, must sing with their mouths full of porridge.

In the morning Perigot rose early and was about to lead his flock back to the river-pasture when a man who looked like a Saracen or an Indian, and who had been lounging by the sheepfold, stopped him and said, "I've heard tell you know a good fighting-cock when you see one, sir?"

Now Perigot was a sportsman, and though till that moment his thoughts had all been of Cleophantis, as soon as the Indian spoke of fighting-cocks a picture rushed into his mind of brave birds tussling in the air—bronze feathers gleaming, spurs clashing—and eagerly he asked, "Have you any to sell or match with mine?"

"Better birds than any in your country," said the Indian.

"I doubt that," answered Perigot, "but I'll have a look at them." And he called Thenot, his younger brother, a freckled boy with a snub nose, and told him to take the sheep to the river-field, and he would follow by-and-by.

So fine were the Indian's birds, and such a heroic main was fought, that the sun was overhead before Perigot remembered his tryst with Cleophantis. Then, in a kind of panic, he threw some silver coins to the Indian and began to run, as fast as he could, up the steep path that led over the hill to the riverside grazing. He knew that he would be late, and though he tried to comfort himself with the thought that a little waiting never did any girl harm, he could not convince himself, for Cleophantis was the Moon King's daughter, and very different from any other nymph or forest-girl he had ever seen.

It was a full hour past noon when he reached the flock, and immediately his young brother called to him in a strange sobbing voice. Thenot's freckled face was tear-stained, and in great distress he gasped, "She's dead, Perigot, she's dead! Oh, why didn't you come in time? She waited for you a little while, walking to and fro, and then she sat down, for she felt weak, and still you did not come, and presently she fainted. I rubbed her hands, but they were so delicate I could not rub them hard. Once she opened her eyes and asked, 'Do you see him coming?' And then she said, 'My heart is breaking,' and she died. Oh, Perigot, she was lovely! Why did you not come in time?"

Perigot, numb with remorse, looked down at her where she lay like a plucked lily on the grass. He could not speak, and his brain was too cold even to frame a proper thought. He just stood and looked at her, and knew that he had never seen such loveliness alive. Suddenly Thenot gave a frightened cry and ran away. Perigot looked up and saw, coming to him from the stream, a tall and dreadful nymph with a black river-squall blowing about her, bending the grass and flowers and chilling the summer air.

"Murderer!" she said. "Killer of my sister!" She raised a wet arm round which a water-snake was twisted. The river-squall howled at her back, and Perigot, shivering with cold, fell to his knees beside the dead girl.

"I never dreamt that such a thing could happen," he cried. "Truly I loved her, and truly I hurried to be in time!"

"Murderer and liar!" said the elder sister in a terrible voice. "An unkind thought could bruise her skin, you must have known that such neglect as yours would kill her. But I'm not easily hurt, and I'm not easily swayed by a handsome face and soft words. Be quiet, murderer, and hear your punishment. Oh, my sister, he who killed you will suffer more than you and ten thousand times as long!"

For a moment the squall was silent, and the dreadful nymph, whose face seemed to Perigot like broken water in its darkness, said in a clear hard voice, "The curse of Shepherd Alken be on you!"

Then the storm howled again, and under its wings the nymph took up her dead sister and carried her, over the broken flowers and bent grasses, back to the dark and sullen stream.

For more than a week Perigot lived in utter misery. His pipe was silent and his flock untended. Wolves stole a lamb or two, and he never heard the woeful bleating of the ewes. But his father, counting the sheep and finding several missing, rated his son with harsh and brutal words.

"You're the fool of the family," he shouted. "You've wasted your time cock-fighting and playing that idiot pipe of yours, and now you blubber for a week because a worthless undine jilts you. I'm ashamed and sick of the sight of you!"

"Then let me go away from here," said Perigot. "I'm tired of keeping your silly sheep. I must do something braver than that, something dangerous and great, to justify my wretched life and perhaps forget, in peril of my own death, the death of Cleophantis."

"H'mph!" said his father. "If you mean what you say— but I doubt it—you'd better go to Gargaphie. The King's in a pretty pickle, and shouting east and west for help."

"No, no!" cried Perigot's mother, "not there, he'd be killed as all the other young men have been killed, and to no purpose at all. You mustn't go there, Perigot!"

"Tell me what is happening in Gargaphie," said Perigot.

"Oh, the usual thing," said his father, that heartless man. "A dragon has gone off with the King's daughter, and killed a dozen young fools who've tried to rescue her. Do you fancy dragon-baiting? She's a well-made girl, I believe, and I suppose you could marry her if you got her away. That's the orthodox reward, isn't it?"

"I shall never marry," said Perigot bitterly. But the thought of so desperate an adventure made him resolute to go to Gargaphie, and when he remembered the sickle that Cleophantis had given him he felt confident of his ability to slay the monster who had stolen the King's daughter; though so far he had never seen a dragon and had only a very vague idea of what one looked like.

His mother wept when he told her of his determination, but finding his intention fixed she made such preparation for his journey as seemed suitable. Perigot polished his magic sickle with a woollen cloth and felt happier than he had been since Cleophantis died. Only the memory of her sister's curse hung like a little cloud over his mind. He had told no one about it. He had, indeed, tried to forget it, and in his preoccupation with grief almost succeeded. But now, for the first time admitting his anxiety, he thought it advisable to discover all he could about the malediction with which he had been saddled.

His old nurse Dorcas was an aged woman with a great reputation for wisdom, and Perigot, on the evening before his journey to Gargaphie, went to the fireside-corner where she sat spinning, and said in a conversational way, "Tell me, Dorcas, have you ever heard of a shepherd called Alken?"

"Indeed and I have, Master Perigot," she answered, very glad of the opportunity to talk and show off her knowledge. "And a wicked old man he was, and hated everybody, and what with sitting by himself for days on end, and talking to serpents and owls and mandrakes, he invented the most horrible curse in the world, partly to punish his poor wife, who was almost as nasty as he was, and partly out of pure spite against all humanity."

"What was the curse?" asked Perigot.

"Well, it was like this," said Dorcas, putting aside her wheel and sucking her old gums. "Shepherd Alken used to think a lot about the misery of his life, and indeed he'd hardships enough, what with sitting all day in the hot sun, and little to drink, while he watched his sheep; and lambing them while the snow was on the ground, and that's hard work; and always the danger of wolves; and knowing he'd be poor to the end of his days. But all he thought about his misery was little to what his wife said about hers, for she'd had eleven children, and those who didn't die brought shame and disgrace to her; and to keep her house clean was heart-breaking, for the fire smoked and the roof leaked and the hens came in through the broken door, so to tell the truth she had something to talk about. But the shepherd hated her for it, and thought his own life was far, far worse. So he made up a curse that turned her into a man, and he sent her out to keep the sheep while he sat at home. And he had the satisfaction of hearing her grumble louder than ever, for she could stand neither the heat nor the cold, and she was terribly frightened of wolves. But though it pleased him to hear her complaining so, he wasn't comfortable at all, for there was no one to cook his supper, and the hens made the floor like a midden, and if there was no smoke in the house that was because the fire was always out. So he thought he would use another kind of curse on himself, and turn himself into a woman, and then housework would come easy and natural to him. Well, he spoke the words, and the very next morning he was a woman. But somehow he didn't like it, and every day he liked it less, and when, old though he was, he found himself in the family way, as they call it, he nearly went off his head altogether. So it seemed to him that if there was one thing harder than being a man it was being a woman; and the way his wife grumbled showed him that the only thing worse than a woman's life was a man's life. And then he thought that if he could put two curses into one handy-like little sentence he could do a lot of harm in the world with it, and that's what he wanted. Well, he talked to his friends the Owl and the Serpent and the Mandrake, and they helped him, and by-and-by he had it, and the first use he made of it was in his own house, and he and his wife changed places once again, and she bore her twelfth child and died of it. But the curse became famous, and wicked folk who know the way of it use it a lot, just saying 'The curse of Shepherd Alken be on you,' and that signifies 'If you're a man, become a woman. If you're a woman, become a man.' And that's enough to spread misery wherever it goes, as you'll learn, Master Perigot, when you're a little older—though there's nothing but good fortune I wish you, as you know.'

Perigot listened to this story with growing consternation,

for he remembered that lately his voice had assumed, once or twice, a curious treble tone, and before he went to bed that night he examined himself anxiously to see if there were any further signs that the malediction was working. He discovered nothing, however, except a little plumpness about his chest, and even that he was not very sure of. The next morning he set off for Gargaphie.

He travelled for a week, and came by degrees to country more mountainous and savage than any he had seen before. In Gargaphie itself there were everywhere signs of grief and mourning faces, for the Princess Amoret had been popular as well as beautiful, and the thought of her durance in the dragon's cave caused great distress to young and old. As soon as Perigot made known his mission he was taken to the King, whose gloom visibly lightened when he heard Perigot's stout assertion of his intention to slay the monster and rescue its poor prisoner. But he was a fair-minded man, and he thought it his duty to warn Perigot of the danger he was about to face.

"That wretched dragon has already killed twelve brave young men, all apt in war," he said.

"I am not afraid," answered Perigot, and the King, seeing his bold attitude, his broad shoulders, and the stern light in his blue eyes, felt there was at least a possibility of his success.

"I have promised my daughter's hand to her rescuer," he said, "and though of course I speak with a father's partiality, I think I may say without fear of contradiction that she is the most beautiful girl in all Gargaphie."

"I shall never marry," said Perigot in a grim way, "and I undertake this adventure without any hope of personal gain."

"I can show you a picture of her, if you don't believe me," said the King, a little testily; but the Queen interrupted him, and said to Perigot, "Your attitude, sir, is a noble example to us all," while to the King she whispered rapidly, "Don't argue! Can't you see that he has had an unfortunate love affair, and will fight all the better for it, being careless of his life?" So the King, who appreciated his wife's good sense, said nothing more except to call very loudly for dinner, which had been put back because of Perigot's arrival.

In the morning the King and his courtiers led Perigot to a high rock from which he could see the dragon's den, and there they waited while he went forward alone, for such fear had the monster spread that none dared go within a mile of the waterfall behind which it lived. But Perigot, feeling perfectly confident, climbed down to the torrent-bed, and thence by a narrow path got to the dragon's lair. Lightly he sprang to a rock that the waterfall sprinkled with its high white splashing, and there, first easing the sickle in his belt, he sat down and began to play upon his pipe. First, in a whimsical mood, he played a serenade, but that had no effect, so he began a little taunting air, full of a gay defiance, with shrill notes in it that suggested a small boy being impudent to his elder brother. And presently, through the rushing veil of the waterfall, Perigot saw two huge and shining eyes.

The dragon poked its head out, and when it snorted the waterfall divided and was blown to left and right in large white fans of mist. Perigot now played an inviting tune called *Tumble in the Hay,* and the dragon, amazed by his fearlessness and somewhat attracted by the melody, pushed farther through the waterfall, that now spread like a snowy cape about its shoulders. Its colour was a changing green, on which the sun glittered wildly, and its eyes were like enormous emeralds. Perigot was dazzled by them, and had he not been aware how exceptionally well he was playing, he would have been frightened. As it was, he changed his tune again, with a flourish of sharp leaping notes, and what he played now was an irresistible ribald air called *Down, Wantons, Down.*

The dragon, surprised, then tickled, then captured by delight, opened its enormous mouth and roared with joy. It plunged into the pool in front of the waterfall, and Perigot was soaked to the skin with the splash it made. But he continued to play, and the dragon rolled and floundered in its bath, and what with the sunlight on the waterfall, and the sun shining on its glimmering hide, it seemed as though someone were throwing great handfuls of diamonds, emeralds, and opals into the pool.

Perigot finished the ribald song and slid cunningly into a tune so honey-sweet, so whispering of drowsy passion, that one thought of nightingales, and white roses heavy with dew, and young love breathless and faint for love. The dragon stopped its whale-like gambols, and sighed luxuriously. It rolled over on to its back, and a dreamy look clouded its emerald eyes. It sighed again, like far-off thunder, and came closer to the rock on which Perigot sat. His pipe sang more sweetly still. A kind of foolish smile twisted the dragon's horrible mouth, and its eyes half-closed. Its head was touching the rock.

Sudden as lightning Perigot drew his moon-made sickle, and slashed fiercely at the monster's thick green throat. The blade went through its tough hide, through muscle and bone, as easily as an ordinary sickle goes through grass; and torrents of black blood stained the pool that the dragon's death-struggle made stormier than a tempest-twisted sea. When the headless body at last was still, and blackness lay like a film on the water, Perigot, first cleaning his sickle, climbed by a way he had discovered through the waterfall and into the cave behind it. There he found the Princess Amoret, tied to a rock but apparently unharmed.

He cut her loose and helped her out of the greenish cave that was full of the noise of falling water. She looked at the dead monster, turned away with a shudder, and still for a minute or two did not speak.

Then she said, "How can I express my gratitude? For words are such little things, mere symbols of conventional emotion that time has defaced. I need new words to thank you, but, alas, I am not a poet and can make none. You are an artist, though—I heard your music—and know how I feel."

"I am only too happy to have been of service to you," said Perigot a little stiffly.

The Princess suddenly knelt and embraced his knees. "You have rid me of the most horrible fear in the world," she said, and when she looked up her eyes were clouded with tears, and her face was radiant with happiness because her life had been saved, and because her rescuer was so handsome, and so gifted a musician.

The path was narrow, and as the Princess was weary from long restraint, and as Perigot found that he could talk to her more easily and with more pleasure than to any girl he had ever met before, they took a long time to return to the rock on which the King and his courtiers waited so anxiously—for at that great distance they had been unable to perceive how the battle went. The King's joy at seeing his daughter again was overwhelming, but when he had satisfied himself that she was unhurt, and embraced her a score of times, and blessed all heaven for her deliverance, he remembered the necessity of thanking her rescuer, and did so very heartily.

"And you thought you wouldn't want to marry her, eh?" he said. "Well, haven't you changed your mind by this time?"

As it happened, Perigot had; and no one who realized the excitement of his battle with the dragon, or observed the beauty of Princess Amoret, accused him of undue fickleness for so quickly forgetting his determination to respect in lifelong celibacy the memory of poor Cleophantis. Nor was he embarrassed by the reminder of what he had said, on the previous evening, about his views on marriage. He merely remarked, with some dignity, "I had no wish to force my attentions on the Princess until I had ascertained the possibility of their welcome."

The courtiers were all impressed by this evidence of a noble temper, and Amoret immediately cried, "Father, let there be no hesitation or pretence about this. We love each other, and we were made for each other!"

"That's the way to speak!" said the King. "There's nothing like honesty, and we'll have a wedding after all. I like weddings."

The Queen, a tolerant and kindly woman, was made so happy by Amoret's return that she hardly cared whom her daughter married, if the match were dictated by love; and thereupon the King, in great spirits, declared that Perigot should wed her that night—"If it's quite convenient for you, my dear?" he added.

"Quite convenient," said Amoret, "and, indeed just what I wish myself."

Preparations for a feast were speedily made, and with much ceremony the marriage took place. At a late hour Perigot and his bride retired to their chamber.

For an hour or two Perigot had been feeling his clothes uncommonly tight about his chest and hips, but he imagined the discomfort was due to somewhat excessive eating and drinking. When he undressed, however, he discovered to his horror that the nymph's curse had taken effect, and he had become, for all practical purposes, a woman.

The shock almost unnerved him, but with a great effort he retained his self-control. His predicament was appalling. Not only was he madly in love with Amoret, but Amoret was madly in love with him. She approached him with endearing words, and when Perigot offered her a slight and distant embrace, which was all he dared to offer for fear of revealing his shameful secret, she accepted it with really pitiful disappointment. He stood for a long time looking out of the window, while Amoret sat on the edge of her bed and wondered why Perigot had turned so cold or if this was all that marriage meant. She could not believe that its mystery cloaked precisely nothing.

After an agonized vigil of the dark sky, Perigot remembered his pipe. He took it from the chimney-piece where he had laid it, and played a gentle phrase or two.

"You must be tired, my dear," he said. "Let me play you to sleep."

Amoret turned her face from him, and wept quietly into her pillow. In a little while, however, Perigot's sweet and mournful lullaby soothed her brain, and drove consciousness away, and presently she slept. Perigot lay awake till morning, so bitter were all his thoughts, and before the sun was up he dressed himself and went out, and left Amoret still dreaming.

The day was embarrassing to them both, for in Gargaphie weddings occasioned a certain jocularity that often made ordinary brides and bridegrooms feel uncomfortable. But no wedded couple had ever been in the curious plight of Amoret and Perigot, and their distress at the customary witticisms was so marked as to make even the wits doubtful of their taste. And the day's embarrassments naturally increased as darkness fell, for Amoret was full of doubt and more affectionate than ever, and Perigot was doubly miserable. That night it took him at least an hour, and he needed every bit of his skill upon the pipe, to play his bride asleep.

This wretched state of affairs continued for several days, until the Queen, seeing how unhappy and even ill her daughter looked, talked seriously to her for a long time, and at last elicited some part of the facts.

"But my poor dear!" she said in amazement.

"I assure you that what I say is true," sobbed Amoret. "Every night he plays his pipe until I fall asleep. Sometimes I wonder if he is a man at all."

"The King must be told immediately," said the Queen with decision, and straightaway went to look for her husband, in spite of Amoret's protests, who still loved Perigot dearly and feared that her father would do him harm.

The King, though normally a genial man, lost his temper completely when he heard what the Queen had to say.

"I suspected something of the sort!" he roared. "Did you hear his voice last night? Squeaking like a girl! The insolent impostor! I'll wring his neck with my own hands, I'll drop him over the battlements, I'll hound him out of Gargaphie!"

"There must be no scandal," said the Queen, quietly but firmly. "Not for Perigot's sake, but for Amoret's. The girl has suffered enough without being made the subject of national gossip. I admit it would be a good thing to get rid of Perigot, but it must be done discreetly. I'm sure that you can think of some clever plan to remove him quietly and without fear of unpleasant comment."

"There's something in what you say," admitted the King, "and as for plans, my head is full of them. It always is, and that's why Gargaphie is a happy and prosperous country. Now what about sending Perigot off to retrieve the golden apples that my great-grandfather lost? He'd never come back from that errand alive."

"You'll never persuade him to start on it," objected the Queen.

"Nonsense," said the King. "All that's needed is a little tact and diplomacy. Just you see."

As soon as the Queen had gone he sent his personal herald to look for Perigot, and when the young man appeared, greeted him in a serious and a friendly way.

"Perigot," he said, "there is a stain on the escutcheon of my house which I think you are the very man to erase. In my great-grandfather's time we had, among our family treasures, three golden apples that were said to confer upon their owners health, wealth, and happiness. Whether or not that was so, they were at least intrinsically valuable, and as objects of art, I believe, incomparable. Unhappily, in an affair that did credit to neither side, they were stolen by the Cloud King and taken by him to his favourite castle, which, as probably you are aware, is seven days' march to the north of Gargaphie. On several occasions enterprising young men have endeavoured to retrieve these apples, but every one of them, I am sorry to say, has perished at the hands, or in the teeth, of a curious monster, half-human and half-dog, that the Cloud King retains as a kind of seneschal or warder. You, however, who kill dragons with such ease, would probably make short work of the Hound-man, and if you can bring back those apples I shall seriously consider making you my heir. I don't want to press you, of course . . ."

"There's no need to," said Perigot, "for I'll go very willingly. When can I start?"

The King was a little astonished by his eagerness to undertake so perilous an expedition, but as he did not want to give Perigot an opportunity to change his mind, he said, as though thinking about it very carefully, "Well, there's a full moon to-night, and if you're really in a hurry you could start at once. I'll give you a guide for the first part of your journey, and after that anyone will tell you your way."

So Perigot said good-bye to Amoret and set out on his desperate enterprise. His hope was partly to forget in danger the embarrassment of his married life, and partly to give healing time a chance to restore him to his normal shape. For the curse, he thought, might be a passing or permanent one.

For seven days he marched through wild and desolate country, where the clouds hung ever closer on towering black mountains, and the crying of eagles came hoarsely through the mist. It was a cold and friendless land, and no sign of his returning manhood, except his intrepid spirit, came to comfort him. On the eighth day he reached the Cloud King's castle, and over it, to his surprise, the sky was clear. The castle was empty and deserted except for the great grey Hound-man lying at the gate.

When Perigot appeared the Hound-man rose and growled, and the brindled hair on its neck bristled terribly.

Perigot took out his pipe and began to play the first tune that came into his mind. The Hound-man lifted his head and howled most dismally. Perigot played something else, and the Hound-man bayed like a pack of hunting-dogs. Clearly music would have no effect on him. So Perigot, putting away his pipe, drew his moon-made sickle and warily advanced.

Showing great fangs like icicles, the Hound-man leapt to kill him, but Perigot neatly evaded its rush and cut off its right arm. Foaming at the mouth the brute again attacked him, but this time Perigot with great skill lopped off both its legs, and the Hound-man fell to the ground and lay dying. Its eyes began to glaze, but the wickedness in its heart still lived, and out of its great throat came a growling voice that said, "The curse of Shepherd Alken be on you!"

"What did you say?" demanded Perigot excitedly.

"The curse of Shepherd Alken on you!" repeated the Hound-man. "If you are a man become a woman, if you are a woman become a man!" And died in that instant.

Perigot was so excited that he almost forgot his errand, but just as he was turning back to Gargaphie he remembered that he had come to look for some golden apples, and breaking into the castle speedily found them in the Cloud King's bedroom. He put them into a satchel he had brought for the purpose, and then, wasting no more time, he began to run southwards down the path he had lately climbed so grimly. He made such speed—for his clothes no longer felt tight about the chest—that he reached Gargaphie on the evening of the fourth day, just at the time when everybody was getting ready to go to bed.

The King was astounded to see him, and despite his pleasure in regaining the golden apples that his great-grand-father had lost, found it difficult to infuse his welcome with any cordiality. But Perigot paid little attention to the King. Amoret, he was told, had taken her candle a few minutes earlier and already retired to her chamber.

She, poor girl, was delighted by his return, for she loved him though he had deceived her, and she had feared he was dead. But after they had embraced each other once or twice she remembered her former disappointment, and a little bitterly she said, "Where is your pipe, Perigot? Aren't you going to play me to sleep?"

"That for my pipe!" said Perigot, and threw it out of the window.

"Perigot!" she said.

"Amoret!" he answered, in a deep manly voice that made her heart flutter strangely.

The following morning it was Amoret who rose first, and left Perigot sleeping. At her chamber door the King and Queen were waiting for her.

"Well, my dear," said the King, "I'm afraid that my attempt to get rid of your so-called husband has failed, well-thought-out though it was. But don't worry. I've plenty more plans in my head, and when he's out of the way we'll get you a proper man."

"A proper man!" said Amoret, laughing happily. "Oh, my dear father and my very dear mother, he's the most wonderful man in the whole wide world. I wouldn't change him for all the husbands in Gargaphie."

❦ T. H. WHITE ❦
(1906-1964)

Terence Hanbury White spent most of his life in a tortured quest for the happiness and stability that were totally lacking in his early years. He was born in Bombay, India, where his father was the District Superintendent of Police. His parents' marriage was a singularly unhappy one. White recalls in his diary (recounted by Sylvia Townsend Warner in her biography of White) his parents quarreling over his crib, pistols in hand, threatening to shoot each other and himself as well. Fortunately, White had to be brought to England in 1911 for health reasons, and there he was raised by grandparents for several years. He compensated for the lack of attention from his parents by excelling in everything to which he turned his attention, whether racing cars, flying planes, or studying. He took a first in the English Honours School at Cambridge in 1929, where he studied under some of the finest scholars of the time, such as E. M. W. Tillyard and I. A. Richards. To gain his first, he wrote an essay on Malory. He taught literature for several years at Stowe Preparatory School and became head of the English Department.

White quit teaching, however, to pursue the more hazardous occupation of a professional writer; he had been writing since the age of twenty. In 1939, he went to Ireland for a holiday and remained there for six highly productive years. His father, Garrick White, had been born in Ireland, and White was perhaps attempting to regain a lost heritage. He flirted with Roman Catholicism but never became a Catholic. For the first several years of World War II, White remained a troubled

pacifist, but finally decided that Hitler must be defeated and
volunteered for service in the Royal Air Force. He was turned
down, however, because of poor health. After the war, he
resided in the Channel Islands, wrote, and lectured. He made
a highly successful and gratifying lecture tour of the United
States in 1963, but weakened himself considerably traveling
around the country. He died shortly after leaving the United
States in 1964. But perhaps he had attained his quest, or a
portion of it anyway; regarding his time in the United States, he
noted in his diary that he had never been happier in his life.

T. H. White is best known for his retelling of Malory's *Morte
d'Arthur*, or perhaps even more so for *Camelot*, the play and
movie adaptation of his book, The *Once and Future King*. This
work, which appeared in 1958, consists of four books, three of
which had been published earlier: *The Sword in the Stone*
(1938)—Walt Disney bought the film rights and later filmed
it in cartoon form; *The Witch in the Wood* (1939), which White
later revised and retitled *The Queen of Air and Darkness*; *The
Ill-Made Knight* (1940); *The Candle in the Wind*, completing
the final 1958 version of the tetralogy. Three other works of
importance are *Mistress Masham's Repose* (1946), *The Gos-
hawk* (1951), and *The Book of the Beasts* (1954). These
command a considerably smaller reading audience, but a very
discerning one.

"The Troll" first appeared in *Gone to Ground* (1935), a
collection of stories told by two men who are 112 years old.
The story probably stems from White's walking tour of Lapland
in 1926. At the end of his first year at Cambridge, he and a
friend picked what they considered to be the least populous area
they could reach for their holiday. The fact that, according to
White's diary, the trip was made miserable by bad weather and
mosquitoes perhaps explains the presence of the Troll, one of
the author's most repulsive creations. The Troll stands out in
hideous relief, framed by the background of commonplace
railroad trains and modern guest houses on the one hand,
and the beautiful landscapes on the other. In this regard, the
story is carefully constructed to accent the reality and the
repulsiveness of the Troll. White's style, which already
promises the master strokes of his *Once and Future King*, is

aptly suited to depicting both the tangible reality and the majesty of the setting. The descriptions, along with the humor and the understatement, further reinforce the grotesqueness of what happens.

The Troll

T. H White

❦

"My father," said Mr. Marx, "used to say that an experience like the one I am about to relate was apt to shake one's interest in mundane matters. Naturally he did not expect to be believed, and he did not mind whether he was or not. He did not himself believe in the supernatural, but the thing happened, and he proposed to tell it as simply as possible. It was stupid of him to say that it shook his faith in mundane affairs, for it was just as mundane as anything else. Indeed the really frightening part about it was the horribly tangible atmosphere in which it took place. None of the outlines wavered in the least. The creature would have been less remarkable if it had been less natural. It seemed to overcome the usual laws without being immune to them.

"My father was a keen fisherman, and used to go to all sorts of places for his fish. On one occasion he made Abisko his Lapland base, a comfortable railway hotel, one hundred and fifty miles within the Arctic Circle. He traveled the prodigious length of Sweden (I believe it is as far from the south of Sweden to the north, as it is from the south of Sweden to the south of Italy) in the electric railway, and arrived tired out. He went to bed early, sleeping almost immediately, although it was bright daylight outside, as it is in those parts throughout the night at that time of the year. Not the least shaking part of his experience was that it should all have happened under the sun.

"He went to bed early, and slept, and dreamt. I may as well make it clear at once, as clear as the outlines of that creature in the northern sun, that his story did not turn out to be a dream in the last paragraph. The division between sleeping and waking

157

was abrupt, although the feeling of both was the same. They were both in the same sphere of horrible absurdity, though in the former he was asleep and in the latter almost terribly awake. He tried to be asleep several times.

"My father always used to tell one of his dreams, because it somehow seemed of a piece with what was to follow. He believed that it was a consequence of the thing's presence in the next room. My father dreamed of blood.

"It was the vividness of the dreams that was impressive, their minute detail and horrible reality. The blood came through the keyhole of a locked door which communicated with the next room. I suppose the two rooms had originally been designed *en suite*. It ran down the door panel with a viscous ripple, like the artificial one created in the conduit of Trumpingdon Street. But it was heavy, and smelled. The slow welling of it sopped the carpet and reached the bed. It was warm and sticky. My father woke up with the impression that it was all over his hands. He was rubbing his first two fingers together, trying to rid them of the greasy adhesion where the fingers joined.

"My father knew what he had got to do. Let me make it clear that he was now perfectly wide awake, but he knew what he had got to do. He got out of bed, under this irresistible knowledge, and looked through the keyhole into the next room.

"I suppose the best way to tell the story is simply to narrate it, without an effort to carry belief. The thing did not require belief. It was not a feeling of horror in one's bones, or a misty outline, or anything that needed to be given actuality by an act of faith. It was as solid as a wardrobe. You don't have to believe in wardrobes. They are there, with corners.

"What my father saw through the keyhole in the next room was a Troll. It was eminently solid, about eight feet high, and dressed in brightly ornamental skins. It had a blue face, with yellow eyes, and on its head there was a woolly sort of nightcap with a red bobble on top. The features were Mongolian. Its body was long and sturdy, like the trunk of a tree. Its legs were short and thick, like the elephant's feet that used to be cut off for umbrella stands, and its arms were wasted: little rudimentary members like the forelegs of a kangaroo. Its head and neck were very thick and massive. On the whole, it looked like a grotesque doll.

That was the horror of it. Imagine a perfectly normal golliwog (but without the association of a Christie minstrel) standing in the corner of a room, eight feet high. The creature was as ordinary as that, as tangible, as stuffed, and as ungainly at the joints, but could move itself about.

"The Troll was eating a lady. Poor girl, she was tightly clutched to its breast by those rudimentary arms, with her head on a level with its mouth. She was dressed in a nightdress which had crumpled up under her armpits, so that she was a pitiful naked offering, like a classical picture of Andromeda. Mercifully, she appeared to have fainted.

"Just as my father applied his eye to the keyhole, the Troll opened its mouth and bit off her head. Then, holding the neck between the bright blue lips, he sucked the bare meat dry. She shriveled, like a squeezed orange, and her heels kicked. The creature had a look of thoughtful ecstasy. When the girl seemed to have lost succulence as an orange she was lifted into the air. She vanished in two bites. The Troll remained leaning against the wall, munching patiently and casting its eyes about it with a vague benevolence. Then it leaned forward from the low hips, like a jackknife folding in half, and opened its mouth to lick the blood up from the carpet. The mouth was incandescent inside, like a gas fire, and the blood evaporated before its tongue, like dust before a vacuum cleaner. It straightened itself, the arms dangling before it in patent uselessness, and fixed its eyes upon the keyhole.

"My father crawled back to bed, like a hunted fox after fifteen miles. At first it was because he was afraid that the creature had seen him through the hole, but afterward it was because of his reason. A man can attribute many nighttime appearances to the imagination, and can ultimately persuade himself that creatures of the dark did not exist. But this was an appearance in a sunlit room, with all the solidity of a wardrobe and unfortunately almost none of its possibility. He spent the first ten minutes making sure that he was awake, and the rest of the night trying to hope that he was asleep. It was either that, or else he was mad.

"It is not pleasant to doubt one's sanity. There are no satisfactory tests. One can pinch oneself to see if one is asleep, but there are no means of determining the other problem. He spent some time opening and shutting his eyes, but the room seemed normal and remained unaltered. He also soused his head in a basin of cold water, without result. Then he lay on his back, for hours, watching the mosquitoes on the ceiling.

"He was tired when he was called. A bright Scandinavian maid admitted the full sunlight for him and told him that it was a fine day. He spoke to her several times, and watched her carefully, but she seemed to have no doubts about his behavior. Evidently, then, he was not badly mad; and by now he had begun thinking about the matter for so many hours that it had begun to get obscure. The outlines were blurring again, and he determined that the whole thing must have been a dream or a temporary delusion, something temporary, anyway, and finished with, so that there was no good in thinking about it longer. He got up, dressed himself fairly cheerfully, and went down to breakfast.

These hotels used to be run extraordinarily well. There was a hostess always handy in a little office off the hall, who was delighted to answer any questions, spoke every conceivable language, and generally made it her business to make the guests feel at home. The particular hostess at Abisko was a lovely creature into the bargain. My father used to speak to her a good deal. He had an idea that when you had a bath in Sweden one of the maids was sent to wash you. As a matter of fact this sometimes used to be the case, but it was always an old maid and highly trusted. You had to keep yourself underwater and this was supposed to confer a cloak of invisibility. If you popped your knee out she was shocked. My father had a dim sort of hope that the hostess would be sent to bathe him one day, and I daresay he would have shocked her a good deal. However, this is beside the point. As he passed through the hall something prompted him to ask about the room next to his. Had anybody, he inquired, taken number 23?

" 'But, yes,' said the lady manager with a bright smile, '23 is taken by a doctor professor from Upsala and his wife, such a charming couple!'

"My father wondered what the charming couple had been doing, whilst the Troll was eating the lady in the nightdress. However, he decided to think no more about it. He pulled himself together, and went in to breakfast. The Professor was sitting in an opposite corner (the manageress had kindly pointed him out), looking mild and shortsighted, by himself. My father thought he would go out for a long climb on the mountains, since exercise was evidently what his constitution needed.

"He had a lovely day. Lake Torne blazed a deep blue below him, for all its thirty miles, and the melting snow made a lacework of filigree round the tops of the surrounding mountain basin. He got away from the stunted birch trees, and the mossy bogs with the reindeer in them, and the mosquitoes, too. He forded something that might have been a temporary tributary of the Abiskojokk, having to take off his trousers to do so and tucking his shirt up round his neck. He wanted to shout, bracing himself against the glorious tug of the snow water, with his legs crossing each other involuntarily as they passed, and the boulders turning under his feet. His body made a bow wave in the water, which climbed and feathered on his stomach, on the upstream side. When he was under the opposite bank a stone turned in earnest, and he went in. He came up, shouting with laughter, and made out a loud remark which has since become a classic in my family. 'Thank God,' he said, 'I rolled up my sleeves.' He wrung out everything as best he could, and dressed again in the wet clothes, and set off up the shoulder of Niakatjavelk. He was dry and warm again in half a mile. Less than a thousand feet took him over the snow line, and there, crawling on hands and knees, he came face to face with what seemed to be the summit of ambition. He met an ermine. They were both on all fours, so that there was a sort of equality about the encounter, especially as the ermine was higher up than he was. They looked at each other for a fifth of a second, without saying anything, and then the ermine vanished. He searched for it everywhere in vain, for the snow was only patchy. My father sat down on a dry rock, to eat his well-soaked luncheon of chocolate and rye bread.

"Life is such unutterable hell, solely because it is sometimes beautiful. If we could only be miserable all the time, if there could be no such things as love or beauty or faith or hope, if I could be absolutely certain that my love would never be returned, how much more simple life would be. One could plod through the Siberian salt mines of existence without being bothered about happiness. Unfortunately the happiness is there. There is always the chance (about eight hundred and fifty to one) that another heart will come by mine. I can't help hoping, and keeping faith, and loving beauty. Quite frequently I am not so miserable as it would be wise to be. And there, for my poor father sitting on his boulder above the snow, was stark happiness beating at the gates.

"The boulder on which he was sitting had probably never been sat upon before. It was a hundred and fifty miles within the Arctic Circle, on a mountain five thousand feet high, looking down on a blue lake. The lake was so long that he could have sworn it sloped away at the ends, proving to the naked eye that the sweet earth was round. The railway line and the half-dozen houses of Abisko were hidden in the trees. The sun was warm on the boulder, blue on the snow, and his body tingled smooth from the spate water. His mouth watered for the chocolate, just behind the tip of his tongue.

"And yet, when he had eaten the chocolate—perhaps it was heavy on his stomach—there was the memory of the Troll. My father fell suddenly into a black mood, and began to think about the supernatural. Lapland was beautiful in the summer, with the sun sweeping round the horizon day and night, and the small tree leaves twinkling. It was not the sort of place for wicked things. But what about the winter? A picture of the Arctic night came before him, with the silence and the snow. Then the legendary wolves and bears snuffled at the far encampments, and the nameless winter spirits moved on their darkling courses. Lapland had always been associated with sorcery, even by Shakespeare. It was at the outskirts of the world that the Old Things accumulated, like driftwood round the edges of the sea. If one wanted to find a wise woman, one went to the rims of the Hebrides; on the coast of Brittany, one sought the mass of St. Secaire. And what an outskirt Lapland was! It was an outskirt not only of Europe, but of civilization.

It had no boundaries. The Lapps went with the reindeer, and
where the reindeer were was Lapland. Curiously indefinite
region, suitable to the indefinite things. The Lapps were not
Christians. What a fund of power they must have had behind
them, to resist the march of mind. All through the missionary centuries they had held to something; something had
stood behind them, a power against Christ. My father
realized with a shock that he was living in the age of the
reindeer, a period contiguous to the mammoth and the fossil.

"Well, this was not what he had come out to do. He dismissed
the nightmares with an effort, got up from his boulder, and
began the scramble back to his hotel. It was impossible that a
professor from Abisko could become a troll.

"As my father was going in to dinner that evening the
manageress stopped him in the hall.

"'We have had a day so sad,' she said. 'The poor Dr. Professor
has disappeared his wife. She has been missing since last
night. The Dr. Professor is inconsolable.'

"My father then knew for certain that he had lost his reason.

"He went blindly to dinner, without making any answer, and
began to eat a thick sour-cream soup that was taken cold with
pepper and sugar. The Professor was still sitting in his corner,
a sandy-headed man with thick spectacles and a desolate
expression. He was looking at my father, and my father, with
the soup spoon halfway to his mouth, looked at him. You
know that eye-to-eye recognition, when two people look
deeply into each other's pupils, and burrow to the soul? It
usually comes before love. I mean the clear, deep, milk-eyed
recognition expressed by the poet Donne. Their eyebeams
twisted and did thread their eyes upon a double string. My
father recognized that the Professor was a troll, and the Professor recognized my father's recognition. Both of them knew that
the Professor had eaten his wife.

"My father put down his soup spoon, and the Professor began
to grow. The top of his head lifted and expanded, like a great
loaf rising in an oven; his face went red and purple, and finally
blue; the whole ungainly upper works began to sway and
topple toward the ceiling. My father looked about him. The
other diners were eating unconcernedly. Nobody else could see

it, and he was definitely mad at last. When he looked at the Troll again, the creature bowed. The enormous superstructure inclined itself toward him from the hips, and grinned seductively.

"My father got up from his table experimentally, and advanced toward the Troll, arranging his feet on the carpet with excessive care. He did not find it easy to walk, or to approach the monster, but it was a question of his reason. If he was mad, he was mad; and it was essential that he should come to grips with the thing, in order to make certain.

"He stood before it like a small boy, and held out his hand, saying, "Good evening.'

"'Ho! Ho!' said the Troll, 'little mannikin. And what shall I have for my supper tonight?'

"Then it held out its wizened furry paw and took my father by the hand.

"My father went straight out of the dining room, walking on air. He found the manageress in the passage and held out his hand to her.

"'I am afraid I have burnt my hand,' he said. 'Do you think you could tie it up?'

"The manageress said, 'But it is a very bad burn. There are blisters all over the back. Of course, I will bind it up at once.'

"He explained that he had burnt it on one of the spirit lamps at the sideboard. He could scarcely conceal his delight. One cannot burn oneself by being insane.

"'I saw you talking to the Dr. Professor,' said the manageress as she was putting on the bandage. 'He is a sympathetic gentleman, is he not?'

"The relief about his sanity soon gave place to other troubles. The Troll had eaten its wife and given him a blister, but it had also made an unpleasant remark about its supper that evening. It proposed to eat my father. Now very few people can have been in a position to decide what to do when a troll earmarks them for its next meal. To begin with, although it was a tangible troll in two ways, it had been invisible to the other diners. This put my father in a difficult position. He could not, for instance, ask for protection. He could scarcely go to the manageress and say, 'Professor Skål is an odd kind of werewolf; he ate his wife last night, and hopes to eat me this evening.' He would have found himself in a looney bin at once. Besides, he was too proud to do this, and still too confused. Whatever the proofs and blisters, he did not find it easy to believe in professors that turned into trolls. He had lived in the normal world all his life, and, at his age, it was difficult to start learning afresh. It would have been quite easy for a baby, who was still coordinating the world, to cope with the troll situation: for my father, not. He kept trying to fit it in somewhere, without disturbing the universe. He kept telling himself that it was nonsense: one did not get eaten by professors. It was like having a fever, and telling oneself that it was all right, really, only a delirium, only something that would pass.

"There was that feeling on the one side, the desperate assertion of all the truths that he had learned so far, the tussle to keep the world from drifting, the brave but intimidated refusal to give in or to make a fool of himself.

"On the other side there was stark terror. However much one struggled to be merely deluded, or hitched up momentarily in an odd pocket of space-time, there was panic. There was the urge to go away as quickly as possible, to flee the dreadful Troll. Unfortunately the last train had left Abisko, and there was nowhere else to go.

"My father was not able to distinguish these trends of thought. For him they were at the time intricately muddled together. He was in a whirl. A proud man, and an agnostic, he stuck to his muddled guns alone. He was terribly afraid of the Troll, but he could not afford to admit its existence. All his mental processes remained hung up, whilst he talked on the terrace, in a state of suspended animation, with an American tourist who had come to Abisko to photograph the midnight sun.

"The American told my father that the Abisko railway was the northernmost electric railway in the world, that twelve trains passed through it every day traveling between Upsala and Narvik, that the population of Abo was 12,000 in 1862, and that Gustavus Adolphus ascended the throne of Sweden in 1611. He also gave some facts about Greta Garbo.

"My father told the American that a dead baby was required for the mass of St. Secaire, that an elemental was a kind of mouth in space that sucked at you and tried to gulp you down, that homeopathic magic was practiced by the aborigines of Australia, and that a Lapland woman was careful at her confinement to have no knots or loops about her person, lest these should make the delivery difficult.

"The American, who had been looking at my father in a strange way for some time, took offense at this and walked away; so that there was nothing for it but to go to bed.

"My father walked upstairs on will power alone. His faculties seemed to have shrunk and confused themselves. He had to help himself with the banister. He seemed to be navigating himself by wireless, from a spot about a foot above his forehead. The issues that were involved had ceased to have any meaning, but he went on doggedly up the stairs, moved forward by pride and contrariety. It was physical fear that alienated him from his body, the same fear that he had felt as a boy, walking down long corridors to be beaten. He walked firmly up the stairs.

"Oddly enough, he went to sleep at once. He had climbed all day and been awake all night and suffered emotional extremes. Like a condemned man, who was to be hanged in the morning, my father gave the whole business up and went to sleep.

"He was woken at midnight exactly. He heard the American on the terrace below his window, explaining excitedly that there had been a cloud on the last two nights at 11:58, thus making it impossible to photograph the midnight sun. He heard the camera click.

"There seemed to be a sudden storm of hail and wind. It roared at his windowsill, and the window curtains lifted themselves taut, pointing horizontally into the room. The shriek and rattle of the tempest framed the window in a crescendo of growing sound, and increasing blizzard directed toward himself. A blue paw came over the sill.

"My father turned over and hid his head in the pillow. He

could feel the domed head dawning at the window and the eyes fixing themselves upon the small of his back. He could feel the places physically, about four inches apart. They itched. Or else the rest of his body itched, except those places. He could feel the creature growing into the room, glowing like ice, and giving off a storm. His mosquito curtains rose in its afflatus, uncovering him, leaving him defenseless. He was in such ecstasy of terror that he almost enjoyed it. He was like a bather plunging for the first time into freezing water and unable to articulate. He was trying to yell, but all he could do was to throw a series of hooting noises from his paralyzed lungs. He became a part of the blizzard. The bedclothes were gone. He felt the Troll put out its hands.

"My father was an agnostic, but, like most idle men, he was not above having a bee in his bonnet. His favorite bee was the psychology of the Catholic church. He was ready to talk for hours about psychoanalysis and the confession. His greatest discovery had been the rosary.

"The rosary, my father used to say, was intended solely as a factual occupation which calmed the lower centers of the mind. The automatic telling of the beads liberated the higher centers to meditate upon the mysteries. They were a sedative, like knitting or counting sheep. There was no better cure for insomnia than a rosary. For several years he had given up deep breathing or regular counting. When he was sleepless he lay on his back and told his beads, and there was a small rosary in the pocket of his pajama coat.

"The Troll put out its hands, to take him round the waist. He became completely paralyzed, as if he had been winded. The Troll put its hand upon the beads.

"They met, the occult forces, in a clash above my father's heart. There was an explosion, he said, a quick creation of power. Positive and negative. A flash, a beam. Something like the splutter with which the antenna of a tram meets its overhead wires again, when it is being changed about.

"The Troll made a high squealing noise, like a crab being boiled, and began rapidly to dwindle in size. It dropped my father and turned about, and ran wailing, as if it had been terribly burnt, for the window. Its color waned as its size decreased. It was one of those air toys now, that expire with a piercing whistle. It scrambled over the window sill, scarcely larger than a little child, and sagging visibly.

"My father leaped out of bed and followed it to the window. He saw it drop on the terrace like a toad, gather itself together, stumble off, staggering and whistling like a bat, down the valley of the Abiskojokk.

"My father fainted.

"In the morning the manageress said, 'There has been such a terrible tragedy. The poor Dr. Professor was found this morning in the lake. The worry about his wife had certainly unhinged his mind.'

"A subscription for a wreath was started by the American, to which my father subscribed five shillings; and the body was shipped off next morning, on one of the twelve trains that travel between Upsala and Narvik every day."

❦ LORD DUNSANY ❦
(1878–1957)

Lord Dunsany continues to be one of the most popular and influential fantasy writers of this century; he is incontestably one of the finest stylists of the genre. Many have tried to match the wry wit or sonorous majesty of his prose, but few, if any, have succeeded. Born Edward John Moreton Drax Plunkett in London, on July 24, 1878, he became the eighteenth Baron Dunsany when his father, an Irish nobleman, died in 1899. His hereditary home of Dunsany Castle was built in 1180, in Dunsany, County Meath. After attending Sandhurst, the English military college, Dunsany served as a front-line officer in the Boer War, and later saw action in World War I. During World War II, Dunsany held the chair of Byron Professor of English Literature at the University of Athens, and was there when Nazi troops invaded and captured the city. He disappeared and, in the nonchalant British manner, was next seen having a meal in his Dublin club.

Dunsany was a handsome, robust, and athletic man who loved to play cricket, hunt foxes and big game as well, and travel. He crisscrossed America on several reading tours, and spent a good deal of time on safari in Africa. He was also an excellent chess player. One can only marvel, in the light of these activities, how Dunsany found time to write more than sixty books. He has fortunately detailed portions of his fascinating life in a series of memoirs: *Patches of Sunlight* (1938), *While the Sirens Slept* (1944), and *The Sirens Wake* (1945). He died in Dublin on October 25, 1957.

While Dunsany is read primarily for his fantasy stories, he initially gained fame as a dramatist. In 1909, at the request of W. B. Yeats, Dunsany wrote a play, *The Glittering Gate,* for production at the Abbey Theatre. A solid success, the play was succeeded by numerous others which were produced in London and New York as well as in Dublin. In addition to his plays, Dunsany wrote and published volumes of poetry (he attacked what he termed the obscurity of modern poetry), as well as numerous essays and his memoirs. His major contribution to literature remains, however, his eight collections of short stories, most of them fantasies. A tribute to Dunsany's popularity is the fact that of these eight, five have been reprinted in recent years: *Time and the Gods* (1906, reprinted by Arno Press in 1972); *A Dreamer's Tales* (1910, reprinted by Owlswick in 1979); *The Book of Wonder* (1912, reprinted by Arno Press in 1976); *Fifty-One Tales* (1915, reprinted by Newcastle in 1974 as *The Food of Death: Fifty-One Tales*); *Tales of Three Hemispheres* (1919, reprinted by Owlswick in 1976). In addition to these reprints, a number of collections have been put together by fantasy editors such as Lin Carter and E. F. Bleiler. Carter is also to be congratulated for reintroducing Dunsany's superlative fantasy novel, *The King of Elfland's Daughter* (1924) in 1969 as part of his adult fantasy series at Ballantine. In 1954 Dunsany, with the assistance of his wife, selected a group of stories, to which is appended the following publisher's note: "The sixteen stories in this book were selected by Lord Dunsany, with the assistance of Lady Dunsany, from various of his books which have long been out of print. They are the stories by which the author most wished to be remembered, and they reflect his gift of fancy most entertainingly." The stories appeared under the title of *The Sword of Welleran and Other Tales of Enchantment* (Devin-Adair).

Included as one of the sixteen tales by which Dunsany wished to be remembered is "The Bride of the Man-horse." One can understand why Dunsany selected this piece for inclusion. It is a paean of sheer sensuous exuberance, a wedding song and a celebration of life made more exquisite by the recognition of death. And the style is Dunsany's at its best, with its rolling sentences building to a crescendo to match the action. In its archaic majesty the style is most like the King James Bible, upon which it is most likely modeled.

While much of Dunsany's fantasy is invented myth, this story is an example of his adapting a tale from traditional sources, though he makes it his own. The origins of the centaurs provide ample precedence for the occurrences in "The Bride." The first centaurs, according to Greek myth, came into being in a roundabout way as a result of Ixion's killing the father of his bride-to-be.

The Bride of the Man-Horse
Lord Dunsany

On the morning of his two hundred and fiftieth year Shepperalk the centaur went to the golden coffer wherein the treasure of the centaurs was and, taking from it the hoarded amulet that his father Jyshak in the years of his prime had hammered from mountain gold and set with opals bartered from the gnomes, he put it upon his wrist, and said no word but walked from his mother's cavern. And he took with him too that clarion of the centaurs, that famous silver horn, that in its time had summoned to surrender seventeen cities of Man and for twenty years had brayed at star-girt walls in the Siege of Tholdenblarna, the citadel of the gods, what time the centaurs waged their fabulous war and were not broken by any force of arms, but retreated slowly in a cloud of dust before the final miracle of the gods that they brought in their desperate need from their ultimate armoury. He took it and strode away, and his mother only sighed and let him go.

She knew that to-day he would not drink at the stream coming down from the terraces of Varpa Niger, the inner land of the mountains, that to-day he would not wonder awhile at the sunset and afterwards trot back to the cavern again to sleep on rushes pulled by rivers that know not Man. She knew that it was with him as it had been of old with his father, and with Goom the father of Jyshak and long ago with the gods. Therefore she only sighed and let him go.

But he, coming out from the cavern that was his home, went for the first time over the little stream and, going round the corner of the crags, saw glittering beneath him the mundane plain. And the wind of the autumn that was gilding the world, rushing up the slopes of the mountain,

172

beat cold on his naked flanks. He raised his head and snorted.

"I am a man-horse now," he shouted aloud; and leaping from crag to crag he galloped by valley and chasm, by torrent-bed and scar of avalanche, until he came to the wandering leagues of the plain and left behind him for ever the Athraminaurian mountains.

His goal was Zretazoola, the city of Sombelenë. What legend of Sombelenë's inhuman beauty or of the wonder of her mystery had ever floated over the mundane plains to the fabulous cradle of the centaurs' race, the Athraminaurian mountains, I do not know. Yet in the blood of man there is a tide, an old sea-current rather, that is somehow akin to the twilight, which brings him rumours of beauty from however far away, as driftwood is found at sea from islands not yet discovered; and this spring-tide or current that visits the blood of man comes from the fabulous quarter of his lineage, from the legendary, the old; it takes him out to the woodlands, out to the hills, he listens to ancient song. So it may be that Shepperalk's fabulous blood stirred in those lonely mountains away at the edge of the world to rumours that only the airy twilight knew and only confided secretly to the bat, for Shepperalk was more legendary even than man. Certain it was that he headed from the first for the city of Zretazoola, where Sombelenë in her temple dwelt; though all the mundane plains, their rivers and mountains, lay between Shepperalk's home and the city he sought.

When first the feet of the centaur touched the grass of that soft alluvial earth he blew for joy upon the silver horn, he pranced and caracolled, he gambolled over the leagues; peace came to him like a maiden with a lamp, a strange and beautiful wonder, the wind laughed as it passed him. He put his head down low to the scent of the flowers, he lifted it up to be nearer the unseen stars, he revelled through kingdoms, took rivers in his stride; how shall I tell you, ye that dwell in cities, how shall I tell you what he felt as he galloped? He felt for strength like the towers of Bel-Narāna; for lightness like those gossamer palaces that the fairy-spider builds twixt heaven and sea along the coasts of Zith; for swiftness like some bird racing up from the morning to sing in some city's spires before daylight breaks, and as the sworn companion of the wind. For joy he was as a song; the lightnings of his legendary sires the earlier gods began to mix with his blood; his hooves thundered. He came to the cities of men, and all men trembled, for they remembered the ancient mythical wars, and now dreaded new battles and feared for the race of man. Not by Clio are these wars recorded, history does not know them, but what of that? Not all of us have sat at historians' feet, but all have learned fable and myth at their mother's knees. And there were none that did not fear strange wars, when they saw Shepperalk swerve and leap along the public ways. So he passed from city to city.

By nights he lay down unpanting in the reeds of some marsh or a forest; before dawn he rose triumphant, and hugely drank of some river in the dark and, splashing out of it, would trot to some high place to find the sunrise and to send echoing eastwards the exultant greetings of his jubilant horn. And lo! the sunrise coming up from the echoes, and the plains new-lit by the day, and the leagues spinning by like water flung from a top, and that gay companion, the loudly laughing wind, and men and the fears of men and their little cities; and, after that, great rivers and waste spaces and huge new hills and then new lands beyond them and more cities of men, and always the old companion, the glorious wind. Kingdom by kingdom slipt by, and still his breath was even. "It is a golden thing to gallop on good turf in one's youth," said the young man-horse, the centaur. "Ha, Ha," said the wind of the hills, and the winds of the plain answered.

Bells pealed in frantic towers, wise men consulted parchments, astrologers sought of the portent from the stars, the aged made subtle properties; "Is he not swift?" said the young. "How glad he is," said children.

Night after night brought him sleep, and day after day lit his gallop, till he came to the lands of the Athalonian men, who live by the edges of the mundane plain, and from them he came to the lands of legend again, such as those in which he was cradled on the other side of the world, and which fringe the marge of the world and mix with the twilight. And there a mighty thought came into

his untired heart, for he knew that he neared Zretazoola
now, the city of Sombelenë.

It was late in the day when he neared it, and clouds
coloured with evening rolled low on the plain before him;
he galloped on into their golden mist, and when it hid from
his eyes the sight of things, the dreams in his heart awoke
and romantically he pondered all those rumours that used
to come to him from Sombelenë because of the fellowship
of fabulous things. She dwelt, said the evening secretly to
the bat, in a little temple by a lone lake-shore. A grove of
cypresses screened her from the city, from Zretazoola of
the climbing ways. And opposite her temple stood her
tomb, her sad lake-sepulchre with open door, lest her
amazing beauty and the centuries of her youth should ever
give rise to the heresy among men that lovely Sombelenë
was immortal: for only her beauty and her lineage were
divine.

Her father had been half centaur and half god, her
mother was the child of a desert-lion and that sphinx that
watches the pyramids, she was more mystical than Woman.

Her beauty was as a dream, was as a song; the one
dream of a lifetime dreamed on enchanted dews, the one
song sung to some city by a deathless bird, blown far from
his native coasts by storm in Paradise. Dawn after dawn on
mountains of romance, or twilight after twilight, could
never equal her beauty; all the glow-worms had not the
secret among them, nor all the stars of the night; poets had
never sung it nor evening guessed its meaning; the morning envied it, it was hidden from lovers.

She was unwed, unwooed.

The lions came not to woo her, because they feared her
strength; and the gods dared not love her, because they
knew she must die.

This was what evening had whispered to the bat, this
was the dream in the heart of Shepperalk as he cantered
blind through the mist. And suddenly there at his hooves in
the dark of the plain appeared the cleft in the legendary
lands, and Zretazoola sheltering in the cleft, a-glitter with
the sunset.

Swiftly and craftily he bounded down by the upper end
of the cleft and, entering Zretazoola by the outer gate,

which looks out sheer on the stars, he galloped suddenly down the narrow streets. Many that rushed out on to balconies as he went clattering by, many that put their heads from glittering windows, are told of in olden song. Shepperalk did not tarry to give greetings, or to answer challenges from martial towers; he was down through the earthward gateway like the thunderbolt of his sires, and, like Leviathan who has leapt at an eagle, he surged into the water between the temple and tomb.

He galloped with half-shut eyes up the temple steps, and only seeing dimly through his lashes, seized Sombelenë by the hair, undazzled as yet by her beauty, and so haled her away, and leaping with her over the floorless chasm where the waters of the lake fall unremembered away into a hole in the world, took her we know not where, to be her slave for all those centuries that are allowed to his race.

Three blasts he gave as he went upon that silver horn that is the world-old treasure of the centaurs. These were his wedding bells.

❧ FÉLIX MARTÍ-IBÁÑEZ ❧
(1912–1972)

While one can find many of Marti-Ibañez's numerous volumes in the science or the literature sections of the library, some in English and others in Spanish, one finds relatively little about the man himself, other than accounts of his contributions to the field of the history of medicine. The following outline is garnered from *The New York Times* obituary and from an autobiographical essay, "Interview with Myself," in *The Mirror of Souls and Other Essays* (1972).

Felix Marti-Ibañez was born in Cartagena, Spain. His father was a teacher and prolific writer of essays. He received his degree in medicine from the University of Madrid and practiced medicine and psychiatry until the outbreak of the Spanish Civil War in 1937, when he became a public health official for the Republican (the anti-Franco) government. Only in later years did he disclose both his flirtations with death during the war and the trauma of uprooting himself from his native soil when Franco came to power. He came to the United States and became a citizen in 1939. A second trauma of which he speaks in his autobiographical essay is the death of his wife from cancer. Throughout his career he wrote and lectured extensively on the history and philsophy of medicine. He edited a medical news magazine called *MD*, which appeared in editions in Canada, Latin America, Southeast Asia, and Australia, as well as in the United States. He became chairman of the department of the history of medicine at the New York Medical College.

The vast majority of Marti-Ibañez's writings are essays on medical history, but he has also written works of history, biography, and fiction. Among this last group is the volume entitled *All the Wonders We Seek: Thirteen Tales of Surprise and Prodigy* (1963), a collection of fantasy stories. He later singled out this collection (written in English) as one of his favorite works. The stories were composed some time between 1954 and 1963; two had been published previously in *Weird Tales*.

"Niña Sol" is one of the thirteen stories in the collection. In it we are treated to what Marti-Ibañez himself described as the three principal characteristics of good writing: "lucidity, simplicity, and euphony." Marti-Ibañez has clearly been influenced, in the theory and practice of the short story, by another doctor-author, W. Somerset Maugham, to whom *All the Wonders We Seek* is dedicated. Maugham had said that if you had to sacrifice sense in order to maintain a mellifluous, smooth-flowing prose, do it. Fortunately, Marti-Ibañez achieves such prose without sacrificing either lucidity or simplicity. Marti-Ibañez also has written about the importance of imagery and metaphor to give life to prose, and he happily follows his own advice in "Niña Sol," which is ablaze with the imagery of light. In theme the story illustrates the ambivalence of human contact with divinity, the wonder as well as the peril of such contact. A sub-theme of the work involves the question which is at the center of much mythology, the issue of whether science or poetry more nearly approaches the truth.

In "Niña Sol" (best translated as "sun child"), Marti-Ibañez draws heavily from Peruvian mythology. Pachacama is a creator god, portrayed as surrounded by the sun's rays. He was the god of the pre-Incas, the Quechuans, and was later adopted by the Incas. Pachacama apparently merged with the sun god and became the chief Peruvian deity and the founder and ancestor of man, according to the Incas. The sun god had temples throughout Peru, and the temples were tended by the virgins of the sun, young girls who lived in convents. A very prominent convent of these virgins existed—the ruins can still be seen —at Cuzco.

Niña Sol

Félix Martí–Ibáñez

❦

Perhaps it was the sun, perhaps the bleat of a goat, but that day I woke up earlier than usual. Through the open window the cool breeze brought me a message of autumn scents. I clambered out of bed and noticed with great joy that the *puna*—that dreaded mountain sickness—had finally tired of grinding my weary bones. After three weeks of fighting the altitude, I was still intact. Now I could think without effort, move without my joints creaking, and breathe without feeling as though there were a forge in each of my lungs. Even my heart was once again a forgotten organ quietly doing its clock work in a crimson chamber.

I looked out of the window hoping to see a bird, but I saw only the *puna*, all gray and gold—gray the earth and grass, gold the fine air—and the solemn llamas grazing in the distance. The llama, the only animal to which dirt lends dignity! The pale sky was like an invisible presence. I sniffed the air as though it were a Lachryma Christi and then breathed in deeply, finished dressing, and finally went to the dining room downstairs.

It was not only the restless spirit of the writer but also love for solitude that had brought me to the inn called Paradero de la Perricholi. While in Lima I had always longed for the Peru of the lofty mountains. For the Spanish conquerors Peru was Lima, a bejeweled town, the City of Kings, with its fabulous treasures; for me Peru was still a legend high up near the clouds, it was the *puna*, cosmic and abrupt, and the wandering llama, and the sky like polished metal.

That accounts for my itinerary: a few days in Lima, just enough to fall in love with the beautiful city, small, perfumed and voluptuous like a *señora criolla*, then on to

Juliaca and Cuzco, and thence by mule to the top of the Ara, a steep hill the very name of which held the promise of a legend. There I found the Paradero, a large house built of stone the color of green olives, with a vast hall that was at once hearth, dining room, and storage room for seeds, harnesses and fodder. Near the fire, which was never allowed to die out, sat two very old women, with as many colored skirts as an onion has layers, and a man—father? brother?—even older than they. A brooding cat and a dog that looked as if he had been silent for years lay sprawled at their feet. The smell of feed, leather, nuts and old wine hovered forever in the air, and a pearly mist rose from a pot, eternally kept on the fire as in a pagan ritual, and mixed with the mumblings—whinings or prayers—of the old women.

This was what I wanted: silence, solitude, time frozen into days without yesterday or tomorrow. Thousands of feet below was the other Peru with its great cities and its silver mountains; here drawing me like a magnet there was only the *puna*, a mysterious titanic prairie of grass and rock where I could roam and dream and let the solitude soothe my nerves, tense and taut like violin strings from being fingered too much by the big cities.

It was with annoyance therefore that I saw another guest sitting at the table, lustily attacking a sizable piece of roast meat. He was on the threshold of the thirties, with a heavy head of hair, the color of ripe corn, and childlike eyes that sparkled like aquamarines. His clothes were simple, a mountaineer's outfit, like mine. Near him there was a wooden box all spotted with paint of many colors, a roll of canvas, and brushes.

He greeted me with a wide smile and his fork, on which a boiled potato was impaled. His voice was as warm and friendly as the fragrant steam escaping from the huge blackened coffeepot.

"Welcome! Pardon my greediness, but I arrived very late last night and could get no dinner. This meat is excellent and the coffee smells superb. Won't you sit down with me? There is enough for two. I have invaded your retreat, but I shall disturb you little. I want to be outdoors all day, painting. The yellows of this landscape are marvelous. What delicious potatoes! My name is Jorge Martínez.

Please call me Jorge. Some day my signature at the bottom
of a Peruvian landscape will be worth a great deal of
money."

He spoke quickly while devouring the contents of his
plate. His ebullience introduced such an incongruous note
in the somber, silent room that I had to smile. I introduced
myself and assured him that, since he was going to paint
and I was going to write, he would have no reason to fear
either competition or intrusion from me. By the time we
had finished our fourth cup of coffee we were chatting like
old friends, and after a barrage of courteous protestations
as to who should have the last potato, we finally divided it
in two.

"What attracts a painter to this part of the country?" I
asked him.

"Light," he answered emphatically. "The mystery of
light fascinates me as it did Rembrandt, if I may be a little
presumptuous. I have traveled all over South America and
never have I seen anywhere such light as that of the Peruvian *puna*. Actually the light here is all the same color,
yellow, but yellow in all shades. The grass is gray-yellow,
the llamas dark yellow, the sun a burning yellow, even the
sky is a faded yellow. I want to paint that, a symphony of
yellows, a canticle to the glorious yellow light of this glorious land, so that it may bring joy to the weary people who
live in gray, gloomy towns."

"It should be a fascinating challenge to transfer to canvas the mysterious quality of the *puna*," I said, a little wary
of his enthusiasm. "In my own way I intend to—"

"Yes," he interrupted me abruptly, following the thread
of his own thoughts, "the secret of the *puna* is not just
silence or solitude. That is part of it, of course. But the real
secret is the light. And I am going to capture it with this,"
and he kicked his box of paints.

We took leave of each other with a handshake, but his
d'Artagnan attitude of attacking the entire realm of the
puna alone irritated me. When I went outside, I saw him
walking in the distance, his hair a bright yellow against the
faded sky.

The narrow plateau around the Paradero was covered
with gray grass, some stunted trees and massive rocks. A
gentle slope led to a wide esplanade where flocks of llamas

grazed. From here one went down to another wide step, and then another and another, until the step-like projections reached the deep, distant valley, where houses pressed together as if they had been poured from the heights in one heavy splash. One's gaze could reach very far, where the land, dressed in green with brown and other colors, rose and fell and then rose again to majestic heights where it was crowned with snow. There was the odor of damp grass, the bleating of goats, and always the faint tolling of bells from the valley mingled with the soft sighs of the breezes from the peaks.

The day passed lazily and quietly. I strolled around, meditated, read and made notes. At noon I had lunch alone at the Paradero, served by one of the melancholy old women. After a short siesta, I was again engulfed by the silence of the afternoon, which though profound was not oppressive. When I was about to go in to dinner, I heard a shout and suddenly saw the young painter emerge from behind a rock. He was out of breath and looked exhausted, but he still burned with the fire of enthusiasm.

"What a country! What light!" he greeted me, flourishing a brush just as he had brandished his fork in the morning. "I have walked miles and miles. I even forgot to eat. Color, color, color everywhere, always the same and always different."

"The *puna* reminds me of the sea," I ventured coldly, for his rebuff of that morning still rankled in my chest. "It is infinite and it can be cruel or kind, depending on the time of day."

"That is true," he granted, wiping off his sweat with a handkerchief as big as a sheet. "The land here seems to move like the sea, according to the light of every hour of the day. It's the light that does it. Such glorious light!"

He pressed my arm with his hot hand.

"Let me show you something." He quickly unrolled two canvases and showed them to me with the same gesture of pride with which Chinese merchants must have displayed their gorgeous silks before Suleiman the Magnificent.

There was not much to them. They were sketches, almost identical, of a lot of grass with some llamas grazing and a low sky thick with clouds the color of chromium oxide.

"What do you think?" he asked proudly.

"Well, not bad."

"Not bad!" He was really astonished.

"Frankly, I have seen better."

He stared at me and then at the canvases, and finally he rolled them up with a gesture of despair.

"You are right. There's something missing. The light. The light. It escapes me. I can't mix the right colors. The customary method is inadequate. One would have to paint this light as Fra Angelico painted heaven—on one's knees."

Seizing my arm he led me back to the house, and the welcome of the dog and the smell of the stew on the fire soon made me forget the anxieties of the painter.

I did not see him again for several days. He always left before I got up and returned after I had retired. As there was no electric light, I fell into the habit of going to bed early, following the custom of the proprietors of the inn. I never asked about him and they told me nothing. I would hear him arrive before I fell asleep, and, listening to the noise of dishes, I imagined him devouring the supper they left him by the fire. Then he would shut himself in his room next to mine and I could hear him mumbling and ripping paper until I fell asleep.

The days passed sweet and solemn. I read all my books; I filled several notebooks with meticulous scribblings. I began to think of going back to Lima, and finally I set a date for my return.

One night, unable to sleep, I lit my candle and sat down to write some letters. I had been writing only a few minutes when I heard the painter arrive. Contrary to his habit, he came upstairs immediately. His boots made the corridor shake. When he reached my door he stopped and knocked. I opened the door.

"What luck to find you up! I saw the light in your room and could not resist the temptation of having a chat with you. May I sit down?"

I found him disturbingly changed. He looked thin, almost emaciated, and there was a feverish look in his eyes. I closed the door. The room, quiet and peaceful before he came in, suddenly seemed to vibrate with the nervousness emanating from his pores.

"I'm happy to see you," I said, pouring two glasses of

sherry, which shimmered like two patches of sun in the flickering light of the candle. "You must be working very hard. I haven't seen a trace of you around the house in the past few days."

He drank the sherry in one gulp. Above the feeble flame of the candle, which shed more shadows than light in the room, his reddened eyes gleamed strangely. In his glass a drop of the golden liquid glittered like a pirate's doblon.

"What do you think of this?" he said suddenly, unrolling a canvas. I looked at it for a moment and then at him. In his eyes I saw an ironical sparkle.

"You think it's a lot of nonsense and that I'm crazy, don't you?"

I was about to reply that he had guessed my thoughts, but his feverish aspect held me back.

"I wouldn't say that," I answered cautiously. "In any case, it's quite different from anything I have ever seen."

The canvas was covered with patches of yellow of so vivid a hue that they cast a glow in the semidarkness of the room. At first I thought they were only random strokes of the brush, but as I studied the canvas further I thought I detected vague shadows and contours amid the yellow blotches. Perhaps it was only my imagination, but in those childish-looking blobs of vivid yellow I thought I perceived strangely disquieting figures and profiles. Suddenly, without any warning, he rolled up the canvas.

"You are very diplomatic," he said sarcastically. "Of course, you don't understand. How can you?"

"You forget," I replied, rather piqued, "that I'm only a writer with only a superficial feeling for painting."

"Of course, of course." In the dancing shadows cast by the leaping flame of the candle, his face looked as if it had escaped from one of Goya's *Caprichos*. "But that is no excuse for not recognizing the marvelous when it's facing you."

I shrugged my shoulders and poured two more glasses of sherry, determined not to be angry but also not to tolerate any more impertinence.

"Let's drink to your paintings," I suggested sarcastically.

"Let's drink to *her*," he said with vehemence.

My glass stopped in mid-air.

"Her?"

"The *Niña Sol*, the girl who inspired this painting," he answered, and again he gulped down his drink.

"And just what does the picture represent?" I inquired.

"The light of the *puna*."

I drank my sherry in silence.

"It's an incredible story," Jorge said. "You probably will not believe me, but I must tell it to someone. Some day you will tell it and no one will believe you either. But I have seen her, I have spoken to her, I shall see her tomorrow and every day. No, I am not drunk, or perhaps I am—with light. Listen. . . ."

The story issued from his lips slowly, hesitantly, as if it were a great effort to tell it. As he had told me earlier, Jorge had come to the *puna* determined to capture the light on his palette. For days he tried again and again to paint what he saw, but his brushes could only capture the form of things, not their light. He wanted the sun of the *puna* to be the protagonist of his pictures, as the air is in *Las Meninas* of Velázquez and the light in Rembrandt's paintings. His hobnailed boots had trod all the mountain paths, leaving behind, scattered everywhere, torn pieces of canvas bright with colors. Every day he climbed new hills always searching for light and more light. Until one afternoon . . .

". . . I had been walking all day in no special direction," said Jorge. "Both my feet and my thoughts were going round in circles. I went down a steep slope to the bottom of a narrow valley wedged between two high walls of rock. On all sides there was gray grass under a sun so luminous that being all light it gave no warmth. If only I could mix the sun on my palette and dip my brushes in it, I kept thinking. I walked the length of the narrow dell and came to a natural rock staircase that went up the opposite slope. I started the ascent. Halfway up I stopped. The side wall was perforated, forming a window in the rock through which I could see a path winding down to another little valley. On the other side of the valley there was a small hill and at the top of the hill a little house. And then, I saw her.

"The hill was like any other hill around here except for its brilliant yellow color, so brilliant that it glittered like burnished metal. Grass the color of new gold covered it completely. On top of the hill there was a small platform to which one climbed along a pathway covered with yellow pebbles. In the middle of the platform stood the little house with walls and roof of bright yellow straw. Yellow-hued flowers swayed in the breeze all around the house. In the midst of this blazing yellow paradise, silent and motionless, stood the girl.

"At first I thought she was a statue. My eyes were so blinded by the sun, which reverberated on the hill and on the house as on a mirror, that I barely saw her silhouette. But after a while, with my hands shading my eyes, I was able to see her quite clearly. She was almost a child, dressed in a sleeveless blouse and a short skirt which glistened as if made of gold. At first I thought she was wearing a helmet on her head, but then I realized that it was her blonde hair on which the sun broke into myriad luminous sparks. But what left me spellbound was her skin. I cannot give you even a remote idea of the color of her arms, her bare legs, her face. They were of the same golden shade as the paradise that surrounded her, but with a gossamer quality, a transparency, an iridescence, that was not of this earth. It was as though she were standing on a blazing throne of gold and she herself were made of such fiery gold that mortal eyes were not meant to look at her and retain their sight.

"When she saw me, she waved an arm. Her loose hair fluttered in the wind like a flaming banner. She showed no surprise; indeed, her greeting was the cheerful welcome accorded to an expected guest. The wings of the wind brought me the merry twinkling of her laughter.

"I remained sitting astride the stone window, unable to move, breathing with difficulty. I cannot explain what I felt. My whole being urged me to go to the girl, but my body refused to move. My eyes would never have withstood the blazing light the hill exhaled under the sun.

"I must have sat there for hours, watching her face turned toward the sun, her eyes wide open. Had she not waved to me, I would have thought her blind, so completely undisturbed were her eyes by the sun.

"When the sun went down she rose and simultaneously a flock of yellow birds, up to then invisible but whose singing had been audible all the time, took flight. For an instant she stood surrounded by dozens of yellow flapping wings like a flame surrounded by eager moths. She then looked at me, waved her hand in farewell and disappeared into the house.

"Only then was I able to move. Half blinded, my entire body burning from the sun, I fled from the place. Instinct must have brought me here. It was night when I arrived.

"The next day and the day after that and still another day I returned to the opening in the rock. And every day the same thing happened. Although at night, throughout the endless hours of insomnia, I swore to myself that the next day I would go up the golden hill and talk to the Sun Girl, as soon as I reached the window in the rock I was again overcome by the same strange paralysis."

The painter mechanically picked up his glass. On the wall his lifted hand projected a monstrous shadow like that of a bat. Through the window the cool night air brought a breath of sanity and reality. The candle flickered wildly and our shadows danced a saraband on the walls. The painter's eyes were burning coals in his shadowed face.

"On the fourth day," he continued, "as soon as I reached the opening I realized that something was different. The girl, wearing a cape this time, sat on the grass weaving a wicker basket. The hill, the house, the flowers, everything was the same. Nevertheless, something had changed. The sun was as brilliant as ever, yet I did not feel the strange sensation that had transfixed me to the window on previous days. And before I realized it I was running down the other side of the stone window, crossing the narrow valley, and, with my heart beating wildly, climbing the little path lined with yellow pebbles.

"When I reached the top of the hill, the girl, smiling, motioned me to sit on the grass a few steps from where she herself was sitting. Her fingers, swiftly and with great skill, kept on braiding the wicker. Birds sang softly all around us. I stared enraptured at her lovely face. Droplets of sun had fallen in her eyes and her skin had a golden luminescence.

" 'You seem surprised,' she finally said in a musical Spanish.

" 'I believe I'm dreaming,' I answered in my faltering Spanish.

" 'Why?' she laughed. 'I am flesh and blood and there is

nothing strange about your presence here. I was expecting you.'

" 'You were expecting me?'

" 'Of course. You looked at me from afar long enough. It was time you made up your mind to come. But I was to blame. Only today did I realize what held you back, and I remedied it.'

"She ignored the astonishment on my face.

" 'You are very sunburned,' she remarked.

" 'It does not matter now that I am here. I don't know why, but I'm glad I came.'

" 'I know why you came. You're looking for light and you came to it.' She pointed to my paintbox. 'Show me your paintings.'

"I unrolled one of my canvases and showed it to her. She looked at it from where she was sitting.

" 'Just what do you want to paint?' she asked.

" 'I don't know. This land, the colors—they fascinate me.'

"Her laughter ran down my spine like a rivulet of silver.

" 'The colors! There is *no* color on the *puna*. Only light.'

" 'Everything here is yellow, all shades of yellow and gold,' I protested.

" 'Everything here is sunlight,' she corrected. 'You think it's yellow because that has always been the color of the sun for painters. But there are no colors here. The house, the birds, the flowers, I, myself—we all are soaked in light. Everything here is sun. This is Peru, the land of the sun, and the *puna* is the closest to the sun. That is why you came here. Without knowing it, you have been following the sun, just as birds fly thousands of miles following the sun. You began seeking color for your paintings and you ended seeking the sun.'

" 'I would gladly give my life if I could paint the light of the sun,' I said.

" 'Why don't you try?'

" 'I have tried but I failed. The color escapes me. If one cannot even look at the sun, how can one paint it?'

" 'I shall help you,' she said with a mocking little laugh. 'I know nothing about painting but I have trod the path of light many times.'

"Leaning toward me, she took my paintbox and pressed

it against her breast as if it were a doll. She then gave it back to me.

" 'You shall now paint the light, and to say the light is to say the sun.' "

Jorge pointed to the canvas he had shown me.

"This is what I have been painting ever since. It means nothing to you, but I know that I am far on the road to capturing the light of the sun on my palette."

"Do you know who this girl is?" I asked in a skeptical tone.

"I don't know. I asked her once. She laughed and answered, 'Does one ask a rock or a mountain what it is? Does one ask the grass or the light? I am as the *puna*, as the condor, the llama and the alpaca, as the pumpkin and the casave—we are all children of the Sun. Pachacama gave life to the Sun and the Sun gave life to me, the *Niña Sol*. My brothers and sisters, the Quechuan *ayllúa*, worshipped the Sun, and later the Incas had a court of virgins, Vestals of the Sun. For many centuries my people lived under the laws of the Sun. What glorious times those were! They danced the *kashua*, and on their clothes, on their metals, even in their liquor, there was a drop of sun.

" 'After the great massacre—even the Sun was dyed vermillion—after the bearded men who came with sword and cross from across the sea had impaled the heads of the last Incas on their pikes, the City of Kings was born in the valley, but the Sun was lost. Only this hill remains, by the will of the first god, Pachacama, and from it one day the lost empire will be born again.' "

"The girl is mad!" I cried out, in my excitement knocking down my glass of sherry. "Can't you see? She is playing the heroine in a tale of fantasy."

Jorge's face turned deathly pale. "At first," he answered, "I, too, thought the same thing, but these canvases—Can't you see? There is light in them! Oh, I'm sure you're wrong. I know you're wrong. When I'm with her I feel as if I am in another world. When I set foot on the hill where she lives something happens—how shall I explain it to you? Time does not exist there, it disappears in a strange relativity, it becomes fused with the clouds, with the sun. Please, please, try to understand."

He nervously pulled an old silver watch out of his pocket.

"See this watch? Today, when I was with her, I took it out to look at the time. She asked me what it was and when I told her she didn't know what a watch was. She asked me to let her look at it and I placed it on the grass near her, for she never allows me to come too close to her. She took it and examined it and finally put it back on the grass and said, 'How strange! You measure time with *that* and yet you called my ancestors savages.'

"There was a sharp note of anger in her voice. Your face, mine, gets red when flushed. Hers turned into a mask of incandescent gold.

" 'You presume to capture time in that absurd little box!' she exclaimed. 'Don't you know yet that time is reckoned not by duration but by intensity? One instant of happiness or of pain lasts longer than ten years of indifference.'

"Pointing to the sun, she said with deep fervor, 'There is the measure of time. According to you, my age should be marked off by that silly little instrument. What madness! Does the sun have an age? Throw away your little metal box and with it your fear of time!' "

With a cry of anguish, Jorge tossed the watch on the table.

"Why am I telling you all this? You can't possibly understand. Can't you see that I am not the same man you met only a few days ago? The Sun Girl has changed my whole life. But you probably don't even believe me. Why have I told you all this?"

"Shall I tell you why?" I answered. "Because you know that that poor girl is mad, that she's playing the part of the Ophelia of the *puna*, that she's no more a fragment of sun than you or I."

What happened then still makes me shiver. The dying candle flickered wildly with a hissing noise and then went out, leaving the room in total darkness. I got up to fetch another candle when Jorge, grabbing my arm, cried out, "Look! The watch! On the table!"

I had already seen it, and wide-eyed I stared at it. In the darkness, the watch was an incandescent ball of such radiance that my eyes could not bear to look at it for long. It was no longer a watch; it was a tiny sun.

Jorge snatched the watch from the table and brought it close to his face. Above the glowing brilliance of the object, he looked at me with wild eyes.

"Now do you believe me?" he shouted. "Now do you believe in her? She held this watch in her hands for one moment only and look at it now! It's a sun, a miniature sun!"

"I am sure that we can explain this rationally," I replied in a tremulous voice. "Give me the watch."

I took it in my hands with some fear, but the watch was cold to the touch. The radiation of light was uniform on both crystal and silver. The light was yellowish, like that of the sun on an autumn day. I rubbed it against my jacket and then against my hands, but it produced no phosphorescence, which eliminated the explanation that had occurred to me.

Jorge was now standing close to me and I could feel the intense heat exuded by his body.

"She said to me," he whispered, "that she carried within her the sun of centuries, that she was all light—*la Niña Sol*, she called herself. Now I understand. When I showed her my painting—He stopped abruptly and then cried, "My paintings, she touched them, she touched my box of paints—"

He seized the roll of canvases from the table and quickly unrolled them. The same thing happened again. The canvases glowed with masses of light, a radiant light, big round blobs of it, as if the canvases were soaked in sun. I passed my hand over them but felt nothing, nor did the light adhere to my skin.

Jorge burst out into wild laughter, rolled up the paintings, and, still laughing, left the room, the roll under his arm and the watch in his hand. I remained facing the closed door, surrounded by darkness, watching through the cracks in the door a patch of bright light slowly move away until it vanished completely.

The next morning I woke up after a short restless sleep preceded by long hours of tossing. The smell of coffee was a reassuring sign of reality. Jorge's door was ajar, and I could see that the young painter had already left.

I ate my breakfast with little appetite and spent the day walking back and forth around the inn, wondering all the time where the hill of the Sun Girl might be. In daylight, the events of the night before seemed like a dream.

Impatiently I saw night descending. Seated by the fire, the old women whispered to each other. I asked questions. No one knew of the hill of the sun nor of any other dwelling in the neighborhood, but then, they admitted that for years they had not been beyond the esplanade on which their llamas grazed.

I retired to my room and opened a book, which I made no attempt to read. I was waiting for the painter. It was not until much later that I heard a noise on the floor below. I ran down the stairs. Jorge was seated by the fire, his eyes staring at the glowing embers. When he saw me he greeted me with a vague nod of the head and continued gazing at the fire.

"What happened today?" I asked, sitting down next to him.

Jorge was so self-absorbed that I had to repeat my question.

"I'm leaving tonight," he replied, kicking a burned log, which fell apart, shooting forth a shower of sparkling stars.

"Where are you going? To Lima?"

He turned to me, and the sight of his face made me gasp. Gone was the deranged look of the night before, gone were the lines of emaciation, the haunted expression, the anguish, the undefined doubts. His face was now radiant with peace. It was sweet and serene. It was the face of one who had received divine grace.

"I'm going with her," he said quietly. "We shall be together forever, and I shall have what no other painter ever had. I shall have light."

There was no maniacal exaltation in his voice. I tried to introduce a note of reality into our strange dialogue.

"Did you tell the Sun Girl what happened last night with the watch and the paintings?"

Jorge smiled a smile of pity, as if he were far above the picayune problems that worried me.

"Yes, I told her," he answered with a voice of condescension. " 'If we dip an object in paint,' she said, 'does it not come out the color of the paint?' To anything she touches she gives her own light."

"But how is it," I asked, making an effort to speak of

this fantastic thing calmly, "that during the day your Sun Girl does not shine like the sun?"

"Because her light is scattered in the atmosphere as that of the sun itself," he replied. "But," he added impatiently, "I'm not concerned about these petty problems that trouble you so much. I'm not looking for tricks. I am a painter who all his life has looked for light and now has found it. I have come for my things and I shall then go to her immediately. I shall live forever on the hill of light with the Sun Girl. Together we shall complete each other. She has in her flesh and soul the solar light that once was religion and law to her race. God has granted me what Rembrandt only adumbrated. He has granted me light. If you," he added almost in a whisper, "had held in your hands, as I did today, the hands of the Sun Girl, if, as I did, you had felt like Parsifal holding the Holy Grail, you would understand why I must return to her."

He got up with a gesture of finality that forbade further talk and walked toward the stairs. When he reached the stairs I uttered a cry. In the darkness of the staircase, which lay beyond the circle of light cast by the fire, both his hands glowed with a bright yellow light. I saw them—two stars of golden fire, ten flaming points—suspended in mid-air as he raised them close to his face to examine them.

"Does it frighten you?" he said quietly. "I told you I held her hands in mine. Tomorrow my whole body will shine with the same light as hers."

A moment later I heard him moving in his room on the floor above. I sat by the fire, biting on my dead pipe. The logs in the hearth snapped and crackled and the brooding cat stared at me with severe eyes. I tried to marshal in my mind everything the painter had told me, seeking in vain a few straws of reality with which to solve the mystery. Heavy boots tramping down the stairs interrupted my thoughts. Jorge came down, his knapsack on his shoulder, a handful of brushes protruding like arrows from the quiver of a wandering archer.

"May I go with you part of the way?" I asked him when he held out his hand.

He shrugged his shoulders. "I won't mind it if you promise not to preach."

"Have no fear," I promised, opening the door of the house.

We walked in silence a long time. The night was cold and remote like a Nordic bride. The stars were but a spangling dust scattered on the dark blue of the sky. The *puna* was in deep sleep. The only noise was made by our boots crushing the damp grass, which shone like polished metal under the pale moon, and the wind, which panted like a tired alpaca.

"Jorge," I finally said, "all this must have a logical explanation."

"Everything in life," he retorted mockingly, "has two explanations: the materialistic—call it scientific if you wish —which is neither complete nor true, and the poetic, which gets to the innermost truth of things. Freud never knew as much about dreams as Poe, nor doctors as much about love as Byron. I only know that my dream has come true. I don't have to burden it with pseudoscientific explanations."

"Couldn't it be," I proceeded, ignoring his words, "that this hill of light of yours contains an unknown radioactive mineral? As time went by, everything on that hill—rocks, flowers, birds—took on the light of that mineral. Even a human being, after years of being charged, like an electric battery, with radioactivity, might have absorbed the light and might communicate it. If this is so, there may be no danger for the girl, but there might be for anyone who came in sudden close contact with her."

He stopped abruptly. "That's all very fantastic," he interrupted me angrily.

"It is not fantastic. You may be in danger. Look at your hands. She touched them only a moment and look how they glow. Tomorrow they may become numb and the next day they may fall off, burned by that satanic force that now illuminates them. Have you thought of what might happen to you when you come close to the Sun Girl, when you touch her, when you embrace her?"

"Be quiet!" he shouted. I paid no attention to him.

"Has it occurred to you that the arms of the Sun Girl, or whatever the devil she is, might make you burn to death horribly?"

I thought he would attack me, so furious did he look,

but suddenly his face relaxed and when he spoke his voice was again quiet.

"Think what you like," he said. "I only know that I have found the source of light and to it I must go though I perish. A woman of light! The only survivor of the extinct Vestals of the Sun. She will give light even to my heart. Even if her embrace were followed by death, can you imagine a more glorious death for a painter? To love the Sun Girl, to embrace her body of light, to drink sunshine from her lips! To die in the embrace of the Sun, to have light within one—that is not death. That is life!"

Only then did I realize that we were standing before the opening in the barrier of rock described by Jorge. He held out his hand and I shook it silently. The moon, stiff with cold, put on a shawl of clouds, engulfing us in partial darkness. The silence was hushed and solemn like that of an empty cradle. Suddenly Jorge gripped my arm with painful violence.

"Look! Over there!" he cried hoarsely.

Opposite us, on the hill looming darkly on the other side of the passage, a statue of light had suddenly appeared. There was nothing frightening about it. Slender and feminine, with flesh a shimmering gold, it was like a block of sun sculptured into the glorious figure of a woman.

"She's going away!" Jorge cried. "She's going away!"

The girl with a slow step disappeared down the other side of the hill. Jorge, shouting after her, plunged through the darkness. I heard him scrambling wildly down to the bottom of the passage, and, hesitating no longer, I ran after him.

I shall never forget that nightmarish race in the dark, scrambling from rock to rock, stumbling down, tearing my clothes and my flesh on the jagged stones. On my hands and knees, still lagging behind Jorge, whom I could hear calling the Sun Girl in the distance, I crossed the bottom of the passage and gropingly sought the way to the top of the hill. In the dark shadows I suddenly saw the path lined with pebbles gleaming with a faint yellow light leading to the golden dollhouse above. Panting, I reached the top of the hill. Jorge stood motionless on the edge of the platform, staring down at the vast black chasm gaping at his feet.

"Jorge," I called, running toward him across a carpet of flowers that glistened like golden crystal.

When I reached his side, he looked at me with eyes filled with despair.

"She's gone, down there," he said in a sobbing voice. "She, too, must have been afraid, afraid to harm me, to consume me in her light. She didn't know that I would gladly give my life to embrace the light of her flesh, to kiss the sun from her lips. But I shall follow her—to the end of the earth, if need be. Look."

He pointed to the ground and I cried out in amazement. Wherever the Sun Girl's feet had trod, they had left footprints as small as those of a child but resplendent in their golden light.

"If I fail to find her before daybreak," Jorge added, I shall wait until night returns, again and again. I shall not rest until I find her. For I do not want life without her. Goodbye, my friend. In the nights to come, until she and I meet, I shall be wandering after her."

And he disappeared down the trail of glowing footsteps.

❦ URSULA K. LE GUIN ❦
(1929 —)

Ursula K. Le Guin, author of numerous award-winning works of science fiction and fantasy literature, established herself, in little more than ten years, as one of America's finest writers. Born in Berkeley, California, the daughter of anthropologist A. L. Kroeber and writer Theodora Kroeber, she received her B.A. from Radcliffe College in 1951 and her M.A. from Columbia University in 1952. A year later, while studying in Paris on a Fulbright Fellowship, she met and married Charles A. Le Guin, an historian. Since the mid-1960s Le Guin has not only maintained a remarkably prolific and brilliant literary career, but has also participated in numerous professional activities and conventions, as well as serving as leader of various writing workshops, including University of Washington's Science Fiction Writer's Workshop. The Le Guins now live in Portland, Oregon, with their family.

Although Le Guin has remarked that she has been writing science fiction and fantasy literature since the age of six, the success of her professional literary career was not assured until 1966, when her first novel, *Rocannon's World,* was published. This science fiction work was followed by a number of others in the same genre: *Planet of Exile* (1966), *City of Illusions* (1967), *The Left Hand of Darkness* (1969), *The Lathe of Heaven* (1971), and more recently, *The Dispossessed* (1974). Illustrative of the high quality of her writing is the fact that *The Left Hand of Darkness* and *The Dispossessed* each received both the Hugo and Nebula awards, the highest honors that can be bestowed upon an sf author.

Her short fiction has fared equally well, with "The Day Before the Revolution" (1974) receiving both the Nebula and

197

Jupiter awards, and "The Ones Who Walk Away from Omelas" (1973) earning a Hugo. In the realm of fantasy literature, Le Guin has published the popular and critically acclaimed *Earthsea Trilogy*, which consists of *A Wizard of Earthsea* (1968 — ALA Notable Book), *The Tombs of Atuan* (1971 — Newberry Honor Book), and *The Farthest Shore* (1972 — National Book Award in children's literature). Moreover, she has published a collection of short stories (containing both sf and fantasy) entitled *The Wind's Twelve Quarters* (1975), a novel, *The Word for World is Forest* (1976), a novelette, *Very Far Away from Anywhere Else* (1976), and *Wild Angels* (1975) a collection of poetry. As might be expected, in the past few years more and more scholarly articles and books have been published about Le Guin's work, including a special Le Guin issue of *Science Fiction Studies* (November, 1975) and George Edgar Slusser's *The Farthest Shores of Ursula Le Guin* (1976).

In her preface to "April in Paris," which appears in *The Wind's Twelve Quarters*, Ursula Le Guin states that: "This is the first story I ever got paid for; the second story I ever got published; and maybe the thirtieth or fortieth story I ever wrote." It is obviously a rather special story to Le Guin, and a special one to us as well. Le Guin has the knack of blending realism and fantasy with extraordinary effect. She manages to create a unique tone and atmosphere in this high fantasy by involving the painfully believable Professor Barry Pennyfeather from Munson College, Indiana, in the black magic of Jehan Lenoir.

This is essentially a humorous story, full of Le Guin's delightful brand of sly wit and biting irony. But it displays a serious side as well, because ultimately this is a story about loneliness. And it is Le Guin's clever but compassionate and understanding treatment of the suffering experienced by social misfits, the "different" of any society, that makes the story so meaningful and moving. The reader cannot help but rejoice with the two very strange, but contented, couples who stroll happily on the banks of the river Seine at the conclusion of this tale.

April in Paris
Ursula K. Le Guin

❦

Professor Barry Pennywither sat in a cold, shadowy garret and stared at the table in front of him, on which lay a book and a breadcrust. The bread had been his dinner, the book had been his lifework. Both were dry. Dr. Pennywither sighed, and then shivered. Though the lower-floor apartments of the old house were quite elegant, the heat was turned off on April 1st, come what may; it was now April 2nd and sleeting. If Dr. Pennywither raised his head a little he could see from his window the two square towers of Notre Dame de Paris, vague and soaring in the dusk, almost near enough to touch: for the Island of Saint-Louis, where he lived, is like a little barge being towed downstream behind the Island of the City, where Notre Dame stands. But he did not raise his head. He was too cold.

The great towers sank into darkness. Dr. Pennywither sank into gloom. He stared with loathing at his book. It had won him a year in Paris—publish or perish, said the Dean of Faculties, and he had published, and been rewarded with a year's leave from teaching, without pay. Munson College could not afford to pay unteaching teachers. So on his scraped-up savings he had come back to Paris, to live again as a student in a garret, to read fifteenth-century manuscripts at the Library, to see the chestnuts flower along the avenues. But it hadn't worked. He was forty, too old for lonely garrets. The sleet would blight the budding chestnut flowers. And he was sick of his work. Who cared about his theory, the Pennywither Theory, concerning the mysterious disappearance of the poet François Villon in 1463? Nobody. For after all his

199

Theory about poor Villon, the greatest juvenile delinquent of all time, was only a theory and could never be proved, not across the gulf of five hundred years. Nothing could be proved. And besides, what did it matter if Villon died on Montfaucon gallows or (as Pennywither thought) in a Lyons brothel on the way to Italy? Nobody cared. Nobody else loved Villon enough. Nobody loved Dr. Pennywither, either; not even Dr. Pennywither. Why should he? An unsocial, unmarried, underpaid pedant, sitting here alone in an unheated attic in an unrestored tenement trying to write another unreadable book. "I'm unrealistic," he said aloud with another sigh and another shiver. He got up and took the blanket off his bed, wrapped himself in it, sat down thus bundled at the table, and tried to light a Gauloise Bleue. His lighter snapped vainly. He sighed once more, got up, fetched a can of vile-smelling French lighter fluid, sat down, rewrapped his cocoon, filled the lighter, and snapped it. The fluid had spilled around a good bit. The lighter lit, so did Dr. Pennywither, from the wrists down. "Oh hell!" he cried, blue flames leaping from his knuckles, and jumped up batting his arms wildly, shouting "Hell!" and raging against Destiny. Nothing ever went right. What was the use? It was then 8:12 on the night of April 2nd, 1961.

A man sat hunched at a table in a cold, high room. Through the window behind him the two square towers of Notre Dame loomed in the Spring dusk. In front of him on the table lay a hunk of cheese and a huge, iron-latched, handwritten book. The book was called (in Latin) *On the Primacy of the Element Fire over the Other Three Elements*. It's author stared at it with loathing. Nearby on a small iron stove a small alembic simmered. Jehan Lenoir mechanically inched his chair nearer the stove now and then, for warmth, but his thoughts were on deeper problems. "Hell!" he said finally (in Late Mediaeval French), slammed the book shut, and got up. What if his theory was wrong? What if water were the primal element? How could you prove these things? There must be some way—some method—so that one could be sure, absolutely sure, of one single fact! But each fact led into others, a monstrous tangle, and the Authorities conflicted, and anyway no one would read his book, not even the wretched pedants at the Sorbonne. They smelled heresy. What was the use? What good this life spent in poverty and alone, when he had learned nothing, merely guessed and theoerized? He strode about the garret, raging, and then stood still. "All right!" he said to Destiny. "Very good! You've given me nothing, so I'll take what I want!" He went to one of the stacks of books that covered most of the floor-space, yanked out a bottom volume (scarring the leather and bruising his knuckles when the overlying folios avalanched), slapped it on the table and began to study one page of it. Then, still with a set cold look of rebellion, he got things ready: sulfur, silver, chalk. . . . Though the room was dusty and littered, his little workbench was neatly and handily arranged. He was soon ready. Then he paused. "This is ridiculous," he muttered, glancing out the window into the darkness where now one could only guess at the two square towers. A watchman passed below calling out the hour, eight o'clock of a cold clear night. It was so still he could hear the lapping of the Seine. He shrugged, frowned, took up the chalk and drew a neat pentagram on the floor near his table, then took up the book and began to read in a clear but self-conscious voice: "Haere, haere, audi me . . . " It was a long spell, and mostly nonsense. His voice sank. He stood bored and embarrassed. He hurried through the last words, shut the book, and then fell backwards against the door, gap-mouthed, staring at the enormous shapeless figure that stood within the pentagram, lit only by the blue flicker of its waving, fiery claws.

Barry Pennywither finally got control of himself and put out the fire by burying his hands in the folds of the blanket wrapped around him. Unburned but upset, he sat down again. He looked at his book. Then he stared at it. It was no longer thin and grey and titled *The Last Years of Villon*: *an Investigation of Possibilities*. It was thick and brown and titled *Incantatoria Magna*. On his table? A priceless manuscript dating from 1407 of which the only extant undamaged copy was in the Ambrosian Library in Milan. He looked slowly around. His mouth dropped slowly open. He observed a stove, a chemist's workbench, two or three dozen heaps of unbelievable leatherbound books, the window, the door. His window, his door. But crouching against his door was a little creature, black and shapeless, from which came a dry rattling sound.

Barry Pennywither was not a very brave man, but he was rational. He thought he had lost his mind, and so he said quite steadily, "Are you the Devil?"

The creature shuddered and rattled.

Experimentally, with a glance at invisible Notre Dame, the professor made the sign of the Cross.

At this the creature twitched; not a flinch, a twitch. Then it said something, feebly, but in perfectly good English—no, in perfectly good French—no, in rather odd French: "Mais vous estes de Dieu," it said.

Barry got up and peered at it. "Who are you?" he demanded, and it lifted up a quite human face and answered meekly, "Jehan Lenoir."

"What are you doing in my room?"

There was a pause. Lenoir got up from his knees and stood straight, all five foot two of him. "This is *my* room," he said at last, though very politely.

Barry looked around at the books and alembics. There was another pause. "Then how did I get here?"

"I brought you."

"Are you a doctor?"

Lenoir nodded, with pride. His whole air had changed. "Yes, I'm a doctor," he said. "Yes, I brought you here. If Nature will yield me no knowledge, then I can conquer Nature herself, I can work a miracle! To the Devil with science, then. I was a scientist—" he glared at Barry. "No longer! They call me a fool, a heretic, well by God I'm worse! I'm a sorcerer, a black magician, Jehan the Black! Magic works, does it? Then science is a waste of time. Ha!" he said, but he did not really look triumphant. "I wish it hadn't worked," he said more quietly, pacing up and down between folios.

"So do I," said the guest.

"Who are you?" Lenoir looked up challengingly at Barry, though there was nearly a foot difference in their heights.

"Barry A. Pennywither. I'm a professor of French at

Munson College, Indiana, on leave in Paris to pursue my studies of Late Mediaeval Fr—" He stopped. He had just realized what kind of accent Lenoir had. "What year is this? What century? Please, Dr. Lenoir—" The Frenchman looked confused. The meanings of words change, as well as their pronunciations. "Who rules this country?" Barry shouted.

Lenoir gave a shrug, a French shrug (some things never change). "Louis is king," he said. "Louis the Eleventh. The dirty old spider."

They stood staring at each other like wooden Indians for some time. Lenoir spoke first. "Then you're a man?"

"Yes. Look, Lenoir, I think you—your spell—you must have muffed it a bit."

"Evidently," said the alchemist. "Are you French?"

"No."

"Are you English?" Lenoir glared. "Are you a filthy Goddam?"

"No. No. I'm from America. I'm from the—from your future. From the twentieth century A.D." Barry blushed. It sounded silly, and he was a modest man. But he knew this was no illusion. The room he stood in, his room, was new. Not five centuries old. Unswept, but new. And the copy of Albertus Magnus by his knee was new, bound in soft supple calfskin, the gold lettering gleaming. And there stood Lenoir in his black gown, not in costume, at home. . . .

"Please sit down, sir," Lenoir was saying. And he added with the fine though absent courtesy of the poor scholar, "Are you tired from the journey? I have bread and cheese, if you'll honor me by sharing it."

They sat at the table munching bread and cheese. At first Lenoir tried to explain why he had tried black magic. "I was fed up," he said. "Fed up! I've slaved in solitude since I was twenty, for what? For knowledge. To learn some of Nature's secrets. They are not to be learned." He drove his knife half an inch into the table, and Barry jumped. Lenoir was a thin little fellow, but evidently a passionate one. It was a fine face, though pale and lean: intelligent, alert, vivid. Barry was reminded of the face of a famous atomic physicist, seen in newspaper pictures up until 1953. Somehow this likeness prompted him to say, "Some are, Lenoir; we've learned a good bit, here and there. . . ."

"What?" said the alchemist, skeptical but curious.

"Well, I'm no scientist—"

"Can you make gold?" He grinned as he asked.

"No, I don't think so, but they do make diamonds."

"How?"

"Carbon—coal, you know—under great heat and pressure, I believe. Coal and diamond are both carbon, you know, the same element."

"Element?"

"Now as I say, I'm no—"

"Which is the primal element?" Lenoir shouted, his eyes fiery, the knife poised in his hand.

"There are about a hundred elements," Barry said coldly, hiding his alarm.

Two hours later, having squeezed out of Barry every dribble of the remnants of his college chemistry course, Lenoir rushed out into the night and reappeared shortly with a bottle. "O my master," he cried, "to think I offered you only bread and cheese!" It was a pleasant burgundy, vintage 1477, a good year. After they had drunk a glass together Lenoir said, "If somehow I could repay you . . ."

"You can. Do you know the name of the poet François Villon?"

"Yes," Lenoir said with some surprise, "but he wrote only French trash, you know, not in Latin."

"Do you know how or when he died?"

"Oh, yes; hanged at Montfaucon here in '64 or '65, with a crew of no-goods like himself. Why?"

Two hours later the bottle was dry, their throats were dry, and the watchman had called three o'clock of a cold clear morning. "Jehan, I'm worn out," Barry said, "you'd better send me back." The alchemist was too polite, too grateful, and perhaps also too tired to argue. Barry stood stiffly inside the pentagram, a tall bony figure muffled in a brown blanket, smoking a Gauloise Bleue. "Adieu," Lenoir said sadly. "Au revoir," Barry replied. Lenoir began to read the spell backwards. The candle flickered, his voice softened. "Me audi, haere, haere," he read, sighed, and looked up. The pentagram was empty. The

candle flickered. "But I learned so little!" Lenoir cried
out to the empty room. Then he beat the open book with
his fists and said, "And a friend like that—a real friend—"
He smoked one of the cigarettes Barry had left him—he
had taken to tobacco at once. He slept, sitting at his
table, for a couple of hours. When he woke he brooded
a while, relit his candle, smoked the other cigarette, then
opened the *Incantatoria* and began to read aloud: "Haere,
haere . . ."

"Oh, thank God," Barry said, stepping quickly out of
the pentagram, and grasping Lenoir's hand. "Listen, I
got back there—this room, this same room, Jehan! but
old, horribly old, and empty, you weren't there—I
thought, my God, what have I done? I'd sell my soul to
get back there, to him—What can I do with what I've
learned? Who'll believe it? How can I prove it? And who
the devil could I tell it to anyhow? Who cares? I couldn't
sleep, I sat and cried for an hour—"

"Will you stay?"

"Yes. Look, I brought these—in case you did invoke
me." Sheepishly he exhibited eight packs of Gauloises,
several books, and a gold watch. "It might fetch a price,"
he explained. "I knew paper francs wouldn't do much
good."

At sight of the printed books Lenoir's eyes gleamed
with curiosity, but he stood still. "My friend," he said,
"you said you'd sell your soul . . . you know . . . so
would I. Yet we haven't. How—after all—how did this
happen? That we're both men. No devils. No pacts in
blood. Two men who've lived in this room . . ."

"I don't know," said Barry. "We'll think that out later.
Can I stay with you, Jehan?"

"Consider this your home," Lenoir said with a gracious gesture around the room, the stacks of books, the
alembics, the candle growing pale. Outside the window,
grey on grey, rose up the two great towers of Notre Dame.
It was the dawn of April 3rd.

After breakfast (bread crusts and cheese rinds) they
went out and climbed the south tower. The cathedral
looked the same as always, though cleaner than in 1961,
but the view was rather a shock to Barry. He looked

down upon a little town. Two small islands covered with houses; on the right bank more houses crowded inside a fortified wall; on the left bank a few streets twisting around the college; and that was all. Pigeons chortled on the sun-warmed stone between gargoyles. Lenoir, who had seen the view before, was carving the date (in Roman numerals) on a parapet. "Let's celebrate," he said. "Let's go out into the country. I haven't been out of the city for two years. Let's go clear over there—" he pointed to a misty green hill on which a few huts and a windmill were just visible— "to Montmartre, eh? There are some good bars there, I'm told."

Their life soon settled into an easy routine. At first Barry was a little nervous in the crowded streets, but, in a spare black gown of Lenoir's, he was not noticed as outlandish except for his height. He was probably the tallest man in fifteenth-century France. Living standards were low and lice were unavoidable, but Barry had never valued comfort much; the only thing he really missed was coffee at breakfast. When they had bought a bed and a razor—Barry had forgotten his—and introduced him to the landlord as M. Barrie, a cousin of Lenoir's from the Auvergne, their housekeeping arrangements were complete. Barry's watch brought a tremendous price, four gold pieces, enough to live on for a year. They sold it as a wondrous new timepiece from Illyria, and the buyer, a Court chamberlain looking for a nice present to give the king, looked at the inscription—Hamilton Bros., New Haven, 1881—and nodded sagely. Unfortunately he was shut up in one of King Louis's cages for naughty courtiers at Tours before he had presented his gift, and the watch may still be there behind some brick in the ruins of Plessis; but this did not affect the two scholars. Mornings they wandered about sightseeing the Bastille and the churches, or visiting various minor poets in whom Barry was interested; after lunch they discussed electricity, the atomic theory, physiology, and other matters in which Lenoir was interested, and performed minor chemical and anatomical experiments, usually unsuccessfully; after supper they merely talked. Endless, easy talks that ranged over the centuries but always ended here, in the shadowy room with its window open to the Spring night, in their friendship. After two weeks they might have known each other all their lives. They were perfectly happy. They knew they would do nothing with what they had learned from each other. In 1961 how could Barry ever prove his knowledge of old Paris, in 1482 how could Lenoir ever prove the validity of the scientific method? It did not bother them. They had never really expected to be listened to. They had merely wanted to learn.

So they were happy for the first time in their lives; so happy, in fact, that certain desires always before subjugated to the desire for knowledge, began to awaken. "I don't suppose" Barry said one night across the table, "that you ever thought much about marrying?"

"Well, no," his friend answered, doubtfully. "That is, I'm in minor orders . . . and it seemed irrelevant. . . ."

"And expensive. Besides, in my time, no self-respecting woman would want to share my kind of life. American women are so damned poised and efficient and glamorous, terrifying creatures. . . ."

"And women here are little and dark, like beetles, with bad teeth," Lenoir said morosely.

They said no more about women that night. But the next night they did; and the next; and on the next, celebrating the successful dissection of the main nervous system of a pregnant frog, they drank two bottles of Montrachet '74 and got soused. "Let's invoke a woman, Jehan," Barry said in a lascivious bass, grinning like a gargoyle.

"What if I raised a devil this time?"

"Is there really much difference?"

They laughed wildly, and drew a pentagram. "Haere, haere" Lenoir began; when he got the hiccups, Barry took over. He read the last words. There was a rush of cold, marshy-smelling air, and in the pentagram stood a wild-eyed being with long black hair, stark naked, screaming.

"Woman, by God," said Barry.

"Is it?"

It was. "Here, take my cloak," Barry said, for the poor thing now stood gawping and shivering. He put the cloak over her shoulders. Mechanically she pulled it round her, muttering, "Gratias ago, domine."

"Latin!" Lenoir shouted. "A woman speaking Latin?"
It took him longer to get over that shock than it did Bota
to get over hers. She was, it seemed, a slave in the household of the Sub-Prefect of North Gaul, who lived on the
smaller island of the muddy island town called Lutetia.
She spoke Latin with a thick Celtic brogue, and did not
even know who was emperor in Rome in her day. A real
barbarian, Lenoir said with scorn. So she was, an ignorant, taciturn, humble barbarian with tangled hair, white
skin, and clear grey eyes. She had been waked from a
sound sleep. When they convinced her that she was not
dreaming, she evidently assumed that this was some prank
of her foreign and all-powerful master, the Sub-Prefect,
and accepted the situation without further question. "Am
I to serve you, my masters?" she inquired timidly but
without sullenness, looking from one to the other.

"Not me," Lenoir growled, and added in French to
Barry, "Go on; I'll sleep in the store-room." He departed.

Bota looked up at Barry. No Gauls, and few Romans,
were so magnificently tall; no Gauls and no Romans ever
spoke so kindly. "Your lamp" (it was a candle, but she
had never seen a candle) "is nearly burnt out," she said.
"Shall I blow it out?"

For an additional two sols a year the landlord let them
use the store-room as a second bedroom, and Lenoir now
slept alone again in the main room of the garret. He observed his friend's idyll with a brooding, unjealous interest. The professor and the slave-girl loved each other with
delight and tenderness. Their pleasure over-lapped Lenoir
in waves of protective joy. Bota had led a brutal life,
treated always as a woman but never as a human. In one
short week she bloomed, she came alive, evincing beneath
her gentle passiveness a cheerful, clever nature. "You're
turning out a regular Parisienne," he heard Barry accuse
her one night (the attic walls were thin). She replied, "If
you knew what it is for me not to be always defending
myself, always afraid, always alone . . ."

Lenoir sat up on his cot and brooded. About midnight,
when all was quiet, he rose and noiselessly prepared the
pinches of sulfur and silver, drew the pentagram, opened

the book. Very softly he read the spell. His face was apprehensive.

In the pentagram appeared a small white dog. It cowered and hung its tail, then came shyly forward, sniffed Lenoir's hand, looked up at him with liquid eyes and gave a modest, pleading whine. A lost puppy . . . Lenoir stroked it. It licked his hands and jumped all over him, wild with relief. On its white leather collar was a silver plaque engraved, "Jolie. Dupont, 36 rue de Seine, Paris VIe."

Jolie went to sleep, after gnawing a crust, curled up under Lenoir's chair. And the alchemist opened the book again and read, still softly, but this time without self-consciousness, without fear, knowing what would happen.

Emerging from his store-room-bedroom-honeymoon in the morning, Barry stopped short in the doorway. Lenoir was sitting up in bed, petting a white puppy, and deep in conversation with the person sitting on the foot of the bed, a tall red-haired woman dressed in silver. The puppy barked. Lenoir said, "Good morning!" The woman smiled wondrously.

"Jumping Jesus," Barry muttered (in English). Then he said, "Good morning. When are you from?" The effect was Rita Hayworth, sublimated—Hayworth plus the Mona Lisa, perhaps?

"From Altair, about seven thousand years from now," she said, smiling still more wondrously. Her French accent was worse than that of a football-scholarship freshman. "I'm an archaeologist. I was excavating the ruins of Paris III. I'm sorry I speak the language so badly; of course we know it only from inscriptions."

"From Altair? The star? But you're human—I think—"

"Our planet was colonized from Earth about four thousand years ago—that is, three thousand years from now." She laughed, most wondrously, and glanced at Lenoir. "Jehan explained it all to me, but I still get confused."

"It was a dangerous thing to try it again, Jehan!" Barry accused him. "We've been awfully lucky, you know."

"No," said the Frenchman. "Not lucky."

"But after all it's black magic you're playing with—
Listen—I don't know your name, madame."

"Kislk," she said.

"Listen, Kislk," Barry said without even a stumble,
"your science must be fantastically advanced—is there
any magic? Does it exist? Can the laws of Nature really
be broken, as we seem to be doing?"

"I've never seen nor heard of an authenticated case
of magic."

"Then what goes on?" Barry roared. "Why does that
stupid old spell work for Jehan, for us, that one spell,
and here, nowhere else, for nobody else, in five—no,
eight—no, fifteen thousand years of recorded history?
Why? Why? And where did that damn puppy come
from?"

"The puppy was lost," Lenoir said, his dark face grave.
"Somewhere near this house, on the Ile Saint-Louis."

"And I was sorting potsherds," Kislk said, also
gravely, "in a house-site, Island 2, Pit 4, Section D. A
lovely Spring day, and I hated it. Loathed it. The day,
the work, the people around me." Again she looked at the
gaunt little alchemist, a long, quiet look. "I tried to explain it to Jehan last night. We have improved the race,
you see. We're all very tall, healthy, and beautiful. No
fillings in our teeth. All skulls from Early America have
fillings in the teeth. . . . Some of us are brown, some
white, some gold-skinned. But all beautiful, and healthy,
and well-adjusted, and aggressive, and successful. Our
professions and degree of success are preplanned for us
in the State Pre-School Homes. But there's an occasional
genetic flaw. Me, for instance. I was trained as an
archaeologist because the Teachers saw that I really didn't
like people, live people. People bored me. All like me on
the outside, all alien to me on the inside. When everything's alike, which place is home? . . . But now I've seen
an unhygienic room with insufficient heating. Now I've
seen a cathedral not in ruins. Now I've met a living man
who's shorter than me, with bad teeth and a short
temper. Now I'm home, I'm where I can be myself, I'm
no longer alone!"

"Alone," Lenoir said gently to Barry. "Loneliness, eh?

Loneliness is the spell, loneliness is stronger. . . . Really it doesn't seem unnatural."

Bota was peering round the doorway, her face flushed between the black tangles of her hair. She smiled shyly and said a polite Latin good-morning to the newcomer.

"Kislk doesn't know Latin," Lenoir said with immense satisfaction. "We must teach Bota some French. French is the language of love, anyway, eh? Come along, let's go out and buy some bread. I'm hungry."

Kislk hid her silver tunic under the useful and anonymous cloak, while Lenoir pulled on his moth-eaten black gown. Bota combed her hair, while Barry thoughtfully scratched a louse-bite on his neck. Then they set forth to get breakfast. The alchemist and the interstellar archaeologist went first, speaking French; the Gaulish slave and the professor from Indiana followed, speaking Latin, and holding hands. The narrow streets were crowded, bright with sunshine. Above them Notre Dame reared its two square towers against the sky. Beside them the Seine rippled softly. It was April in Paris, and on the banks of the river the chestnuts were in bloom.

❦ ISAAC BASHEVIS SINGER ❦
(1904-1991)

Recipient of the Nobel Prize for literature in 1978, Isaac Bashevis Singer was the most prominent and popular Yiddish writer in the world today. His many stories and novels have been translated into dozens of languages, including Hebrew, French, Dutch, Norwegian, Finnish, Italian, German, and English. This international acceptance offers convincing proof that even though most of Singer's fiction deals with the somewhat esoteric culture of Polish Jewry of the past three centuries, it acquires universality through its sensitive treatment of common human concerns. Yiddish may be slowly dying, but there is no doubt that Singer's stories will live on.

Although Singer lived in the United States for most of his adult life, he was born in Radzymin, Poland, on July 14, 1904. His family was financially poor, but abundantly rich in religious heritage: Isaac's father and his maternal and paternal grandfathers were all rabbis. In 1908, the four-year-old Isaac moved with his family to a ghetto tenement in the Polish capital city of Warsaw. There his religious education began in earnest. Although he received his formal education from the Tachenioni Rabbinical Seminary, Singer probably learned as much, if not more, from the spirited discussions taking place in his own home. In a biographical statement made to *World Authors* Singer reminisces:

> My elder brother, I. J. Singer, who later wrote *The Brothers Ashkenazi*, began in Warsaw to paint, to write secular stories and to express doubts about the

213

> Jewish dogmas. My parents advocated religion with all their power and I listened to these discussions. In order to strengthen the cause of faith, my parents told many tales of *dybbuks*, possessions, haunted houses, wandering corpses. I was fascinated both with my brother's rationalism and with my parents' mysticism (p. 1321).

His parents' stories made a deep impression upon Singer and later became the raw material for much of his own fiction.

At the age of thirteen Singer moved, with his mother and younger brother, to the Jewish village of Bilgoray, the home of his maternal grandfather. He spent a few years in this tiny *shtetl*, and then in the early 1920s, returned to Warsaw to live with his older brother, Israel. From his early youth Isaac had been interested in literature and writing, and had already tried his hand at both poetry and short fiction, writing mostly in Hebrew. Now, while working as a proofreader for the *Literarishe Bletter*, he began practicing his craft in earnest, publishing several stories and book reviews in both Yiddish and Hebrew. He became more and more immersed in a literary life-style, becoming co-editor of the literary magazine *Globus*, in 1932. It was in this journal that sections of his first novel, *Satan in Goray*, were published, along with several of his early pieces of short fiction.

The mid-thirties were difficult years for Singer: his brother Israel, with whom he had established a very close relationship, moved to New York in 1934; ominous sounds were coming from Hitler's Germany; and Singer's wife, Rachel, had decided to become a Communist. By 1935 the situation had deteriorated to such an extent that Singer packed his few belongings and set sail for New York, leaving behind his job, his wife and son, and his beloved homeland. Once in New York he joined his brother, Israel, and began working as a columnist for the *Jewish Daily Forward*. It is in this publication, New York City's leading Yiddish newspaper, that most of Singer's fiction has first appeared. Singer became an American citizen in 1943 and subsequently lived with his second wife, Alma, in New York for much of his life.

Singer's literary output is indeed prodigious. He has written a number of fine novels, including *The Family Moskat* (1950), *Satan in Goray* (1955), *The Magician of Lublin* (1959), and *The Slave* (1962). Two other closely related novels, *The Manor* (1967) and *The Estate* (1969), were serialized as a single long work between 1952 and 1955. It is his short stories, however, for which Singer is best known. Some of his finest short fiction has been collected in such volumes as *Gimpel the Fool* (1957), *The Spinoza of Market Street* (1961), *Short Friday* (1964), *A Friend of Kafka* (1970), and the award-winning *A Crown of Feathers* (1973). His *A Day of Pleasure: Stories of a Boy Growing Up in Warsaw* received the 1970 National Book Award for children's literature as the best children's book of the year.

An anthology of Christian fantasy would not be complete without a story reflecting Christianity's rich Judaic literary heritage. "Jachid and Jechidah," embodying a number of tenets and concepts central to both Judaism and Christianity, is such a story. The key concept of reincarnation, or transmigration of souls, is one that, over the centuries, has provoked rather vehement disagreement among both Judaic and Christian theologians. This fact, we feel, makes "Jachid and Jechidah" all the more attractive as a selection.

The reader will find all of the Singer hallmarks in "Jachid and Jechidah": a vigorous, tightly woven narrative; evocative descriptions; and subtle character delineation. Perhaps the most intriguing aspect of the tale, however, is its use of reversal of perspective. Readers familiar with C. S. Lewis's description of Earth (*Out of the Silent Planet*) as a dead spot in a sea of space suffused with heavenly vitality and life will immediately see the similarity between this treatment of our planet and Singer's treatment in "Jachid and Jechidah." Lewis's Oyarsa reveals that Earth is the dominion of the Bent One (Satan) and calls it the "Silent Planet"; similarly, Singer has the Souls of Heaven refer to Earth as

Sheol, the abode of the dead. The reversal of perspective goes even further in Singer's tale: what we think of as life is really a kind of death, and what we usually consider to be death is really true life. "Death," we learn, "is a laboratory for the rehabilitation of souls"; a "preparation of a new existence." Page after page shocks us into seeing life and death from a different perspective. Have you ever, for example, considered the Earth as a "large necropolis where corpses are prepared for all kinds of mortuary functions"? "Jachid and Jechidah," a powerful moral fable, will force you to consider that very possibility.

Jachid and Jechidah
Issac Bashevis Singer
(Translated by Issac Bashevis Singer and Elizabeth Pollet)

❦

In a prison where souls bound for Sheol—Earth they call it there—await destruction, there hovered the female soul Jechidah. Souls forget their origin. Purah, the Angel of Forgetfulness, he who dissipates God's light and conceals His face, holds dominion everywhere beyond the Godhead. Jechidah, unmindful of her descent from the Throne of Glory, had sinned. Her jealousy had caused much trouble in the world where she dwelled. She had suspected all female angels of having affairs with her lover Jachid, had not only blasphemed God but even denied him. Souls, she said, were not created but had evolved out of nothing: they had neither mission nor purpose. Although the authorities were extremely patient and forgiving, Jechidah was finally sentenced to death. The judge fixed the moment of her descent to that cemetery called Earth.

The attorney for Jechidah appealed to the Superior Court of Heaven, even presented a petition to Metatron, the Lord of the Face. But Jechidah was so filled with sin and so impenitent that no power could save her. The attendants seized her, tore her from Jachid, clipped her wings, cut her hair, and clothed her in a long white shroud. She was no longer allowed to hear the music of the spheres, to smell the perfumes of Paradise and to meditate on the secrets of the Torah, which sustain the soul. She could no longer bathe in the wells of balsam oil. In the prison cell, the darkness of the nether world already surrounded her. But her greatest torment was her longing for Jachid. She could no longer reach him telepathically. Nor could she send a message to him, all of her servants having been taken away. Only the fear of death was left to Jechidah.

Death was no rare occurrence where Jechidah lived but it befell only vulgar, exhausted spirits. Exactly what hap-

217

pened to the dead, Jechidah did not know. She was convinced that when a soul descended to Earth it was to extinction, even though the pious maintained that a spark of life remained. A dead soul immediately began to rot and was soon covered with a slimy stuff called semen. Then a grave digger put it into a womb where it turned into some sort of fungus and was henceforth known as a child. Later on, began the tortures of Gehenna: birth, growth, toil. For according to the morality books, death was not the final stage. Purified, the soul returned to its source. But what evidence was there for such beliefs? So far as Jechidah knew, no one had ever returned from Earth. The enlightened Jechidah believed that the soul rots for a short time and then disintegrates into a darkness of no return.

Now the moment had come when Jechidah must die, must sink to Earth. Soon, the Angel of Death would appear with his fiery sword and thousand eyes.

At first Jechidah had wept incessantly, but then her tears had ceased. Awake or asleep she never stopped thinking of Jachid. Where was he? What was he doing? Whom was he with? Jechidah was well aware he would not mourn for her for ever. He was surrounded by beautiful females, sacred beasts, angels, seraphim, cherubs, ayralim, each one with powers of seduction. How long could someone like Jachid curb his desires? He, like she, was an unbeliever. It was he who had taught her that spirits were not created, but were products of evolution. Jachid did not acknowledge free will, nor believe in ultimate good and evil. What would restrain him? Most certainly he already lay in the lap of some other divinity, telling those stories about himself he had already told Jechidah.

But what could she do? In this dungeon all contact with the mansions ceased. All doors were closed: neither mercy, nor beauty entered here. The one way from this prison led down to Earth, and to the horrors called flesh, blood, marrow, nerves, and breath. The God-fearing angels promised resurrection. They preached that the soul did not linger forever on Earth, but that after it had endured its punishment, it returned to the Higher Sphere. But Jechidah, being a modernist, regarded all of this as superstition. How would a soul free itself from the corruption of the body? It was scientifically impossible. Resurrection was a dream, a silly comfort of primitive and frightened souls.

One night as Jechidah lay in a corner brooding about Jachid and the pleasures she had received from him, his kisses, his caresses, the secrets whispered in her ear, the many positions and games into which she had been initiated, Dumah, the thousand-eyed Angel of Death, looking just as the Sacred Books described him, entered bearing a fiery sword.

"Your time has come, little sister," he said.

"No further appeal is possible?"

"Those who are in this wing always go to Earth."

Jechidah shuddered. "Well, I am ready."

"Jechidah, repentance helps even now. Recite your confession."

"How can it help? My only regret is that I did not transgress more," said Jechidah rebelliously.

Both were silent. Finally Dumah said, "Jechidah, I know you are angry with me. But is it my fault, sister? Did I want to be the Angel of Death? I too am a sinner, exiled from a higher realm, my punishment to be the executioner of souls. Jechidah, I have not willed your death, but be comforted. Death is not as dreadful as you imagine. True, the first moments are not easy. But once you have been planted in the womb, the nine months that follow are not painful. You will forget all that you have learned here. Coming out of the womb will be a shock; but childhood is often pleasant. You will begin to study the lore of death, clothed in a fresh, pliant body, and soon will dread the end of your exile."

Jechidah interrupted him. "Kill me if you must, Dumah, but spare me your lies."

"I am telling you the truth, Jechidah. You will be absent no more than a hundred years, for even the wickedest do not suffer longer than that. Death is only the preparation for a new existence."

"Dumah, please. I don't want to listen."

"But it is important for you to know that good and evil exist there too and that the will remains free."

"What will? Why do you talk such nonsense?"

"Jechidah, listen carefully. Even among the dead there are laws and regulations. The way you act in death will determine what happens to you next. Death is a laboratory for the rehabilitation of souls."

"Make an end of me, I beseech you."

"Be patient, you still have a few more minutes to live and must receive your instructions. Know, then, that one may act well or evilly on Earth and that the most pernicious sin of all is to return a soul to life."

This idea was so ridiculous that Jechidah laughed despite her anguish.

"How can one corpse give life to another?"

"It's not as difficult as you think. The body is composed of such weak material that a mere blow can make it disintegrate. Death is no stronger than a cobweb; a breeze blows and it disappears. But it is a great offense to destroy either another's death or one's own. Not only that, but you must not act or speak or even think in such a way as to threaten death. Here one's object is to preserve life, but there it is death that is succored."

"Nursery tales. The fantasies of an executioner."

"It is the truth, Jechidah. The Torah that applies to Earth is based on a single principle: another man's death must be as dear to one as one's own. Remember my words. When you descend to Sheol, they will be of value to you."

"No, no, I won't listen to any more lies." And Jechidah covered her ears.

Years passed. Everyone in the higher realm had forgotten Jechidah except her mother who still continued to light memorial candles for her daughter. On Earth Jechidah had a new mother as well as a father, several brothers and sisters, all dead. After attending a high school, she had begun to take courses at the university. She lived in a large necropolis where corpses are prepared for all kinds of mortuary functions.

It was spring, and Earth's corruption grew leprous with blossoms. From the graves with their memorial trees and cleansing waters arose a dreadful stench. Millions of creatures, forced to descend into the domains of death, were becoming flies, butterflies, worms, toads, frogs. They buzzed, croaked, screeched, rattled, already involved in the death struggle. But since Jechidah was totally inured to the habits of Earth, all this seemed to her part of life. She sat on a park bench staring up at the moon, which from the darkness of the nether world is sometimes recognized as a memorial candle set in a skull. Like all female corpses, Jechidah yearned to perpetuate death, to have her womb become a grave for the newly dead. But she couldn't do that without the help of a male with whom she would have to copulate in the hatred which corpses call love.

As Jechidah sat staring into the sockets of the skull above her, a white-shrouded corpse came and sat beside her. For a while the two corpses gazed at each other, thinking they could see, although all corpses are actually blind. Finally the male corpse spoke:

"Pardon, Miss, could you tell me what time it is?"

Since deep within themselves all corpses long for the termination of their punishment, they are perpetually concerned with time.

"The time?" Jechidah answered. "Just a second." Strapped to her wrist was an instrument to measure time but the divisions were so minute and the symbols so tiny that she could not easily read the dial. The male corpse moved nearer to her.

"May I take a look? I have good eyes."

"If you wish."

Corpses never act straightforwardly but are always sly and devious. The male corpse took Jechidah's hand and bent his head toward the instrument. This was not the first time a male corpse had touched Jechidah but contact with this one made her limbs tremble. He stared intently but could not decide immediately. Then he said: "I think it's ten minutes after ten."

"Is it really so late?"

"Permit me to introduce myself. My name is Jachid."

"Jachid? Mine is Jechidah."

"What an odd coincidence."

Both hearing death race in their blood were silent for a long while. Then Jachid said: "How beautiful the night is!"

"Yes, beautiful!"

"There's something about spring that cannot be expressed in words."

"Words can express nothing," answered Jechidah.

As she made this remark, both knew they were destined to lie together and to prepare a grave for a new corpse. The fact is, no matter how dead the dead are there remains some life in them, a trace of contact with that knowledge which fills the universe. Death only masks the truth. The sages speak of it as a soap bubble that bursts at the touch of a straw. The dead, ashamed of death, try to conceal their condition through cunning. The more moribund a corpse the more voluble it is.

"May I ask where you live?" asked Jachid.

Where have I seen him before? How is it his voice sounds so familiar to me? Jechidah wondered. *And how does it happen that he's called Jachid? Such a rare name.*

"Not far from here," she answered.

"Would you object to my walking you home?"

"Thank you. You don't have to. But if you want . . . It is still too early to go to bed."

When Jachid rose, Jechidah did, too. Is this the one I have been searching for? Jechidah asked herself, the one destined for me? But what do I mean by destiny? According to my professor, only atoms and motion exist. A carriage approached them and Jechidah heard Jachid say:

"Would you like to take a ride?"

"Where to?"

"Oh, just around the park."

Instead of reproving him as she intended to, Jechidah said: "It would be nice. But I don't think you should spend the money."

"What's money? You only live once."

The carriage stopped and they both got in. Jechidah knew that no self-respecting girl would go riding with a strange man. What did Jachid think of her? Did he believe she would go riding with anyone who asked her? She wanted to explain that she was shy by nature, but she knew she could not wipe out the impression she had already made. She sat in silence, astonished at her behavior. She felt nearer to this stranger than she ever had to anyone. She could almost read his mind. She wished the night would continue for ever. Was this love? Could one really fall in love so quickly? And am I happy? she asked herself. But no answer came from within her. For the dead are always melancholy, even in the midst of gaiety. After a while Jechidah said: "I have a strange feeling I have experienced all this before."

"*Dejà vu*—that's what psychology calls it."

"But maybe there's some truth to it. ...."

"What do you mean?"

"Maybe we've known each other in some other world."

Jachid burst out laughing. "In what world? There is only one, ours, the earth."

"But maybe souls do exist."

"Impossible. What you call the soul is nothing but vibrations of matter, the product of the nervous system. I should know, I'm a medical student." Suddenly he put his arm around her waist. And although Jechidah had never permitted any male to take such liberties before, she did not reprove him. She sat there perplexed by her acquiescence, fearful of the regrets that would be hers tomorrow. I'm completely without character, she chided herself. But he is right about one thing. If there is no soul and life is nothing but a short episode in an eternity of death, then why shouldn't one enjoy oneself without restraint? If there is no soul, there is no God, free will is meaningless. Morality, as my professor says, is nothing but a part of the ideological superstructure.

Jechidah closed her eyes and leaned back against the upholstery. The horse trotted slowly. In the dark all the corpses, men and beasts, lamented their death—howling, laughing, buzzing, chirping, sighing. Some of the corpses staggered, having drunk to forget for a while the tortures of hell. Jechidah had retreated into herself. She dozed off, then awoke again with a start. When the dead sleep they once more connect themselves with the source of life. The illusion of time and space, cause and effect, number and relation ceases. In her dream Jechidah had ascended again into the world of her origin. There she saw her real mother, her friends, her teachers. Jachid was there, too. The two greeted each other, embraced, laughed and wept with joy. At that moment, they both recognized the truth, that death on Earth is temporary and illusory, a trial and a means of purification. They traveled together past heavenly mansions, gardens, oases for convalescent souls, forests for divine beasts, islands for heavenly birds. No, our meeting was not an accident, Jechidah murmured to herself. There is a God. There is a purpose in creation. Copulation, free will, fate—all are part of His plan. Jachid and Jechidah passed by a prison and gazed into its window. They saw a soul condemned to sink down to Earth. Jechidah knew that this soul would become her daughter. Just before she woke up, Jechidah heard a voice:

"The grave and the grave digger have met. The burial will take place tonight."

❦ LLOYD ALEXANDER ❦
(1924-)

Lloyd Alexander was born and brought up in Philadelphia. As a boy he loved to read fairy tales, folklore, legends, and, especially, the adventures of King Arthur and his knights of the round table. His interest in literature was so strong that while still a teenager he decided to become a writer, and subsequently spent long evening hours hunched over his writing desk. After a brief and uneventful stay at Westchester State College, he joined the army, hoping to find there a more exciting and adventurous life style—one which might provide the raw materials for later works of fiction. His assignments in military intelligence carried him first to England, and later to Wales. It was most certainly the rugged grandeur of the Welsh landscapes which inspired the settings of the *Chronicles of Prydain*. When the war ended, Alexander was stationed in Paris, where he met and married a French girl, Janine. Still enthusiastically pursuing his career as writer, he attended the University of Paris with the intention of learning more about his craft. A short time later the decision was made to return to the city of his youth. In Philadelphia, the aspiring young writer held a number of different jobs while attempting to get his works published. For the next seventeen years he experienced only moderate success with his adult fiction, but then he turned to children's literature with *The Time Cat* (1963), and his fortunes took a dramatic turn for the better. Since that publication, he has written a number of popular and award-winning fantasy works, but he is best known for the five volumes which comprise the "Prydain Cycle": *The Book of*

Three (1964), *The Black Cauldron* (1965), *The Castle of Llyr* (1966), *Taran Wanderer* (1967), and *The High King* (1968) which was the recipient of the 1969 Newberry Award. Alexander was for a time writer-in-residence at Temple University, Philadelphia, Pennsylvania.

Tolkien has his Middle Earth, Lewis his Narnia, and Alexander his Prydain. Each is a classic example of the key ingredient of high fantasy—a magical other-world. "The Foundling" is only one of the many stories Alexander has set in that wondrous world of Prydain, where all things are possible. It is a brief, but rich, tale which is especially noteworthy for its mythic underpinnings. It should not take the reader long to discover the similarities between the tree crones who find and rear Dallben, "greatest of enchanters of Prydain," and the three Fates of classical mythology. But Orddu, Orwen, and Orgoch are not the cold and impersonal figures of the myth. Rather, they are three garrulous old women with unforgettable and distinctive human personalities. The Alexander touch is also evident in the wry humor which permeates the narrative. The story is entertaining, but also instructive. It is a thoughtful commentary on the curious admixture of anguish, suffering, hope, and joy which characterizes every man's existence.

The Foundling
Lloyd Alexander

This is told of Dallben, greatest of enchanters in Prydain: how three black-robed hags found him, when he was still a baby, in a basket at the edge of the Marshes of Morva. "Oh, Orddu, see what's here!" cried the one named Orwen, peering into the wicker vessel floating amid the tall grasses. "Poor lost duckling! He'll catch his death of cold! Whatever shall we do with him?"

"A sweet morsel," croaked the one named Orgoch from the depths of her hood. "A tender lamb. I know what I should do."

"Please be silent, Orgoch," said the one named Orddu. "You've already had your breakfast." Orddu was a short, plump woman with a round, lumpy face and sharp black eyes. Jewels, pins, and brooches glittered in her tangle of weedy hair. "We can't leave him here to get all soggy. I suppose we shall have to take him home with us."

"Oh, yes!" exclaimed Orwen, dangling her string of milky white beads over the tiny figure in the basket. "Ah, the darling tadpole! Look at his pink cheeks and chubby little fingers! He's smiling at us, Orddu! He's waving! But what shall we call him? He mustn't go bare and nameless."

"If you ask me——" began Orgoch.

"No one did," replied Orddu. "You are quite right, Orwen. We must give him a name. Otherwise, how shall we know who he is?"

"We have so many names lying around the cottage,"

227

said Orwen. "Some of them never used. Give him a nice, fresh, unwrinkled one."

"There's a charming name I'd been saving for a special occasion," Orddu said, "but I can't remember what I did with it. No matter. His name—his name: Dallben."

"Lovely!" cried Orwen, clapping her hands. "Oh, Orddu, you have such good taste."

"Taste, indeed!" snorted Orgoch. "Dallben? Why call him Dallben?"

"Why not?" returned Orddu. "It will do splendidly. Very good quality, very durable. It should last him a lifetime."

"It will last him," Orgoch muttered, "as long as he needs it."

And so Dallben was named and nursed by these three, and given a home in their cottage near the Marshes of Morva. Under their care he grew sturdy, bright, and fair of face. He was kind and generous, and each day handsomer and happier.

The hags did not keep from him that he was a foundling. But when he was of an age to wonder about such matters, he asked where indeed he had come from, and what the rest of the world was like.

"My dear chicken," replied Orddu, "as to where you came from, we haven't the slightest notion. Nor, might I say, the least interest. You're here with us now, to our delight, and that's quite enough to know."

"As to the rest of the world," Orwen added, "don't bother your pretty, curly head about it. You can be sure it doesn't bother about you. Be glad you were found instead of drowned. Why, this very moment you might be part of a school of fish. And what a slippery, scaly sort of life that would be!"

"I like fish," muttered Orgoch, "especially eels."

"Do hush, dear Orgoch," said Orddu. "You're always thinking of your stomach."

Despite his curiosity, Dallben saw there was no use in questioning further. Cheerful and willing, he went about every task with eagerness and good grace. He drew pails of water from the well, kept the fire burning in the hearth, pumped the bellows, swept away the ashes, and dug the garden. No toil was too troublesome for him. When Orddu spun thread, he turned the spinning wheel. He helped Orwen measure the skeins into lengths and held them for Orgoch to snip with a pair of rusty shears.

One day, when the three brewed a potion of roots and herbs, Dallben was left alone to stir the huge, steaming kettle with a long iron spoon. He obeyed the hags' warning not to taste the liquid, but soon the potion began boiling so briskly that a few drops bubbled up and by accident splashed his fingers. With a cry of pain, Dallben let fall the spoon and popped his fingers into his mouth.

His outcry brought Orddu, Orwen, and Orgoch hurrying back to the cottage.

"Oh, the poor sparrow!" gasped Orwen, seeing the boy sucking at his blistered knuckles. "He's gone and burned himself. I'll fetch an ointment for the sweet fledgling, and some spider webs to bandage him. What did you do with all those spiders, Orgoch? They were here only yesterday."

"Too late for all that," growled Orgoch. "Worse damage is done."

"Yes, I'm afraid so," Orddu sighed. "There's no learning without pain. The dear gosling has had his pain; and now, I daresay, he has some learning to go along with it."

Dallben, meanwhile, had swallowed the drops of liquid scalding his fingers. He licked his lips at the taste, sweet and bitter at the same time. And in that instant he began to shake with fear and excitement. All that had been common and familiar in the cottage he saw as he had never seen before.

Now he understood that the leather bellows lying by the hearth commanded the four winds; the pail of water in the corner, the seas and oceans of the world. The earthen floor of the cottage held the roots of all plants and trees. The fire showed him the secrets of its flame, and how all things come to ashes. He gazed awe-struck at the enchantresses, for such they were.

"The threads you spin, and measure, and cut off," Dallben murmured, "these are no threads, but the lives of men. I know who you truly are."

"Oh, I doubt it," Orddu cheerfully answered. "Even we aren't always sure of that. Nevertheless, one taste of that magical brew and you know as much as we do. Almost as much, at any rate."

"Too much for his own good," muttered Orgoch.

"But what shall we do?" moaned Orwen. "He was such a sweet, innocent little robin. If only he hadn't swallowed the potion! Is there no way to make him un-swallow it?"

"We could try," said Orgoch.

"No," declared Orddu. "What's done is done. You know that as well as I. Alas, the dear duckling will have to leave us. There's nothing else for it. So many people, knowing so much, under the same roof? All that knowledge crammed in, crowded, bumping and jostling back and forth? We'd not have room to breathe!"

"I say he should be kept," growled Orgoch.

"I don't think he'd like your way of keeping him," Orddu answered. She turned to Dallben. "No, my poor chicken, we must say farewell. You asked us once about the world? I'm afraid you'll have to see it for yourself."

"But, Orddu," protested Orwen, "we can't let him march off just like that. Surely we have some little trin-ket he'd enjoy? A going-away present, so he won't for-get us?"

"I could give him something to remember us by," began Orgoch.

"No doubt," said Orddu. "But that's not what Or-wen had in mind. Of course, we shall offer him a gift. Better yet, he shall choose one for himself."

As Dallben watched, the enchantress unlocked an iron-bound chest and rummaged inside, flinging out all sorts of oddments until there was a large heap on the floor.

"Here's something," Orddu at last exclaimed. "Just the thing for a bold young chicken. A sword!"

Dallben caught his breath in wonder as Orddu put the weapon in his hands. The hilt, studded with jewels, glittered so brightly that he was dazzled and nearly blinded. The blade flashed, and a thread of fire ran along its edges.

"Take this, my duckling," Orddu said, "and you shall be the greatest warrior in Prydain. Strength and power, dear gosling! When you command, all must obey even your slightest whim."

"It is a fine blade," Dallben replied, "and comes easily to my hand."

"It shall be yours," Orddu said. "At least, as long as you're able to keep it. Oh, yes," the enchantress went on, "I should mention it's already had a number of owners. Somehow, sooner or later, it wanders back to us. The difficulty, you see, isn't so much getting power as holding on to it. Because so many others want it, too. You'd be astonished, the lengths to which some will go. Be warned, the sword can be lost or stolen. Or bent out of shape—as, indeed, so can you, in a manner of speaking."

"And remember," put in Orwen, "you must never let it out of your sight, not for an instant."

Dallben hesitated a moment, then shook his head. "I think your gift is more burden than blessing."

"In that case," Orddu said, "perhaps this will suit you better."

As Dallben laid down the sword, the enchantress handed him a golden harp, so perfectly wrought that he no sooner held it than it seemed to play of itself.

"Take this, my sparrow," said Orddu, "and be the greatest bard in Prydain, known throughout the land for the beauty of your songs."

Dallben's heart leaped as the instrument thrilled in his arms. He touched the sweeping curve of the glowing harp and ran his fingers over the golden strings. "I have never heard such music," he murmured. "Who owns this will surely have no lack of fame."

"You'll have fame and admiration a-plenty," said Orddu, "as long as anyone remembers you."

"Alas, that's true," Orwen said with a sigh. "Memory can be so skimpy. It doesn't stretch very far; and, next thing you know, there's your fame gone all crumbly and mildewed."

Sadly, Dallben set down the harp. "Beautiful it is," he said, "but in the end, I fear, little help to me."

"There's nothing else we can offer at the moment," said Orddu, delving once more into the chest, "unless you'd care to have this book."

The enchantress held up a large, heavy tome and blew away the dust and cobwebs from its moldering leather binding. "It's a bulky thing for a young lamb to carry. Naturally, it would be rather weighty, for it holds everything that was ever known, is known, and will be known."

"It's full of wisdom, thick as oatmeal," added Orwen. "Quite scarce in the world—wisdom, not oatmeal —but that only makes it the more valuable."

"We have so many requests for other items," Orddu said. "Seven-league boots, cloaks of invisibility, and such great nonsense. For wisdom, practically none. Yet whoever owns this book shall have all that and more, if he likes. For the odd thing about wisdom is the more you use it the more it grows; and the more you share, the more you gain. You'd be amazed how few understand that. If they did, I suppose, they wouldn't need the book in the first place."

"Do you give this to me?" Dallben asked. "A treasure greater than all treasures?"

Orddu hesitated. "Give? Only in a manner of speaking. If you know us as well as you say you do, then you also know we don't exactly *give* anything. Put it this way: We shall *let* you take that heavy, dusty old book if that's what you truly want. Again, be warned: The greater the treasure, the greater the cost. Nothing is given for nothing; not in the Marshes of Morva—or anyplace else, for the matter of that."

"Even so," Dallben replied, "this book is my choice."

"Very well," said Orddu, putting the ancient volume in his hands. "Now you shall be on your way. We're sorry to see you go, though sorrow is something we don't usually feel. Fare well, dear chicken. We mean this in the polite sense, for whether you fare well or ill is entirely up to you."

So Dallben took his leave of the enchantresses and set off eagerly, curious to see what lay in store not only in the world but between the covers of the book. Once the cottage was well out of sight and the marshes far behind him, he curbed his impatience no longer, but sat down by the roadside, opened the heavy tome, and began to read.

As he scanned the first pages, his eyes widened and his heart quickened. For here was knowledge he had never dreamed of: the pathways of the stars, the rounds of the planets, the ebb and flow of time and tide. All secrets of the world and all its hidden lore unfolded to him.

Dallben's head spun, giddy with delight. The huge book seemed to weigh less than a feather, and he felt so light-hearted he could have skipped from one mountaintop to the next and never touched the ground. He laughed and sang at the top of his voice, bursting with gladness, pride, and strength in what he had learned.

"I chose well!" he cried, jumping to his feet. "But why should Orddu have warned me? Cost? What cost can there be? Knowledge is joy!"

He strode on, reading as he went. Each page lightened and sped his journey, and soon he came to a village where the dwellers danced and sang and made holiday. They offered him meat and drink and shelter for the coming night.

But Dallben thanked them for their hospitality and shook his head, saying he had meat and drink enough in the book he carried. By this time he had walked many miles, but his spirit was fresh and his legs un-weary.

He kept on his way, hardly able to contain his hap-piness as he read and resolving not to rest until he had come to the end of the book. But he had finished less than half when the pages, to his horror, began to grow dark and stained with blood and tears.

For now the book told him of other ways of the world; of cruelty, suffering, and death. He read of greed, hatred, and war; of men striving against one an-other with fire and sword; of the blossoming earth trampled underfoot, of harvests lost and lives cut short. And the book told that even in the same village he had passed, a day would come when no house would stand; when women would weep for their men, and children for their parents; and where they had offered him meat and drink, they would starve for lack of a crust of bread.

Each page he read pierced his heart. The book, which had seemed to weigh so little, now grew so heavy that his face faltered and he staggered under the burden. Tears blinded his eyes, and he stumbled to the ground.

All night he lay shattered by despair. At dawn he stirred and found it took all his efforts even to lift his head. Bones aching, throat parched, he crept on hands and knees to quench his thirst from a puddle of water. There, at the sight of his reflection, he drew back and cried out in anguish.

His fair, bright curls had gone frost-white and fell below his brittle shoulders. His cheeks, once full and flushed with youth, were now hollow and wrinkled, half hidden by a long, gray beard. His brow, smooth yesterday, was scarred and furrowed, his hands gnarled and knotted, his eyes pale as if their color had been wept away.

Dallben bowed his head. "Yes, Orddu," he whis-pered, "I should have heeded you. Nothing is given without cost. But is the cost of wisdom so high? I thought knowledge was joy. Instead, it is grief beyond bearing."

The book lay nearby. Its last pages were still unread and, for a moment, Dallben thought to tear them to shreds and scatter them to the wind. Then he said:

"I have begun it, and I will finish it, whatever else it may foretell."

Fearfully and reluctantly, he began to read once more. But now his heart lifted. These pages told not only of death, but of birth as well; how the earth turns in its own time and in its own way gives back what is given to it; how things lost may be found again; and how one day ends for another to begin. He learned that the lives of men are short and filled with pain, yet each one a priceless treasure, whether it be that of a prince or a pig-keeper. And, at the last, the book taught him that while nothing was certain, all was possible.

"At the end of knowledge, wisdom begins," Dallben murmured. "And at the end of wisdom there is not grief, but hope."

He climbed to his withered legs and hobbled along his way, clasping the heavy book. After a time a farmer drove by in a horse-drawn cart, and called out to him:

"Come, Grandfather, ride with me if you like. That book must be a terrible load for an old man like you."

"Thank you just the same," Dallben answered, "but I have strength enough now to go to the end of my road."

"And where might that be?"

"I do not know," Dallben said. "I go seeking it."

"Well, then," said the farmer, "may you be lucky enough to find it."

"Luck?" Dallben answered. He smiled and shook his head. "Not luck, but hope. Indeed, hope."

❧ JOAN AIKEN ❧
(1924-   )

"It is so much more fun inventing the word for it than doing the job! I think that is the main reason why I love writing.... It is so much better inventing a whole new world—*just* the way you want it—than doing the jobs that are waiting to be done.... The very thought of all those awful little jobs is enough to make one sit down and write 'Once upon a time—.'" This is how Joan Aiken, English novelist, short-story writer, and author of children's books, rather playfully explains her motivation for writing in an interview in *Cricket: The Magazine for Children* (March, 1977). Considering the entertainment and pleasure she has brought to countless readers of every age over the past quarter of a century, we are thankful for the existence of those "awful little jobs."

Born September 4, 1924, in Rye, Sussex, the daughter of the distinguished poet Conrad Potter Aiken and Jessie (MacDonald) Aiken, Joan Aiken received her higher education at Wychwood School, Oxford (1936-41). After completing her work there, she joined the British Broadcasting Corporation for a one-year stint, and then moved on to the United Nations London Information Office, where she served as a research assistant in the Library (1943-49). It was here that she met and fell in love with Ronald George Brown, a press officer in the Information Office. They were married on July 7, 1945, but only ten years later, Brown died of lung cancer; the young widow was left to care for two small children. Shortly after her husband's death, Aiken found employment with *Argosy Magazine* (1955-60). In 1961 she joined the J. Walter Thompson Advertising Agency, but that same year decided to take her chances as a freelance writer. Since then she has established herself as one of the finest, and most prolific, English writers of the twentieth century.

In a brief autobiographical statement in *Contemporary Authors* Aiken explains: "I always intended to be a writer; when I was five I went to the village store and spent two shillings (a huge sum then) on a large, thick writing-block in which to write poems, stories, and thoughts, as they occurred. It lasted for years. . . and when it was finished I bought another and then another." Although she published a short story as early as 1941, when she was just seventeen years old, her first major publication was *All You've Ever Wanted* (1953), a collection of children's short stories. Among her many other short-story collections are *A Necklace of Raindrops, and Other Stories* (1968), *Smoke From Cromwell's Time, and Other Stories* (1970), and *A Harp of Fishbones, and Other Stories* (1972). Her most popular novels include *The Wolves of Willoughby Chase* (1962), which earned the Lewis Carroll Award; *The Whispering Mountain* (1968), which received the Manchester Guardian Award and was runner-up for the Carnegie Award; *Night Fall* (1972), winner of the Mystery Writers of America Award; and *Midnight Is a Place* (1974), which prompted Timothy Foote to write ". . . the author proves once again that she writes about children in distress better than anyone since Dickens." (*Time*, 23 Dec. 1974). Besides her novels and short stories, Aiken has written poetry and a child's play, *Winterthing* (1972). She enjoys reading, painting, cooking, gardening, and listening to classical music, especially Handel and Purcell.

Some time ago Aiken wrote: "Thinking back over my children's books and my adult thrillers (if thrillers are adult) I honestly can't recall any difference at all in the actual writing process. . . . If ever I find myself writing anything . . . with less than the total care and skill I can command, I shall take this as a sign that I have written enough, and shall turn to some other profession."(*Contemporary Authors,*

1974). This literary philosophy, reminiscent of the attitude of other fantasists such as C. S. Lewis and J. R. R. Tolkien, serves to remind us of the major strength and significance of "A Harp of Fishbones" and other quality fantasy works: All exhibit a universality which allows readers of all ages to enjoy, and profit from, them.

"A Harp of Fishbones" is a delightful fairy tale which clearly exhibits Aiken's consummate craftsmanship. The plot is energetic, tightly woven, and filled with surprises (note the ending); the characterization is handled with a deft and careful touch; the secondary world is convincingly described, with an admirable inner consistency; and the themes are concretely illustrated through the actions of the characters. Aiken is a marvelous scene writer, and although many of the scenes in this story are vividly drawn, the episode featuring Nerryn's successful breaking of the mountain goddess' spell is especially moving and memorable. Those familiar with Lewis's Narnian Chronicles will immediately be reminded of Chapter XVI of *The Lion, The Witch, and the Wardrobe*, where Aslan breathes life into the multitude of creatures turned into lifeless statues by the malevolent White Witch. Both scenes, with their strong archetypal underpinnings, illustrate the power of high fantasy to elicit a sense of awe and wonder.

A Harp of Fishbones

Joan Aiken

❦

Little Nerryn lived in the half-ruined mill at the upper end
of the village, where the stream ran out of the forest. The
old miller's name was Timorash, but she called him uncle.
Her own father and mother were dead, long before she
could remember. Timorash was no real kin, nor was he
particularly kind to her; he was a lazy old man. He never
troubled to grow corn as the other people in the village
did, little patches in the clearing below the village before
the forest began again. When people brought him corn to
grind he took one-fifth of it as his fee and this, with wild
plums which Nerryn gathered and dried, and carp from
the deep millpool, kept him and the child fed through the
short bright summers and the long silent winters.

Nerryn learned to do the cooking when she was seven or
eight; she toasted fish on sticks over the fire and baked
cakes of bread on a flat stone; Timorash beat her if the
food was burnt, but it mostly was, just the same, because
so often half her mind would be elsewhere, listening to the
bell-like call of a bird or pondering about what made the
difference between the stream's voice in winter and in
summer. When she was little older Timorash taught her
how to work the mill, opening the sluice-gate so that the
green, clear mountain water could hurl down against the
great wooden paddle-wheel. Nerryn liked this much better, since she already spent hours watching the stream end-
lessly pouring and plaiting down its narrow passage. Old
Timorash had hoped that now he would be able to give
up work altogether and lie in the sun all day, or crouch by
the fire, slowly adding one stick after another and dreaming about barley wine. But Nerryn forgot to take flour in

240

payment from the villagers, who were in no hurry to remind her, so the old man angrily decided that this plan would not answer, and sent her out to work.

First she worked for one household, then for another. The people of the village had come from the plains; they were surly, big-boned, and lank, with tow-coloured hair and pale eyes; even the children seldom spoke. Little Nerryn sometimes wondered, looking at her reflection in the millpool, how it was that she should be so different from them, small and brown-skinned with dark hair like a bird's feathers and hazelnut eyes. But it was no use asking questions of old Timorash, who never answered except by grunting or throwing a clod of earth at her. Another difference was that she loved to chatter, and this was perhaps the main reason why the people she worked for soon sent her packing.

There were other reasons too, for, though Nerryn was willing enough to work, things often distracted her.

"She let the bread burn while she ran outside to listen to a curlew," said one.

"When she was helping me cut the hay she asked so many questions that my ears have ached for three days," complained another.

"Instead of scaring off the birds from my corn-patch she sat with her chin on her fists, watching them gobble down half a winter's supply and whistling to them!" grumbled a third.

Nobody would keep her more than a few days, and she had plenty of beatings, especially from Timorash, who had hoped that her earnings would pay for a keg of barley wine. Once in his life he had had a whole keg, and he still felt angry when he remembered that it was finished.

At last Nerryn went to work for an old woman who lived in a tumbledown hut at the bottom of the street. Her name was Saroon and she was by far the oldest in the village, so withered and wrinkled that most people thought she was a witch; besides, she knew when it was going to rain and as the only person in the place who did not fear to venture a little way into the forest. But she was growing weak now, and stiff, and wanted somebody to help dig her corn-patch and cut wood. Nevertheless she hardly seemed to welcome help when it came. As Nerryn moved about at the tasks she was set, the old woman's little red-rimmed eyes followed her suspiciously; she hobbled round the hut watching through cracks, grumbling and chuntering to herself, never losing sight of the girl for a moment, like some cross-grained old animal that sees a stranger near its burrow.

On the fourth day she said,

"You're singing, girl."

"I—I'm sorry," Nerryn stammered. "I didn't mean to —I wasn't thinking. Don't beat me, please."

"Humph," said the old woman, but she did not beat Nerryn that time. And next day, watching through the window-hole while Nerryn chopped wood, she said,

"You're not singing."

Nerryn jumped. She had not known the old woman was so near.

"I thought you didn't like me to," she faltered.

"I didn't say so, did I?"

Muttering, the old woman stumped off to the back of the hut and began to sort through a box of mildewy nuts. "As if I should care," Nerryn heard her grumble, "whether the girl sings or not!" But next day she put her head out of the door, while Nerryn hoed the corn patch, and said,

"Sing, child!"

Nerryn looked at her, doubtful and timid, to see if she really meant it, but she nodded her head energetically, till the tangled grey locks jounced on her shoulders, and repeated,

"Sing!"

So presently the clear, tiny thread of Nerryn's song began again as she sliced off the weeds; and old Saroon came out and sat on an upturned log beside the door, pounding roots for soup and mumbling to herself in time to the sound. And at the end of the week she did not dismiss the girl, as everyone else had done, though what she paid was so little that Timorash grumbled every time Nerryn brought it home. At this rate twenty years would go by before he had saved enough for a key of barley wine.

One day Saroon said,

"Your father used to sing."

This was the first time anyone had spoken of him.

"Oh," Nerryn cried, forgetting her fear of the old woman. "Tell me about him."

"Why should I?" old Saroon said sourly. "He never did anything for *me*." And she hobbled off to fetch a pot of water. But later she relented and said,

"His hair was the colour of ash buds, like yours. And he carried a harp."

"A harp, what is a harp?"

"Oh, don't pester, child. I'm busy."

But another day she said, "A harp is a thing to make music. His was a gold one, but it was broken."

"Gold, what is gold?"

"This," said the old woman, and she pulled out a small, thin disc which she wore on a cord of plaited grass round her neck.

"Why!" Nerryn exclaimed. "Everybody in the village has one of those except Timorash and me. I've often asked what they were but no one would answer."

"They are gold. When your father went off and left you and the harp with Timorash, the old man ground up the harp between the millstones. And he melted down the gold powder and made it into these little circles and sold them to everybody in the village, and bought a keg of barley wine. He told us they would bring good luck. But I have never had any good luck and that was a long time ago. And Timorash has long since drunk all his barley wine."

"Where did my father go?" asked Nerryn.

"Into the forest," the old woman snapped. "I could have told him he was in for trouble. I could have warned him. But he never asked *my* advice."

She sniffed, and set a pot of herbs boiling on the fire. And Nerryn could get no more out of her that day.

But little by little, as time passed, more came out.

"Your father came from over the mountains. High up yonder, he said, there was a great city, with houses and palaces and temples, and as many rich people as there are fish in the millpool. Best of all, there was always music playing in the streets and houses and in the temples. But then the goddess of the mountain became angry, and fire burst out of a crack in the hillside. And then a great cold came, so that people froze where they stood. Your father said he only just managed to escape with you by running very fast. Your mother had died in the fire."

"Where was he going?"

"The king of the city had ordered him to go for help."

"What sort of help?"

"Don't ask *me*," the old woman grumbled. "You'd think he'd have settled down here like a person of sense, and mended his harp. But no, on he must go, leaving you behind so that he could travel faster. He said he'd fetch you again on his way back. But of course he never did come back—one day I found his bones in the forest. The birds must have killed him."

"How do you *know* they were my father's bones?"

"Because of the tablet he carried. See, here it is, with his name on it, Heramon the harper."

"Tell me more about the harp!"

"It was shaped like this," the old woman said. They were washing clothes by the stream, and she drew with her finger in the mud. "Like this, and it had golden strings across, so. All but one of the strings had melted in the fire from the mountain. Even on just one string he could make very beautiful music, that would force you to stop whatever you were doing and listen. It is a pity he had to leave the harp behind. Timorash wanted it as payment for looking after you. If your father had taken the harp with him, perhaps he would have been able to reach the other side of the forest."

Nerryn thought about this story a great deal. For the next few weeks she did even less work than usual and was mostly to be found squatting with her chin on her fists by the side of the stream. Saroon beat her, but not very hard. Then one day Nerryn said,

"I shall make a harp."

"Hah!" sniffed the old woman. "You! What do you know of such things?"

After a few minutes she asked,

"What will you make it from?"

Nerryn said, "I shall make it of fishbones. Some of the biggest carp in the millpool have bones as thick as my wrist, and they are very strong."

"Timorash will never allow it."

"I shall wait till he is asleep, then."

So Nerryn waited till night, and then she took a chunk of rotten wood, which glows in the dark, and dived into the deep millpool, swimming down and down to the depths where the biggest carp lurk, among the mud and weeds and old sunken logs.

When they saw the glimmer of the wood through the water, all the fish came nosing and nibbling and swimming round Nerryn, curious to find if this thing which shone so strangely was good to eat. She waited as long as she could bear it, holding her breath, till a great barrel-shaped monster slid nudging right up against her; then, quick as a flash, she wrapped her arms round his slippery sides and fled up with a bursting heart to the surface.

Much to her surprise, old Saroon was there, waiting in the dark on the bank. But the old woman only said,

"You had better bring the carp to my hut. After all, you want no more than the bones, and it would be a pity to waste all that good meat. I can live on it for a week." So she cut the meat off the bones, which were coal-black but had a sheen on them like mother-of-pearl. Nerryn dried them by the fire, and then she joined together the three biggest, notching them to fit, and cementing them with a glue she made by boiling some of the smaller bones together. She used long, thin, strong bones for strings, joining them to the frame in the same manner.

All the time old Saroon watched closely. Sometimes she would say,

"That was not the way of it. Heramon's harp was wider," or "You are putting the strings too far apart. There should be more of them, and they should be tighter."

When at last it was done, she said,

"Now you must hang it in the sun to dry."

So for three days the harp hung drying in the sun and wind. At night Saroon took it into her hut and covered it with a cloth. On the fourth day she said,

"Now, play!"

Nerryn rubbed her finger across the strings, and they gave out a liquid murmur, like that of a stream running over pebbles, under a bridge. She plucked a string, and the noise was like that a drop of water makes, falling in a hollow place.

"That will be music," old Saroon said, nodding her

head, satisfied. "It is not quite the same as the sound from your father's harp, but it is music. Now you shall play me tunes every day, and I shall sit in the sun and listen."

"No," said Nerryn, "for if Timorash hears me playing he will take the harp away and break it or sell it. I shall go to my father's city and see if I can find any of his kin there."

At this old Saroon was very angry. "Here have I taken all these pains to help you, and what reward do I get for it? How much pleasure do you think I have, living among dolts in this dismal place? I was not born here, any more than you were. You could at least play to me at night, when Timorash is asleep."

"Well, I will play to you for seven nights," Nerryn said.

Each night old Saroon tried to persuade her not to go, and she tried harder as Nerryn became more skilful in playing, and drew from the fishbone harp a curious watery music, like the songs that birds sing when it is raining. But Nerryn would not be persuaded to stay, and when she saw this, on the seventh night, Saroon said,

"I suppose I shall have to tell you how to go through the forest. Otherwise you will certainly die, as your father did. When you go among the trees you will find that the grass underfoot is thick and strong and hairy, and the farther you go, the higher it grows, as high as your waist. And it is sticky and clings to you, so that you can only go forward slowly, one step at a time. Then, in the middle of the forest, perched in the branches, are vultures who will drop on you and peck you to death if you stand still for more than a minute."

"How do you know all this?" Nerryn said.

"I have tried many times to go through the forest, but it is too far for me; I grow tired and have to turn back. The vultures take no notice of me, I am too old and withered, but a tender young piece like you would be just what they fancy."

"Then what must I do?" Nerryn asked.

"You must play music on your harp till they fall asleep; then, while they sleep, cut the grass with your knife and go forward as fast as you can."

Nerryn said, "If I cut you enough fuel for a month, and catch you another carp, and gather you a bushed of nuts, will you give me your little gold circle, or my father's tablet?"

But this Saroon would not do. She did, though, break off the corner of the tablet which had Heramon the harper's name on it, and give that to Nerryn.

"But don't blame me," she said sourly, "if you find the city all burnt and frozen, with not a living soul to walk its streets."

"Oh, it will all have been rebuilt by this time," Nerryn said. "I shall find my father's people, or my mother's, and I shall come back for you, riding a white mule and leading another."

"Fairy tales!" old Saroon said angrily. "Be off with you, then. If you don't wish to stay I'm sure *I* don't want you idling about the place. All the work you've done this last week I could have done better myself in half an hour. Drat the woodsmoke! It gets in a body's eyes till they can't see a thing." And she hobbled into the hut, working her mouth sourly and rubbing her eyes with the back of her hand.

Nerryn ran into the forest, going cornerways up the mountain, so as not to pass too close to the mill where old Timorash lay sleeping in the sun.

Soon she had to slow down because the way was so steep. And the grass grew thicker and thicker, hairy, sticky, all twined and matted together, as high as her waist. Presently, as she hacked and cut at it with her bone knife, she heard a harsh croaking and flapping above her. She looked up, and saw two grey vultures perched on a branch, leaning forward to peer down at her. Their wings were twice the length of a man's arm and they had long, wrinkled, black, leathery necks and little fierce yellow eyes. As she stood, two more, then five, ten, twenty others came rousting through the branches, and all perched round about, craning down their long black necks, swaying back and forth, keeping balanced by the way they opened and shut their wings.

Nerryn felt very much afraid of them, but she unslung the harp from her back and began to play a soft, trickling tune, like rain falling on a deep pool. Very soon the vultures sank their necks down between their shoulders and closed their eyes. They sat perfectly still.

When she was certain they were asleep, Nerryn made haste to cut and slash at the grass. She was several hundred yards on her way before the vultures woke and came cawing and jostling through the branches to cluster again just overhead. Quickly she pulled the harp round and strummed on its fishbone strings until once again, lulled by the music, the vultures sank their heads between their grey wings and slept. Then she went back to cutting the grass, as fast as she could.

It was a long, tiring way. Soon she grew so weary that she could hardly push one foot ahead of the other, and it was hard to keep awake; once she only just roused in time when a vulture, swooping down, missed her with his beak and instead struck the harp on her back with a loud strange twang that set echoes scampering through the trees.

At last the forest began to thin and dwindle; here the tree-trunks and branches were all draped about with grey-green moss, like long dangling hanks of sheepswool. Moss grew on the rocky ground, too, in a thick carpet. When she reached this part, Nerryn could go on safely; the vultures rose in an angry flock and flew back with harsh croaks of disappointment, for they feared the trailing moss would wind round their wings and trap them.

As soon as she reached the edge of the trees Nerryn lay down in a deep tussock of moss and fell fast asleep.

She was so tired that she slept almost till nightfall, but then the cold woke her. It was bitter on the bare mountainside; the ground was all crisp with white frost, and when Nerryn started walking uphill she crunched through it, leaving deep black footprints. Unless she kept moving she knew that she would probably die of cold, so she climbed on, higher and higher; the stars came out, showing more frost-covered slopes ahead and all around, while the forest far below curled round the flank of the mountain like black fur.

Through the night she went on climbing and by sunrise she had reached the foot of a steep slope of ice-covered boulders. When she tried to climb over these she only slipped back again.

What shall I do now? Nerryn wondered. She stood blowing on her frozen fingers and thought, "I must go on

or I shall die here of cold. I will play a tune on the harp
to warm my fingers and my wits."

She unslung the harp. It was hard to play, for her fingers were almost numb and at first refused to obey but,
while she had climbed the hill, a very sweet, lively tune
had come into her head, and she struggled and struggled
until her stubborn fingers found the right notes to play it.
Once she played the tune—twice—and the stones on the
slope above began to roll and shift. She played a third
time and, with a thunderous roar, the whole pile broke
loose and went sliding down the mountain-side. Nerryn
was only just able to dart aside out of the way before the
frozen mass careered past, sending up a smoking dust of
ice.

Trembling a little, she went on up the hill, and now she
came to a gate in a great wall, set about with towers. The
gate stood open, and so she walked through.

"Surely this must be my father's city," she thought.

But when she stood inside the gate, her heart sank, and
she remembered old Saroon's words. For the city that
must once have been bright with gold and coloured stone
and gay with music was all silent; not a soul walked the
streets and the houses, under thick covering of frost, were
burnt and blackened by fire.

And, what was still more frightening, when Nerryn
looked through the doorways into the houses, she could
see people standing or sitting or lying, frozen still like
statues, as the cold had caught them while they worked,
or slept, or sat at dinner.

"Where shall I go now?" she thought. "It would have
been better to stay with Saroon in the forest. When night
comes I shall only freeze to death in this place."

But still she went on, almost tiptoeing in the frosty
silence of the city, looking into doorways and through
gates, until she came to a building that was larger than any
other, built with a high roof and many pillars of white
marble. The fire had not touched it.

"This must be the temple," she thought, remembering
the tale Saroon had told, and she walked between the
pillars, which glittered like white candles in the light from
the rising sun. Inside there was a vast hall, and many
people standing frozen, just as they had been when they

came to pray for deliverance from their trouble. They had
offerings with them, honey and cakes and white doves and
lambs and precious ointment. At the back of the hall the
people wore rough clothes of homespun cloth, but farther
forward Nerryn saw wonderful robes, embroidered with
gold and copper thread, made of rich materials, trimmed
with fur and sparkling stones. And up in the very front,
kneeling on the steps of the altar, was a man who was
finer than all the rest and Nerryn thought he must have
been the king himself. His hair and long beard were
white, his cloak was purple, and on his head were three
crowns, one gold, one copper, and one of ivory. Nerryn
stole up to him and touched the fingers that held a gold
staff, but they were ice-cold and still as marble, like all
the rest.

A sadness came over her as she looked at the people
and she thought, "What use to them are their fine robes
now? Why did the goddess punish them? What did they
do wrong?"

But there was no answer to her question.

"I had better leave this place before I am frozen as
well," she thought. "The goddess may be angry with me
too, for coming here. But first I will play for her on my
harp, as I have not brought any offering."

So she took her harp and began to play. She played all
the tunes she could remember, and last of all she played
the one that had come into her head as she climbed the
mountain.

At the noise of her playing, frost began to fall in white
showers from the roof of the temple, and from the rafters
and pillars and the clothes of the motionless people. Then
the king sneezed. Then there was a stirring noise, like the
sound of a winter stream when the ice begins to melt.
Then someone laughed—a loud, clear laugh. And, just as,
outside the town, the pile of frozen rocks had started to
move and topple when Nerryn played, so now the whole
gathering of people began to stretch themselves, and turn
round, and look at one another, and smile. And as she
went on playing they began to dance.

The dancing spread, out of the temple and down the
streets. People in the houses stood up and danced. Still
dancing, they fetched brooms and swept away the heaps

of frost that kept falling from the rooftops with the sound of the music. They fetched old wooden pipes and tabors out of the cellars that had escaped the fire, so that when Nerryn stopped playing at last, quite tired out, the music still went on. All day and all night, for thirty days, the music lasted, until the houses were rebuilt, the streets clean, and not a speck of frost remained in the city.

But the king beckoned Nerryn aside when she stopped playing and they sat down on the steps of the temple.

"My child," he said, "where did you get that harp?"

"Sir, I made it out of fishbones after a picture of my father's harp that an old woman made for me."

"And what was your father's name, child, and where is he now?"

"Sir, he is dead in the forest, but here is a piece of a tablet with his name on it."

And Nerryn held out the little fragment with Heramon the harper's name written. When he saw it, great tears formed in the king's eyes and began to roll down his cheeks.

"Sir," Nerryn said, "what is the matter? Why do you weep?"

"I weep for my son Heramon, who is lost, and I weep for joy because my grandchild has returned to me."

Then the king embraced Nerryn and took her to his palace and had robes of fur and velvet put on her, and there was great happiness and much feasting. And the king told Nerryn how, many years ago, the goddess was angered because the people had grown so greedy for gold from her mountain that they spent their lives in digging and mining, day and night, and forgot to honour her with music, in her temple and in the streets, as they had been used to do. They made tools of gold, and plates and dishes and musical instruments; everything that could be was made of gold. So at last the goddess appeared among them, terrible with rage, and put a curse on them, of burning and freezing.

"Since you prefer gold, got by burrowing in the earth, to the music that should honour me," she said, "you may keep your golden toys and little good may they do you! Let your golden harps and trumpets be silent, your flutes and pipes be dumb! I shall not come among you again until I am summoned by notes from a harp that is not made of gold, nor of silver, nor any precious metal, a harp that has never touched the earth but came from deep water, a harp that no man has ever played."

Then fire burst out of the mountain, destroying houses and killing many people. The king ordered his son Heramon, who was the bravest man in the city, to cross the dangerous forest and seek far and wide until he should find the harp of which the goddess spoke. Before Heramon could depart a great cold had struck, freezing people where they stood; only just in time he caught up his little daughter from her cradle and carried her away with him.

"But now you are come back," the old king said, "you shall be queen after me, and we shall take care that the goddess is honoured with music every day, in the temple and in the streets. And we will order everything that is made of gold to be thrown into the mountain torrent, so that nobody ever again shall be tempted to worship gold before the goddess."

So this was done, the king himself being the first to throw away his golden crown and staff. The river carried all the golden things down through the forest until they came to rest in Timorash's millpool, and one day, when he was fishing for carp, he pulled out the crown. Overjoyed, he ground it to powder and sold it to his neighbours for barley wine. Then he returned to the pool, hoping for more gold, but by now he was so drunk that he fell in and was drowned among a clutter of golden spades and trumpets and goblets and pickaxes.

But long before this Nerryn, with her harp on her back and astride of a white mule with knives bound to its hoofs, had ridden down the mountain to fetch Saroon as she had promised. She passed the forest safely, playing music for the vultures while the mule cut its way through the long grass. Nobody in the village recognized her, so splendidly was she dressed in fur and scarlet.

But when she came to where Saroon's hut had stood, the ground was bare, nor was there any trace that a dwelling had ever been there. And when she asked for Saroon, nobody knew the name, and the whole village declared that such a person had never been there.

Amazed and sorrowful, Nerryn returned to her grandfather. But one day, not long after, when she was alone, praying in the temple of the goddess, she heard a voice that said,

"Sing, child!"

And Nerryn was greatly astonished, for she felt she had heard the voice before, though she could not think where.

While she looked about her, wondering, the voice said again,

"Sing!"

And then Nerryn understood, and she laughed, and, taking her harp, sang a song about chopping wood, and about digging, and fishing, and the birds of the forest, and how the stream's voice changes in summer and in winter. For now she knew who had helped her to make her harp of fishbones.

❦ PETER SOYER BEAGLE ❦
(1939-   )

Peter Beagle, one of the younger American writers of fantasy, supports himself by writing, in addition to fiction, book reviews and essays on a wide variety of topics ranging from cockfighting to love. His essays provide the best insights available into his background. He was born of a middle-class Jewish family in the Bronx and remained quite attached to both his family and the Bronx until he decided that he had to break away to gain a different perspective. He received his B.A. from the University of Pittsburgh in 1959 and spent a year on a writing fellowship at Stanford (1960-1961). After living and traveling for some time in Europe, he returned to the United States and settled in Santa Cruz, California. He has been chairman of the local branch of the American Civil Liberties Union —one of his pet peeves is censorship; he likes music, plays the guitar, and composes ballads. He continues to live in the San Francisco Bay area.

His review essay of Tolkien's *Lord of the Rings* trilogy (*Holiday*, June 1966), later incorporated in part into his introduction to *The Tolkien Reader*, is of particular interest to readers of Tolkien and of fantasy in general. Beagle comments that the reason people, the young in particular, find Tolkien so appealing is that they recognize that Tolkien believes in what he is writing, that is, in the ethical standards and humanistic attitudes expressed in his books. Two examples of such standards and attitudes are: safeness or complacency corrupts, and every individual is a vital part of the whole of humankind and is responsible for its well-being. Both of these principles underlie much of Beagle's own fiction.

Beagle's output of fiction has been steady, but not at all

prolific. One suspects the reasons for this are the demands the author places upon himself for quality writing. His first book, still in print, is *A Fine and Private Place* (1960), published when he was just twenty-one. It is a highly unusual ghost story that blends fine characterization and a good measure of delightful humor with the themes of love and responsibility. The New York City graveyard setting of this book, however, hardly prepares the reader for the elegance of his next full-length novel, *The Last Unicorn* (1968), a medieval fantasy set entirely in a secondary world inhabited by kings, wizards, and unicorns. The humor, however, is there, as are the fine character delineations and the powerful themes. In between these two novels, Beagle wrote "Come Lady Death," a fantasy short story that was nominated for an O'Henry Award in 1963. His subsequent short fantasy work was "Lila the Werewolf" (1974), which returns to the style and setting of his first book. In addition to his fiction, Beagle has written two entertaining works of nonfiction: *I See by My Outfit* (1965) and *The California Feeling* (1969). Beagle is currently writing for movies and television. He co-authored the script for Ralph Bakshi's film version of Tolkien's *Lord of the Rings*. He has notified us that he has completed a script of the film version of "Lila the Werewolf," as well.

The tone of ironic humor pervades "Lila the Werewolf." As the narrator states in the story, "you could have either werewolves or Pyrex nine-cup percolators in the world, but not both, surely." Yet in this fantasy both do exist; although one could interpret the story as a psychological allegory, there is no doubt about the reality of both werewolf and percolator. It is one of Peter Beagle's greatest talents that here, as elsewhere, he combines the flippant with the serious, the comical with the ghastly. His unexpected images and comparisons are the tools with which he creates his humor, makes real the smell and feel of the werewolf's breath, and yokes the impossible with the real.

Lila the Werewolf
Peter S. Beagle

❧

Lila Braun had been living with Farrell for three weeks before he found out she was a werewolf. They had met at a party when the moon was a few nights past the full, and by the time it had withered to the shape of a lemon Lila had moved her suitcase, her guitar, and her Ewan MacColl records two blocks north and four blocks west to Farrell's apartment on Ninety-eighth Street. Girls sometimes happened to Farrell like that.

One evening Lila wasn't in when Farrell came home from work at the bookstore. She had left a note on the table, under a can of tunafish. The note said that she had gone up to the Bronx to have dinner with her mother, and would probably be spending the night there. The coleslaw in the refrigerator should be finished up before it went bad.

Farrell ate the tunafish and gave the coleslaw to Grunewald. Grunewald was a half-grown Russian wolfhound, the color of sour milk. He looked like a goat, and had no outside interests except shoes. Farrell was taking care of him for a girl who was away in Europe for the summer. She sent Grunewald a tape recording of her voice every week.

Farrell went to a movie with a friend, and to the West End afterward for beer. Then he walked home alone under the full moon, which was red and yellow. He reheated the morning coffee, played a record, read through a week-old "News of the Week in Review" section of the Sunday Times, and finally took Grunewald up to the roof for the night, as he always did. The dog had been accustomed to sleep in the same bed with his mistress, and the point was not negotiable. Grunewald

257

mooed and scrabbled and butted all the way, but Farrell pushed him out among the looming chimneys and ventilators and slammed the door. Then he came back downstairs and went to bed.

He slept very badly. Grunewald's baying woke him twice; and there was something else that brought him half out of bed, thirsty and lonely, with his sinuses full and the night swaying like a curtain as the figures of his dream scurried offstage. Grunewald seemed to have gone off the air— perhaps it was the silence that had awakened him. Whatever the reason, he never really got back to sleep.

He was lying on his back, watching a chair with his clothes on it becoming a chair again, when the wolf came in through the open window. It landed lightly in the middle of the room and stood there for a moment, breathing quickly, with its ears back. There was blood on the wolf's teeth and tongue, and blood on its chest.

Farrell, whose true gift was for acceptance, especially in the morning, accepted the idea that there was a wolf in his bedroom and lay quite still, closing his eyes as the grim, black-lipped head swung toward him. Having once worked at a zoo, he was able to recognize the beast as a Central European subspecies — smaller and lighter-boned than the northern timber wolf variety, lacking the thick, ruffy mane at the shoulders, and having a more pointed nose and ears. His own pedantry always delighted him, even at the worst moments.

Blunt claws clicking on the linoleum, then silent on the throw rug by the bed. Something warm and slow splashed down on his shoulder, but he never moved. The wild smell of the wolf was over him, and that did frighten him at last—to be in the same room with that smell and the Miró prints on the walls. Then he felt the sunlight on his eyelids, and at the same moment he heard the wolf moan softly and deeply. The sound was not repeated, but the breath on his face was suddenly sweet and smoky, dizzyingly familiar after the other. He opened his eyes and saw Lila. She was sitting naked on the edge of the bed, smiling, with her hair down.

"Hello, baby," she said. "Move over, baby. I came home."

Farrell's gift was for acceptance. He was perfectly willing to believe that he had dreamed the wolf; to believe Lila's story of boiled chicken and bitter arguments and sleeplessness on Tremont Avenue; and to forget that her first caress had been to bite him on the shoulder, hard enough so that the blood crusting there as he got up and made breakfast might very well be his own. But then he left the coffee perking and went up to the roof to get Grunewald. He found the dog sprawled in a grove of TV antennas, looking more like a goat than ever, with his throat torn out. Farrell had never actually seen an animal with its throat torn out.

The coffeepot was still chuckling when he came back into the apartment, which struck him as very odd. You could have either werewolves or Pyrex nine-cup percolators in the world, but not both, surely. He told Lila, watching her face. She was a small girl, not really pretty, but with good eyes and a lovely mouth, and with a curious sullen gracefulness that had been the first thing to speak to Farrell at the party. When he told her how Grunewald had looked, she shivered all over, once.

"Ugh!" she said, wrinkling her lips back from her neat white teeth. "Oh baby, how awful. Poor Grunewald. Oh, poor Barbara." Barbara was Grunewald's owner.

"Yeah," Farrell said. "Poor Barbara, making her little tapes in Saint-Tropez." He could not look away from Lila's face.

She said, "Wild dogs. Not really wild, I mean, but with owners. You hear about it sometimes, how a pack of them get together and attack children and things, running through the streets. Then they go home and eat their Dog Yummies. The scary thing is that they probably live right around here. Everybody on the block seems to have a dog. God, that's scary. Poor Grunewald."

"They didn't tear him up much," Farrell said. "It must have been just for the fun of it. And the blood. I didn't know dogs killed for the blood. He didn't have any blood left."

The tip of Lila's tongue appeared between her lips, in the unknowing reflex of a fondled cat. As evidence, it wouldn't have stood up even in old Salem; but Farrell knew the truth then, beyond laziness or rationalization, and went on buttering toast for Lila. Farrell had nothing against werewolves, and he had never like Grunewald.

He told his friend Ben Kassoy about Lila when they met in the Automat for lunch. He had to shout it over the clicking and rattling all around them, but the people sitting six inches away on either hand never looked up. New Yorkers never eavesdrop. They hear only what they simply cannot help hearing.

Ben said, "I told you about Bronx girls. You better come stay at my place for a few days."

Farrell shook his head. "No, that's silly. I mean, it's only Lila. If she were going to hurt me, she could have done it last night. Besides, it won't happen again for a month. There has to be a full moon."

His friend stared at him. "So what? What's that got to do with anything? You going to go on home as though nothing had happened?"

"Not as though nothing had happened," Farrell said lamely. "The thing is, it's still only Lila, not Lon Chaney or somebody. Look, she goes to her psychiatrist three afternoons a week, and she's got her guitar lesson one night a week, and her pottery class one night, and she cooks eggplant maybe twice a week. She calls her mother every Friday night, and one night a month she turns into a wolf. You see what I'm getting at? It's still Lila, whatever she does, and I just can't get terribly shook about it. A little bit, sure, because what the hell. But I don't know. Anyway, there's no mad rush about it. I'll talk to her when the thing comes up in the conversation, just naturally. It's okay."

Ben said, "God damn. You see why nobody has any respect for liberals anymore? Farrell, I know you. You're just scared of hurting her feelings."

"Well, it's that too," Farrell agreed, a little embarrassed. "I hate confrontations. If I break up with her now, she'll think I'm doing it because she's a werewolf. It's awkward, it feels nasty and middle-class. I should have broken up with her the first time I met her mother, or the second time she served the eggplant. Her mother, boy, there's the real werewolf, there's somebody I'd wear wolfbane against, that woman. Damn, I wish I hadn't found out. I don't think I've ever found out anything about people that I was the better for knowing."

Ben walked all the way back to the bookstore with him, arguing. It touched Farrell, because Ben hated to walk. Before they parted, Ben suggested, "At least you could try some of that stuff you were talking about, the wolfbane. There's garlic, too — you put some in a little bag and wear it around your neck. Don't laugh, man. If there's such a thing as werewolves, the other stuff must be real too. Cold iron, silver, oak, running water —"

"I'm not laughing at you," Farrell said, but he was still grinning. "Lila's shrink says she has a rejection thing, very deep-seated, take us years to break through all that scar tissue. Now if I start walking around wearing amulets and mumbling in Latin every time she looks at me, who knows how far it'll set her back? Listen, I've done some things I'm not proud of, but I don't want to mess up anyone's analysis. That's the sin against God." He sighed and slapped Ben lightly on the arm. "Don't worry about it. We'll work it out, I'll talk to her."

But between that night and the next full moon, he found no good, casual way of bringing the subject up. Admittedly, he did not try as hard as he might have: it was true that he feared confrontations more than he feared werewolves, and he would have found it almost as difficult to talk to Lila about her guitar playing, or her pots, or the political arguments she got into at parties. "The thing is," he said to Ben, "it's sort of one more little weakness not to take advantage of. In a way."

They made love often that month. The smell of Lila flowered in the bedroom, where the smell of the wolf still lingered almost visibly, and both of them were wild, heavy zoo smells, warm and raw and fearful, the sweeter for being savage. Farrell held Lila in his arms and knew what she was, and he was always frightened; but he would not have let her go if she had turned into a wolf again as he held her. It was a relief to peer at her while she slept and see how stubby and childish her fingernails were, or that the skin around her mouth was rashy because she had been snacking on chocolate. She loved secret sweets, but they always betrayed her.

It's only Lila after all, he would think as he drowsed off. Her mother used to hide the candy, but Lila always found it.

Now she's a big girl, neither married nor in a graduate school, but living in sin with an Irish musician, and she can have all the candy she wants. What kind of a werewolf is that. Poor Lila, practicing *Who killed Davey Moore? Why did he die? . . .*

The note said that she would be working late at the magazine, on layout, and might have to be there all night. Farrell put on about four feet of Telemann laced with Django Reinhardt, took down *The Golden Bough*, and settled into a chair by the window. The moon shone in at him, bright and thin and sharp as the lid of a tin can, and it did not seem to move at all as he dozed and woke.

Lila's mother called several times during the night, which was interesting. Lila still picked up her mail and most messages at her old apartment, and her two roommates covered for her when necessary, but Farrell was absolutely certain that her mother knew she was living with him. Farrell was an expert on mothers. Mrs. Braun called him Joe each time she called and that made him wonder, for he knew she hated him. Does she suspect that we share a secret? Ah, poor Lila.

The last time the telephone woke him, it was still dark in the room, but the traffic lights no longer glittered through rings of mist, and the cars made a different sound on the warming pavement. A man was saying clearly in the street, "Well, I'd shoot'm. I'd shoot'm." Farrell let the telephone ring ten times before he picked it up.

"Let me talk to Lila," Mrs.Braun said.

"She isn't here." What if the sun catches her, what if she turns back to herself in front of a cop, or a bus driver, or a couple of nuns going to early Mass? "Lila isn't here, Mrs. Braun."

"I have reason to believe that's not true." The fretful, muscular voice had dropped all pretense of warmth. "I want to talk to Lila."

Farrell was suddenly dry-mouthed and shivering with fury. It was her choice of words that did it. "Well, I have reason to believe you're a suffocating old bitch and a bourgeois Stalinist. How do you like them apples, Mrs. B?" As though his anger had summoned her, the wolf was standing two feet away from him. Her coat was dark and lank with sweat, and yellow saliva was mixed with the blood that strung from her jaws. She looked at Farrell and growled far away in her throat.

"Just a minute," he said. He covered the receiver with his palm. "It's for you," he said to the wolf. "It's your mother."

The wolf made a pitiful sound, almost inaudible, and scuffed at the floor. She was plainly exhausted. Mrs. Braun pinged in Farrell's ear like a bug against a lighted window. "What, what? Hello, what is this? Listen, you put Lila on the phone right now. Hello? I want to talk to Lila. I know she's there."

Farrell hung up just as the sun touched a corner of the window. The wolf became Lila. As before, she only made one sound. The phone rang again, and she picked it up without a glance at Farrell. "Bernice?" Lila always called her mother by her first name. "Yes — no, no — yeah, I'm fine. I'm all right, I just forgot to call. No, I'm all right, will you listen? Bernice, there's no law that says you have to get hysterical. Yes you are." She dropped down on the bed, groping under her pillow for cigarettes. Farrell got up and began to make coffee.

"Well, there was a little trouble," Lila was saying. "See, I went to the zoo, because I couldn't find — Bernice, I know, I *know*, but that was, what, three months ago. The thing is, I didn't think they'd have their horns so soon. Bernice, I had to, that's all. There'd only been a couple of cats and a — well, sure they chased me, but I — well, Momma, Bernice, what did you want me to do? Just what did you want me to do? You're always so dramatic — why do I shout? I shout because I can't get you to listen to me any other way. You remember what Dr. Schechtman said — what? No, I told you, I just forgot to call. No, that is the reason, that's the real and only reason. Well, whose fault is that? What? Oh, Bernice. Jesus Christ, Bernice. All right, *how* is it Dad's fault?"

She didn't want the coffee, or any breakfast, but she sat at the table in his bathrobe and drank milk greedily. It was the first time he had ever seen her drink milk. Her face was sandy pale, and her eyes were red. Talking to her mother left her looking as though she had actually gone ten rounds with the woman. Farrell asked, "How long has it been happening?"

"Nine years," Lila said. "Since I hit puberty. First day, cramps; the second day, this. My introduction to womanhood." She snickered and spilled her milk. "I want some more," she said. "Got to get rid of that taste."

"Who knows about it?" he asked. "Pat and Janet?" They were the two girls she had been rooming with.

"God, no. I'd never tell them. I've never told a girl. Bernice knows, of course, and Dr. Schechtman — he's my head doctor. And you now. That's all." Farrell waited. She was a bad liar, and only did it to heighten the effect of the truth. "Well, there was Mickey," she said. "The guy I told you about the first night, you remember? It doesn't matter. He's an acidhead in Vancouver, of all the places. He'll never tell anybody."

He thought: I wonder if any girl has ever talked about me in that sort of voice. I doubt it, offhand. Lila said, "It wasn't too hard to keep it secret. I missed a lot of things. Like I never could go to the riding camp, and I still want to. And the senior play, when I was in high school. They picked me to play the girl in *Liliom*, but then they changed the evening, and I had to say I was sick. And the winter's bad, because the sun sets so early. But actually, it's been a lot less trouble than my goddamn allergies." She made a laugh, but Farrell did not respond.

"Dr. Schechtman says it's a sex thing," she offered. "He says it'll take years and years to cure it. Bernice thinks I should go to someone else, but I don't want to be one of those women who runs around changing shrinks like hair colors. Pat went through five of them in a month one time. Joe, I wish you'd say something. Or just go away."

"Is it only dogs?" he asked. Lila's face did not change, but her chair rattled, and the milk went over again. Farrell said, "Answer me. Do you only kill dogs, and cats, and zoo animals?"

The tears began to come, heavy and slow, bright as knives in the morning sunlight. She could not look at him, and when she tried to speak she could only make creaking, cartilaginous sounds in her throat. "You don't know," she whispered at last. "You don't have any idea what it's like."

"That's true," he answered. He was always very fair about that particular point.

He took her hand, and then she really began to cry. Her sobs were horrible to hear, much more frightening to Farrell than any wolf noises. When he held her, she rolled in his arms like a stranded ship with the waves slamming into her. I always get the criers, he thought sadly. My girls always cry, sooner or later. But never for me.

"Don't leave me!" she wept. "I don't know why I came to live with you — I knew it wouldn't work — but don't leave me! There's just Bernice and Dr. Schechtman, and it's so lonely. I want somebody else, I get so lonely. Don't leave me, Joe. I love you, Joe. I love you."

She was patting his face as though she were blind. Farrell stroked her hair and kneaded the back of her neck, wishing that her mother would call again. He felt skilled and weary, and without desire. I'm doing it again, he thought.

"I love you," Lila said. And he answered her, thinking, I'm doing it again. That's the great advantage of making the same mistake a lot of times. You come to know it, and you can study it and get inside it, really make it yours. It's the same good old mistake, except this time the girl's hang-up is different. But it's the same thing. I'm doing it again.

The building superintendent was thirty or fifty: dark, thin, quick, and shivering. A Lithuanian or a Latvian, he spoke very little English. He smelled of black friction tape and stale water, and he was strong in the twisting way that a small, lean animal is strong. His eyes were almost purple, and they bulged a little, straining out — the terrible eyes of a herald angel stricken dumb. He roamed in the basement all day, banging on pipes and taking the elevator apart.

The superintendent met Lila only a few hours after Farrell did: on that first night, when she came home with him. At the sight of her the little man jumped back, dropping the two-legged chair he was carrying. He promptly fell over it, and did not try to get up, but cowered there, clucking and gulping, trying to cross himself and make the sign of the horns at the same time. Farrell started to help him up, but he screamed. They could hardly hear the sound.

It would have been merely funny and embarrassing, except

for the fact that Lila was equally as frightened of the superintendent from that moment. She would not go down to the basement for any reason, nor would she enter or leave the house until she was satisfied that he was nowhere near. Farrell had thought then that she took the superintendent for a lunatic.

"I don't know how he knows," he said to Ben. "I guess if you believe in werewolves and vampires, you probably recognize them right away. I don't believe in them at all, and I live with one."

He lived with Lila all through the autumn and the winter. They went out together and came home, and her cooking improved slightly, and she gave up the guitar and got a kitten named Theodora. Sometimes she wept, but not often. She turned out not to be a real crier.

She told Dr. Schechtman about Farrell, and he said that it would probably be a very beneficial relationship for her. It wasn't, but it wasn't a particularly bad one either. Their lovemaking was usually good, though it bothered Farrell to suspect that it was the sense and smell of the Other that excited him. For the rest, they came near being friends. Farrell had known that he did not love Lila before he found out that she was a werewolf, and this made him feel a great deal easier about being bored with her.

"It'll break up by itself in the spring," he said, "like ice."

Ben asked, "What if it doesn't?" They were having lunch in the Automat again. "What'll you do if it just goes on?"

"It's not that easy." Farrell looked away from his friend and began to explore the mysterious, swampy innards of his beef pie. He said, "The trouble is that I know her. That was the real mistake. You shouldn't get to know people if you know you're not going to stay with them, one way or another. It's all right if you come and go in ignorance, but you shouldn't know them."

A week or so before the full moon, she would start to become nervous and strident, and this would continue until the day preceding her transformation. On that day, she was invariably loving, in the tender, desperate manner of someone who is going away; but the next day would see her silent, speaking only when she had to. She always had a cold on the last day, and looked gray and patchy and sick, but she usually went to work anyway.

Farrell was sure, though she never talked about it, that the change into wolf shape was actually peaceful for her, though the returning hurt. Just before moonrise she would take off her clothes and take the pins out of her hair and stand waiting. Farrell never managed not to close his eyes when she dropped heavily down on all fours; but there was a moment before that when her face would grow a look that he never saw at any other time, except when they were making love. Each time he saw it, it struck him as a look of wondrous joy at not being Lila any more.

"See, I know her," he tried to explain to Ben. "She only likes to go to color movies, because wolves can't see color. She can't stand the Modern Jazz Quartet, but that's all she plays the first couple of days afterward. Stupid things like that. Never gets high at parties, because she's afraid she'll start talking. It's hard to walk away, that's all. Taking what I know with me."

Ben asked, "Is she still scared of the super?"

"Oh, God," Farrell said. "She got his dog last time. It was a Dalmatian — good-looking animal. She didn't know it was his. He doesn't hide when he sees her now, he just gives her a look like a stake through the heart. That man is a really classy hater, a natural. I'm scared of him myself." He stood up and began to pull on his overcoat. "I wish he'd get turned on to her mother. Get some practical use out of him. Did I tell you she wants me to call her Bernice?"

Ben said, "Farrell, if I were you, I'd leave the country. I would."

They went out into the February drizzle that sniffled back and forth between snow and rain. Farrell did not speak until they reached the corner where he turned toward the bookstore. Then he said very softly, "Damn, you have to be so careful. Who wants to know what people turn into?"

May came, and a night when Lila once again stood naked at the window, waiting for the moon. Farrell fussed with dishes and garbage bags and fed the cat. These moments were always awkward. He had just asked her, "You want to save what's left of the rice?" when the telephone rang.

It was Lila's mother. She called two and three times a week now. "This is Bernice. How's my Irisher this evening?"

"I'm fine, Bernice," Farrell said. Lila suddenly threw back her head and drew a heavy, whining breath. The cat hissed silently and ran into the bathroom.

"I called to inveigle you two uptown this Friday," Mrs. Braun said. "A couple of old friends are coming over, and I know if I don't get some young people in we'll just sit around and talk about what went wrong with the Progressive Party. The Old Left. So if you could sort of sweet-talk our girl into spending an evening in Squaresville —"

"I'll have to check with Lila." She's *doing* it, he thought, that terrible woman. Every time I talk to her, I sound married. I see what she's doing, but she goes right ahead anyway. He said, "I'll talk to her in the morning." Lila struggled in the moonlight, between dancing and drowning.

"Oh," Mrs. Braun said. "Yes, of course. Have her call me back." She sighed. "It's such a comfort to me to know you're there. Ask her if I should fix a fondue."

Lila made a handsome wolf: tall and broad-chested for a female, moving as easily as water sliding over stone. Her coat was dark brown, showing red in the proper light, and there were white places on her breast. She had pale green eyes, the color of the sky when a hurricane is coming.

Usually she was gone as soon as the changing was over, for she never cared for him to see her in her wolf form. But tonight she came slowly toward him, walking in a strange way, with her hindquarters almost dragging. She was making a high, soft sound, and her eyes were not focusing on him.

"What is it?" he asked foolishly. The wolf whined and skulked under the table, rubbing against the leg. Then she lay on her belly and rolled, and as she did so the sound grew in her throat until it became an odd, sad, thin cry, not a hunting howl, but a shiver of longing turned into breath.

"Jesus, don't do that!" Farrell gasped. But she sat up and howled again, and a dog answered her from somewhere near the river. She wagged her tail and whimpered.

Farrell said, "The super'll be up here in two minutes flat.

What's the matter with you?" He heard footsteps and low frightened voices in the apartment above them. Another dog howled, this one nearby, and the wolf wriggled a little way toward the window on her haunches, like a baby, scooting. She looked at him over her shoulder, shuddering violently. On an impulse, he picked up the phone and called her mother.

Watching the wolf as she rocked and slithered and moaned, he described her actions to Mrs. Braun. "I've never seen her like this," he said. "I don't know what's the matter with her."

"Oh, my God," Mrs. Braun whispered. She told him.

When he was silent, she began to speak very rapidly. "It hasn't happened for such a long time. Schechtman gives her pills, but she must have run out and forgotten — she's always been like that, since she was little. All the thermos bottles she used to leave on the school bus, and every week her piano music —"

"I wish you'd told me before," he said. He was edging very cautiously toward the open window. The pupils of the wolf's eyes were pulsing with her quick breaths.

"It isn't a thing you tell people!" Lila's mother wailed in his ears. "How do you think it was for me when she brought her first little boyfriend —" Farrell dropped the phone and sprang for the window. He had the inside track, and he might have made it, but she turned her head and snarled so wildly that he fell back. When he reached the window, she was already two fire escape landings below, and there was eager yelping waiting for her in the street.

Dangling and turning just above the floor, Mrs. Braun heard Farrell's distant yell, followed immediately by a heavy thumping on the door. A strange, tattered voice was shouting unintelligibly beyond the knocking. Footsteps crashed by the receiver and the door opened.

"My dog, my dog!" the strange voice mourned. "My dog, my dog, my dog!"

"I'm sorry about your dog," Farrell said. "Look, please go away. I've got work to do."

"I got work," the voice said. "I know my work." It climbed and spilled into another language, out of which English words jutted like broken bones. "Where is she? Where is she? She kill my dog."

"She's not here." Farrell's own voice changed on the last word. It seemed a long time before he said, "You'd better put that away."

Mrs. Braun heard the howl as clearly as though the wolf were running beneath her own window—lonely and insatiable, with a kind of gasping laughter in it. The other voice began to scream. Mrs. Braun caught the phrase *silver bullet* several times. The door slammed, then opened and slammed again.

Farrell was the only man of his own acquaintance who was able to play back his dreams while he was having them: to stop them in mid-flight, no matter how fearful they might be — or how lovely — and run them over and over studying them in his sleep, until the most terrifying reel became at once utterly harmless and unbearably familiar. This night that he spent running after Lila was like that.

He would find them congregated under the marquee of an apartment house, or romping around the moonscape of a construction site: ten or fifteen males of all races, creeds, colors, and previous conditions of servitude; whining and yapping, pissing against tires, inhaling indiscriminately each other and the lean, grinning bitch they surrounded. She frightened them, for she growled more wickedly than coyness demanded, and where she snapped, even in play, bone showed. Still they tumbled on her and over her, biting her neck and ears in their turn; and she snarled but she did not run away.

Never, at least, until Farrell came charging upon them, shrieking like any cuckold, kicking at the snuffling lovers. Then she would turn and race off into the spring dark, with her thin, dreamy howl floating behind her like the train of a smoky gown. The dogs followed, and so did Farrell, calling and cursing. They always lost him quickly, that jubilant marriage procession, leaving him stumbling down rusty iron ladders into places where he fell over garbage cans. Yet he would come upon them as inevitably in time, loping along Broadway or trotting across Columbus Avenue toward the park; he would hear them in the tennis courts near the river, breaking down the nets over Lila and her moment's Ares. There were dozens of them now, coming from all directions. They stank of their joy, and he threw stones at them and shouted, and they ran.

And the wolf ran at their head, on sidewalks and on wet grass, her tail waving contentedly, but her eyes still hungry, and her howl growing ever more warning than wistful. Farrell knew that she must have blood before sunrise, and that it was both useless and dangerous to follow her. But the night wound and unwound itself, and he knew the same things over and over, and ran down the same streets, and saw the same couples walk wide of him, thinking he was drunk.

Mrs. Braun kept leaping out of a taxi that pulled up next to him, usually at corners where the dogs had just piled by, knocking over the crates stacked in market doorways and spilling the newspapers at the subway kiosks. Standing in broccoli, in black taffeta, with a front like a ferryboat —yet as lean in the hips as her wolf-daughter — with her plum-colored hair all loose, one arm lifted, and her orange mouth pursed in a bellow, she was no longer Bernice but a wronged fertility goddess getting set to blast the harvest. "We've got to split up!" she would roar at Farrell, and each time it sounded like a sound idea. Yet he looked for her whenever he lost Lila's trail, because she never did.

The superintendent kept turning up too, darting after Farrell out of alleys or cellar entrances, or popping from the freight elevators that load through the sidewalk. Farrell would hear his numberless passkeys clicking on the flat piece of wood tucked into his belt.

"You see her? You see her, the wolf, kill my dog?" Under the fat, ugly moon, the army .45 glittered and trembled like his own mad eyes.

"Mark with a cross." He would pat the barrel of the gun and shake it under Farrell's nose like a maraca. "Mark with a cross, bless by a priest. Three silver bullets. She kill my dog."

Lila's voice would come sailing to them then, from up in Harlem or away near Lincoln Center, and the little man would whirl and dash down into the earth, disappearing into the crack between two slabs of sidewalk. Farrell understood quite clearly that the superintendent was hunting Lila underground, using the keys that only superintendents have to take elevators down to the black sub-sub-basements, far below the bicycle rooms and the wet, shaking laundry rooms, and below the furnace rooms, below the passages walled with electricity meters and roofed with burly steam pipes; down to the realms where the great dim water mains roll like whales, and the gas lines hump and preen, down where the roots of the apartment houses fade together; and so along under the city, scrabbling through secret ways with silver bullets, and his keys rapping against the piece of wood. He never saw Lila, but he was never very far behind her.

Cutting across parking lots, pole-vaulting between locked bumpers, edging and dancing his way through fluorescent gaggles of haughty children; leaping uptown like a salmon against the current of the theater crowds; walking quickly past the random killing faces that floated down the night tide like unexploded mines, and especially avoiding the crazy faces that wanted to tell him what it was like to be crazy — so Farrell pursued Lila Braun, of Tremont Avenue and CCNY, in the city all night long. Nobody offered to help him, or tried to head off the dangerous-looking bitch bounding along with the delirious raggle of admirers streaming after her; but then, the dogs had to fight through the same clenched legs and vengeful bodies that Farrell did. The crowds slowed Lila down, but he felt relieved whenever she turned toward the emptier streets. *She must have blood soon, somewhere.*

Farrell's dreams eventually lost their clear edge after he played them back a certain number of times, and so it was with the night. The full moon skidded down the sky, thinning like a tatter of butter in a skillet, and remembered scenes began to fold sloppily into each other. The sound of Lila and the dogs grew fainter whichever way he followed. Mrs. Braun blinked on and off at longer intervals; and in dark doorways and under subway gratings, the superintendent burned like a corposant, making the barrel of his pistol run rainbow. At last he lost Lila for good, and with that it seemed that he woke.

It was still night, but not dark, and he was walking slowly home on Riverside Drive through a cool, grainy fog. The moon had set, but the river was strangely bright — glittering gray as far up as the bridge, where headlights left shiny, wet paths like snails. There was no one else on the street.

"Dumb broad," he said aloud. "The hell with it. She wants to mess around, let her mess around." He wondered whether werewolves could have cubs, and what sort of cubs they might be. Lila must have turned on the dogs by now, for the blood. Poor dogs, he thought. They were all so dirty and innocent and happy with her.

"A moral lesson for all of us," he announced sententiously. "Don't fool with strange, eager ladies, they'll kill you." He was a little hysterical. Then, two blocks ahead of him, he saw the gaunt shape in the gray light of the river, alone now, and hurrying. Farrell did not call to her, but as soon as he began to run, the wolf wheeled and faced him. Even at that distance, her eyes were stained and streaked and wild. She showed all the teeth on one side of her mouth, and she growled like fire.

Farrell trotted steadily toward her, crying, "Go home, go home! Lila, you dummy, get on home, it's morning!" She growled terribly, but when Farrell was less than a block away she turned again and dashed across the street, heading for West End Avenue. Farrell said, "Good girl, that's it," and limped after her.

In the hours before sunrise on West End Avenue, many people came out to walk their dogs. Farrell had done it often enough with poor Grunewald to know many of the dawn walkers by sight, and some to talk to. A fair number of them were whores and homosexuals, both of whom always seem to have dogs in New York. Quietly, almost always alone, they drifted up and down the Nineties, piloted by their small, fussy beasts, but moving in a kind of fugitive truce with the city and the night that was ending. Farrell sometimes fancied that they were all asleep, and that this hour was the only true rest they ever got.

He recognized Robie by his two dogs, Scone and Crumpet. Robie lived in the apartment directly below Farrell's, usually unhappily. The dogs were horrifying little homebrews of Chihuahua and Yorkshire terrier, but Robie loved them. Crumpet, the male, saw Lila first. He gave a delighted yap of welcome and proposition (according to Robie, Scone bored him, and he liked big girls anyway) and sprang to meet her, yanking his leash through Robie's slack hand. The wolf was almost upon him before he realized his fatal misunderstanding and scuttled desperately in retreat, meowing with utter terror.

Robie wailed, and Farrell ran as fast as he could, but Lila knocked Crumpet off his feet and slashed his throat while he was still in the air. Then she crouched on the body, nuzzling it in a dreadful way.

Robie actually came within a step of leaping upon Lila and trying to drag her away from his dead dog. Instead, he turned on Farrell as he came panting up, and began hitting him with a good deal of strength and accuracy. "Damn you, damn you!" he sobbed. Little Scone ran away around the corner, screaming like a mandrake.

Farrell put up his arms and went with the punches, all the while yelling at Lila until his voice ripped. But the blood frenzy had her, and Farrell had never imagined what she must be like at those times. Somehow she had spared the dogs who had loved her all night, but she was nothing but thirst now. She pushed and kneaded Crumpet's body as though she were nursing.

All along the avenue, the morning dogs were barking like trumpets. Farrell ducked away from Robie's soft fists and saw them coming, tripping over their trailing leashes, running too fast for their stubby legs. They were small, spoiled beasts, most of them, overweight and short-winded, and many were not young. Their owners cried unmanly pet names after them, but they waddled gallantly toward their deaths, barking promises far bigger than themselves, and none of them looked back.

She looked up with her muzzle red to the eyes. The dogs did falter then, for they knew murder when they smelled it, and even their silly, nearsighted eyes understood vaguely what creature faced them. But they knew the smell of love too, and they were all gentlemen.

She killed the first two to reach her — a spitz and a cocker spaniel — with two snaps of her jaws. But before she could settle down to her meal, three Pekes were scrambling up to her, though they would have had to stand on each others' shoulders. Lila whirled without a sound, and they fell away, rolling and yelling but unhurt. As soon as she turned, the Pekes were at her again, joined now by a couple of valiant poodles. Lila got one of the poodles when she turned again.

Robie had stopped beating on Farrell, and was leaning against a traffic light, being sick. But other people were running up now: a middle-aged black man, crying; a plump youth in a plastic car coat and bedroom slippers, who kept whimpering, "Oh God, she's eating them, look at her, she's really eating them!"; two lean, ageless girls in slacks, both with foamy beige hair. They all called wildly to their unheeding dogs, and they all grabbed at Farrell and shouted in his face. Cars began to stop.

The sky was thin and cool, rising pale gold, but Lila paid no attention to it. She was ramping under the swarm of little dogs, rearing and spinning in circles, snarling blood. The dogs were terrified and bewildered, but they never swerved from their labor. The smell of love told them that they were welcome, however ungraciously she seemed to receive them. Lila shook herself, and a pair of squealing dachshunds, hobbled in a double harness, tumbled across the sidewalk to end at Farrell's feet. They scrambled up and immediately towed themselves back into the maelstrom. Lila bit one of them almost in half, but the other dachshund went on trying to climb her hindquarters, dragging his ripped comrade with him. Farrell began to laugh.

The black man said, "You think it's funny?" and hit him. Farrell sat down, still laughing. The man stood over him, embarrassed, offering Farrell his handkerchief. "I'm sorry, I shouldn't have done that," he said. "But your dog killed my dog."

"She isn't my dog," Farrell said. He moved to let a man pass between them, and then saw that it was the superintendent, holding his pistol with both hands. Nobody noticed him until he fired; but Farrell pushed one of the foamy-haired girls, and she stumbled against the superintendent as the gun went off. The silver bullet broke a window in a parked car.

The superintendent fired again while the echoes of the first shot were still clapping back and forth between the houses. A Pomeranian screamed that time, and a woman cried out, "Oh, my God, he shot Borgy!" But the crowd was crumbling away, breaking into its individual components like pills on television. The watching cars had sped off at the sight of the gun, and the faces that had been peering down from windows disappeared. Except for Farrell, the few people who remained were scattered halfway down the block. The sky was brightening swiftly now.

"For God's sake, don't let him!" the same woman called from the shelter of a doorway. But two men made shushing gestures at her, saying, "It's all right, he knows how to use that thing. Go ahead, buddy."

The shots had at last frightened the little dogs away from Lila. She crouched among the twitching splotches of fur, with her muzzle wrinkled back and her eyes more black than green. Farrell saw a plaid rag that had been a dog jacket protruding from under her body. The superintendent stooped and squinted over the gun barrel, aiming with grotesque care, while the men cried to him to shoot. He was too far from the werewolf for her to reach him before he fired the last silver bullet, though he would surely die before she dies. His lips were moving as he took aim.

Two long steps would have brought Farrell up behind the superintendent. Later he told himself that he had been afraid of the pistol, because that was easier than remembering how he had felt when he looked at Lila. Her tongue never stopped lapping around her dark jaws, and even as she set herself to spring she lifted a bloody paw to her mouth. Farrell thought of her padding in the bedroom, breathing on his face. The superintendent grunted and Farrell closed his eyes. Yet even then he expected to find himself doing something.

Then he heard Mrs. Braun's unmistakable voice. "*Don't you dare!*" She was standing between Lila and the superintendent — one shoe gone, and the heel off the other one; her knit dress torn at the shoulder, and her face tired and smudgy. But she pointed a finger at the startled superintendent, and he stepped quickly back, as though she had a pistol too.

"Lady, that's a wolf," he protested nervously. "Lady, you please get, get out of the way. That's a wolf, I go shoot her now."

"I want to see your license for that gun." Mrs. Braun held out her hand. The superintendent blinked at her, muttering in despair. She said, "Do you know that you can be sent to prison for twenty years for carrying a concealed weapon in this state? Do you know what the fine is for having a gun without a license? The fine is Five. Thousand. Dollars." The men down the street were shouting at her, but she swung around to face the creature snarling among the little dead dogs.

"Come on, Lila," she said. "Come on home with Bernice. I'll make tea and we'll talk. It's been a long time since we've really talked, you know? We used to have nice long talks when you were little, but we don't anymore." The wolf had stopped growling, but she was crouching even lower, and her ears were still flat against her head. Mrs. Braun said, "Come on, baby. Listen, I know what — you'll call in sick at the office and stay for a few days. You'll get a good rest, and maybe we'll even look around a little for a new doctor, what do you say? Schechtman hasn't done a thing for you, I never liked him. Come on home, honey. Momma's here, Bernice knows." She took a step toward the silent wolf, holding out her hand.

The superintendent gave a desperate wordless cry and pumped forward, clumsily shoving Mrs. Braun to one side. He leveled the pistol point-blank, wailing, "My dog, my dog!" Lila was in the air when the gun went off, and her shadow sprang after her, for the sun had risen. She crumpled down across a couple of dead Pekes. Their blood dabbled her breasts and her pale throat.

Mrs. Braun screamed like a lunch whistle. She knocked the superintendent into the street and sprawled over Lila, hiding her completely from Farrell's sight. "Lila, Lila," she keened her daughter, "poor baby, you never had a chance. He killed you because you were different, the way they kill everything different." Farrell approached her and stooped down, but she pushed him against a wall without looking up. "Lila, Lila, poor baby, poor darling, maybe it's better, maybe you're happy now. You never had a chance, poor Lila."

The dog owners were edging slowly back, and the surviving dogs were running to them. The superintendent squatted on the curb with his head in his arms. A weary, muffled voice said, "For God's sake, Bernice, would you get up off me? You don't have to stop yelling, just get off."

When she stood up, the cars began to stop in the street again. It made it very difficult for the police to get through.

Nobody pressed charges, because there was no one to lodge them against. The killer dog — or wolf, as some insisted — was gone, and if she had an owner, he could not be found. As for the people who had actually seen the wolf turn into a young girl when the sunlight touched her; most of them managed not to have seen it, though they never really forgot. There were a few who knew quite well what they had seen, and never forgot it either, but they never said anything. They did, however, chip in to pay the superintendent's fine for possessing an unlicensed handgun. Farrell gave what he could.

Lila vanished out of Farrell's life before sunset. She did not go uptown with her mother, but packed her things and went to stay with friends in the village. Later he heard that she was living on Christopher Street, and later still, that she had moved to Berkeley and gone back to school. He never saw her again.

"It had to be like that," he told Ben once. "We got to know too much about each other. See, there's another side to knowing. She couldn't look at me."

"You mean because you saw her with all those dogs? Or because she knew you'd have let that little nut shoot her?" Farrell shook his head.

"It was that, I guess, but it was more something else, something I know. When she sprang, just as he shot at her that last time, she wasn't leaping at him. She was going straight for her mother. She'd have got her too, if it hadn't been sunrise."

Ben whistled softly. "I wonder if her old lady knows."

"Bernice knows everything about Lila," Farrell said.

Mrs. Braun called him nearly two years later to tell him that Lila was getting married. It must have cost her a good deal of money and ingenuity to find him (where Farrell was living then, the telephone line was open for four hours a day), but he knew by the spitefulness in the static that she considered it money well spent.

"He's at Stanford," she crackled. "A research psychologist.

They're going to Japan for their honeymoon."

"That's fine," Farrell said. "I'm really happy for her, Bernice." He hesitated before he asked, "Does he know about Lila? I mean, about what happens? — "

"Does he know?" she cried. "He's proud of it — he thinks it's wonderful! It's his field!"

"That's great. That's fine. Good-bye, Bernice. I really am glad."

And he was glad, and a little wistful, thinking about it. The girl he was living with here had a really strange hang-up.

❦ SYLVIA TOWNSEND WARNER ❦
(1893-1978)

Sylvia Townsend Warner, poet, novelist, short-story writer, and biographer, is one of England's most versatile and brilliant authors. Born at Harrow-on-the-Hill, Middlesex, the daughter of a schoolmaster, she was educated privately. Acquiring an interest in music very early in life, she spent an entire decade, from her early twenties through her early thirties, compiling, with three other editors, an impressive ten-volume work entitled *Tudor Church Music*. As might be expected, this rather definitive research project brought her widespread recognition as an expert on Renaissance music.

At the age of twenty-nine, Warner began writing poetry, and three years later, in 1925, she published her first collection, *The Espalier*. Although her writing career can be said to have begun with this warm and witty book of poems, her real breakthrough as an author came in 1926 with the fantasy novel *Lolly Willowes*, which had the distinction of being the initial selection of the American Book-of-the-Month Club. Following this popular work were other novels such as the rather philosophical *Mr. Fortune's Maggot* (1927), a Literary Guild selection; *The True Heart* (1929); *Summer Will Show* (1936); and *The Flint Anchor* (1954). Many commentators consider *The Corner That Held Them* (1948), a fascinating and informative novel about life in a medieval English convent, to be the finest of her endeavors in this genre. Her novels, like her poems, are characterized by a polished style and an urbane, whimsical wit. Her collections of short fiction include *A Garland of Straw* (1943), *The Museum of Cheats* (1947), *The Innocent and the Guilty* (1971), and, most recently, *Kingdoms of Elfin* (1977), a collection of several delightful works of fantasy, most of which were originally published as a series in *The New Yorker*. Warner also gained published as a series in *The New Yorker*. Warner also gained considerable prestige and renown as a biographer. Although her work on a biography of one of her great admirers, T. F. Powys, was not completed, she published an extraordinarily fine biography of T. H. White (1968).

Although well into her eighties, this remarkable scholar, wit, and author extraordinaire continued to delight her many devoted readers with a steady flow of fine writing. Warner died May 1, 1978, in Dorset, England.

In a letter we received in 1978 from Warner, she reacted to our inclusion of "Elphenor and Weasel" in this volume by stating that we had "picked a story [I myself] would have chosen for such an anthology." It is not difficult to understand why this tale is one of Warner's favorites. There is a gentleness, a delicacy, a charm, that is more apparent here than in most of her other Elfin Kingdom stories, which often stress the more sinister, cruel, and malevolent elements of faerie. Quite simply, this is a beautiful and touching love story.

But it is also a great deal more. Warner's particular fantasy formula calls for an interaction of Elfin beings and mortals that very effectively puts in bold relief the essential qualities of the human condition. This is certainly true of "Elphenor and Weasel." We see, quite clearly, both the good, and the bad, of man's lot. The deceit, charlatanry, greed, suspicion, and religious hypocrisy are poignantly displayed during the course of the narrative; but so too is the "agreeably terminal" nature of our existence, and also its infinite variety. (Elphenor finds that "there [is] better entertainment in the mortal world. Mortals [pack] more variety into their brief lives—perhaps because they [know] them to be brief.") But perhaps above all else, this is a story about intolerance, and the alienation, suffering, bitterness, and loneliness resulting from it. Just as in our own world, the Kingdoms of Elfin discriminate against those of different colored skins and different beliefs. "Two Stranger Children"—what a world of sad meaning is in that Register of Burials epithet.

Elphenor and Weasel
Sylvia Townsend Warner

❧

The ship had sailed barely three leagues from IJmuiden when the wind backed into the east and rose to gale force. If the captain had been an older man he would have returned to port. But he had a mistress in Lowestoft and was impatient to get to her; the following wind, the waves thwacking the stern of the boat as though it were the rump of a donkey and tearing on ahead, abetted his desires. By nightfall, the ship was wallowing broken-backed at the mercy of the storm. Her decks were awash and cluttered with shifting debris. As she lurched lower, Elphenor thrust the confidential letter inside his shirt, the wallet of mortal money deeper in his pocket, and gave his mind to keeping his wings undamaged by blows from ripped sails and the clutches of his fellow-passengers. Judging his moment, he took off just before the ship went down, and was alone with the wind.

His wings were insignificant: he flew by the force of the gale. If for a moment it slackened he dropped within earshot of the hissing waves, then was scooped up and hurled onward. In one of these descents he felt the letter, heavy with seals, fall out of his breast. It would be for-ever private now, and the world of Elfin unchanged by its contents. On a later descent, the wallet followed it. His clothes were torn to shreds, he was benumbed with cold, he was wet to the skin. If the wind had let him drown he would have drowned willingly, folded his use-less wings and heard the waves hiss over his head. The force of the gale enclosed him, he could hardly draw breath. There was no effort of flight; the effort lay in be-

ing powerlessly and violently and almost senselessly conveyed—a fragment of existence in the drive of the storm.
Once or twice he was asleep till a slackening of the wind
jolted him awake with the salt smell of the sea beneath
him. Wakened more forcibly, he saw a vague glimmer
on the face of the water and supposed it might be the
light of dawn; but he could not turn his head. He saw
the staggering flight of a gull, and thought there must be
land not far off.

The growing light showed a tumult of breakers ahead,
close on each other's heels, devouring each other's bulk.
They roared, and a pebble beach screamed back at them,
but the wind carried him over, and on over a dusky flat
landscape that might be anywhere. So far, he had not
been afraid. But when a billow of darkness reared up in
front of him, and the noise of tossing trees swooped on
his hearing, he was suddenly in panic, and clung to a
bough like a drowning man. He had landed in a thick
grove of ilex trees, planted as a windbreak. He squirmed
into the shelter of their midst, and heard the wind go on
without him.

Somehow, he must have fallen out of the tree without
noticing. When he woke, a man with mustachios was
looking down on him.

"I know what you are. You're a fairy. There were
fairies all round my father's place in Suffolk. Thieving
pests, they were, bad as gypsies. But I half liked them.
They were company for me, being an only child. How
did you get here?"

Elphenor realized that he was still wearing the visibility he had put on during the voyage as a measure against
being jostled. It was too late to discard it—though the
shift between visible and invisible is a press-button affair.
He repressed his indignation at being classed with gypsies
and explained how the ship from IJmuiden had sunk and
the wind carried him on.

"From IJmuiden, you say? What happened to the rest
of them?"

"They were drowned."

"Drowned? And my new assistant was on that ship!
It's one calamity after another. Sim's hanged, and Jacob

Kats gets drowned. Seems as though my stars meant me to have you."

It seemed as though Elphenor's stars were of the same mind. To tease public opinion he had studied English as his second language; he was penniless, purposeless, breakfastless, and the wind had blown his shoes off. "If I could get you out of any difficulties—" he said.

"But I can't take you to Walsham Borealis looking like that. We'll go to old Bella, and she'll fit you out."

Dressed in secondhand clothes too large for him and filled with pork pie, Elphenor entered Walsham Borealis riding pillion behind Master Elisha Blackbone. By then he knew he was to be assistant to a quack in several arts, including medicine, necromancy, divination, and procuring.

Hitherto, Elphenor, nephew to the Master of Ceremonies at the Elfin Court of Zuy, had spent his days in making himself polite and, as far as in his tailor lay, ornamental. Now he had to make himself useful. After the cautious pleasures of Zuy everything in this new life, from observing the planets to analyzing specimens of urine, entertained him. It was all so agreeably terminal: one finished one thing and went on to another. When Master Blackbone's clients overlapped, Elphenor placated those kept waiting by building card houses, playing the mandora, and sympathetic conversation—in which he learned a great deal that was valuable to Master Blackbone in casting horoscopes.

For his part, Master Blackbone was delighted with an assistant who was so quick to learn, so free from prejudice, and, above all, a fairy. To employ a fairy was a step up in the world. In London practice every reputable necromancer kept a spiritual appurtenance—fairy, familiar, talking toad, airy consultant. When he had accumulated the money, he would set up in London, where there is always room for another marvel. For the present, he did not mention his assistant's origin, merely stating that he was the seventh son of a seventh son, on whom any gratuities would be well bestowed. Elphenor was on the footing of an apprentice; his keep and training were sufficent wages. A less generous master would have demanded the gratuities, but Master Blackbone had his eye on a golden future, and did not care to imperil it by more than a modest scriptural tithe.

With a fairy as an assistant, he branched out into larger developments of necromancy and took to raising the Devil as a favour. The midnight hour was essential and holy ground desirable—especially disused holy ground: ruined churches, disinhabited religious foundations. The necromancer and the favoured clients would ride under cover of night to Bromholm or St. Benet's in the marshes. Elphenor, flying invisibly and dressed for the part, accompanied them. At the Word of Power he became visible, pranced, menaced, and lashed his tail till the necromancer ordered him back to the pit. This was for moonlight nights. When there was no moon, he hovered invisibly, whispering blasphemies and guilty secrets. His blasphemies lacked unction; being a fairy he did not believe in God. But the guilty secrets curdled many a good man's blood. A conscience-stricken clothier from a neighbouring parish spread such scandals about the iniquities done in Walsham Borealis that Master Blackbone thought it wisest to make off before he and Elphenor were thrown into jail.

They packed his equipment—alembics, chart of the heavens, book of spells, skull, etc.—and were off before the first calm light of an April morning. As they travelled southward Elphenor counted windmills and church towers and found windmills slightly predominating. Church towers were more profitable, observed Master Blackbone. Millers were rogues and cheats, but wherever there was a church you could be sure of fools; if Elphenor were not a fairy and ignorant of Holy Writ he would know that fools are the portion appointed for the wise. But for the present they would lie a little low, shun the Devil, and keep to love philtres and salves for the itch, for which there is always a demand in spring. He talked on about the herbs they would need, and the henbane that grew round Needham in Suffolk, where he was born and played with fairies, and whither they were bound. "What were they like?" Elphenor asked. He did not suppose Master Blackbone's fairies were anything resplendent. Master Blackbone replied that they came out of a hill and were green. Searching his memory, he added that they smelled like elderflowers. At Zuy, elderflowers were used to flavour gooseberry jam—an inelegant conserve.

At Zuy, by now, the gardeners would be bringing the tubs of myrtle out of the conservatories, his uncle would be conducting ladies along the sanded walks to admire the hyacinths, and he would be forgotten; for in good society failures are smoothly forgotten, and as nothing had resulted from the confidential letter it would be assumed he had failed to deliver it. He would never be able to go back. He did not want to. There was better entertainment in the mortal world. Mortals packed more variety into their brief lives—perhaps because they knew them to be brief. There was always something going on and being taken seriously: love, hate, ambition, plotting, fear, and all the rest of it. He had more power as a quack's assistant then ever he would have attained to in Zuy. To have a great deal of power and no concern was the life for him.

Hog's grease was a regrettable interpolation in his career. Master Blackbone based his salves and ointments on hog's grease, which he bought in a crude state from pork butchers. It was Elphenor's task to clarify it before it was tinctured with juices expressed from herbs. Wash as he might, his hands remained greasy and the smell of grease hung in his nostrils. Even the rankest-smelling herbs were a welcome change, and a bundle of water peppermint threw him into a rapture. As Master Blackbone disliked stooping, most of the gathering fell to him.

It is a fallacy that henbane must be gathered at midnight. Sunlight raises its virtues (notably efficacious against toothache, insomnia, and lice), and to be at its best it should be gathered in the afternoon of a hot day. Elphenor was gathering it in a sloping meadow that faced south. He was working invisibly—Master Blackbone did not wish every Tom, Dick, and Harry to know what went into his preparations. Consequently, a lamb at play collided with him and knocked the basket out of his hand. As it stood astonished at this sudden shower of henbane, Elphenor seized it by the ear and cuffed it. Hearing her lamb bleat so piteously, its mother came charging to the rescue. She also collided with Elphenor and, being heavy with her winter fleece, sent him sprawling. He was still flat on his back when a girl appeared from nowhere, stooped over him, and slapped his face, hard and accurately. To assert his manly dignity he pulled her down on top of him—and saw that she was green.

She was a very pretty shade of green—a pure delicate tint, such as might have been cast on a white eggshell by the sun shining through the young foliage of a beech tree. Her hair, brows, and lashes were a darker shade; her lashes lay on her green cheek like a miniature fern frond. Her teeth were perfectly white. Her skin was so nearly transparent that the blue veins on her wrists and breasts showed through like some exquisitely marbled cheese.

As they lay in an interval of repose, she stroked the bruise beginning to show on his cheek with triumphant moans of compassion. Love did not heighten or diminish her colour. She remained precisely the same shade of green. The smell, of course, was that smell of elderflowers. It was strange to think that exactly like this she may have been one of the fairies who played with Elisha Blackbone in his bragged-of boyhood, forty, fifty years back. He pushed the speculation away, and began kissing her behind the ear, and behind the other ear, to make sure which was the more sensitive. But from that hour love struck root in him.

Eventually he asked her name. She told him it was Weasel. "I shall call you Mustela," he said, complying with the lover's imperative to rename the loved one; but in the main he called her Weasel. They sat up, and saw that time had gone on as usual, that dusk had fallen and the henbane begun to wilt.

When they parted, the sheep were circling gravely to the top of the hill, the small grassy hill of her tribe. He flew leisurely back, swinging the unfilled basket. The meagre show of henbane would be a pretext for going off on the morrow to a place where it grew more abundantly; he would have found such a place, but by then it was growing too dark for picking, and looking one way while flying another he had bruised his cheek against a low-growing bough. At Zuy this artless tale would not have supported a moment's scrutiny; but it would pass with a mortal, though it might be wise to substantiate it with a request for the woundwort salve. For a mortal, Master Blackbone was capable of unexpected intuitions.

The intuitions had not extended to the reverence for age and learning which induced Elphenor to sleep on a pallet to the windward. Toward morning, he dreamed that he was at the foot of the ilex; but it was Weasel who was looking down at him, and if he did not move she would slap his face. He moved, and woke. Weasel lay asleep beside him. But at the same time they were under the ilex, for the waves crashed on the screaming pebble beach and were Master Blackbone's snores.

At Zuy the English Elfindom was spoken of with admiring reprehension: its magnificence, wastefulness, and misrule, its bravado and eccentricity. The eccentricity of being green and living under a hill was not included. A hill, yes. Antiquarians talked of hill dwellings, and found evidence of them in potsherds and beads. But never, at any time, green. The beauties of Zuy, all of them white as bolsters, would have swooned at the hypothesis. Repudiating the memory of past bolsters, he looked at Weasel, curled against him like a caterpillar in a rose leaf, green as spring, fresh as spring, and completely contemporary.

She stirred, opened her eyes, and laughed.

"Shush!"

Though invisible, she might not be inaudible, and her voice was ringing and assertive as a wren's. She had come so trustingly it would be the act of an ingrate to send her away. Not being an ingrate he went with her, leaving Master Blackbone to make what he would of an early-rising assistant. They breakfasted on wild strawberries and a hunk of bread he had had the presence of mind to take from the bread crock. It was not enough for Weasel, and when they came to a brook she twitched up a handful of minnows and ate them raw. Love is a hungry emotion, and by midday he wished he had not been so conventional about the minnows. As a tactful approach, he began questioning her about life in the hill, it's amenities, its daily routine. She suddenly became evasive: he would not like it; it was dull, old-fashioned, unsociable.

"All the same, I should like to visit it. I have never been inside a hill."

"No! You can't come. It's impossible. They'd set on you, you'd be driven out. *You're not green.*"

Etiquette.

"Don't you understand?"

"I was wondering what they would do to you if they found out where you woke this morning."

"Oh, that! They'd have to put up with it. Green folk don't draw green blood. But they'd tear *you* in pieces."

"It's the same where I come from. If I took you to Zuy, they might be rather politer, but they'd never forgive you for being green. But I won't take you, Weasel. We'll stay in Suffolk. And if it rains and rains and rains—"

"I don't mind rain—"

"We'll find a warm, dry badger sett."

They escaped into childishness and were happy again, with a sharpened happiness because for a moment they had so nearly touched despair.

As summer became midsummer, and the elder blossom outlasted the wild roses and faded in its turn till the only true elderflower scent came from her, and the next full moon had a broader face and shone on cocks of hay in silvery fields, they settled into an unhurried love and strolled from day to day as through a familiar landscape. By now they were seldom hungry, for there was a large crop of mushrooms, and Elphenor put more system into his attendances on Master Blackbone, breakfasting soundly and visibly while conveying mouthfuls to the invisible Weasel (it was for the breakfasts that they slept there). Being young and perfectly happy and pledged to love each other till the remote end of their days, they naturally talked of death and discussed how to contrive that neither should survive the other. Elphenor favoured being struck by lightning as they lay in each other's arms, but Weasel was terrified by thunder—she winced and covered her ears at the slightest rumble—and though he talked soothingly of the electric fluid and told her of recent experiments with amber and a couple of silk stockings, one black, one white, she refused to die by lightning stroke.

And Master Blackbone, scarcely able to believe his ears, madly casting horoscopes and invoking the goddess

Fortuna, increasingly tolerant of Elphenor's inattention, patiently compounding his salves unassisted, smiling on the disappearances from his larder, was day after day, night after night, more sure of his surmise—till convinced of his amazing good fortune he fell into the melancholy of not knowing what best to do about it, whether to grasp fame single-handed or call in the help of an expert and self-effacingly retire on the profits. He wrote a letter to an old friend. Elphenor was not entrusted with this letter, but he knew it had been written and was directed to London. Weasel was sure Master Blackbone was up to no good— she had detested him at first sight. They decided to keep a watch on him. But their watch was desultory, and the stranger was already sitting in Master Blackbone's lodging and conversing with him when they flew in and perched on a beam.

The stranger was a stout man with a careworn expression. Master Blackbone was talking in his best procuring voice.

"It's a Golconda, an absolute Golconda! A pair of them, young, in perfect condition. Any manager would snap at them. But I have kept it dark till now. I wanted you to have the first option."

"Thanks, I'm sure," said the stranger. "But it's taking a considerable chance."

"Oh no, it isn't. People would flock to see them. You could double the charges—in fact you should, for it's something unique—and there wouldn't be an empty seat in the house. Besides, it's a scientific rarity. You'd have all the illuminati. Nobs from the colleges. Ladies of fashion. Royal patronage."

The stranger said he didn't like buying pigs in pokes.

"But I give you my word. A brace of fairies—lovely, young, amorous fairies. Your fortune would be made."

"How much do you want?"

"Two-thirds of the takings. You can't say that's exorbitant. Not two-thirds of the profits, mind. Two-thirds of the takings and a written agreement."

The stranger repeated that he didn't like buying pigs in pokes, the more so when he had no warrant the pigs were within.

"Wait till tonight! They come every night and cuddle on

that pallet there. They trust me like a father. Wait till they're asleep and throw a net over them, and they're yours."

"But when I've got them to London, suppose they are awkward, and won't perform? People aren't going to pay for what they can't see. How can I be sure they'll be visible?"

Master Blackbone said there were ways and means, as with performing animals.

"Come, Weasel. We'll be off."

The voice was right overhead, loud and clear. Some cobwebs drifted down.

Elphenor and Weasel were too pleased with themselves to think beyond the moment. They had turned habitually toward their usual haunts and were dabbling their feet in the brook before it occurred to Elphenor that they had no reason to stay in the neighbourhood and good reason to go elsewhere. Weasel's relations would murder him because he was not green, Master Blackbone designed to sell them because they were fairies. Master Blackbone might have further designs: he was a necromancer, though a poor one; it would be prudent to get beyond his magic circle. Elphenor had congratulated himself on leaving prudence behind at Zuy. Now it reasserted itself and had its charm. Prudence had no charm whatever for Weasel; it was only by representing the move as reckless that he persuaded her to make it.

With the world before them, he flew up for a survey and caught sight of the sea, looking as if ships would not melt in its mouth—which rather weakened the effect of his previous narrative of the journey from IJmuiden to the ilexes. Following the coastline they came to Great Yarmouth, where they spent several weeks. It was ideal for their vagrant purposes, full of vigorous, cheerful people, with food to be had for the taking—hot pies and winkles in the marketplace, herring on the quayside where the fishing boats unloaded. The air was rough and cold, and he stole a pair of shipboy's trousers and a knitted muffler for Weasel from a marine store near the Custom House. He was sorry to leave this kind place. But Weasel showed such a strong inclination to go to sea, and found it so amusing to flaunt her trousers on the quayside and startle her admirers with her green face, that she was becoming notorious, and he was afraid Master Blackbone might hear of her. From Yarmouth they flew inland, steering their course by church towers. Where there is a church tower you can be sure of fools, Master Blackbone had said. True enough; but Elphenor tired of thieving—though it called for more skill in villages—and he thought he would try turning an honest penny, for a change. By now he was so coarsened and brown-handed that he could pass as a labouring man. In one place he sacked potatoes, in another baled reeds for thatching. At a village called Scottow, where the sexton had rheumatism, he dug a grave. Honest-pennying was no pleasure to Weasel, who had to hang about invisibly, passing the time with shrivelled blackberries. In these rustic places which had never seen a circus or an Indian peddler, her lovely green face would have brought stones rattling on their heels.

Winter came late that year and stealthily, but the nights were cold. Nights were never cold in Suffolk, she said. He knew this was due to the steady temperature under the hill, but hoping all the same she might be right he turned southward. He had earned more than enough to pay for a night at an inn. At Bury St. Edmunds he bought her a cloak with a deep hood, and telling her to pull the hood well forward and keep close to his heels he went at dusk to a respectable inn and hired the best bedroom they had. All went well, except that they seemed to look at him doubtfully. In his anxiety to control the situation he had reverted to his upper-class manner, which his clothes did not match with. The four-poster bed was so comfortable that he hired the room for a second night, telling the chambermaid his wife had a headache and must not be disturbed. It was certainly an elopement, she reported; even before she had left the room, the little gentleman had parted the bed curtains and climbed in beside the lady. After the second night there was no more money.

They left on foot, and continued to walk, for there was a shifting, drizzling fog which made it difficult to keep each other in sight if they flew. Once again they stole a dinner, but it was so inadequate that Elphenor decided to try begging. He was rehearsing a beggar's whine when they saw a ruddy glow through the fog and heard a ham-

mer ring on an anvil. Weasel as usual clapped her hands
to her ears; but when they came to a wayside forge the
warmth persuaded her to follow Elphenor, who went in
shivering ostentatiously and asked if he and his wife could
stand near the blaze: they would not get in the way, they
would not stay long. The blacksmith was shaping horse-
shoes. He nodded, and went on with his work. Elphenor
was preparing another whine when the blacksmith remarked it was no day to be out, and encouraged Weasel,
who stood in the doorway, to come nearer the fire.

"Poor soul, she could do with a little kindness," said
Elphenor. "And we haven't met with much of it today. We
passed an inn, farther back"—it was there they had stolen
the heel of a Suffolk cheese—"but they said they had no
room for us."

Weasel interrupted. "What's that black thing ahead,
that keeps on showing and going?"

The blacksmith pulled his forelock. "Madam. That's
the church."

They thanked him and went away, Elphenor thinking
he must learn to beg more feelingly. The blacksmith stood
looking after them. At this very time of year, too. He
wished he had not let slip the opportunity of a Hail Mary
not likely to come his way again.

The brief December day was closing when they came
to the church. The south porch, large as a room, was
sheltered from the wind, and they sat there, huddled in
Weasel's cloak. "We can't sleep here," Elphenor said. For
all that, he got up and tried the church door. It was
locked. He immediately determined to get in by a window. They flew round the church, fingering the cold
panes of glass, and had almost completed their round and
seen the great bulk of the tower threatening down on
them, when Weasel heard a clatter overhead. It came
from one of the clerestory windows, where a missing pane
had been replaced by a shutter. They wrenched the shutter open, and flew in, and circled downward through darkness, and stood on a flagstone pavement. Outlined against
a window was a tall structure with a peak. Fingering it,
they found it was wood, carved, and swelling out of a
stem like a goblet. A railed flight of steps half encircled
the stem. They mounted the steps and found themselves

in the goblet. It was an octagonal cupboard, minus a top but carpeted. By curling round each other, there would be room to lie down. The smell of wood gave them a sense of security, and they spent the night in the pulpit.

He woke to the sound of Weasel laughing. Daylight was streaming in, and Weasel was flitting about the roof, laughing at the wooden figures that supported the cross-beams—carved imitations of fairies, twelve foot high, with outstretched turkey wings and gaunt faces, each uglier than the last. "So that's what they think we're like," she said. "And look at *her!*" She pointed to the fairy above the pulpit, struggling with a trumpet.

Exploring at floor level, Elphenor read the Ten Commandments, and found half a bottle of wine and some lozenges. It would pass for a breakfast; later, he would stroll into the village and see what could be got from there. While he was being raised as the Devil at Walsham Borealis, he had learned some facts about the Church of England, one of them that the reigning monarch, symbolically represented as a lion and a unicorn, is worshipped noisily on one day of the week and that for the rest of the week churches are unmolested. There was much to be said for spending the winter here. The building was windproof and weatherproof, Weasel was delighted with it, and, for himself, he found its loftiness and spaciousness congenial, as though he were back in Zuy— a Zuy improved by a total removal of its inhabitants. He had opened a little door and discovered a winding stone stairway behind it when his confidence in Church of England weekdays was shaken by the entrance of two women with brooms and buckets. He beckoned to Weasel, snatched her cloak from the pulpit, and preceded her up the winding stairs, holding the bottle and the lozenges. The steps were worn; there was a dead crow on one of them. They groped their way up into darkness, then into light; a window showed a landing and a door open on a small room where some ropes dangled from the ceiling. Weasel seized a rope and gave it a tug, and would have tugged at it more energetically if Elphenor had not intervened, promising that when the women had gone away she could tug to her heart's content. Looking out of the cobwebbed window, he saw the churchyard far below and

realized they must be a long way up the tower. But the
steps wound on into another darkness and a dimmer lightness, and to another landing and another door open on
another room. This room had louvred windows high up in
the wall, and most of its floor space was taken up by a
frame supporting eight bells, four of them upside down
with their clappers lolling in their iron mouths. This was
the bell chamber, he explained. The ropes went from the
bells into the room below, which was the ringing chamber. There was a similar tower near Zuy; mortals thought
highly of it, and his tutor had taken him to see it.

Weasel began to stroke one of the bells. As though she
were caressing some savage sleeping animal, it presently
responded with a noise between a soft growl and a purr.
Elphenor stroked another. It answered at a different pitch,
deeper and harsher, as though it were a more savage animal. But they were hungry. The bells could wait. The
light from the louvred windows flickered between bright
and sombre as the wind tossed the clouds. It was blowing
up for a storm.

They would be out of the wind tonight and for many
nights to come. January is a dying season, there would be
graves to dig, and with luck and management, thought
Elphenor, he might earn a livelihood and be a friend to
sextons here and around. Weasel would spare crumbs
from the bread he earned, scatter them for birds, catch
the birds, pluck and eat them: she still preferred raw food,
with the life still lively in it. On Sundays, she said, they
would get their week's provisions; with everybody making a noise in church, stealing would be child's play. The
pulpit would be the better for a pillow, and she could
soon collect enough feathers for a pillow, for a feather
mattress even: one can always twitch a pillowcase from
the washing line. The wine had gone to their heads; they
outbid each other with grand plans of how they would
live in the church, and laughed them down, and imagined
more. They would polish the wooden fairies' noses till
they shone like drunkards' noses; they would grow water-
cresses in the font; Elphenor would tell the complete
story of his life before they met. Let him begin now! Was
he born with a hook nose and red hair? He began, obedi-
ently and prosily. Weasel clamped her eyes open, and

suppressed yawns. He lost the thread of his narrative.
Drowsy with wine, they fell asleep.

He woke to two appalling sounds. Weasel screaming
with terror, a clash of metal. The bell ringers had come to
practise their Christmas peal, and prefaced it by sounding
all the bells at once. The echo was heavy on the air as
they began to ring a set of changes, first the scale descending evenly to the whack of the tenor bell, then in
patterned steps to the same battle-axe blow. The pattern
altered; the tenor bell sounded midway, jolting an arbi-
trary finality into the regular measure of eight. With each
change of position the tenor bell accumulated a more
threatening insistency, and the other bells shifted round
it like a baaing flock of sheep.

Weasel cowered in Elphenor's arms. She had no
strength left to scream with; she could only tremble before
the impact of the next flailing blow. He felt his senses
coming adrift. The booming echo was a darkness on his
sight through which he saw the bells in their frame heaving and evading, evading and heaving, under a dark sky.
The implacable assault of the changing changes pursued
him as the waves had pursued the boat from IJmuiden.
But here there was no escape, for it was he who wallowed
broken-backed at the mercy of the storm. Weasel lay in
his arms like something at a distance. He felt his pro-
tectiveness, his compassion, ebbing away; he watched
her with a bloodless, skeleton love. She still trembled, but
in a disjointed way, as though she were falling to pieces.

He saw the lovely green fade out of her face. "My darling," he said, "death by lightning would have been easier." He could not hear himself speak.

The frost lasted on into mid-March. No one went to
the bell chamber till the carpenter came to mend the
louvres in April. The two bodies, one bowed over the
other, had fallen into decay. No one could account for
them, or for the curious weightless fragments of a sub-
stance rather like sheet gelatine which the wind had
scattered over the floor. They were buried in the same
grave. Because of their small stature and light bones they
were entered in the Register of Burials as *Two Stranger
Children.*

❧ EVANGELINE WALTON ENSLEY ❧
(1907-   )

For over thirty years Evangeline Walton Ensley quietly, but determinedly, pursued a writing career that brought her very little recognition, either from the critics or the reading public. It was not until 1970, with the reprinting of *The Virgin and the Swine* under the new title, *The Island of the Mighty*, that her literary fortunes soared. Since then, her works have been given the kind of critical and popular attention they have always deserved. Patrick Merla's assessment of Ensley in his landmark essay on fantasy literature, "'What Is Real?' Asked the Rabbit One Day" (*Saturday Review*, November 4, 1972), is fairly typical of the kind of praise now being lavished upon Ensley. Merla declares that Ensley's "... three books (*The Island of the Mighty*, *The Children of Llyr*, and *The Song of Rhiannon*), together with C. S. Lewis's *Out of the Silent Planet*, *Perelandra*, and *That Hideous Strength* and T. H. White's *The Once and Future King*, are not only the best fantasies of the twentieth century, they are also great works of fiction." But although Ensley (Walton is a family name she uses as her pseudonym) is now recognized as one of our finest contemporary fantasists, very little has been published about her life and writings. Much of the biographical material included here, for example, has been gleaned from correspondence.

Born in Indianapolis in November 24, 1907, Evangeline Ensley quickly revealed her literary bent. At the tender age of six she began composing stories that her mother transcribed and later sent (when Evangeline was eight) to an Indianapolis publisher, who praised the works but judged them not yet ready for publication. Because of her poor health (she suffered from pneumonia nearly every winter) Evangeline was unable to attend school. Consequently, her entire education was received at home under the careful tutelage of her great aunt, Calista Fellows. The young pupil's appetite for books was voracious, and thus, in her own words, she read "anything I could lay hands on." Particular favorites were L. Frank Baum's Oz books, Rider Haggard's exotic adventure stories, and Lord Dunsany's tales of glamour. Closest to her heart, though, were the works of the Irish poet and story writer, James Stephens, whom she still regards as her literary mentor.

However, the work destined to have the single greatest impact upon her literary career was that remarkable collection of medieval Welsh tales called the *Mabinogion*. It was her reading of the rich repository of Celtic myth and legend that inspired the writing, in 1936, of *The Virgin and the Swine*, a beautiful retelling of the fourth "branch" of the *Mabinogion*. For nearly thirty-five years *Virgin* was known only to a small coterie of dedicated readers. Then, in 1970, Paul Spencer, of the James Branch Cabell Society, brought the novel to the attention of Lin Carter, who reissued the book as part of the Ballantine Adult Fantasy Series (the reprinting already referred to). Reader response to the paperback reprint was enthusiastic, and the Ballantine editors asked Ensley if she had more such fiction. "Yes," was the answer. She then proceeded to practice her literary magic on the other three branches of the *Mabinogion* by retelling their tales in *The Children of Llyr* (1971), *The Song of Rhiannon* (1972), and *The Prince of Annwn* (1974). Other works by Ensley include *Witch House* (1945), the first volume in the "Library of Arkham House Novels of Fantasy and Terror"; *The Cross and the Sword* (1956), a historical novel of epic proportions; an unpublished novel, *The Prince of Air*; an unpublished verse drama, *Swan-Wife*; and a small number of stories and critical essays. Since 1970, Ensley has been reworking a Theseus trilogy that she had written but has put aside previously when Mary Renault's *The King Must Die* (1958) was published first. The project is now complete, and the first volume, *The Sword is Forged*, was published in 1983. The author currently lives in a cozy bungalow with a mountain view in Tucson, Arizona, her home for the past forty-six years.

"The Mistress of Kaer-Mor" is one of the very few short fantasies written by Ensley, and one of her first works of fiction. Composed when Ensley was in her early twenties, the story remained hidden in an attic until about fourteen years ago, when we invited Ensley to contribute a fantasy short story to our *The Fantastic Imagination* II. Her subsequent search through some old papers and manuscripts uncovered both "Kaer-Mor" and "Above Ker-Is," the latter seeing print for the first time in the aforementioned anthology. "Kaer-Mor" appeared in print for the first time in *The Phoenix Tree* (1980). Both stories, companion pieces really, make heavy use of Celtic myth and legend. The central legend drawn upon is that of the submerged city of Ys, which, as the story goes, now lies buried beneath the waters of Brittany's Bay of Douarnenez. According to the legend, Ys was a prosperous and flourishing coastal city of the fifth century that was protected from the sea by a long dike. There was only one key to the main sluice gate of this dike, and that was worn round the neck of King Gradlon. Gradlon was a good ruler who had been converted to Christianity by St. Guenole, but he had an evil daughter, Ahes (Dahut in some sources), who still practiced pagan rites. In addition, she was notorious for her lechery, entertaining lover after lover in her castle rooms, and then strangling them after they had satisfied her lust. One night Ahes stole the fabled silver key from her father, opened the floodgate, and thus allowed the waters to pour over the sleeping city. Gradlon awoke and tried to save his daughter from the approaching flood, but she was pushed into the waters by St. Guenole, who saw in her the workings of the devil. Only Gradlon escaped the avalanche of water; Ys and all its inhabitants perished. Interpretations differ regarding Princess Ahes and her actions. Some see her as a romantic young girl who accidentally opened the sluice gate while attempting to let her lover into the city, while others see her as a demon princess who purposely destroyed the city. It is the latter interpretation that informs "Kaer-Mor" and helps explain Alienor's personality and actions. We are grateful to Ms. Ensley for providing us with a story dealing with this most mysterious and intriguing of Breton myths.

The Mistress of Kaer-Mor
Evangeline Walton Ensley

There is a grisly jest in the fact that when I went to
Brittany in 1918 I was seeking peace. For over two years I
had been nursing the wounded, and I had had enough of
war and reality. I am neither young nor strong, and I felt
entitled to peace: the peace of a grey misty countryside so
steeped in the fabulous Celtic past that childless women
still supplicate a stone, the famous *Groach H'ouard*, with
rites as secret as the Eleusinian Mysteries. I found instead
the theatre of the oldest and darkest warfare known to
man.

I was to visit a woman I had known in her girlhood, a
Madame de Saint-Saens, and she had sent down young
Ronan Kerodec, a schoolboy when I had last seen him, to
meet me at Merlevenez and drive me to her home near
Carnac.

"Still a civilian, Ronan?" I asked, when we had greeted
each other. I missed the familiar uniform.

The boy flushed. "Alienor—Mme. de Saint-Saens—has
helped me to obtain my exemption. They found a defect in
my heart. I feel that I can be of more use to my country—
to the world—by trying to give it back some beauty with
my poetry than by perhaps dying in the trenches. It is not
that I am better than others—it is only that I have been
entrusted with a torch that they have not." He ended with
a rather pleading note in his voice. "I had hoped you
would understand, Mme. Foster, you who are American,
not blind with suffering like our people. It is not that I
have fear. I think it would be easier to die than to face the
people who do not understand."

"Yes, Ronan," I said gently. The pathetic earnestness
behind the rather bombastic words touched me. "Perhaps

303

gifted men ought to be spared. But who can blame you if your heart—"

He looked away. "Tudual does—my brother. And you could move the great menhir above Kaer-Mor as easily as Tudual. He thinks the examination a dishonest one. Because the men to whom Alienor sent me found a condition our family doctor had never found. He calls me a shirker, a traitor, a—*coward!*"

"But how does he happen to be at home himself?" I was too startled to think of anything else to say. I knew Tudual Kerodec's lifelong devotion to his young brother; their parents had died when he was a boy in his teens and Ronan a small child.

"He was wounded—one arm may always be stiff. He blames Alienor for using influence he says she should not have had. Unjustly. She has had trouble enough."

"You mean the husband she left?" I said slowly. "That marriage that her family arranged?" I could not say more to the boy; I think no man could have understood the full hideousness of Alienor de Saint-Saens's marriage. "Tudual used to be one of her greatest champions, I remember. Does the change in him trouble her?"

"Nothing troubles her, whatever is said against her—and it is shameful!" His eyes lit like lamps in their adoring championship. "Every servant in her house has come from Paris. Our people here say that she is a witch who can move things without touching them. That lunacy began because a young fellow who had given her notice—a brainless, impudent young ox!—was killed by a paleolith that fell on him when he was moving the table beneath it."

"Wasn't Kaer-Mor always supposed to be haunted?" Some vague stir of foreboding moved in me.

For the first time his frankness left him; his manner showed evasion, and an odd constraint. "It is a grim old place. I used to feel my skin creep there, in loathing. . . . And yet lately I have come to see how wonderful a setting it is for Alienor—how she shines against its darkness. Light needs darkness."

I said nothing. Jacques de Pontorsin, an ancestor of Alienor's, had built Kaer-Mor in 1484. He had been a friend of Gilles de Rais, equally guilty of the outraging and murdering of children, of sorcery, Black Masses, and all the rest of it. But he is not as famous—he only offered a baker's dozen or so of children to his Unknown God, not Gilles's hundreds. Or was he only more careful, harder to catch?

We drove on in silence—a weird, oppressive journey through a grey ghost-world of mist. The fog, always common in Carnac, made sight impossible, and only the sea, crooning in soft, cruel menace, and as invisible as the desolate moors around us, broke the grave-like stillness. Every turn of the wheels seemed to be carrying us farther away from the war-torn present, back into the old druidic Brittany. Yet I felt no relief, only a curious, sinister expectancy.

Alienor met us in the great stone hall at Kaer-Mor, the firelight catching eagerly at her blue-green dress and yellow hair. Her eyes shone green in it too, startling me who had remembered them as clear, transparent bluish-grey. There had once been something rather touching about the way she welcomed guests—a glad, eager desire to make friends and be approved of, the heritage of that long bitter time when she had been trying to escape from her husband and her family had taken his side. But there was no trace of that left. She sparkled like sunlit water. One had a queer feeling that there was the same kind of wildness in her that there is in water. An elemental rushing power hidden beneath the softness. I thought I must be imagining things; after several years, one can't expect a friend to seem quite the same.

She had always been an artist of considerable merit, and after dinner she showed me a portfolio of her sketches, Ronan proudly looking over our shoulders and pointing out each excellence. They were her conception of the legendary submersion of the city of Ys: pictures whose lovely delicacy of line had a weird and unforgettable power. One showed the demon-princess, the dread Breton sea-goddess incarnate, opening the dikes to flood the city. Alienor had used her own face as model; the beauty and the elvish remorselessness of the waves were in it, neither malicious planning nor any human fright or pity, only a kind of glorious drunkenness, a delight in the use of power. In sweeping away everything she knew, every power for good or bad that ever had regulated her world. Well, perhaps that

too is human in its way. But it was what first really
brought home to me the change in the living face. To cover
my shock I asked why there were so many empty pages
between the sketches.

"You are venturing on forbidden ground, madame.
Some pictures are for our uninitiated mortal eyes—others
are not."

Tudual Kerodec was looking down upon us from the
doorway that his great shoulders almost filled, his swarthy,
square-jawed face grimly mocking in the firelight.

"Tudual!" Alienor started up and glided to him, laughing. "You are late—and wicked—you who were my espe-
cial surprise for madame, our friend."

"Old friends first, madame," he laughed. Swinging her
hands away from him, he strode toward me.

I am past the time for love, but I felt curiously warmed
and relieved to see him there. Many strong men are only
brawny hulks, commanding no more respect than oxen,
but this man was round, complete. He was tall, I do not
think there was an ounce of fat on him, yet he was so
broad-shouldered that he looked stocky. Power seemed to
be part of him, the elemental power of Earth itself.

"You startled us horribly, Tudual," Ronan's voice held a
rather pathetic appeal for friendliness. "You came so suddenly that I took you for Alienor's poltergeist—the one
that frightens the maids."

"It did more than frighten poor Jean." Tudual's gaze
went past his brother to the great stone axe that hung
above a table at the end of the room. "I see you left the
thing hanging there, Alienor. But have no fear, madame,"
he turned to me again, "he—or it—is only one of Alienor's
innovations of the last year or two. Not a tradition."

"You are wrong, Tudual." Alienor shrugged, with a glint
of malice in her eyes that were now as blue-green as her
dress. "You know the old tales of mysterious sounds and
movements very well. The etheric influence was on the
wane when I first came here, because I suppose, Kaer-Mor
had been long unoccupied."

"Until now it never has been regularly occupied since
Baron Henri de Pontorsin died in the Bastille." Ronan,
who had been watching his brother with the dark, hurt
eyes of a whipped child, came to her support eagerly.

"After he had been convicted of invoking Satan," his brother answered drily. "Kaer-Mor has always had the opposite of an ennobling effect on its masters. Let us be thankful that it has a mistress now." He bowed to Alienor with exaggerated, mocking gallantry.

"Perhaps Jacques built Kaer-Mor here because Carnac was a sacred country in pre-Christian days," I put in, anxious to dispel under-currents that I couldn't understand. "The home of the priests and the dead, where the tribes went only to perform holy rites and to bury their chieftains."

"True," Tudual agreed, "He may have believed that by building his—*temple*—in a place already steeped in religious associations, he immeasurably strengthened its power. Nobody really knows what God it was that he and Gilles de Rais invoked so bloodily, though the priests still cry 'Satanism.' "

"They would," Alienor spoke with lazy scorn. "But greedy Christianity has not killed the old Breton faith yet —think of the variety of things that peasants still do around the menhirs. And it is not in very good health itself. People may yet turn back to something in which they can find real strength."

Tudual laughed shortly. "In Jacques's or Henri's day you'd have been burned for the witch you are, Alienor."

"I can believe that you would have done it!" She rose to curtsy mockingly. "Hear! Cijava's son, St. Tudual, sits in judgment. 'And if our good St. Tudual is not God the Father, it is because he did not wish to be.' "

In the rainbow flames of the driftwood fire her peacock draperies shimmered like water, her bare white arms and breast had a greenish translucence. She was radiant, all seduction, yet I had a queer, repellent feeling that her flesh would have been as unhumanly cold as the waves to any touch.

"Would you have helped your brother stack the faggots, Ronan?" Her laughter foamed over him.

"I would have burned with you!" His rapt boy's eyes were already afire as they clung worshipingly to her face.

"If I had permitted you to do so," Tudual said drily. "This is a rather melodramatic plane of 'woulds.' "

Later, when Ronan had accompanied Alienor to her

studio to get some more pictures, his brother and I were left alone.

"Tudual," I said, "you may say this is none of my business, but you're being hard with Ronan. How can you be sure there's nothing wrong with his heart?"

"There is plenty wrong with it. Alienor." For the first time since I had known him he used an American idiom.

"You think—"

"I know." His calm was as unshakable as the moors outside. "I am hard, but it is with a purpose. His arguments—which are really hers—are good enough."

"Then you don't really think him a coward?"

"No. If I could think a thing like that about him I wouldn't know him well enough to care what happened to him. I put on what you'd call an act—a cruel and ugly one, I admit—to storm and shame him into the army. Anything to get him away from *her*." His jaw clamped.

As I stared he relaxed; smiled wryly.

"Not that I am so moral. I wouldn't mind their merely becoming lovers. Not if she were what she was when you knew her. But in spite of yourself I think you must be beginning to see that she has—changed."

I felt suddenly, queerly cold. "I don't understand, Tudual. People do change—through the years—"

"If I told you what I think and guess," he laughed harshly, "it would be enough to bring me before a lunacy commission. But one thing I do know, indisputably. The lady is—deliciously impartial. My brother's genius is a weapon she wants badly, but I, too, could have been her lover."

"You too! Then they are—"

"Not yet." He spoke the one clipped syllable with great finality. "Once they are he will be lost, spiritually devoured. Not even her death, unless it were immediate, could save him. I have given her to understand that in that case, regardless of such obstacles as hell and the guillotine, her death will be just that—immediate."

I had much to think of when I undressed in my vaulted stone room that night. Were Tudual and I both going crazy, and were Ronan and Alienor to be pitied?

I also had the curious, uneasy feeling which was never

to leave me during my stay in that house: the sense of being watched by unseen eyes. By some dark life stored in the ancient walls and ceilings: a semi-conscious, malignant life.

I left the lamp burning low when I got into bed. I never have liked to sleep in utter darkness.

It was past midnight when I started up, shivering; as if sleep had been a lapse from some queer, uncomprehended vigilance. Had someone knocked? Rising, I turned the lamp high and made myself open the door, though I never have hated to do anything more. But the long, narrow corridor, pitch black and quiet as the bottom of a well, was empty as far as eye could see. Lifeless as only stone can be lifeless. Then suddenly the lamp behind me flickered as if unseen hands had clutched at the flames. I whirled round, slamming and locking the door as if the space outside were filled with monsters.

And saw that the lamp was burning as steadily as ever. . . .

Then, just when my hand was falling from the key, I heard it—a low tapping on the thick oak panels behind me. No one could have reached the door since I had looked out into the passage; that knocking could come from no human hand.

And it was coming—low and soft, but insistent. I seemed to feel it upon my flesh like blows; they did not hurt, but they were breath-taking. Something seemed to be fighting to get in, to pour its darkness into me, to fuse from itself and myself another *me*.

I do not think I remember all the horror of that moment; perhaps no mind could hold it and live. It taught me the futility of all man-made tyrannies; dreadful as they may be, they must rule from without, and so leave us the one possession so integral we never fear for it: *oneself*. But somehow at last the torture ceased; there was no more sound. I got back into bed, sickly sure that the vitality that had ebbed from me had gone into the power behind that knocking. That it would be, not death, but utter personal annihilation, to turn out the lamp or go to sleep.

"I've met your poltergeist," I told Alienor next morning, with a poor attempt at laughter. And then explained.

She did not answer at once. A troubled, remembering

look came over her face, a *human* look. "I know. I used to hear it—often." Then the uncanny beauty flashed back into her face, the unhuman silvery notes rippled in her voice. "But have no fear, madame. It will not come again for many nights."

She ended on a faintly amused, faintly patronizing note; I was reminded of a tactful missionary reassuring a savage frightened by the Christian hell. The charming child-woman of old days, with her pathetic self-uncertainties, her wistful friendliness, was gone—as completely gone as the dead. I think I knew then that I would never see her again.

Yet I did sleep well for many nights thereafter. Sleep was never hard to come by at Kaer-Mor. . . . And the days, when I try to remember them, have the quality of a dream. Ronan was forever in and out, his mesmerized eyes following Alienor. In the eerie, wildly beautiful poems that he said she inspired an ever fiercer cry of passion kept growing. And while he read them aloud she would watch him with an uncanny, hungry brooding; I wondered how much longer she could hold in the fires that I felt sure charged her body. She had a different look for Tudual during his less frequent visits: a baffled look, which held fear and forming menace, but also an abnormally fierce response to the elemental magnificence of his manhood.

Then he came one afternoon when Alienor and Ronan were out on the moors. And that was the beginning of the end.

"I have enjoyed others more," I answered dryly when he inquired about my visit. "Tudual, I am afraid that I too am ready for a lunacy commission."

He heard my story, then said only, "But you do not think she had anything to do with the knocking?"

"I don't think she had to," I confessed. "Kaer-Mor is—quite capable—in itself."

"Yet Flammarion's theory was that such phenomena could manifest itself only through the vitality of a young person." He spoke of the great French astonomer who tried so hard to find a scientific basis for the unseen and the unknown. "Witnesses have testified that mediums, bound hand and foot, could move objects several feet away from them. Perhaps some force as yet unexplained—but as natural as radio or electricity—makes it possible."

I shivered. Had the axe's fall on poor Jean been Kaer-Mor's claiming of the old blood sacrifice? Had the Dark Powers, bodiless and hungrily grasping at every human being within reach, drawn strength to act from the body of a new medium?

"You think that she—Alienor—uses that force? Perhaps unconsciously?"

"I wish that were all I thought! There is a thing that I must do." His dark, life-ful eyes transfixed mine. "Madame, will you go with me to Alienor's studio? As a witness, or as a fellow-snooper, whichever way you prefer to put it?"

At first I thought that the great stone studio looked exactly as I remembered it. Then I noticed a shrouded figure near the wall and gasped. "Tudual, what on earth is that?"

He smiled. "Not a corpse, madame, though the peasants used to credit it with making many corpses. God knows where Alienor got it; the only extant figure of l'Ankou, the Death-God, is supposed to be hidden in a clergyman's loft in Ploumilliau. He put it away because so many people were coming to it to pray for the death of their enemies."

He did not go near l'Ankou. He strode straight to the old cabinet in which Alienor stored her work, and began rummaging through the portfolios. I snatched at *The Submersion of Ys*, but the picture at which it fell open was not one I knew. I gave a choking cry. . . .

Alienor had not shown us how fully she had illustrated the old legend. The licentious revelries of the demon-princess—those which had preceded the city's crowning—were shown in voluptuous and highly varied detail. Whatever sex shrinkings had embittered Alienor's married life were obviously gone. And yet, through all the horror and the vileness ran the familiar fairy-like delicacy of line, the same background of ethereal beauty.

"She wanted beauty, Tudual," I babbled. "She wanted—back into fairyland. You remember her. Life had been unkind. And then—this place—that knocking—think of it, Tudual! Night after night—upon her door—"

"But she stayed." His voice was as hard as the stone walls. "Because she had the terrible curiosity you had not, the thirst for the unknown. For power, not just for beauty."

"And finally—*it got in!*"

"There can be no doubt of that. Look here." He pointed to some more pictures. The princess, loyal to the Old Gods from whom her Christian father had turned, had offered them sacrifice. With a great stone axe like that which had killed Jean Rozel. The victim had been young and strong, remarkably strong, and his face had not been very intelligent. But I looked into Tudual's eyes and knew.

"He was just bright enough to have got into the army if she hadn't used this influence of hers—the influence she always is able to get, because it's difficult to find high places—especially small local high places—without corruption in them. He wasn't bright, but he had strength. Strength enough to feed anything."

Yes, he had been strong; it had taken him quite awhile to die. There were several detailed pictures of his dying, all drawn with exquisite, painstaking care.

"Tudual, she let him lie there—when he fell. *She didn't call for help!*" Shuddering and nauseated, I hid my face in my hands.

"I am sorry, madame. I should not have brought you." His voice was quiet. "I expected horror, but not this. These pictures should be enough to cure my brother—set him free."

He had to help me to the door. In passing I brushed against l'Ankou, caught a glimpse of red before the displaced shroud fell back. Tudual did not notice, and soon I was to wish that I had told him. Would it have had a difference if I had? I will never know.

Back in the great hall he frowned and looked at his watch. "How long have she and my charming brother been gone? You can hardly see through this fog."

"Too long." I was seeing, as he was seeing, the desolate moor outspread like a wide bed, and those alone beneath the cloaking mist.

"I'll go look for them." His jaw set. "She always loved the cliff above the castle."

I know that everything was moving by pre-arrangement then, moving swiftly, towards an inevitable end. Then, standing by the window after he had gone, I only knew that I was afraid. Afraid for *him*. There were uncanny shiftings and spiralings in that mist: things it would not have been good for a nervous child to see. I remembered that some occultists say that blood-offerings can bring Powers other than those the caller originally meant to call upon: Beings whom blood strengthens. And then I saw Alienor coming out of the mist; in her clinging, blue-green draperies she looked like a wave come up from the sea, gliding over land on some unnatural errand.

Her exquisite, dehumanized face had the immobility of a picture when I ran out to meet her. "I sent Ronan to the village to get something for me. And Tudual is out on those slippery cliffs looking for us, you say? I had better go after the fool."

The great peacock eyes flamed mockingly, cruelly into mine for a second, and then she was gone; the fog swallowed her up. And suddenly, sickeningly, I remembered what the red paint on l'Ankou meant; worshippers painted the image that color when they desired to bring about a death.

I ran after her, out into the fog. God knows what I thought I could do. But the mist seemed to confuse me purposely, with white curdlings and weird twistings. Only the gulls answered my cries, and the waves. That sound of the not-too-distant waters grew into a roar, like that of fog-hidden sacrificial drums.

Then a far-off halloo answered mine. I stumbled toward it, gasping, "Ronan!"

"Madame Foster, what have you?" He caught my hands in his, his voice like a frightened child's. "Nothing has happened to her—to Alienor—"

It was then that it happened. The mists parted suddenly, like the deliberate opening of a window. We saw the towering cliffs above us, and the grey-green sea below. Alienor was there, on a steep sloping ledge not far ahead of us, her eyes a green blaze in her white face. Above her was a jutting spur of rock, on which a great round boulder was poised, like a cap. I had never seen her so beautiful, and yet her beauty had a terribleness that made me shiver.

She saw us. With a gesture as fairylike as it was unspeakably cruel, she kissed her hand to me. I understood, for Tudual had seen her when the mists parted, and was climbing towards her.

The end came quickly then. We could only watch, too far away to reach them in time. As he came toward her she laughed, as if in defiance, then swayed, her foot evidently twisting on the uneven ground. As she fell Ronan cried out, and Tudual automatically did what any other man would have done; he sprang forward to catch her. Into the shadow of that jutting rock. And the great cap of stone, that the strongest man's strength could barely have stirred, shook, trembled, and fell forward.

"Tudual!" I screamed, but I do not think he heard me. He must have seen, for he turned and tried to spring aside. Then, with tigerish swiftness, she was on him, no longer falling, but springing forward, a live projectile that struck him and hurled him back, straight into the path of that downward-hurtling stone. Yet he had been a little quicker than she expected; the coinciding of their efforts overbalanced her. The stone hurtled down upon them both.

When we reached the ledge Tudual was stumbling uncertainly to his feet; he had been knocked against the cliff wall. With Ronan I stepped quickly to the edge of the precipice; we peered over.

Far below, on the narrow beach, the rock lay, and from beneath it, in a wide, reddening pool, something protruded. A limp thing in stained blue-green, with a crimsoning head of gold.

And then the fog fell again, mercifully, as if the force that had rolled it back were gone.

🍒 VERA CHAPMAN 🍒
(1898-   )

Vera Chapman has become a veteran in the field of fantasy literature since 1976. Between 1976 and 1979, she had six novels published. She is nearing completion on two full-length works.

The present story is the second that Mrs. Chapman has written specially for one of our anthologies. The first, "Crusader Damosel," appeared in *The Fantastic Imagination* II (Avon, 1978). At that time, she graciously wrote a brief autobiography that is still, for the most part, current.

> I was born in 1898, in Bournemouth, Hampshire, England. I went to Oxford (Lady Margaret Hall) in 1918, and was one of the very first women to be granted full membership of Oxford University in 1919, to wear the gown, and to graduate in 1921. I married a Clergyman of the Church of England in 1924, and my first married home was in Lourenco Marques, which was then Portuguese East Africa (Mozambique). I returned to England in 1925, and for many years lived in country vicarages. Shortly after the 1940 war, I worked in the Colonial Office as a student welfare officer. I have now been retired for many years. I live in a Council flat (apartment) in Camden Town, London, and I have two children and four grandchildren. My first novel, *The Green Knight*, was published in 1976, and was followed by *The King's Damosel* and *King Arthur's Daughter*, and in 1977 *Judy and Julia*. The first three are published as 'children's stories,' but are really not intended for children; the fourth, *Judy and Julia*, really is a children's book.

In her self-portrait, Mrs. Chapman also commented on her becoming a new author in her late seventies.

> There are several reasons why I have not attained publication until so late in life: chiefly that although I always meant to write, I have had so many other things to do—and also that until recently, there has not been much opening for 'fantasy' writing—I had to wait till the present interest in imaginative writing gave me a chance.
>
> I have certainly accumulated the proverbial 'rejection slips enough to paper a room.'

One of the activities that apparently prompted her to start writing was her founding of The Tolkien Society in London in 1969 to provide a forum for discussing the works of J. R. R. Tolkien. Tolkien, with whom Mrs. Chapman was personally acquainted, accepted the position of Honorary President of the group in 1972.

Since she wrote her autobiographical sketch for us in 1978, Mrs. Chapman has, if anything, become even more productive. She has produced two novels, *The Wife of Bath* (Avon, 1978) and *Blaedud the Birdman* (Rex Collings, 1978). She is currently working on two books, both featuring the delightful Abbess of Shaston, a character who appeared in a secondary role in "Crusader Damosel." The Abbess is a cross between Alice of Bath and Madame Eglentyne, Chaucer's two famous female pilgrims. Mrs. Chapman herself, if one can judge by her letters, is something like the Abbess, vibrant, charming, and witty. One looks forward to the appearance of these books to become better acquainted with both the Abbess and Vera Chapman.

"The Thread" is an interpretive retelling or, to use Mrs. Chapman's term, a "realisation" of a "well-known classical myth." Actually, she combines two separate Theseus myths in her tale, the Theseus-Minotaur-Ariadne and the Theseus-Pirithous-Persephone myths. There are numerous versions of the Theseus-Minotaur-Ariadne myth, but main outline is fairly uniform. The Minotaur was the half-human, half-bull offspring of Pasiphae and a bull.

Pasiphae was the wife of Minos, King of Crete; thus the Minotaur was half-brother to Ariadne, daughter of Pasiphae and Minos. Minos built the labyrinth to contain the Minotaur, and he required a yearly tribute of seven young men and seven young women of Athens to be sent into the labyrinth to their certain doom. Ariadne, however, helped Theseus, with whom, according to most sources, she had fallen in love, to destroy the Minotaur and to break the power of Minos. Ariadne then joined Theseus on the journey to Athens, but Theseus left her on a small island, for reasons which students of mythology can only guess.

The second Theseus myth that Chapman uses involves the attempt by Theseus and Pirithous to kidnap Persephone from Hades, the underworld where she had been taken by force by Pluto to be his bride. Pirithous, according to some versions, wanted to wed Persephone, since his own wife had been killed by the centaurs. Another version states that Persephone was the mother of Dionysus and that Dionysus had taken pity on the abandoned Ariadne and married her. Still another thread of the myth, an earlier one, has Dionysus, not Pluto, as the one who raped and carried off Persephone to an underworld, but a happy underworld. Dionysus was prominent in the Eleusinian mysteries, rituals that involved a happy underworld ("eleusis" means underworld in the sense of a place of happy arrival).

What Mrs. Chapman does in "The Thread" is to integrate these various strands of the Theseus-Pirithous-Persephone myth into a meaningful whole and to relate this composite story to the myth involving Theseus, the Minotaur, and Ariadne. Her highly original suggestions, such as Ariadne's being consecrated to Dionysus, are bold but remain consistent with the myths as we know them, and they help her to weave two traditional Theseus myths into a well-structured and unified story. Chapman's merging of Ariadne with Persephone to join the two stories is a masterful stroke. And while some of her original interpretations rationalize away supernatural causality, Chapman remains consciously ambiguous regarding the causality at the end. This in fact is her strategy, to leave her readers wondering, like Theseus himself, if Theseus's mockery of women and disbelief in their goddess were in fact disastrous errors.

The Thread

Vera Chapman

❦

Naturally, Theseus had let go of the thread when he fought the Minotaur. A man couldn't fight for his life against that horror and still hold a thread in one hand. Ariadne ought to have thought of that.

And now here he was, in the glimmering twilight of that subterranean maze, with the Minotaur dead at his feet, and its decapitated head in his hand—lost in the dark.

He cursed, and flung the head away, and, pulling himself up to the low stony roof, crawled out through one of the ragged interstices through which a little light filtered in—and came to the surface.

It was not an encouraging prospect. Far away to the northward he could make out the palace—very dimly—the red and blue pillars, the yellow architraves, gleamed; mere spots of colour, otherwise all the rest was too far off to see. A long day's march if one could go straight there, but—all the country between, he could see, consisted of the broken ground under which lay the half-buried maze he had traversed. The Old Palace, far older and vaster than that where King Minos now lived, and totally unexplored except by that repulsive creature, the Minotaur. As he pursued his quarry, Theseus had taken note, in the practical way a hunter would, of the nature of the place—dark tunnels, dark empty rooms, sometimes faintly lit by light-wells, but these were mostly choked with the heavy vegetation above them. Places here and there where the track came to the surface, in a courtyard or a terrace, but all buried in bushes and creepers and thorns, dense and venomous. Stairways, and long, long tunnels underground, where sometimes the roof had cracked and let daylight in—other places that seemed to be deep below, under solid

318

masonry. Down there, the beast-man had led him along
tracks which it knew, unerringly; the thread had unrolled
behind him, and of course this would lead him back the
way he had come—but the thread had run out—it wasn't
long enough—and had left him with nó more than an
awkward end, and then he had dropped it, as anyone
would. . . .

No going back underground, then—and overground?
miles of treacherous underfoot jungle, sharp edges and
ridges, pitfalls, screes, precipices, wells, traps—as easy to
try walking over a reef of jagged rocks at low tide. No man
could do it, and—the sun was past its noon. A broken neck
at the bottom of one of those concealed shafts, that was
the least horrible fate that awaited him.

He shuddered, and cursed again. Out there in the red-
pillared palace, they would wait for him, his loyal seven
men and seven women, who had conquered in the Bull
Dance, and all those others, slaves and captives and enemies of cruel old Minos; all those who had only waited for
Theseus the Prince to give them a lead. They would be
waiting and ready now, at the moment of sunset, to fire the
palace, while the ships he had summoned in secret lay in
waiting outside the harbour. But he would not be there.
He'd be dying of thirst and hunger, out there in the rough
country, and the hyenas would pick his bones.

And Ariadne would wait. Ariadne! strange girl. Not
really attractive to him—and yet, a pretty girl was a pretty
girl—with her tiny waist, and exuberant breasts worn
shamelessly bare. . . . She had come to him in prison, and
coolly conspired with him to overthrow her father, and her
father's kingdom, and her brother. . . . Her brother! He
shuddered again—that horrible half-human creature, *that*
was her brother. Half-brother, then—of course that ridiculous story about Queen Pasiphae and the bull was just an
obscene jest handed about among the people. The father of
Minotaurus was the sea-rover who called himself the Bull.
But, on the other hand—the people of Crete had a Bull-
God. Such things had happened. . . .

Ariadne—yes, a very strange girl. She had seemed so
eager, amorous he would have thought, and yet—not quite
that. Her eyes were far away, and she would not let him

touch her. But she had begged him to take her away—to take her to Athens—and had promised him a rich reward if he would do so. Yes, and kill the Minotaur—her brother! —and for that purpose she had given him the thread, and planned everything. And now, because he had relied on that damned thread, he was to die here. . . . Far off, the sight of the sea mocked him.

Oh well, just one more look and feel around. He descended, stiff with weariness, into the darkness the way he had come—and at first could see nothing, and stumbled over the corpse of the Minotaur. His fingers encountered the head. He lifted it by the hair. "Oh yes, I'll have to take you with me, ugly mug, whether I like it or not," he muttered. Something brushed his wrist, hanging from the creature's hair. It was the thread.

Through the darkness, the ships ploughed their way north and westward towards Greece. Behind them, Knossos was burning. The other ships surrounded and convoyed that on which Theseus and Ariadne sailed. They would hasten to Athens with news of Crete broken, Crete with its heart plucked out, Crete ripe for conquest by the kings of Aegina and Sparta and Mycenae.

At the stern of Theseus's ship a rich pavilion had been erected, closed all round with wooden lattices and embroidered curtains, and inside this, on a bed of down and silk, lay Ariadne, worn out with the fatigues and terrors of the escape from Knossos. She had laid aside the belt that braced in her tiny waist, and her snake bracelets and hieratic jewels; and her dark red hair lay spread on the pillow. Theseus came quietly through the curtains. She gave a cry, and covered herself with a mantle.

"Now, my love," he said.

"No—no, Theseus. Never touch me. Leave me alone."

"But my dear—I have rescued you as I said I would. You are my bride—wasn't that your wish?"

"No. No. You don't understand. I never asked you that. I never promised you that."

"You promised me a rich reward."

"You have a rich reward. Your ships are full of the

spoils of the palace. That's reward enough. I never promised—"

"Why, I understood—"

"You misunderstood. No, don't lay a finger on me. Don't come any nearer. Theseus, I am consecrated. I am the bride of a god."

"What is this? What god? Not the Bull-God?"

"Oh no, the Gods forbid. But Theseus, understand this. Many years back, the holy Bacchus came to Crete—he is Dionysus and Zagreus and Iacchos—he came with his band, bringing his message of joy, and he absolved my sin."

"Your sin? What sin?"

"A grievous sin. For it was I who loosed the Minotaur on the island. He had been kept fast in prison, but I—in pity and foolishness—set him free. And so he ravaged all Crete—and it was because of me. None knew it, or I think the people would have stoned me to death. But Bacchus cleansed me from my sin, and plighted me to him as his bride. But that very night the Minotaur broke from hiding and slew Bacchus. He slew my God, and rent him in pieces.—But I know that Bacchus does not die. If I can go to his sanctuary at Eleusis, by Athens, I shall see him again and be truly wedded to him. That is why I prayed you to take me to Athens, and that is why you must not touch me. Did you think that I was in love with you?"

He gave an inarticulate cry and turned from her.

"The Furies take you, woman! *Woman!* Who can understand a woman? How could you serve me so? I don't know why I don't throw you overboard—"

He looked back at her. That red hair, those protuberant eyes—he recalled the Minotaur's head in his hand, and himself saying, "I've got to take you with me . . . whether I like it or not."

He went to the forward end of the ship—hardly master of his emotions—and gave certain instructions to his servants.

When Ariadne woke, it was from a deep oblivious sleep. Her last recollection had been of one of Theseus's slaves handing her a cup of wine, spiced and very sweet. Now as she woke she was dull-witted and bewildered. She had no idea where she was. Silk curtains were all around her, and she lay on a silken bed, but she did not feel as if she were on the ship. The sun shone through the silk curtains—she was in a tent, and the sun was high. With her head still reeling, she rose, parted the curtains, and looked out.

She was at the door of a richly decorated pavilion—but she was alone. Quite alone. All round her was open grassland, overlooking the sea—certainly on an island, and for a long way around her, no trees, walls, houses—and no people. She could not take it in at first. Nobody? But how could there be nobody? She looked all round the tent, inside and out. It was firmly pitched, as to shelter her; there was a heap of vessels, jars of wine, bundles of various kinds of food, gold and silver vessels too, scattered in careless profusion, as if to leave her ironical gifts in her loneliness. Loneliness! All at once the full force of it struck her, and she sank to the ground with a sob.

Left behind. That was what he had done—left her behind, on this island. Gone, gone. And not a soul, not a living soul near her.

At first she sat, and tried to collect her thoughts, to control her rising panic. She would not shriek and run about—she would not. Come now, there was food and drink and shelter to last a day or two. Ships would come by—perhaps he would come back for her? But she knew only too well that he would not. Oh no, he would not come back for her.

The sun was high and fierce—she was intensely thirsty, and her head ached. She drank from one of the wine jars—it made her head throb and reel, and ache still more. She began to sob, quietly at first, then more and more wildly—then she walked, aimlessly, barefoot and lightly clothed as she was, along the line of the cliffs. Upwards, as the line of the cliff went. Was that music she could hear? Oh, if it were music—if only it were music! She quickened her pace, up the shoulder of the down. There she came to a place where her way was barred by a deep cleft, where the sea came in below. The other side of the cleft was another grassy slope, a fathom's length across the chasm. And along this grassy ridge she saw them coming—

Bacchus and all his beautiful people. It was as if they grew out of the quivering heat-haze. There were the lovely long-haired Maenads, and the little Fauns, and the tall young men, the Kouri, and the jolly old men on donkeys—and there at their head was the Heavenly Lover, Bacchus himself—the face she had loved long ago, once dead, now alive forever. He stood and called to her across the gulf.

"Come across. Come to me, my love—it is only a step. Come!"

With a wild cry she stepped across the abyss—and was caught up into great joy and felicity.

There were so many years behind Theseus now—twenty —thirty years since Crete and the Minotaur. Years of conquest and kingship, battles, love and death and heartbreak. Hippolyta had come and gone out of his life, and poor Phaedra, and Hippolytus—ah, that had hurt. He had forgotten that Phaedra was Ariadne's sister—it was all so long ago.

Pirithous was his comfort now—Pirithous, whom all Greece acknowledged to be the handsomest man in all the land, even now when he was no longer young. They made a fine pair together. Pirithous! Worth more to him than all the women. Pirithous kept him young, led him into bold adventures and absurd pranks like schoolboys. It was increasingly hard now to rouse his heart to feel anything worth while—he had known everything. But Pirithous found him new interests, new sensations—new vices, too. Theseus was ruler of Athens—called without any resentment the Tyrant—and could be held blameless for many things that no doubt ought to have been blamed.

Yes, Theseus was bored, without denial he was bored. So he sat on the porch of his great white marble house in Athens, and drank with Pirithous, who alone could find means to relieve his boredom.

Below them they watched the long procession forming up, to set out on the way to Eleusis for the Mysteries.

"I hate all that," Theseus said. "Priests and mysteries and women."

"Especially women," said Pirithous.

"Yes. It's all dark, and devious, and secret—it gives me

the horrors. Why is it secret? If there's anything good in it, they should let all the world know. If not, there must be something bad. Unspeakably bad.—As Tyrant of Athens, I've tried to put it down, but the priests are too strong for me."

An uneasy silence fell. Below them a street singer passed. Not everyone was occupied with the preparations for the Mysteries. This man preferred the popular hero-songs about Theseus and Pirithous. They heard him sing:

> Theseus and Pirithous, the lovers,
> They are so brave they would go down to Hell
> And drag up thence Persephone,
> The Queen of the Dead herself . . .

The two men turned to each other and laughed.

"Why, that's what we ought to do," said Pirithous.

"What do you men—fetch up Persephone from Hell? We can't do that." An unaccountable shiver ran over him.

"We can and we will—don't you see? Eleusis—the Priestess of the Mysteries. They say the initiates are taken down into Hell, through that cave they speak of—and there they come into the presence of Persephone, the Queen of the Dead. What else can she be but the chief priestess, whom no one ever sees? Theseus, you say you want to put down all this priestcraft and superstition. That's the way we'll do it."

"But how? No one can go there but the initiates."

"Then we'll become initiates."

"What? No, we couldn't—"

"We could. We'll go through all their solemn mummery, and then we'll break the whole thing wide open, and bring this Persephone of theirs up to light—poor thing, you'd think she'd be glad to come! And perhaps, who knows," he added with a sour laugh, "we might induce her to make the spring stay all the year round."

It caused a sensation when it was known that Theseus and Pirithous were candidates for the Mysteries. To their admirers, whatever they did was right. Many who admired them less took this as evidence that virtue and piety had won a victory over them. All rejoiced, and the number of applicants for the Mysteries doubled, and the gifts flowed into the treasury of Eleusis.

But certainly the two friends had to submit at least to the appearance of virtue. The preparation was long and serious. Fasting and watching, prayer and meditation, instruction and abstinence—they had to keep reminding each other of their eventual objective.

First came the Lesser Mysteries, in spring, when the holy image of Iacchos, or Dionysus, or Bacchus, was brought from Athens to Eleusis in procession. This was a cheerful seed-time festival, and Theseus and Pirithous went through the first degree of the Mysteries without much trouble. Afterwards in private, Pirithous laughed and made mockery of it. But Theseus's laughter began to be a little hollow. More than once he thought of leaving the whole thing—no, not to go through with it in earnest, but to withdraw from it altogether, driven by the sense of the uncanny, the holy terror, that began to haunt him. But once embarked on the Mysteries you could not draw back —he had become a "mystos," one whose eyes and lips were sealed, and he must go and become an "epoptos," one whose eyes were opened, though never his lips. And Pirithous urged him on, and laughed at his misgivings.

Autumn came, and the time of the Greater Mysteries. Now it began—the long torchlight procession under the full moon, all the people of Athens, men, women, and children, in holiday mood, streaming out along the Sacred Way, with food and drink, garlands and musical instruments, in feast-day clothes, bearing smoking torches, making a cheerful babble along the brilliant ribbon of light under the translucent dark blue sky. In the midst, in their white robes, quiet in all the excitement, went the Mystoi. At the Bridge there was the customary halt, where buffoons and clowns broke upon the sacred procession with wild fooling and the most obscene of jokes, for this was in memory of the Goddess's servant, who had jested to her to make her smile, that she should not die of sorrow.

"Laugh now," said the hierophant priest who had charge of the candidates, "laugh your fill, for you will not laugh for many days after."

Pirithous nudged Theseus. "Oh yes," he whispered, "we'll laugh all right afterwards. That we will!"

But Theseus did not return the nudge.

Revelling and dancing and shouting, the crowd escorted the Mystoi into the precincts of Eleusis at midnight. The torches marked the sky with flame and smoke. The ritual words were said, and the candidates for the Greater Mysteries—twelve in all, eight men and four women—were led through the great swing doors that creaked in their grooves on the marble floors. Dim lights showed from inside, but the people outside tried in vain to get a glimpse of what lay within. The same great doors closed behind the Mystoi, inexorably. Outside, the folk would revel and feast till daybreak, thankful to the Mystoi, who would ensure for them the fertility of the Mother and the happy return of the Daughter next year. But inside, the Mystoi must spend a holy night of quiet preparation.

Daybreak brought the echoing, hollow cry over the bay: "To the sea, all Mystoi!" and, hardly roused from sleep, they came, almost naked, the men in one line, the women, far off, in another, and with the early sun dazzling them, plunged into the cold sea. Each one, grotesquely, carried a small squealing pig, for this was the accustomed sacrifice. Theseus and Pirithous struggled awkwardly with their pigs, and Pirithous swore, and hit his pig so violently with the edge of his great hand that it was dead before he laid it in the sacrificial trench. Now they were all clothed in new white garments, as purified, and the rite proceeded.

In the afternoon they were allowed a rest in the little cells set up for them. As a rule the initiates were kept in strict seclusion, but because Theseus and Pirithous were who they were, the hierophants allowed them to spend an hour together.

As the door closed upon them, Theseus exclaimed, "Pirithous, I'm not going on with this."

"What? Oh, nonsense. I know it's tedious, but look, it's nearly over. It's just tonight, after midnight—first there's that interminable long procession, the 'Search for Persephone'—then the initiates go down into the Cavern, two by two, and come before the Goddess—as they call her.

That's our time. That's when we bring her out to all the
people and show them she's no Goddess at all. Finish the
whole sorry affair, once and for all. Everything you hate—
priests, women, mysteries. And what a feast we'll have
afterwards! Why, the people will call us Gods ourselves."

"No." Theseus stood up and confronted his friend,
hands on hips, stubbornly.

"What do you mean—no?"

"I don't like it, and I won't go on with it. It's not right,
it's not . . . well, I'm sure it's not lucky. Bad things will
come of it. I feel it in my blood—it shouldn't be done. I'm
going through with the Mysteries, but I'll do it properly,
and I'll have no part in it—what you said we'd do."

"Theseus!" Pirithous sprang from where he sat, and confronted his friend, red-faced. "Do you mean to say—it
can't be that you've let all this rubbish influence you? The
oaths and all that? Words, Theseus, nothing but words.
Easy enough to say. Why, you're not—afraid are you?"

Theseus gave a growl of rage and sprang with his hands
at Pirithous's throat. Pirithous looked him straight in the
eyes, and calmly put his own hands over his friend's hands
that were about to throttle him.

"Oh, none of that, none of that. Don't be a fool." The
clutching hands relaxed. "Don't you see—there's no going
back now? I shall do what we planned, and if you don't,
can you imagine what will happen?"

A loud knock on the cell door interrupted them. Their
personal hierophant, robed in white and with his head covered, stood at the door.

"Pirithous, it's time you went to your own cell. Come
with me."

They had quickly turned their hostile grip into the semblance of an emotional leave-taking.

"Farewell, then, till we meet again," said Pirithous. And
a terrible foreboding of grief came over Theseus.

As dusk fell, out over the precincts of Eleusis floated a
single lonely voice.

"Oi-moi. Oi-moi. Oi-moi."

And a deep chorus of men's voices took it up, not loud,
but penetrating. "Oi-moi, oi-moi, oi-moi." It was the chant

of the forsaken Mother seeking the Daughter, Winter seeking Spring, Age seeking her own lost youth. As the moon
rose, the procession wound its way along the dark pathways; the torches, always the torches, blinking in a windless night.

And now they reached the low archway of the cavern,
the way down to the place where Hades was King—he
whose name was so dreaded that it was never spoken—he
was called The Rich One, Pluto. Here the procession
halted while the ominous sacrifice of a black goat was
made. In the dimness and crowd, all that most of the
worshippers could see was the dark horned shape, rearing
up and then falling—they could hear the hiss and splash of
the blood as it ran into the low trench. Then, stepping over
the trench where the sacrifice still lay, the first two initiates
were led in, and the doors closed against the rest.

At first Theseus and Pirithous found themselves in total
darkness—then, as unseen hands led them forward, they
turned a corner, and there was a dim green light from a
brazier.

It was a small, low room, and in it were just six people
—their two selves, the hierophant who was leading them,
and at the far end, up three stone steps, two tall guards, in
the long straight dress that proclaimed them as eunuchs,
stood each armed with a stone mace—and between them
the High Priestess, the Goddess, with a black veil over her
face.

"Now!" said Pirithous, and in one movement the two
rushed forward. They had no weapons, but relied on hands
and fists and the power of surprise. Pirithous, one pace in
front of Theseus, seized the Priestess by the waist and the
knees, and lifted her from the ground. She screamed on a
piercing high note, and in the same instant the two eunuchs brought their maces down on Pirithous's head. As he
fell like a poleaxed beast, the Priestess disappeared behind
a curtain.

Theseus fell on his knees beside his friend.

"Pirithous, Pirithous—oh, the best friend a man ever
had. Dead, dead—smashed like an eggshell by a horrible
eunuch!" His sobs broke the silence.

Then he looked up. The Priestess had come back. Without a word she resumed her throne and lifted her veil. She stood very still and looked down on the scene. Her snake bracelets were not bracelets but living snakes, and they hissed. He looked up and saw her face.

Worn and ravaged with years, the eyes blank, remote, crazy—still he knew her. It was Ariadne.